Friends
&
Lovers Trilogy

Angie,
always believe in
Happily Ever after!

&
Bethany Ryan

Penned Con '14

Friends & Lovers Trilogy

Books by Bethany Lopez

Stories about Melissa - series
Ta Ta for Now.
xoxoxo
Ciao

Friends & Lovers Trilogy
Make it Last
I Choose You
Trust in Me

Nissa: a contemporary fairy tale

Friends & Lovers Trilogy

Copyright 2013

Published March 2013

ISBN: 978-1482729559

Cover Design by b design

This is a work of fiction. Names, characters, places, and incidents either are the product of the author's imagination or are used fictitiously, and any resemblance to actual persons, living or dead, businesses, companies, events, or locales is entirely coincidental.

Visit the author's website: www.bethanylopez.blogspot.com

Friends & Lovers Trilogy

Thanks to Raine, Autumn, Lyn, and Tee. This trilogy wouldn't be the same without the four of you!

Friends & Lovers Trilogy

Make it Last
(Brianna & Colin)

Friends & Lovers Trilogy

Prologue

Briana looked up at him, tears forming in her eyes. Colin felt his resolve begin to crumble, but reminded himself why he'd come to this decision. He was about to leave for college and Bree was beginning her senior year of high school. It made sense to end it now, rather than try to have a long distance relationship. Colin thought about the pro and con list he'd made, and it made sense to break up now, but looking into Briana's beautiful brown eyes he began to question his decision.

Colin shook his head to attempt to clear the doubt from his mind, he knew he had to try and make a clean break now.

"Look Bree, I just can't be tied down right now," he explained, not quite meeting her eyes. He was sure that if he did, she'd see his uncertainty. "I'm leaving tomorrow. Going out together was cool while we were in high school, but we're about to be on different paths. I'm going to need to focus on football and keeping my grades up."

She turned her head and bit her lip, the way she did when she was trying to sort things out in her head. Finally she looked back at him, her face full of confusion.

"Is this because I wouldn't have sex with you?" Tears streamed down her face, and he felt like a complete ass. He should have known she would go there. He'd been trying to have sex with her for the past few months. They'd been dating for a long time, and he was a teenage guy after all. But he understood her reasons for wanting to wait. Especially now.

"Of course not. I just don't think a long distance relationship will work. A clean break now would be best, you know?" he replied, looking at something just over her head.

"Colin, the least you could do is look at me when you're being a total douche," she said tightly.

He looked down at her and his face softened. How could he not love her? She always called him on his shit.

Colin tried to block the thoughts from his mind and stiffened his resolve. "Don't make this harder than it needs to be, Bree."

"Are you being serious right now?" she asked. "We've been dating for over a year. You said that you loved me. Now, all of a sudden, you want to break up? This is coming out of nowhere, Colin."

Everything she was said true. They had planned to continue dating and seeing each other on breaks and holidays, but after thinking about it, making lists, and talking to his friends and family, Colin realized that it would be best for both of them to go their separate ways now. He just needed to make her believe that he believed that.

He let out a long sigh, as if she was the one being unreasonable. "Bree, I'm about to be thousands of miles away. Don't you want to be free to enjoy your senior year? I won't be able to come back and go to dances and stuff with you, ya know?" He shrugged he shoulders in an effort to appear unaffected by his words.

"We always knew you'd be leaving. I don't know why you're acting like this is a new development. We've talked about having a long distance relationship. What's changed?" Colin tried not to smile at her words. He should have known that she wouldn't give up without a fight. His stomach turned. He felt nauseous at the thought of what he was going to say next.

"Fine Bree, you're right. I want to be free to see other people while I'm at college." He tried to sound exasperated, and saw her face fall as he continued to speak. "I'm going to be playing football and looking at joining a fraternity. I don't want to end up cheating or doing something stupid. It just makes more sense to end it now. It'll be better in the long run, you'll see." He put his hand out as if to pat her shoulder, but she backed away.

"You don't get to touch me anymore, Colin," she stated, wiping her face with the back of her hand.

He hated the thought of hurting her and tried to think of something to say that would soften the blow. "Bree, don't be upset. I'll always love you. This is just the way it has to be."

She sniffed and continued wiping her cheeks. She stood up as tall as her five-foot, four-inch frame allowed and looked him in the eyes. "You'll regret this, Colin. One day you'll come back looking for a second chance, but it's never going to happen. I'm not going to forget this day."

He felt a lump form in his throat at her words.

Wavering about his decision, he reached his hand out to touch her again, then stopped himself.

"You're right," he said softly. "I wouldn't deserve a second chance."

He looked at her one last time, memorizing her delicate features. Her long hair flowed around her shoulders, just the way he liked it. His thoughts were tinged with regret, but he knew that breaking it off now was the only way to make sure they didn't end up hurting each other even more in the long run. Dropping his hand to his side, he walked away and left her behind.

Friends & Lovers Trilogy

Four Years Later...

Friends & Lovers Trilogy

Chapter One

Briana hated Wednesday nights. Twenty-five cent wings meant that not only was the Bar & Grill packed all evening, but that the fryers were absolutely disgusting. Although she loved good wings as much as the next person, it was her job to clean the fryers, so she dreaded her shift anytime she was scheduled for a Wednesday night.

She watched as Kara locked up behind the last customer, and then went behind the bar to turn up the music.

Other than the cleaning, Briana loved closing time. That's when the employees got together to chit-chat about their customers, made plans for what they were going to do after shift, and finally had the chance to enjoy their night.

The night manager, Pam, was pretty cool. She stayed in the back, counting the money and making sure everything balanced out, and then put it in the envelope to make the drop at the bank on her way home.

As long as they didn't leave until everything was spotless, she didn't give them a hard time about hanging out.

Briana joined Kara and Pete, one of the bar backs, over by the bar once she set the fryer to drain.

"What a night," Pete started, putting shots in front of Briana and Kara as they settled onto the stools.

"You can say that again," Kara replied, a big grin on her face. "I made two hundred in tips tonight. Gotta love twenty-five cent wings."

Kara worked the front of the house, not the back, so her view of Wednesday was a lot different than Briana's. As a waitress, Kara got to turn on her charm and flirt with the customers, one of her favorite pastimes, thus reaping the rewards of a busy Wednesday night.

The view from the back of the house was a lot different. During shift, Briana cooked all of the orders, so she spent her evenings covered in grease, ketchup, and everything else she spilled while making the food.

Her job was nowhere near as glamorous or profitable as Kara's, but she didn't think she could ever be a waitress. Just the thought of making a mistake and having a customer yell at her or something was enough to keep her in the back.

She didn't mind being a short-order cook though; she figured it was giving her experience that would only help her once she finally gained the courage and the funds to apply for culinary school.

She and Kara toasted each other's amber colored glasses, then Pete's, before downing the shot.

"Holy shit," Briana exclaimed, as the whiskey burned its way down her throat.

"Oops. Sorry, Bree. I forgot you don't like whiskey." Pete chuckled, not looking a single bit sorry as he took out a bottle of the vodka she preferred, and poured them each another shot.

They took the shots and then separated to start cleaning. Briana and Kara were having a party of sorts at their apartment after work, so they wanted to finish up quicker than usual.

Once the stainless steel of the fryer gleamed and the floors were scrubbed down, Briana took one last look around the kitchen and deemed it spotless.

She went out to see if Kara, Pete, or any of the others needed her help getting their side work done.

Kara was just finishing up rolling her silverware and Pete was turning off the radio when she walked up.

"You guys ready?" Briana asked.

A chorus of "Hell, yeah's" were shouted and they all headed out, calling goodnight to Pam.

She and Kara rode together back to their apartment over the flower shop. Their Texas town was small enough that getting to the other side meant they only had to drive for five minutes to get wherever they needed to go.

They parked and ran up the stairs, racing to see who would get to the shower first.

Briana won by half a foot and yelled, "Sorry, sucker," as she began stripping off her clothes, eager to get rid of the greasy stench.

She showered as quickly as she could, while still scrubbing the smells of the kitchen out of her hair and off of her body.

When she was done, Kara was waiting for her turn, and handed Briana a towel as they switched spots.

Briana ran down the short hallway to her room, rubbing the towel over herself as she mentally went through her wardrobe.

She decided that cutoff shorts and a frilly tank would do quite nicely on this hot summer night, and dug through her dresser trying to find the pair she was looking for.

Once she was dressed, she brushed out her chestnut colored hair and pulled it up into a high ponytail. She put minimal makeup on, then threw on her flip flops and hurried out to the kitchen to check the status of their provisions.

It was BYOB, so most of the people would have their own drinks, but a random moocher always showed up and needed some alcohol.

They had a bottle of wine, a twelve pack of Bud Light, and a bottle each of cherry vodka and Sprite.

They were good to go.

She took out a couple bags of chips, put them in bowls, and placed them around the living room.

She threw the blankets, a random sock, and the magazines that were littering the floor into the big hope chest that served as their coffee table.

She was considering running the vacuum when Kara came out, dressed in a sweet sunshine yellow sundress, her blond hair tousled around her face.

"Thanks, Bree, the place looks great. Do you think we should vacuum?"

"I was just thinking the same thing. Then I remembered who was coming over, and realized we'll probably have countless items spilled on the carpet before morning comes, so what's the point?" Brian laughed.

"Very true," Kara said. "Pre-game?"

"Absolutely," Briana replied, following Kara back to the kitchen to make herself a drink.

She'd barely taken her first sip of cherry vodka and Sprite when the front door opened and a group of people piled in. It didn't take long for the music to be turned up and the sound of laughter and chatter to fill the room.

Briana was talking to someone she had taken a college course with a few years ago, when she felt someone come up behind her and softly kiss her neck.

She turned and looked up at Kent over the rim of her glass.

"What's going on, Hot Stuff?" he asked with his cocky grin.

At six feet, he towered over Briana, and his unruly blond hair and self-assured manner always drew her to him.

"Not much, Kent, just getting the party started."

She and Kent enjoyed each other when neither of them was in a serious relationship. Briana hadn't had one since Colin broke up with her in high school, so she was always ready to enjoy Kent.

Sometimes he tried to get too serious for her, and that was when she would tell him it was time to get him a girlfriend.

They weren't an item, and they weren't exclusive, but he was the only guy in this town with whom Briana knew she could enjoy an uncomplicated relationship.

"You here alone?" she asked him.

"Not anymore," he replied, taking her hand and leading her into the kitchen, where he made himself a drink.

Once Kent had his Captain and Coke mixed, he leaned down to give Briana a quick kiss before they headed back into the living room.

"That's a promise of things to come," he whispered against her lips.

Briana mingled and got caught up on all the town gossip. She was going back to fill up her glass when she caught site of Kara going into her room with Pete.

"Well, that's new," she thought with a smile.

As she was filling her glass, the girl she had been talking to earlier when Kent interrupted, came into the kitchen.

She couldn't for the life of her remember the girl's name. Kendra or Kylie, maybe. She'd just think of her as Kendrie.

"Hey, Bree, I didn't get a chance to tell you earlier because that gorgeous guy pulled you away, but I'd wondered if you'd heard the news."

"What news?" she asked absently.

"About Colin." Kendrie seemed unable to control the glee that came out with that statement.

Briana ran into this a lot. In high school, most of the girls were jealous of her because she was dating Colin. Once he left for school, dumping her in the process, those same girls pretended to feel sorry for her, but she could tell that they really loved the fact that he'd dumped her.

Since their town was small, she knew anytime Colin came home on break. Everyone was more than eager to tell her about it.

Judging by the girl's tone, she figured Colin must be home for the summer. It didn't matter. She had successfully avoided him so far. She could manage to do so for another summer.

"What about him?" she asked, making her voice sound as bored as possible.

"He's moving back for good." Briana's stomach dropped to the floor. She only half listened as Kendrie rambled on.

"He hurt his knee during the last game of the season and can't play football anymore. He graduated and everything, but his dream of going on to play professional ball is over, so he's coming back here. They say he's going to work with his dad or something. I think he got in last night." Kendrie continued to prattle on, not realizing that Briana was no longer listening to her.

Briana topped off her drink and walked out of the kitchen, leaving the girl to stare after her, her words still hanging in the air.

She walked in the opposite direction of the crowd in the living room, down the hall and into her room. She didn't bother to shut the door, but opened her window and crawled out onto the roof. She sat down and leaned back against the roof tiles, looking out over the lights of her town.

She drank from her glass as she thought about Colin.

How dare he come back here permanently? This was her town. Sure, he'd grown up here, but he'd always planned to get out and never look back. He wanted to go off to school and play football, then make it big and move off to a city somewhere. He'd always planned to visit once he'd left, but he'd never planned to live here forever.

She'd taken comfort in that fact, and now he was coming back to stay.

Well, things had changed, and Colin had better watch his step where she was concerned. She had no plans to welcome him back with open arms.

Friends & Lovers Trilogy

Chapter Two

Briana rolled out of bed at two in the afternoon, a headache giving her grief. She wandered out of her room and groaned at the sight that met her in the rest of the apartment.

Plastic cups and paper plates littered every surface, and just as she'd predicted, the carpet was a mess of spilled drink and food. Some moron had even used one of her favorite Aggie mugs as an ashtray. Gross.

She went into the kitchen and grimaced at the mess in there, but figured it was best to focus on one thing at a time. She grabbed a trash bag to get started in the living room.

She was about halfway done cleaning up when Kara came strolling in through the front door.

"Hey, Bree, you're up. Thanks for getting started in here. I just ran out to get some provisions," she stated, holding out a to-go coffee cup.

"Oh, thank God," Briana exclaimed, grabbing the cup and drinking as if her life depended on it.

Kara chuckled. "I knew that would brighten up your day. Gosh, what a bunch of slobs, huh? I can't believe this place looks so nasty. I'll just put these muffins in the kitchen and help you out."

"Wait… there are muffins? The kitchen is just as bad. You don't want to put them in there. We'd better just eat them now." Briana grabbed for the bag that Kara was keeping just out of reach.

Kara laughed again and took out a steaming banana nut muffin, Briana's favorite.

"I'll give you this on one condition."

"Anything," Briana said.

"We don't mention what happened last night with Pete. Like, ever."

"Deal," she said, grabbing the muffin and finding a clean corner of the couch to sit on.

Kara sat on the edge of the hope chest and began nibbling on her blueberry muffin.

"What happened to you last night?" she asked. "Kent was looking for you, but I had no idea where you went."

"After that weird girl from my Literary Dimensions on Film class dropped her bomb on me, I kinda disappeared for the night."

Kara sat up, looking interested. "Do tell."

"I shouldn't have let it get to me, but she told me that Colin is moving home for good. Or, I guess he already did, a couple days ago."

"Get out. I noticed you were gone when I came out of my room last night." Kara just looked at Briana. "At first I figured you were with Kent, but then he came up to me and asked where you were. I didn't know and I didn't see you in your room, so I told him so. He hung out for a bit and then I lost track of him. I wondered if you two had ever hooked up. Wow. So…Colin, huh?"

"Yeah. I was on the roof. I just couldn't stand the thought of that girl watching me and waiting for me to break down or react to her news. She was so excited to tell me, you know? It just pissed me off."

"You should have told her to get lost," Kara said, getting angry for her. "It's our place. She can take her gossiping ass someplace else."

Briana laughed. Kara always made her feel better when she was down.

"Anyway, I stayed out there most of the night. I wasn't in the mood to see Kent, especially when I was thinking so much about Colin." Briana was starting to lose her appetite.

"Look, I know this town is small as hell, and you're going to run into him. But, Bree, it's been four years. You're a grown woman with a job, and apartment, and a hot man at your beck and call. You don't need his shit. Just ignore him."

Kara had never met Colin. She moved to town their senior year, after he left for school, and they had been best friends ever since. She never knew Briana and Colin as a couple; she just saw how Briana was affected after he left. She wasn't his biggest fan.

"That's easier said than done, Kara. That girl said that he was going to be working for his daddy. That means he'll be working right down the street and he's gonna come in to eat all the time." The thought made Briana's stomach hurt even more.

"Stop, Bree. You're not seventeen anymore. Let him eat where he wants. Don't let him bother you. You have the upper hand here."

"You're right. I know you are. I'm just scared to see him. It's been so long. What if when I see him I feel just like I did when he left? I never want to feel that way again," Briana said softly, looking up at Kara and hating how pathetic she sounded.

"Then don't," Kara said sternly. "In fact, we've spent enough time on the topic already. Let's finish cleaning this pigsty up so we can relax a bit before work tonight."

"Okay."

Once they had everything spic and span again, they threw on their bikinis and went outside to lie out. They didn't have a pool or a yard, so they laid their towels out on the driveway and made do.

Kara brought out her iPod and Briana brought the tanning oil and the water. They relaxed, enjoying the music and the sun, until the alarm went off, signaling it was time to go in and get washed up for work.

They reluctantly headed into work, motivated by the fact that it was Thursday night, so shouldn't be too crowded, and that they had plans to meet up with some of their friends and go to the gravel pits after work. They brought their bikinis in their bags and sported fresh tan skin to show off in the moonlight.

It looked like it was going to be a pretty good night.

Chapter Three

About two hours into her shift, Briana realized just how wrong she had been.

She'd just finished an order and was rounding the corner to tell Kara that the burger and fries were up, when she caught sight of Colin's family coming in the front door.

Mrs. Grayson looked as sweet as ever, holding her husband's hand and smiling up at him as they waited for the rest of their party to come through the door. He bent over to say something to her, then they both looked over towards the entrance.

Briana had been swept up watching them, remembering a million different conversations that she'd had with the Grayson's, so she didn't immediately follow their gaze. When she did, her breath caught in her throat. She froze.

Kara came up beside her to check on the order. She started waving her hands in front of Briana's face when she saw how still Briana was.

"Hello? Earth to Bree. Is my order up?" Kara chuckled lightly, and turned to see what had caught her attention. "Who's that?"

Briana squeaked, so overcome by emotion that she couldn't form a thought. Then Colin looked up, catching her stare, and she was released. She took off in a flurry of movement, anxious to get back to the safety of the kitchen.

Once behind the swinging door, she braced herself against the stainless steel table and hung her head, breathing in and out.

"Was that him?" Kara asked, scrambling in after her. "Colin?"

"Yup," she managed.

"Crap. I have to take out this order; Kara added a side of ketchup and mustard to the plate before picking it up. "I'll be back, though. Maybe I'll tell Nicole to seat them in my section."

"No," Briana said loudly. "Don't make a scene, please."

Kara tried her best to look innocent. "Who, me?" Then she walked out with a smile on her lips and a swing to her hips.

"Oh, God." Briana held her head in her hands for a moment. "Pull it together, Bree. It's been a long time," she whispered. She stepped back from the table and shook her head, as if to shake the memories out.

She busied herself with the incoming orders, and was just starting to breath normally again, when Kara came back into the kitchen.

"So, Nicole did sit him in my section, but I swear I didn't ask her to," Kara said. "Holy crap, Bree, he is freakin' HOT."

"Shut up, Kara."

"No, seriously… tall, dark, and freakishly handsome! I mean, those dimples… I just want to lick him," Kara said dreamily.

"Jesus, Kara," Briana snapped, "Are you kidding me right now?"

Kara laughed wickedly. "Not about the fact that he's crazy hot, but yes, I'm kidding about wanting to lick him. You know I'd never poach."

"Ugh, I know." Briana closed her eyes. "She really sat them in your section?"

"Yup, all twelve of them. Can you say, 'Big tip?'" Kara said, doing a little booty shake around the kitchen.

"Did they see me? Did they say anything?" Briana asked, hoping the answer was no.

"Well…" Kara began, finally standing still and twirling her finger around a lock of her blonde hair. "I did hear Colin mention that he saw you, and that you looked good."

"He did not."

"Uh, yeah, he did."

"Oh, my gosh. Is that all he said?"

"So far," Kara replied. "I just put in their order, and I have to get back to my other customers. But I'll come back with updates."

Kara sauntered back out into the dining room, leaving Briana momentarily distracted by what she'd just told her. Briana knew that she didn't want to see Colin or talk to him, but she couldn't help but feel some satisfaction upon hearing that he thought she looked good.

Good. Maybe he'd regret breaking her heart.

Briana went back to filling orders and waited for the next update from Kara. The word must have spread, because as the other servers came in to pick up their orders and grab condiments, they couldn't help but make comments to Briana about Colin being in the other room.

"Damn, Bree, you used to date him?"

"That man is *fine*, Bree. If you don't want him, I'd like to take him out for a spin."

"Colin is lookin' good, Bree. You sure you don't want to relive the high school days?"

Briana was starting to lose it when Pete walked in.

"Don't say it, Pete. I swear to God, I'll kill you if you say *anything* about Colin," she said.

Pete put his hands up, as if he were under arrest. "I wasn't going to, I promise," he answered. "Kara is over there with them now. Rich just walked in and joined them."

Rich and Colin had been best friends growing up. Briana got to know Rich pretty well when she dated Colin, and they both went to Texas A & M together. Rich was one of the only people she'd known when she got to college, so they were pretty close during her short stint there.

Pete went to high school with all of them, too, but he hadn't run with the same crowd they did, so they'd never hung out. But he knew Colin and Rich.

"Oh, yeah?" Briana asked. "I haven't seen Rich in ages. I didn't know he was back in town."

"I overheard him telling Mrs. Grayson that he was home for the summer. He only has one year left at A & M."

Briana paused for a minute, trying to ignore the ache in her chest when she realized that she would also be that close to finishing college if she'd stayed.

"Anyway, I didn't come back to talk about Colin and Rich, although I should have realized you were back here freaking out," Pete said.

"I'm not freaking out," she tried to play it off. "What's up?"

"Um…I wanted to ask about Kara," Pete said, his skin starting to match the shade of his hair. "You know, um, if she said anything to you about last night."

"Not really, Pete. You know Kara. She doesn't take that stuff seriously." Briana said. "She's not a relationship kind of girl."

Pete looked over her head and nodded. "Yeah, that's kinda what I figured."

He walked back out.

"Pete," Briana called, but he didn't turn back.

She hoped he didn't end up getting hurt. Kara made sure that the guys she was with knew the score before they did anything, but Briana knew that Pete was different from the guys that Kara usually hung out with.

Pete was one of the good ones.

Kara came in a few minutes later. "Okay, Mr. Hot Stuff has an equally gorgeous friend. This is his order. Can you make it up now so it goes out with the rest of the orders?"

"Sure," Briana replied. "Mr. Gorgeous is Rich. We were all friends in high school. He and I went to A & M together, actually."

"Wait. A. Minute," Kara stated, pulling Briana so that they faced each other. "Is Mr. Gorgeous the A & M guy that you told me about?" she asked, eyes wide.

"Yes, "Briana admitted. "But you have to keep that to yourself. Seriously, no one else knows about that."

"Wow."

Briana shushed Kara when a couple of servers walked in to pick up their orders. She looked over as Bert came in from the back to join her for the night shift.

"So happy you could make it, Bert," she said sarcastically, watching Kara as she backed out of the room.

"What?" Bert asked, stoned as usual.

"You were supposed to be here two hours ago. I've been slammed."

"Whoa…chill, Bree. I just walked in and you're going all 'Nagging Mom' on me," Bert countered, holding up his hands.

What was with the guys at work today?

"Okay, well, since you're here now, I'm going to take a quick break," she said, trying to decide if she should go out the back door, or stop being a chicken and go through the dining room.

She held her head up and walked out the swinging door into the dining room. She tried to look straight ahead, but could hear the sound of Colin's dad's laugh and had to smile. She turned her head slightly and caught Rich's eye.

Shit.

He put his hand up as if to wave, then stood and pushed away from the table. He said something to Colin, causing him to look over at her. He kept looking at Briana as Rich walked up to her, but she focused on Rich.

"Hey, Bree," Rich said as he got closer, opening his arms to pull her into a hug.

She let herself be enveloped by his arms, her head barely coming to the middle of his chest. She smiled as she smelled his familiar cologne and was surprised by how happy she was to see him.

"Hi, Richie," She said as she pulled back and smiled up at him.

"Girl, you're the only one who can call me that and live," he said, returning her smile.

He really was hot, she thought, studying his shaggy brown hair, hazel eyes, and the sweet little cleft in his chin. He put his finger under her chin, holding her face up so she kept looking at him.

"You doin' good, Bree?"

"Yeah, I'm okay."

"I miss you at school," he admitted dropping his hand and putting both hands in his pockets as he rocked back on his heels.

"I've missed you, too." She looked at him for another moment, then said, "I only have a couple minutes left on my break, so I've gotta run. But we need to catch up while you're home."

"Sounds good. See ya, Bree," he said, grinning as he walked backwards towards his table.

Briana grinned back, then looked over and saw that Colin still watched her. Her grin vanished. She walked out the front door, hoping to get some air before going back into the kitchen.

Luckily the rest of the night was uneventful, and after dealing with a hangover that morning and the craziness of her shift, Briana opted to go home rather than go out.

Friends & Lovers Trilogy

Chapter Four

"So, what was all of that last night with Bree?" Colin asked Rich, who was pulling himself up into Colin's truck.

Rich looked over at him and shrugged. "Nothin' much. I just haven't seen her in a while. She left A & M pretty abruptly and I haven't been home a lot since then, so I wanted to see how she's been doing. Why?"

Colin looked at him thoughtfully, then back out at the road as he pulled away from Rich's folk's house. "I don't know. You guys seemed pretty tight is all," he said. "I've never seen you hug her like that."

"It was no big deal, man. Just sayin' hi." Rich shrugged again and propped his boots up on the dashboard.

Colin knew that he should just let it go. He'd lost any claim he had on Bree four years ago, but he couldn't help but feel like there was more to the story.

"Okay. Did she say she was doing all right?" he asked. Despite his vow to leave her alone now that he was back home for good, he couldn't stop thinking about her. Seeing her at the restaurant last night had brought back all sorts of memories, and he couldn't help but notice how good she'd looked. He also couldn't forget the sick feeling he got in the pit of his stomach every time he thought about the way he'd ended it between them.

"Yeah, she's cool," Rich responded. "We're supposed to hook up before I head back to school." When Colin looked sharply at him, he amended his statement. "I just meant that we're going to hang out."

Colin didn't know how he felt about Briana and Rich being buddy-buddy. Rich was a good guy, but a real player. He didn't want Briana getting tangled up with him.

"When?" he asked, trying to keep his tone light.

"She invited me to go to a party at the gravel pits on Saturday. You know, to catch up and stuff. Some of the people she works with and guys from school will be there. No big deal. You should come," Rich said, as laid-back as usual.

"Yeah, right," Colin said with a laugh. "I don't think Bree would be too happy about that."

"Dude, you guys broke up like a million years ago. I doubt she'll be upset if you show up at the same party as her."

"I'll think about it," Colin answered, as they pulled into the parking lot of his dad's store. "You sure you want to work here for the summer? I thought you'd be looking forward to a summer of parties and girls."

"Oh, I am, brother, don't you worry." Rich said with his signature grin. "There will be plenty of parties and girls, but I need to have some extra cash. When your dad brought it up last night, I figured, why not?"

Colin turned off his truck and opened the door, ready to start the job that he'd always told himself, he'd never do. He'd always dreamed about leaving this town and making it big, whether it was in football or doing something else. He hadn't cared, as long as it wasn't this.

The General Store had been in this town since it was first settled, and it had always been run by Grayson's. When he was little, he used to think it was wonderful to come in and help his dad stock the shelves and clean the store, but when he got old enough to work there every day after school, the store lost its appeal.

Colin tried to appease himself by saying that working there was only temporary, but everyone knew the truth. He was back now, His father could retire in a few years, and Colin was going to end up behind that counter for the rest of his life.

"Come on, man. You look like you're going to a funeral," Rich said, waiting for him at the entrance to the store. "We're gonna have a great time."

Colin looked up at the building he had loved as a child, then down the street at the Bar & Grill. Well, at least he'd have an excuse to see Briana, since he'd be right down the street.

With one last sigh, he followed Rich into the store, ready to begin his sentence.

"Howdy, boys," Colin's father boomed. "It's been pretty slow this morning, so why don't you show Rich the ropes, Colin? We'll have him running the soda fountain so he can talk up the customers. With his pretty face behind the counter, I see sales a-risin'."

Mr. Grayson let out a big laugh and then turned back to the counter as Colin ushered Rich into the back room to show him around.

"This is pretty cool, dude. I mean, I've been in the store a million times, but this time I'll be serving the kids at the counter, just like Roberta used to serve me." Rich looked tickled at the thought and Colin just shook his head. He wished he could be as excited as Rich about being there, but he couldn't help but think of all of the possibilities that were lost to him now.

"Come on, man," he said. "Let's get you set up before the customers roll in and Dad loses it because we're not ready."

Colin took him around the back room and showed him where they kept the inventory, specifically, everything Rich needed to run the soda fountain. They offered only shakes, malts, and ice cream sundaes, so it was a pretty easy gig for Rich.

Once they had the cart loaded with the supplies they needed, Colin took Rich out to show him how to stock the counter and make the items on the menu. Just as they finished, they heard the jingle of the door opening and saw a lady come in with her little twin girls.

"Ice cream. Ice cream, Mama, please," the girls sang in unison, as they made their way to the back of the store.

"Okay, girls, but you have to sit there and eat it all while mommy gets her shopping done, all right?" the young mother answered.

"Okay, Mama, we promise," they said.

As they got to the counter and boosted themselves up on the stools, Rich turned on the charm.

"Good morning, ladies, what can I get for you on this fine day?"

The twins giggled and looked back at their mother, as if asking permission to speak.

"Go ahead, girls, tell the young man what you'd like," she coaxed with a smile.

Colin gave Rich a slight nod and then walked off to find his father. The girls' giggles followed him, as Rich laid on the charm. He couldn't help but laugh at the sound.

"Hey, Pop," he said as he approached the counter.

"Rich all set up?" his father asked.

Colin looked back over his shoulder where Rich was making up a couple of sundae's, talking to the girls as he worked.

"Oh, yeah, he'll be fine."

"I thought he'd be a good fit," Mr. Grayson replied. "It's just too bad he'll only be here for the summer."

"It's not like he'd want to work a soda fountain for the rest of his life, Pop. It's a temporary kind of job. I was thinking rather than trying to hire someone on like Roberta, we should focus on kids. No one wants to work a job like that for as long as she did, anymore. I think we should look at it as more of a temporary position."

His father looked at him and smiled. "You're probably right. Roberta was one of a kind, that's for sure. I know that no one wants to work for minimum wage for long if they don't have to, I just hate the thought of constantly having to train new people."

"If it's a part-time position, we could hire a few kids to work. That way, we'd always have someone with experience and they could do the training as the job turns over."

"See, Son? I knew you'd take to running this business like a dog to water." His father grinned, slapping his hand on his back.

Colin couldn't help but chuckle. "I don't think that's the expression, Pop."

He couldn't retain his foul mood with his dad so happy that he was there, and the sounds of Rich smooth-talking the customers coming from the back. He just hoped he could find a way to retain that happiness.

Friends & Lovers Trilogy

Chapter Five

Briana started her shift, happy that not only was it Friday, but that it was actually *her* Friday. Getting weekends was rare, and rarer still was getting weekends off with her friends so that they could barbecue at the gravel pits.

Pam had allowed Briana, Kara, and Pete to switch shifts with some of the more seasoned workers, who had the prime shifts already locked. Most of them were happy to pick up a weekend now and then. It was a lot more packed and they usually made better money.

It was busy, even for a Friday, but Briana had plenty of help in the kitchen, so she didn't feel like she was overwhelmed. Just busy, which was how she liked it.

Kara came sauntering back into the kitchen to pick up an order. "So, Bree, is Mr. Gorgeous going to be at the pits tomorrow?"

"Rich?" Briana asked absently, putting the finishing touches on the grilled chicken wrap for Kara's order. "Yeah, he said he was going to stop by."

Kara walked up to her, forcing her to look up and focus. She had an odd look on her face and didn't say anything for a minute.

"What?" Briana asked her. "I've got a lot of orders to finish, Kara. Why are you acting weird?"

"I'm not, I was just wondering if you would be upset if I talked to him, that's all."

"Who, Rich? No. Why would I care?" Briana looked at her and Kara gave her a look that said, "You know why."

"Kara, I told you about that. It was just a one-time deal. We never dated or had a relationship. It wasn't like that. I have no claim on him. It's fine, I swear."

"Okay, cool," Kara said with a smile and a bounce. "I didn't want to poach. I just wanted to make sure there was nothing there. You know I'd never do that to you."

"I do. Now get this wrap and get out of here. I've got work to do," Briana said, trying to push her back out into the dining room.

Briana worked diligently, getting orders out as fast as she could until it was break time. She decided to go out into the dining room. Pam didn't mind if they took their breaks out there, as long as it didn't cause a problem for the customers.

Briana grabbed a Coke from Pete and was about to find a seat when she found herself face to face with Colin.

"Hey, Bree."

This was the moment she'd been dreading, but now that it was there, she found that she knew just how to handle it.

"Hi, Colin," She replied, and started to walk around him.

"Wait," he said, putting his hand on her arm to stop her from walking away. "Can't we talk?"

She looked pointedly at his hand and then up at his face, not saying anything until he removed it.

"We don't have anything to talk about, Colin," she said, hoping her face looked bored because her nerves were bouncing all over the place. "Besides, I'm working."

"Looks like you're on break," he replied. "C'mon, Bree, just give me a couple minutes."

She was about to tell him to shove it, when she felt someone come up behind her and two strong arms wrapped around her.

"Hey, Babe, I've been wondering if Pam was ever gonna give you a break." Kent whispered in her ear

He said it loud enough for Colin to hear, and Briana noticed him stiffen at Kent's words and his obvious familiarity.

"Yeah, I've got a quick one." Briana turned and gave him a grateful look, before going up on her tip toes to meet him for a brief kiss.

She thought she heard a grunt or something come from Colin, so she turned to give him a smile and an introduction.

"Oh, sorry," she said, though she wasn't in the least. "Kent, this is Colin. We went to high school together. Colin, this is Kent."

"What's up, man?" Kent asked, extending his hand for a shake.

Colin looked at the offered hand, then back at Kent who may have been an inch shorter than him and shook it.

"Not much. You must be new around here." Colin said.

Briana tried to hide a smirk at Colin's discomfort. It looked like he wanted to punch Kent in the face.

"I've been here for about two years. I work over at the paper. You know, just temporary, to gain some experience and move on to a bigger gig."

He seemed happy to hear that Kent was just a transient and that he'd be moving on eventually.

Briana couldn't help but think that Colin had no right to be jealous of anyone in her life. He was the one who walked all of those years ago.

"Cool, man. Well, I'll leave you two to your business and I'll see you around," Colin said, eager to get out of there. "Bye, Bree."

"Yup," was her only response. She pretended to ignore him as he walked away, focusing her attention on Kent. "Thanks for coming to my rescue."

"Who was that guy?" Kent asked, looking up at Colin's retreating back before looking back down at her. "At first I thought he was your date or something, but the look on your face changed my mind. It looked like you wanted out of the situation. I hope you didn't mind me coming up behind you like that. It just seemed to fit the situation."

"No, I didn't mind, I appreciated it. We dated in high school and I really hoped I'd never have to see him again. Pretty stupid, considering how small the town is, but he'd never planned to move back here."

Kent was quiet for a moment. "Oh, so he's the douche from high school." He looked up again, as if wishing Colin was still standing in front of him.

"Yeah, but it's no big deal. It was a long time ago. He just took me by surprise, is all." As did the feelings she'd had when his hand touched her. It didn't seem fair that the one person she never wanted to see again was the one person who could set her body on fire with one innocent touch.

"All right, Babe. You know that I'm here for you anytime you need me. If you want to tell him we're together, feel free," Kent said with his cocky little grin lighting up his face.

Briana touched her hand to his cheek and smiled, wishing she felt the things for Kent that she'd felt for Colin.

"Thanks, but I'll be okay. I don't want to cramp your style and ruin your chance with the ladies," she responded playfully, trying to soften her negative response.

Kent looked down at her seriously, his heart in his eyes. "Bree, you know all you have to do is say the word, and there will be no other ladies."

She nodded, wishing she could give him the answer he wanted.

He smiled again, all seriousness leaving his face. "You still want me to pick you up at one tomorrow?"

"You sure you still want to go?" she asked, giving him an out if he wanted one. "If you have other plans, I'll understand."

"Nope," he replied. "I'm all yours."

"Okay. One o'clock will be perfect." She tip toed up to give him a quick kiss before turning to go back to the kitchen. "I'll see you then."

Friends & Lovers Trilogy

Chapter Six

Briana and Kent were among the first people to arrive at the gravel pits. They parked along the side of the dirt road and unloaded the stuff from the car. Kent grabbed the charcoal grill and started walking.

"Hey, Bree, if you can bring the bags and blanket, I'll come back for the food and charcoal," he grunted back at her, as he carried his heavy load.

"Okay," she replied, grabbing the backpacks and following him down the lane.

Once they reached the end of the path, they walked through a hole in the chain-link fence. It opened up to a large pool of crystal blue water.

Kent walked up to their usual spot by the water and set the grill down. He turned and stopped to kiss Briana's forehead before heading back to the car to get the rest of their stuff.

She set up their blanket and put their backpacks down to hold it in place. It was a pretty hot day already, so she pulled her hair back into a ponytail and put her sunglasses on, then applied some sunscreen and chapstick. When she saw Kent coming back in through the fence, she went over to grab a bag from him.

"Kara texted and said that she and Pete are almost here. They just stopped to put ice in the cooler," Briana said.

"Sounds good. I'll just get the charcoal started. That way it'll be hot enough to start cooking when everyone gets here. If you want to jump in while you have the place to yourself, go ahead."

Briana loved swimming, and Kent knew she cherished these moments of solitude in the water. Pretty soon the pits would be filled with people, so she decided to take him up on his offer.

She looked out over the water as she shimmied out of her cutoff shorts, so she didn't see the look on Kent's face as he watched her get undressed. She took her top off next, then ran to the water and dove in.

She swam around, enjoying the feel of the cool water on her hot skin. When she came up for air, she turned back to say something to Kent, and saw that Pete and Kara had arrived. They were setting up next to Kent. She swam back towards the shore to get out and join them.

She walked out of the water, her hair slicked back with droplets cascading down her body.

That was the image that greeted Colin when Rich ushered him in through the fence. He stopped abruptly. Rich ran into his back, and Colin stood there, mouth open, as he watched her.

"Dude," Rich yelled. "What the hell?"

Briana looked up at the sound of Rich's voice and saw Colin watching her. The look on his face was enough to make her body tingle, and she couldn't help but feel some satisfaction in the stupefied look on his face.

Kent looked up at Rich's shout as well, and was less than happy to see the way Colin stared at Briana. The only one who seemed oblivious was Rich, who was still trying to shove Colin through the gate.

"Colin, I can't walk through you, dude."

Rich's voice finally registered, and Colin said, "Sorry, man," as he got out of the way.

Briana walked over to her friends and pulled Kara off to the side. "What the hell is Colin doing here?" she asked, trying to keep her voice down. "Did you know he was coming?"

"No, I had no idea," Kara replied. "I'm sure Rich invited him. It'll be fine. There will be so many people here that you'll never have to talk to him."

Kara walked back over to finish setting up her blanket and unpacking her things. Briana watched Colin and Rich go up to Pete and slap hands to say hello. They all started talking, probably catching up since they last saw each other, and she took the opportunity to look Colin over while he was distracted.

He wore solid blue swim trunks with a tank top in the same shade. His arms looked really good, toned and tan. She felt that tingle run through her again and she couldn't help but remember what it felt like to touch his body.

Back when she'd the ability to touch him whenever she wanted, she'd always loved to run her hands over his back and feel the taut muscles underneath. She'd always thought his body was amazing, thanks to the training he'd had to do every day.

She looked around and realized that there would be a lot of eye candy for the ladies today. Between Colin, Kent, Rich, and Pete there wasn't an inch of body fat. She couldn't wait until it was time to go swimming.

Maybe she would just enjoy the day and not worry about Colin. The town was small, but it was big enough for the both of them. Since they were bound to run into each other often, she might as well make the most of it.

Kent started grilling the food as the rest of the people started showing up. Everyone cracked open the beers and malt beverages. Kara put on some tunes and everyone started to enjoy the water and the company.

Briana was sitting on her blanket talking to Pete, when they noticed Kara walking over to where Rich and Colin stood talking.

"Don't take it personally, Pete," Briana said quietly to him.

"I don't," Pete replied. "I've known Kara a long time, Bree, and I know that she thinks that she can't have a serious relationship because her mother never could. But she's wrong."

"Her mother's a bitch, and Kara is nothing like her. But you're right; she doesn't think that she's relationship material."

"I'm a patient guy," Pete said with a sad smile as he watched Kara pull Rich towards the water. "I can wait. I plan to be there when she realizes how much she has to offer."

Briana looked over at him and put her hand up to ruffle his hair. "You're the sweetest guy I know."

"I know," he said with a laugh, looking pointedly around. "But that's not saying much."

She laughed with him and punched him goodheartedly in the arm. "These guys aren't so bad," she replied.

They watched Kara and Rich splashing in the water until it became too much for Pete. He excused himself to go help Kent with the food.

Briana laid back on her blanket, eyes closed, soaking up the sun. After a few minutes she felt a shadow pass over her, as someone sat down on the blanket next to her. She knew it was Colin even before she opened her eyes. It was like her senses were still attuned to him and every nerve in her body stood at attention when he got close.

"Hey, Bree, I hope you don't mind that Rich invited me here today," he said in a quiet voice.

She didn't open her eyes. "It's a free country."

He let out a deep sigh and tried to look out at the water, but all he wanted to do was take in the sight before him. Briana's small frame was tanned and perfectly proportioned. He felt his body tightening as his eyes wandered, and he forced his gaze back out.

"I realize that, Bree, but I don't want to ruin your party or anything. I haven't done much since I've been home and when Rich invited me, it sounded like a good time. But I'm not trying to piss you off."

Briana peeked up at him. Then, realizing he wasn't leaving, she sat up and turned towards him.

"It's a small town, Colin. We're bound to run into each other. We still have a lot of the same friends. You should feel comfortable going and doing whatever you want. Don't worry about me. I'll be okay."

"Cool," he said with a small smile, his dimples flashing. "I'm glad to hear you say that. I know I ended things badly Bree, but, shit I was just a kid. I'm sorry."

Briana looked out over the water. "Look, Colin, I know we'll run into each other, but that doesn't mean that I want to rehash everything that happened four years ago. I'm not ready to be your buddy."

With that said she stood up to leave. As she walked down to the water she heard him say, "I've really missed you."

She ran and dove in, trying to swim as far away from him and his damned words as she could.

Friends & Lovers Trilogy

Chapter Seven

Briana was sitting on the couch, drinking coffee and watching E! News the next morning, when Rich poked his head out of Kara's bedroom.

"Walk of shame, Rich?" Briana asked with a chuckle, not looking away from the TV.

"Shit. I was hoping you'd still be asleep, Bree."

"No such luck, Romeo."

He walked out with his pants slung around his hips, still unbuttoned, and his shirt in his hand. Briana looked back briefly and turned away when she saw his six pack rippling and started to inadvertently follow his happy trail with her eyes.

"Can you put your shirt on?" she pleaded.

He smiled at that and cocked his head to the side as he strolled over to her.

"What is it, baby? See something you like?" Rich could flirt in any situation, no matter how awkward or inappropriate. It was part of his charm.

"Been there, done that," she retorted.

He sat down next to her on the couch, his cocky smile gone, a serious look in its place.

"About that. You never said anything to Colin, did you?"

"No. I haven't talked to him in four years, Rich. When would it have come up?"

"I don't know, but I never told him, either. I don't know if we should."

"Rich, I doubt it would ever enter a conversation, but if it does, I won't lie to him," she said, looking him in the eye. "It shouldn't matter to him, anyway. Don't worry about it."

He looked unsure for a minute, then glanced back towards Kara's door.

"Does she know?" he asked.

"Yeah, she knows. She knew before she met you," Briana replied. "It's no big deal, Rich. Seriously, stop worrying."

"Alright," he said finally, then looked back at her, his cocky grin back in place. "You know I'll always love you, right, Babe?"

Briana smiled back, but her look turned serious. "I know that, Richie. I'll always love you too. You're one of my best friends." She leaned in to give him a hug, then realized he still didn't have his shirt on. "I appreciate the fact that you work out and your body is *awesome*, but can you please put your shirt on? It's hard to concentrate."

Rich looked pleased at that. He stood up to go into the kitchen for coffee, throwing his shirt over his head along the way.

Kara came stumbling out moments late and grunted at Briana on her way to get some coffee.

"You'd better have left me some coffee," she grumbled at Rich.

"Dang, girl, you're lookin' rough." Rich stated with a laugh, running out of the kitchen to avoid Kara's wrath.

"Shove it, Rich," was Kara's reply. She walked in holding the warm cup up to her face inhaling briefly, before taking her first sip. "Don't mess with me before I've had my coffee."

"Noted," he replied, as he sat back down on the couch with his mug.

"So, ladies, what's on your agenda today?"

Kara was still waiting for the coffee to take effect and didn't reply, so Briana answered.

"Nothing much. I'm off today, so I'm planning to lie out in the sun and read. But Kara has to work."

"Yeah, me too. I'll be serving up some delicious treats at The General Store if you guys want to stop by," he offered with a wink.

Kara looked at him blandly over her steaming mug. "No, thanks."

"Yeah, I'll pass, too," Briana said with a look of regret. "Sorry, but although I know I'm going to run into Colin now that he's back, that doesn't mean I'm going to seek him out."

"You're not still mad at him for what happened four years ago, are you?" Rich questioned her. "Bree that was a long time ago. You guys have been apart way longer than you were ever together."

"I loved him, Rich," Briana replied quietly. "He really hurt me."

"I know that. Believe me, if anyone knows how much he hurt you, it's me. But give the dude a chance. It's been a long time. He's grown up, and I know he regrets hurting you."

"I don't know if I'm ready yet. A lot of time may have passed, but I've only just started to see him again. It's like seeing him has brought back all of those feelings of hurt and resentment, as if it just happened."

"Just think about it." Rich stood up and took his cup back to the kitchen, then came back out to give them each a hug. "Well, ladies, I hate to break it to you, but I have to get going. Work is a'waitin'."

"You're working at a soda fountain," Kara said, finally waking up enough to get snarky. "It's not like the city will crumble if you don't get to work on time."

"Hey, Ms. Grumpy Pants, this is my last summer before I'm a college graduate and have to get a real job, with all of the stress and long hours that come along with it. I plan to make the most of my time at the counter, and vow to have the happiest customers in town," he declared with a wink and a smile. Then he walked out the door.

Briana couldn't help but giggle at his dramatic exit.

"You shouldn't encourage that clown." Kara said dryly.

"Hey, that clown is one of my best friends. Be nice."

"Sorry. Didn't get a lot of sleep last night," Kara said with a satisfied smile.

"Please, spare me the details about two of my best friends' night of passion," Briana begged her. "This situation is strange enough without getting the play-by-play."

"Yeah, you're probably right."

"You gonna see him again?"

"Nah… We talked it out last night. It was just a casual thing between friends, no big deal." Kara got to her feet and walked out. "Gotta grab a shower."

Briana knew that it was hypocritical, but she couldn't help but wish that Kara would give a guy a chance. She had so much to offer and Briana knew that Kara would be a wonderful girlfriend for any guy, but Kara didn't see it that way. Her mother had spent her life telling her that she would never be good enough for anyone, and Kara believed every word. She figured her mother knew her better than anyone, but she couldn't have been more wrong. Kara was the most loving, loyal, and funny person that Briana had ever met, and she wished that she would allow herself to fall in love.

Although Briana would be the first one to say that love really did hurt, and that hurting really sucked, the love part really made it all worth it.

Having someone who listened to you, really listened. Who cared what happened to you. Who offered you comfort when you needed it. Someone you could laugh or cry hysterically with, someone who would allow you to just be yourself, no matter what. There was nothing like kissing someone that you truly loved. It made her sigh just thinking about it.

That was really the reason why Briana hadn't had a serious relationship since Colin. No one else made her feel the way that she had when they were together. She worried that no one else ever could.

Friends & Lovers Trilogy

Chapter Eight

Colin knew that it was a thinly veiled excuse to stop by and see Briana, but a guy had to eat, didn't he?

He'd talked Rich into heading down to the Bar & Grill after work. It didn't really take that much convincing; Rich was always ready to eat. He seemed especially after the work out he'd been treated to that morning.

When they walked into the crowded restaurant, Colin scanned the room for signs of Briana. He knew she'd more than likely be in the back, but he still hoped for a glimpse. He hadn't seen her in a few days, and he'd missed the sight of her.

He realized that he wasn't going to get to see her yet, so he walked up to where Rich was chatting up the hostess.

"C'mon, sweet Nicole. I'm sure you can find us a table somewhere in this place. There are just two of us."

The blonde hostess turned red at Rich's flirting and said that she'd see what she could do to find them a table right away.

"Leave that poor girl alone, Rich," Colin said as Nicole scurried off in search of a table. "She looks pretty sweet. I don't think she knows how to handle the likes of you."

"No harm," Rich smiled. "And see? It worked. She's fixin' something up for us right now."

Colin couldn't help but chuckle softly as they were led to their seats. Rich could charm the pants off anyone, and very nearly had.

They thanked Nicole, and she flushed again, murmuring, "You're welcome," as she walked back to her post.

They didn't need to look at the menu. It was Wednesday after all, so wings were pretty much a given.

"Well, lucky me. Two of the most eligible bachelors in town, sitting at my table," Kara drawled with a sexy grin.

"Hey, Kara," Colin said. "How you doin'?"

"Can't complain," she replied. "Can I start ya'll off with a beer?"

"Yes, ma'am." This was delivered by Rich, with a sexy grin of his own.

"Comin' right up, Sugar." They both took a moment to watch Kara sashay to the bar. "She's the female version of you," Colin said shaking his head and turning back to Rich.

Rich just leaned back and grinned. "Ain't that the truth."

They got their beer and watched the game for a bit, drinking and talking. While they waited for their wings to come out, Rich asked Colin if he felt better about working at The General Store.

"No, man," Colin said with a frown. "I love my parents and this town and everything, but I can't help but resent the fact that I'm here doing the one thing I swore I'd never do."

"Then why are you?"

"Everything just went to hell when I got hurt. I focused on finishing school, but then I just had to get out of there. I couldn't stand to face the team and my coaches, knowing that I wasn't a part of the game anymore."

"It's not like coming here and running the store is your only option. If you hate it so much, look for something else," Rich offered.

Colin took a long drink, then replied, "Nothing means as much to me as football, so I might as well be miserable here, where I know people."

"That's a shitty way to look at it," Rich argued. "Dude, I know you're pissed, I would be too, but playing football isn't the only way to be involved in the game."

"Yeah, I guess you're right." Colin said thoughtfully. "I could look into coaching or something; I just don't know where to start."

"Well, you're gonna start at the bottom, but at least you'll be happy," Rich replied. Then he looked up at someone approaching their table.

Figuring it was Kara, Colin didn't look up. Then he heard Kent's voice.

"Hey, guys. How's it goin'?" he said when he got to the table. He had his arm slung around a beautiful girl with long blonde hair and amazing gray eyes. She smiled and Colin noticed she had a dimple on the left side of her face. "This is my sister, Roni. She's staying with me for a while and I wanted to introduce her around, make her feel welcome."

Colin and Rich stood up and shook her hand. Rich held on long enough for Kent to narrow his eyes at him.

Rich just smiled and said, "It's nice to meet you, Roni. You need anything, you just look for me."

Kent bent down to say something to Roni and she turned and walked back towards the bar.

"All right. The real reason I wanted to introduce you is because Roni will be at Kara and Bree's party tonight, and I wanted you both to know that she's my sister, so hands off," Kent said. "Especially you, Rich. I didn't like the way you were looking at her."

"No harm, man," Rich said, holding his hands up as if to prove he was no threat. "You're sister's pretty man, that's all. I'll leave her alone."

Kent looked at Colin, who just nodded.

Kent nodded back at both of them and said, "Later," as he walked back in the direction his sister went.

They both sat down and Rich whistled. "Holy, shit. That was the most beautiful girl I have ever seen up close." He declared with a look of wonder.

"I wouldn't mess with Kent if I were you. He looked pretty serious."

Rich was saved from answering when Kara arrived with their food, but Colin noticed that he couldn't help but look over to where the tall, slender blonde leaned against the bar talking with Pete.

Chapter Nine

Briana was thrilled when they finally closed for the night. She felt so greasy and gross that she couldn't wait to get home and shower.

She put the finishing touches on her dish, then took it out to the bar to share with her co-workers.

"That looks so good, Bree," Kara moaned from her perch at the bar. She'd kicked off her heels and was rubbing her sore feet. "I'm so hungry, I could eat that whole plate of pasta."

"Get in line," Pete said as he poured some drinks to go with their meal.

"Wine for me, please," Nicole chimed in as she walked to the back of the room. "I can't wait to get everything cleaned and head to your place. I was so bummed I had to miss out last week, but I had to go home to watch my brothers and sisters."

"No problem," Briana said. "At least you're free tonight." Then she turned to Pete, "Wine sounds good. Would you pour me the red?"

They all sat down to enjoy the food and drinks, then went about cleaning up the front and back of the house as quickly as possible so they could head to Kara and Briana's apartment. They yelled goodnight to Pam, who thanked Briana for the pasta, then locked up behind them.

Kara and Briana hosted this get together most Wednesdays, so they knew the routine and got themselves and the apartment ready when they got home. Pretty soon the place was filled with people and the party was in full swing.

Briana and Kara both opted for sundresses, since it was a hot Texas night. When Nicole arrived wearing her hostess uniform, Briana offered to loan her something to wear.

When Nicole walked out wearing the dress, she looked uncertainly at Briana.

"I think it's too small."

"No, you just have bigger boobs than I do. It's perfect," Briana assured her. She fluffed out Nicole's hair to give it a fuller look, and told her to stop standing with her hands crossed over her chest.

"C'mon, let's go get you a drink. Stop worrying. You look amazing."

They went out to join the party and ran into Kent and Roni in the hall. Kent paused momentarily, taking in Nicole's drastic change in appearance. They all stood there for a moment, until Nicole blushed and looked down, and Roni cleared her throat.

"Oh, ahh, hey. What's up?" Kent said hoarsely, before clearing his throat. "Nicole, you met my sister, Roni, but Roni, you didn't get a chance to meet Bree yet."

Briana smiled at Roni, surprised at the striking resemblance between the two. It almost hurt to look at the pair of them, they were so beautiful.

"Wow, Kent, you never said you had a sister." Briana said, wondering what other things they'd never shared with each other.

"Yeah, Roni's my twin. She's going to be staying with me for a while," he said with a smile for his sister. He tried not to stare at Nicole's amazing body.

"Hi, Roni. It's great to meet you. Would you like something to drink?" Briana offered, taking her arm and steering her towards the kitchen.

That left Kent and Nicole standing in the hallway, her eyes on the floor and his on the ceiling.

"Um, I'm going to go get a drink," Nicole said softly, excusing herself and following the girls.

Kent gave himself a moment to regain control, before turning and heading to join Pete and Kara in the living room.

Briana strolled around her apartment, talking with people and sipping on a beer. Eventually, she decided she'd ignored the corner where Colin and Rich sat deep in conversation, long enough.

She couldn't believe that it had only been a week since she first found out that Colin was back in town. Now he was in her living room. Weird.

There were a couple of empty beer cans next to their seats, and she heard them talking about college as she got closer.

"Hey guys," she said when she got close enough to be heard over the noise of the room.

They both stood up. She walked stepped closer to Rich to give him a hug. They embraced each other and murmured hello before pulling away and smiling.

When she turned away from Rich, she noticed Colin staring at them with a strange expression on his face.

"You guys never used to be that close before. I mean, back in high school we all hung out, but you guys were never on a hugging basis. Anyone watching would think that you were more than just friends," he stated, looking guarded.

"She's one of my best friends." Rich said, trying not to make a big deal out of Colin's observation.

"Hmm. Okay, I guess." Colin still looked confused. "It's just, Bree only went to A & M for like, a year, right? And you've been gone this whole time. When have you guys had time to get so close?"

"What's your point, Colin?" Briana asked, starting to get frustrated with the way he was acting.

"All I'm saying is that it seems like there's more to the story." He took a deep breath, then asked, "Did you guys hook up or something?"

Briana and Rich looked at each other and then looked at him. Both silent, but with expressions of guilt and regret.

"Are you fucking serious?" Colin asked in a low voice. "I was fishing! Did something really happen between the two of you?"

"Bro…" Rich started.

"Don't *Bro*, me, Rich. Answer the fucking question."

Briana stepped in between the two guys. "It was just one time, Colin. It was never anything serious," she said.

"That's. Just. Fucking. Great," he managed before turning and storming out of the apartment.

Briana turned to Rich, who had gone ashen with regret.

"Shit," he said simply, before sitting back down in his chair.

Briana went to find Kara, Kent, or Pete, but ran into Roni first.

"Roni," she said, grabbing her hand and pulling her over to Rich. "Can you keep an eye on him for me? Make sure he doesn't leave this apartment, okay?"

"Sure," Roni replied, looking anything but sure as she looked at the gorgeous guy sitting there like he'd just seen a ghost.

"Thanks." Briana ran to her room to grab the car keys.

"What's up, Bree?" Kara asked from the kitchen. She followed Briana into her room, noting her friend's frantic movement.

"Who does he think he is?" she asked out loud. "He's the one who dumped me! He has no right to act all pissed off, like we did something terrible to him."

"What are we talking about?" Kara tried to get her attention, but she was scouring the room like a crazy person.

"Son of a bitch. Where are the keys?"

"Probably in your purse. Are you going somewhere?" Kara asked, picking up Briana's purse and handing it to her.

"Yeah. I'm going to have it out with Colin, once and for all."

Friends & Lovers Trilogy

Chapter Ten

Briana knew that Colin was staying at the apartments behind The General Store from a conversation she'd had with Rich. She just hoped that that's where he went after he left the party. Then she pulled behind the store and saw his truck, so she parked behind it.

She stormed up the steps and pounded on the door.

It swung open as she raised her fist to knock again.

"Not now, Bree." Colin said swinging the door closed again.

She put her foot in the doorway and pushed the door as hard as she could, shoving past him and walking in, before turning to look at him with her hands on her hips.

"Yes, *now*, Colin," she countered.

He slammed the door shut and looked down at her small angry form.

"Fine, you wanna go?" he yelled, storming past her, his arms emphasizing his words. "Let's go."

"No," she turned on him, standing up on tip toe so she could get in his face. "You don't get to be mad here, Colin. You left me, not the other way around, and I doubt you've been celibate for the last four years. Tell me, are you still a *virgin*, Colin?"

"That's not the point, *Briana,* I don't care that you're not a virgin. I didn't expect you to stay a virgin forever. The point is that you slept with Rich - my best friend. Or should I say, my former best friend."

"Oh, give me a break. Rich is still your best friend. You aren't going to let one night three years ago ruin the friendship you've had your whole life."

Colin turned from her to walk over to the window.

"Colin, listen," she pleaded, her voice softening at the look on his face. "We were both away from home for the first time. I was upset because I was still missing you and I'd heard you had started seeing someone. He was upset because he'd been riding the bench all year. We were hanging out and drinking, and it just happened. It was only once, and it was really awkward afterwards. We agreed that we only wanted to be friends, and have been ever since. Don't be mad at him."

Colin looked at her, his heart heavy and jealousy coursing through his veins. "What about you, should I be mad at you?"

She felt her blood start to rise again, angry that he was trying to make her feel guilty when she had no reason to be.

"I don't care if you're mad at me or not, but it would sure be hypocritical of you, now wouldn't it?"

He sighed loudly. "What did you come here for, Bree? Go back to your boyfriend and leave me be."

"I don't have a boyfriend," she retorted. "I haven't had the stomach for one since you left."

Colin took a step closer. "That Kent guy isn't your boyfriend?"

"No," she responded. "Look, I came here because I was pissed that you got mad at us. You have no reason to be mad. I don't get why you are. You're the one who left. You didn't want me then, so why do you care now?"

With that she whirled towards the door. She only made it a couple steps before Colin grabbed her arm and whirled her back. He walked her quickly backwards until she was stopped by the door.

Before she could register what was happening, she was flat against the door. His mouth was on hers.

She didn't think, she just reacted.

Her hands came up around his neck. His fastened under her bottom and lifted her up. She wrapped her legs around his waist, to get stabilized, then met his hot, hungry mouth with her own.

They kissed frantically, as if they had been starved for the contact. When his mouth left hers to trail kisses down her throat, her head fell back to allow him better access. As he licked his way back up to her mouth, she groaned loudly and he paused to look at her.

"Wanting you was never the problem," he stated, eyes black with need. Then he dove back in and began to drive her slowly crazy.

Her whole body thrummed with need and desire. She rocked against him, reveling in the fact that his body responded to her in a way that it never had before.

Suddenly, the door was no longer at her back as he turned and carried her through the rooms to his bed, his mouth never leaving hers. Once they got to his bed, he laid her down and stayed on top of her in one swift motion.

Prone on the bed, she had the ability to use her trembling hands to explore his rock hard body. She quickly drew his shirt over his head, but when he inhaled deeply and reached for her shirt, she put her hand on top of his to stop him from undressing her.

"I'm not ready for this." Briana looked up at him from beneath full lashes, trying to catch her breath as she spoke.

Colin kneeled back on the bed, running his hands over his face and through his hair. He closed his eyes and nodded, then opened them with a smile.

"Okay." He moved around on the bed so he could lie next to her, picking up her hand and lacing his fingers through hers. "We'll do this on your terms, Bree."

He laid back and patted his chest. She scooted over and placed her head over his racing heart and smiled. He traced his fingers over her shoulder and arm. She dozed off reveling in the smell and feel of him.

Briana opened her eyes to Colin's face peaceful with sleep. She realized that she hadn't seen him look this peaceful since he'd come back home.

She felt a rush of sadness for him that he'd fallen short of his childhood dream. For as long as she'd known him, football had been his life. It was as much a part of him as breathing. She'd loved his dedication to the sport and the fulfillment that it had given him.

She smiled as she remembered Colin and Rich at the first pep rally of his senior year. They had been in front of the entire school, pumped up for their game. Colin was named Captain of the team, and Briana had never been so proud.

Now, she enjoyed having the opportunity to really look at him. They'd never spent the night together, so she'd never seen him look this vulnerable. It tugged at something inside of her, something she'd tried for years to contain.

He began to shift and stretch, then he opened his eyes. He blinked, as if to focus, and when he shifted his hand, it touched her leg, causing him to turn his head towards her.

His face blossomed and his dimples flashed.

"Good morning," he said softly, his voice still rough with sleep.

"Good morning." She smiled back at him, caught up in the moment.

"I'm happy that you're here," he said, bringing his hand up to sweep the hair from her face.

"Me too," she admitted.

"I've missed you."

Briana didn't say anything to that. She wasn't ready to delve too deep into their relationship.

"What happened? With football?" she asked softly

"It was the last game of the season and I got hit. Hard. I went down wrong and messed up my knee pretty bad again. The doctor said that I have to stop playing, or I'll have permanent damage. So that's it. No more ball, well at least no more ball as a player."

"Does that mean you're thinking about still being involved with football, but in another capacity?"

"Yeah. Rich and I were just talking about this actually, and I've been doing some research online. I was thinking about trying to coach." Colin's eyes shone with excitement as he spoke. "I'd have to start as an assistant, but it would be great to still have the opportunity to be part of a team."

Briana couldn't help but be excited for him, but that also meant that his time here would be short-lived.

"That's great. Have you said anything to you folks?"

"Nah, not yet. I know Dad will be disappointed. He was pretty happy when I came home, and he loves the idea of me running the store, but I know that ultimately they both want what's best for me." Colin brought her hand up to his lips and kissed it gently. "What about you? What happened at A & M?"

Briana felt the familiar regret when she answered.

"You've heard the story before: girl goes to college, girl doesn't go to class as much as she should, and doesn't do well when she does. Girl doesn't get good enough grades to keep her financial aid, so girl returns home with her tail between her legs."

"Hey," he said, lifting her face so that he could look in her eyes. "Don't do that. You're not just any girl. You're smart, capable, and confident. Sometimes shit happens, but you're great."

She smiled at him, then leaned in to kiss him softly on the lips.

"Thanks. I've been thinking about going back to school," she admitted shyly. "Not back to university, but to culinary school."

"Really? That's wonderful."

"Yeah, there's one in Austin that I've been looking at."

"You should do it, Bree. You'll be great."

"I've been saving up and my mom said she'd pay half, so I should have the money soon. I've been putting together the application."

"How is your mother?" he asked with a grin. He and her mother had always been very fond of each other.

"She's great. She moved with Ray, her new husband, out to a farm about thirty miles away. I don't get to see her as often as I'd like, but I'm planning on heading out there this weekend."

"I'm glad she's happy. She deserves it." Colin and Briana had just started dating when Briana's father died of a brain aneurysm. He'd passed away in his sleep. It had been a total shock for Briana and her mother. Colin had been a wonderful source of support for them both, and Briana would always love him for that.

Her heart swelled at the memory and her eyes started to fill. She leaned in to kiss him again, with more force and feeling this time. It didn't take much coaxing before Colin was resting on top of her, the weight of him causing the rest of her body to come alive.

The morning passed too quickly, and before she knew it, Briana had to leave so she could get some errands done before work that night.

Colin walked her to the door; his jeans unbuttoned and slung low on his hips.

She took a moment to appreciate the sight and feel of him before tearing herself away and reaching for the door handle.

"Will you go out with me Friday night?" he asked before she walked out the door.

She turned and looked up at him, "Like on a date?"

"Yes. I'll pick you up and we can go to dinner, or whatever you'd like." He looked so unsure of her answer that she couldn't help the smile that blossomed on her face.

"I'd like that," she replied. "But I'm leaving early on Saturday to go to my Mom's house, so it can't be a really late night."

"No problem," Colin said, grinning widely, his eyes sparkling with pleasure. "I'll pick you up at six."

"Okay, I'll see you then." She leaned in for a quick kiss, but paused before turning to go. "Go easy on Rich, all right? He loves you."

Colin just nodded as she walked away.

Friends & Lovers Trilogy

Chapter Eleven

Colin walked into work the next day with a skip in his step and a smile on his face. He was excited at the prospect of his date that evening with Bree, and hoped to continue to rebuild her trust in him.

He was heading towards the back room when he noticed Rich at the counter talking with a pretty blonde as he made a sundae. He knew that they needed to talk, but figured it best to have it out after Rich was done with his customers.

When he got to the back office he booted up the computer and checked his email. He deleted all of the spam and random giveaways, but paused, when he saw an email from his ex.

He'd met Shawn during Greek Week. Her sorority was having a rush party and he and some of the team were out hitting up all of the parties on Greek Row.

Shawn was definitely beautiful; there was no question about that. So when she pursued him, he hadn't put up a fight.

She made it pretty clear that she liked the fact that he was on the team and she enjoyed the perks and status that went along with dating him. He was totally focused on football and wasn't looking for a serious relationship, so she'd suited him just fine.

It didn't take long after he was injured, before it became apparent that his career in football was over, or for her to break off their relationship and move on.

It had hurt his pride a bit, especially on the tail-end of losing his dream of playing career ball, but there were no lasting effects.

When he saw her email address pop up in his inbox, he opened it with mild curiosity, figuring she had a question or something. When it said that she really wanted to see him, he deleted it without replying.

When he was finished in the office, he stood to go on the floor and was met by Rich coming in the back. Rich looked nervous and unsure, so Colin spoke first.

"Hey, man. I'm sorry about the other night, I was outta line."

Rich looked relieved, but still said guiltily, "No. You had every right to be mad. I slept with your ex, and that is totally against man-code."

"Rich, we'd been broken up for a year. Don't sweat it. I shouldn't have gotten so upset, but when you guys admitted that you'd been together, I was totally jealous. It was my gut reaction."

"It's understandable. She was your girl and I'm your best friend. You're like a brother to me, man. It never should have happened."

"Bree explained everything to me, so no hard feelings, all right?" Colin pulled Rich in for a quick hug, and looked at him with a smile. "Let's just never talk about it again, okay?"

Rich grinned back, "Deal."

The day went by pretty quickly, and at exactly six o'clock, Colin knocked on Briana's door.

His breath caught when he took in her short skirt that billowed around her sexy legs. She looked fresh and beautiful as she greeted him with a smile.

He leaned in to kiss her cheek and said, "You look amazing," which caused her smile to widen.

He held her hand as they walked down the stairs to his car. "Thanks for agreeing to go out with me, Bree."

She stopped for a moment and said, "This is the only second chance you're going to get, Colin. Don't disappoint me."

His stomach fluttered at her words, and he hoped that he wouldn't.

"I won't."

When they got to the restaurant, he walked around to open her door and offered his hand in assistance.

"Thank you, Sir," she said with a giggle. She tried to keep her skirt down as she got out of the truck.

"Anytime, Ma'am," he replied, playing along.

She smiled as they walked up to the entrance. "You remembered that I love seafood."

"I remember everything, Bree," he assured her as he opened the door.

When they were escorted to their table, he pulled out Briana's seat for her, and sat across from her. Her delighted grin made him happy that he'd been taking care to be a gentleman for her.

They ordered their food and caught up as they nibbled on spinach dip.

"So," Briana began, "how are your parents doing?"

"They seem happier than they've ever been," he answered. "Mom started playing tennis and has made a beautiful garden in their yard. She's taking more time for herself, since I'm out of the house, which is really good for her. Since she's so happy, that makes Dad happy. They're going out on date nights now and everything."

"That's wonderful. They're such a great couple. I've always looked up to them for that," Briana admitted. "When I get married, I hope my marriage is as great as theirs."

"Me, too," Colin replied, reaching over the table to hold her hand. "I know I've said this already, but I've really missed you, Bree."

She looked down at the joined hands and then back up into his dark eyes.

"I'm sure you've had plenty of company over the last few years," she said softly, not voicing the question that was apparent in her face.

"I'm not going to lie and say that I didn't date after we broke up. I kept things pretty casual for the most part, but I did have one girlfriend while I was in school. It was more of a status thing. We liked each other, but we weren't in love. It was nothing like my relationship with you, Bree. You're the only girl that I've ever been in love with."

Briana blushed at that, and couldn't help the smile that formed at his words. She'd always assumed that he'd see other girls while he was away, and she'd figured that unlike her, he would have another relationship. But she couldn't help the uneasy feeling that came with hearing he'd had another girlfriend.

"What happened?" she asked. "Why'd you break up?"

"She was only interested in dating me because I played football and was getting scouted. Once I got injured, there was nothing that I could do to help her get what she wanted."

"That sucks," she said, getting angry on his behalf. "She sounds like a terrible person."

Colin chuckled at her reaction. "Nah, she's not that bad," he replied. "Like I said, we knew what our relationship was, so the only thing that was injured when she dumped me was my pride."

Briana squeezed his hand, then let it go when their food arrived and they both began to eat.

They talked a bit more while they ate; catching up on things they'd missed in each other's lives since they'd last spoken. As they waited for the waiter to return with their bill, Briana talked to him about Pete's love for Kara.

"I feel so bad. He's been in love with her for over a year, and every time she brings another guy around, she crushes him a little bit more."

"Does she know how he feels?" Colin asked.

She frowned. "She thinks he has a crush, so she doesn't take him seriously. She says that she wants to stay single and just enjoy life, but I don't think she is enjoying life. I think she would love to have someone, but that she's afraid of being hurt."

After he signed the bill, Colin took her hand and said, "You have to let them work this out. If you interfere, you're just going to upset Kara."

"I know," she admitted, "but I know that Pete is exactly what she needs. I just wish she'd give him a chance."

They walked out of the restaurant, but Colin paused before they got to his truck.

"I know that you have to get up early to go to your Moms, but I'm not ready for our night to end." He pushed a strand of hair behind her ear as he spoke.

"It's still early," she responded. "What did you have in mind?"

"I have a bottle of wine in the truck. How about the gravel pits?" he suggested.

"Okay," she agreed with a smile, reaching up to give him a soft kiss on the lips. "Thanks for dinner."

He leaned into her and deepened the kiss. "My pleasure."

When they got to the gravel pits and snuck through the fence, Colin opened his bag and produced a blanket, a bottle of wine, a corkscrew and two glasses.

"Looks like you thought of everything," Briana said, pleasure lighting up her face.

He spread out the blanket near the edge of the water and opened the bottle as she got comfortable. He poured her a glass and handed it to her, sitting down so their thighs touched.

He held his glass up to her and said, "To second chances, and to the most amazing woman I know."

"To second chances," she toasted.

She took a sip and looked out over the water. "It's a beautiful night. I love the way the moon shines out over the water. It's magical."

Colin looked at her face reflected in the moonlight as he tried his wine. He felt the familiar longing and contentment that he always had when he was with her.

"Hey." She turned to him with a wicked grin. "Wanna go swimming?"

"We don't have our suits."

"You gonna let that stop you?" she asked as she stood up and placed her glass on a nearby rock and began to pull her shirt over her head.

Colin watched, awestruck, as she shimmied out of her skirt, then walked to the water and looked over her shoulder at him as she took off her bra and threw it on the ground next to her.

She gave him a come-hither smile. He jumped to his feet and yanked his shirt over his head. When he pulled at his buckle, he watched as she strode to the water and dove in, her gorgeous body softly glowing in the moonlight.

He almost tripped in his eagerness to get his pants off, but quickly righted himself and finished taking off the rest of his clothing. It seemed he was no longer capable of rational thought. His sole focus was on getting in that water as fast as possible.

He barely registered the chill of the water as he dove in the direction that Briana had gone. When he surfaced, she was a few feet away from him, treading water as she waited.

He swam up to her and pulled her to him. She wound her arms around his neck.

Their lips met frantically, both of them reveling in the feel of their wet bodies meeting beneath the water, forgetting momentarily to kick their legs in order to stay above water.

They stayed in the kiss for a moment, as their heads submerged, then pulled apart and resurfaced with a few kicks.

They were both laughing as they came up for air, then began to slowly swim towards the shallow end. When they reached solid ground, they came together, bodies hot and eager to touch.

Briana moaned into his mouth, as Colin began to lose control. Their hands were everywhere, the silky feel of her body turning him on more than he'd ever been. He broke from her lips and trailed kisses along her jaw and neck as her hands roamed freely under the surface.

The light shining in his face barely registered, as Colin licked and nibbled eagerly along Briana's shoulder, fueled by the soft sounds emitting from her throat.

But when he heard a voice say, "Come out of the water and leave the premises, you're on private property," the fog in his brain began to clear.

They broke apart and looked over towards the voice, which had come from a police officer. He shined his flashlight in their direction.

"Come out of the water folks," the officer said again.

Colin was almost to the shore when he realized that he and Briana were naked. She hid shyly behind his body.

"Um, Sir, we're going to exit the water, but would you mind turning off the flashlight and allowing my date to get her clothes?" Colin said loudly, trying to sound firm but respectful at the same time. He didn't want to anger the cop and get them in any further trouble.

The light went out and the policeman turned. They ran from the water to their clothes and dressed as quickly as possible, their bodies' slick and no towels available to dry off.

Once they were dressed, Colin threw everything back into the bag and thanked the officer as they made their way back towards the fence.

"Just remember this is private property and it's not safe to be out here at night," the police officer called after them. "Don't let me catch you here again."

"Yes, Sir," they both yelled back at him as they scurried down the road to Colin's truck.

When they got inside, they both started laughing, and soon Briana was overcome by giggles.

"I was so scared when he started talking," she managed. "I never heard him come up."

"Neither did I. I almost had a heart attack when I realized what was happening."

Briana giggled all the way back to her house. She tried to make her hair look presentable, but without access to a mirror and brush, she just threw it up in a bun on her head.

When he parked in front of her house, he turned to her and asked, "Can I walk you to your door?"

"Of course."

He smiled, his dimples causing her heart to flutter in her chest. He held her hand up the stairs and turned her towards him when they reached her door.

"Thanks again for coming out with me, Bree. I had a wonderful time, cops and all."

"So did I," she agreed. "I can't remember the last time I had so much fun."

He leaned down slowly, watching her eyes as he drew near. He brought his hands up to either side of her face and held her gently, as his lips touched hers.

She brought her hands to his hips, digging her fingers in as the kiss melted every bone in her body. As he deepened the kiss, she moaned in his mouth, which caused his head to feel light and his pants to grow too tight.

He took a few more minutes to torture himself, but stopped when he still had it in him to do so.

"Call me when you get back from your mother's?" he asked her, leaning his forehead against hers so he could catch his breath.

"I will." She reached up for one last kiss before she opened the door and closed it on him leaving him with a sexy smile.

Colin stood there for a moment, staring at the place her beautiful face had just been, and realized that he may be in over his head this time.

Friends & Lovers Trilogy

Chapter Twelve

Briana rose early the next morning and got ready to drive out to her mother's. As she was getting dressed, she couldn't help but think back to her date with Colin.

She felt herself softening towards him. When they were together it felt just like it used to, comfortable and right, with a hint of sexual tension.

She worried about letting him get close to her again. She'd been hurt so badly when he'd broken up with her, but she had to admit that she was starting to like him for the man he was now, not just the boy he'd been. He'd been through a lot over the past few years, and he'd had to grow up and realize that the dream he'd always pursued would never come true now.

She was really enjoying spending time with him, and she had to admit, kissing him now was hotter than it had ever been when they were in high school. She just hoped she wasn't making a mistake by trusting him again.

She called goodbye to Kara as she walked out the door, and smiled at the grunt that answered her. It only took thirty minutes until she turned down the long, dirt road that led to her mother's farm.

When she got out and shut her car door, she smelled cooking bacon coming from inside the house.

She loved breakfast at her mother's. When she walked through the door, she was overcome by the feelings of safety and security that she remembered from her youth.

The décor was a mix of items from Briana's childhood and the new furniture that her mom and Ray had purchased together. The house was full of warmth and charm, and screamed of comfort and happiness. It was one of Briana's favorite places.

She walked into the kitchen, tiptoed across the floor, and wrapped her arms around her mother, squeezing her tight.

"Oh, Briana," her mother said breathlessly. "You startled me."

Her mother turned and threw her arms around her, hugging her close and kissing her cheek.

"It's good to see you, Baby Girl," she said with a big grin.

Briana thought her mother was gorgeous, with her grey hair styled in a sleek bob, and her face a map of years of laughter and happiness. Other than during the period of time after her father passed away, her mother had always been the happiest, most optimistic person that Briana knew.

She loved her to pieces.

"It's good to see you too, Mama."

"Come on over and have a seat. I'll call Ray and we can all sit down and enjoy our breakfast."

Briana sat down at the table and poured herself some coffee, putting a little cream and sugar in it.

When Ray walked into the room he went right over to kiss the top of Briana's head, before sitting in his seat.

"Hello, Bree," he said with a smile. "It's good to see you again. Your mama's been missing you."

"Now, Ray, I know Briana is a busy girl with a life of her own," her mother countered. "But I always welcome her visits."

"I'm sorry it's been so long, Mama. I've just been so caught up in work," Briana explained, feeling a tug of guilt at her mother's words. "I almost have my application finished for culinary school."

"That's wonderful, dear," her mother said, patting her hand. "And don't worry about coming to see me all of the time. You need to live your life, and I need to get used to you being far away again. When you get accepted to that school and move to Austin, I won't get to see you as much."

"I'll come home whenever I can."

"I'm sure you will. Now, tell me... what's this I hear about Colin being back in town?"

Briana blushed though she should have known that her mother's friends from town would be keeping her up-to-date on all of the latest gossip.

"He's back," Briana admitted. "He got injured and won't be able to play football anymore, so he came home. He's helping his daddy at the store now. But you know him, Mama. Running the store isn't what he wants to do for the rest of his life. He's thinking about trying to coach."

Briana's mother looked at Ray with a smile and then back at her daughter. "Sounds like you sure know a lot about it," she said with a wink.

Briana shoveled a piece of French toast into her mouth, trying to buy herself some time to compose herself. She couldn't prevent her embarrassed flush.

"That's okay. I can wait," her mother said with a smirk.

Ray just chuckled and helped himself to some more bacon.

Briana swallowed and took a swig of her coffee, trying to dampen her suddenly dry mouth. "Um, yeah, I've seen him," she stuttered.

"Really?" her mother asked gleefully. She'd always loved Colin and had expressed the hope that Briana would get back together with him someday. "That's wonderful, Bree. Are you two getting along?"

"Yes, Mama. We've talked a bit and I'm giving him the benefit of the doubt."

"I'm so happy, dear. The two of you were always such a good match."

Satisfied that her mother was going to leave the conversation after having said her piece, Briana enjoyed breakfast and then joined her mother for a walk around the farm. They spent a nice day together, catching up and talking about Briana's plans for her culinary school application. As they sat at her mother's favorite bench overlooking the pond, she brought up Colin again.

"So, when you said you've talked a bit, what does that mean?" her mother asked. She nudged Briana's arm and smiled.

"We went on a date."

"Really?" She drew the word out. "That's interesting. How'd that go?"

"It was really nice, Mama. I'm comfortable with him. When we talk, it feels just like it always did, like we haven't been apart all of these years."

"You said he's had to deal with a lot of changes," her mother prompted.

Briana held onto her mother's hand and looked out over the water. "Yeah. He's had to let go of his dream and find a new one. He's really changed, Mama. He was always sweet, but even I can admit that he was pretty self-involved in high school. He knew what he wanted and was willing to do whatever he needed to do to make it happen. Now he seems to be putting his parents' needs ahead of his own. He's grown and realized the consequences of his actions. I'm really enjoying getting to know the man he's become."

Briana's mom just made a hmmming sound and they sat there in silence for a while, enjoying each other's company. When she walked Briana to the car, her mother engulfed her in one last hug before pulling back to look at her, brushing the hair off of Briana's forehead.

"Give Colin a second chance, Baby Girl," her mother said softly. "Your father and I always liked him. You complimented each other so well."

Briana just smiled and kissed her mother on the cheek, before getting in her car to drive back home.

She spent the next thirty minutes thinking about what her mother had said, and trying to decide how she felt about it.

Friends & Lovers Trilogy

Chapter Thirteen

When Briana got home on Saturday night, Kara told her that Rich had put together an impromptu barbecue at his parents' house for the next afternoon. They were out of town for a few weeks, so he thought it would be the perfect time to get everyone together.

Briana got up and went to the grocery store to pick up a few items that she could contribute to the party. She decided to make a spinach and raspberry salad and trifle for desert. Just as Briana wrapped up the dishes, Kara came out in a blue-green summer dress with strappy sandals.

"Ready?" Kara asked as she coated her lips with a shimmery gloss.

"Yup. I just need to grab my bag. You have your clothes for work?"

Kara patted the small backpack that she carried, frowning as she said, "Yes. It stinks that we have to work tonight. We're going to have to leave just when the party gets goin'."

Briana ran to her room and grabbed her stuff, then met Kara at the car to load everything. When they arrived at the party there were already quite a few cars lining the streets in front of the house. They followed the sound of the music and the smell of the grill around the side of the house and let themselves in through the gate. Pete and Nicole were sitting and talking at one of the folding tables, while Rich manned the grill. Colin, Kent and Roni stood awkwardly by a long table of food, talking intermittently.

Briana and Kara headed towards the table to put the dishes down and said, "Hi," to Pete and Nicole as they passed.

Kent walked over to Briana and leaned down to give her a kiss. She stood still, conscious of the fact that Colin was watching and unsure of how the next few minutes were going to play out. Kent pulled back and looked down at her face.

"Everything all right, Bree?" he asked confusion showing on his face.

"Yeah," she responded. "Everything's fine."

She couldn't stop her eyes from darting to Colin and Roni. Kent followed her gaze and then turned back to her.

"Is there something going on that I should know about?" He looked like he was trying not to get upset.

"Um, let's go inside and talk," she responded leading him through Rich's sliding glass door.

"Don't tell me you fell for his shit already, Bree," Kent started before she had a chance to close the door.

She saw Colin start, as if he was about to follow them inside, but she shook her head at him and turned to Kent. She looked up at him, her gaze taking in his blond hair and beautiful grey eyes. He'd always been so good to her, never pressuring her for more than she was ready to give. She felt horrible that she couldn't give him the one thing he'd always hoped for.

Her.

"Kent, it's not about Colin," she began. "I love you, and I always will, but we both know that this thing we've been doing for the past few years isn't good for either of us."

He dragged his hand through his hair as he paced around the room. "Don't tell me it's not about him. Things were great before he got here. Look, Bree, we have an understanding… we always have. If one of is with someone, we back off. It's fine. I'll let you have your fun with Colin, then I'll be here for you when it's done."

He stopped in front of her and she saw the hope on his face. She knew then that she had to let him go. He deserved better than what she had to offer him.

She walked closer until their bodies were almost touching and placed her hand on his cheek. "You deserve better than this, Kent. Better than me. You're a wonderful guy. You deserve to be with a girl who will give you all of the love that she has to offer. Who will appreciate how kind and amazing you are." She looked into his eyes, "We can't do this anymore. Whether or not things work out with Colin, I won't be back to use you as my crutch. But I will always cherish you as my friend."

Kent closed his eyes, then turned away. "Can you give me a minute?" he asked gruffly.

Briana didn't say anything, just turned and went back outside. She didn't meet Colin's eyes as she walked over to where Pete, Nicole, and Kara sat. She sat down, but didn't join their conversation. She couldn't help but picture Kent's crestfallen expression before he'd turned from her.

Before she knew it, the backyard was full of people and she went in search of Kara. She walked up to where Pete stood alone and asked him if he'd seen Kara. He nodded his head towards the tree line of the backyard, where Kara was making out with some tall, lanky guy that Briana didn't recognize.

"She's drunk," Pete stated.

"What?" Briana asked incredulously. "We have to be to work in an hour."

"I don't think she's gonna make it."

Briana walked over to Kara and tugged on her arm. "Kara. Kara. Stop. We have to go."

The stranger pulled away long enough to say, "Fuck off," then went back to slobbering all over Kara.

"Kara." Briana tried getting closer and tapped her on the back. "We have to get to work."

Kara looked back at her and said, "Hey, Bree," then she giggled and turned back to resume her make-out session.

Pete approached from behind Briana and yanked Kara off the guy. He pushed her behind him and stood to face The Asshole.

The Asshole towered over him by a few feet and looked menacing, his jaw clenched and neck bulging.

"What's your problem, Ginger?" Asshole yelled.

"You are," Pete retorted. "You shouldn't be taking advantage of Kara when she's had too much to drink."

"Shut up, Pete," Kara shouted clawing at Pete's back. "This is none of your business."

"Why don't you listen to her, Ginger?" Asshole said.

"Kara, just let me handle this. You deserve better," Pete said to her over his shoulder.

Kara's face turned red. She started to beat on Pete's back. "Don't tell me what I deserve."

"How 'bout you kick rocks and leave us be?" Asshole stated, trying to reach around Pete to grab Kara.

Then everything seemed to happen at once. Colin, Kent and Rich finally noticed what was going on and ran over to assist Pete. Pete knocked Asshole's hand away from Kara, causing Asshole's face to turn a bright shade of red. Kara continued to pound on Pete's back.

Briana watched in horror as Asshole reared back, then punched Pete square on his jaw. The impact caused Pete to fall back, toppling Kara over. Pete turned to the side in order to avoid falling on top of her.

The other guys grabbed Asshole and held him back as Kara and Briana rushed over to Pete. He sat up and looked dazed, but other than a red mark on his jaw, he was fine.

Kara stroked his jaw. She looked into his eyes and started to cry.

"I'm so sorry, Pete. I should have listened to you."

Pete pulled her to him and held her as she cried. Briana got up and walked away to let them have some privacy as the guys hustled Asshole out of the backyard through the gate.

"What the hell was that?" Roni asked. "What happened?"

"That guy got too rough and hit Pete, so they escorted him out," Briana said, trying to play off the situation.

Nicole came running over. "Is Pete okay?" she asked.

"Yeah, but I don't think Kara's going to be able to work tonight. Pam lets you serve sometimes, right? Do you think you'd be able to cover for her tonight?"

"Sure," Nicole said with a shrug. "I don't have any plans after this." She glanced up as the guys walked back through the gate.

Briana recognized the look of longing on her face, but didn't have time to wonder what had caused it. She was just grateful that Nicole agreed to cover for Kara so Kara didn't get in trouble. She thanked Nicole, then walked over to meet Colin, Rich, and Kent.

"Hey, guys, Nicole is going to cover for Kara at work tonight, so we need to get going. Can you keep an eye on Kara and Pete and make sure they get home okay?"

They all nodded. Briana gathered her things and told Nicole she'd see her in a few minutes at the restaurant. Before she made it to the car she heard Colin calling after her and paused.

"I really have to get to work, Colin. I'm going to be late as it is."

"I'll just take a second, Bree," he said quickly.

"Okay."

"When can I see you again?"

"Um, I work the next few nights, but we can hang out before work, or we can get together on my day off."

"Great." He smiled. "Give me a call tomorrow."

"Sounds good," she said, and started back towards her car.

"Hey, Bree," he called after her, causing her to look over her shoulder at him. "What happened with Kent?"

"I told him I couldn't see him anymore," she replied, then got in her car and drove away.

When she looked in her rearview mirror, Colin was still standing in the same spot with a huge grin on his face.

Chapter Fourteen

When Briana woke up the next morning, she stayed in bed for a few minutes, replaying the previous day in her mind.

She couldn't believe the way things had played out at the party: Kara getting drunk, even when she knew they had to work; the Asshole being belligerent; and Pete standing up for Kara and getting punched for his efforts.

Pam had been cool with Nicole covering for Kara. She said that she had been considering promoting Nicole to server, so it would give her a chance to see how she handled herself on the floor. Before closing for the night and heading home, Briana had thanked Nicole again for agreeing to help Kara out as they sat down and had a drink after work.

"No problem," Nicole said. "I'm sorry about what happened at the party, but I made out great in tips tonight. It was fun."

"That's great," Briana replied. Then she studied Nicole, taking in her good looks and the way she carried herself, as if she'd been born to privilege. "So, what's your story, Nicole? No offense, but you don't seem like the type to be working as a hostess at a bar and grill in the middle of nowhere."

Nicole had turned pink, then looked down at the napkin that she was slowly tearing to pieces. "Well, I grew up in Dallas. My parents are wealthy and I went to private schools all my life. It was expected that I would go to SAGU and study Youth Ministries, then come home and marry my high school sweetheart, and we would start a congregation together. The problem was that I don't love Jake, and I couldn't go through with my parents' plans for me. I studied English in school and broke it off with Jake. My parents were very disappointed in me and I just couldn't go back, so I came here to start a life on my own."

"Wow. Did you know anyone here before you came?"

Nicole smiled and giggled a bit, as if still amazed by her decision. "No. I just picked a random spot on the map and showed up. I had a little money saved up, so I was able to rent an apartment, but even with the money I make as a hostess, it is started to become a struggle. That is why I'm hoping to move up to a serving position, and I'm thinking about getting a roommate."

Briana looked at her in amazement. "You're so brave. I don't think I could ever do what you did, not in a million years."

"Thanks, but it's no big deal." Nicole said with an embarrassed shrug.

Thinking back on the conversation, Briana was impressed about Nicole and the decisions she'd made in order to be happy.

Deciding it was time to get some coffee; she rolled out of bed and headed to the kitchen. When she walked in, she saw that Pete was already there making a pot.

"Hey," she said with a yawn. "What are you doing here?"

When Pete turned, she saw that his jaw was colorful with the bruises that were starting to form.

"Ouch."

"It's not so bad," he replied, gingerly touching his jaw. "I brought Kara home and stayed over. She was pretty shook up last night, and I wanted to make sure she was okay."

"Is she?"

"Yeah," he said smiling to himself as he made two cups of coffee. "She's great."

Before Briana could ask him about that smile, he wandered out of the kitchen and into Kara's room, shutting the door behind him. She looked at the shut door for a moment, then shrugged and poured herself a cup of coffee.

Once she'd gotten her caffeine fix, she looked at the clock and decided that it was late enough to give Colin a call.

"'Lo," he said gruffly, answering on the third ring.

"Hey, Colin, it's Bree. You asked me to give you a call." Even though that was true, she felt nervous now that she was talking to him.

His voice got softer. "Good mornin'. I'm glad you called. I was just getting dressed, so I didn't even look to see who it was before I answered it. I'm happy it's you."

She smiled at his response, and felt herself grow warm at the thought of him pulling his clothes on after a hot shower.

She cleared her throat. "Um… well, I was wondering if you wanted to do something today. I have to work tonight, but not until five."

"That would be great. I'm working later tonight, too, because we have inventory, so that works out perfectly."

Briana swore that she heard a smile in his voice. "Well," she began, "I was thinking that I could come over and make you lunch. I'll pick up everything at the market, then come by. Will that work for you?"

"That sounds great."

"Okay, I'll be there in a little bit." She smiled as she disconnected, then ran to the bathroom so she could shower and get ready. She shaved, lotioned, and primped. She put on a red sundress with white sandals and blew her hair dry. She was trying to look effortlessly casual. It took a lot of work.

When she finished she headed to the market and picked up ingredients for Chicken Milano, with fettuccini noodles, salad, and asparagus. As an afterthought she grabbed a bottle of red wine, and headed to the register. She really wanted to impress Colin with this meal.

When she arrived at his place, she felt butterflies in her stomach as she carried the bags up the stairs.

Before she could knock, the door flew open, and Colin stood before her, all sexy and smiling. She took in his bare feet, cargo shorts, and grey T-shirt, before reaching his face and the flash of dimples. It was all she could do not to sigh and stare, but she gathered her wits and smiled up at him, lifting the grocery bags to show him what she'd brought.

He leaned over and kissed her on the cheek, as he took the bags from her hands and moved to the side to allow her access inside.

"Hi," he said as she walked past him.

"Hi," she said back, her smile still in place.

They walked back in to the kitchen and Colin began taking the items out of the grocery bags. "What do you need me to do?" he asked when everything was lined up on the counter.

"If you want to start cutting the vegetables for the salad, I can get started on the main course. Is it okay if I rummage through your kitchen to find what I need?"

"Sure. Mi casa, es su casa. My mom loaded it up when I moved in, so I should have everything that you need."

"Cool."

Briana started to prep the chicken. While she worked, she was conscious of Colin standing next to her chopping and building the salad. Her body seemed to hum and her pulse quickened at his nearness. She watched his bicep flex with every slice of the blade, and started to feel lightheaded.

She cleared her throat and focused on the chicken, getting it breaded and placed in the sauce so she could put it in the oven. Once that was done, she put the pasta water on to boil.

"Do you have a grill?" she asked.

He stopped cutting and looked up at her. It seemed like a current passed through the air, and she knew that he was as aware of the sexual tension as she was.

"Hmm?" he asked. "Did you say something?"

She laughed, her eyes blurring a bit as she met his gaze.

"Do you have a grill?" she asked again.

"Yeah. Do you need me to light it up?" he asked, placing the knife on the cutting board and waiting for her answer.

"Um, yeah." Her lips felt as dry as her mouth and she licked them quickly out of habit. His gaze followed the flick of her tongue and stayed there for a moment, as he hoped she'd do it again. Her throat tightened and she struggled to remember what they were talking about.

"Oh, um… yeah. I wanted to grill the asparagus."

"Sure." His movements seemed slow, as he went out the back door to where she assumed he kept his grill.

Briana shook her head to try and clear the fog then got out the asparagus and coated it with olive oil, pepper, and salt.

When Colin came back in she asked, "Is it gas or do I need to wait for the coals to warm up?"

"It's gas."

She picked up the plate of asparagus and walked by him, accidently brushing her arm against his taut stomach. She heard his quick intake of breath, and bit back the groan that started in the back of her throat. She rushed out and put the asparagus on the grill.

When she got back into the kitchen, she looked at the timer and saw that the chicken still had forty-five minutes to bake, so she turned off the water that had begun to boil. Apparently being in the kitchen with Colin was making forget the basics.

"Shoot."

Colin came up behind her, as if to try and get close enough to hear what she'd said.

"What is it?"

"I put the asparagus on too early. The chicken won't be done for a while and I don't need to cook the asparagus and the noodles yet."

Colin went back outside and came back in a few seconds later.

"No problem. I turned off the grill and we can set it up again when you're ready."

"Thanks."

"So," Colin began, "Does that mean we have some time to kill before we have to do the rest?"

Briana looked at the timer again. "Yeah, about thirty minutes."

She'd barely gotten the words out, when Colin pulled her against him. Her arms went around him eagerly and her mouth eagerly found his. He backed her up against the counter and she felt the long hard length of him against her.

His mouth was everywhere, her neck, her jaw, her earlobe. Her head fell back to allow him better access, and her hands began an exploration of their own.

His hands found their way to her bottom and he lifted her easily, causing her to wrap her legs around his waist. He set her on the countertop, and she shifted down, so she could feel his erection press against her. She began to thrust as she tried to work his shirt up and off of him.

He broke away from her to help her, tearing the shirt over his head and coming back to meet her lips with his.

Her hands thrilled in the feel of his bare skin. She loved the muscles that rippled with each movement and started to feel crazy with need.

She struggled with the straps of her dress. He reached down to help her, pushing the straps and the fabric down over her stomach, and taking her bra off in the process.

When their bare skin touched it was like a fire erupted inside of her. She rocked against him again, causing Colin to moan and he leaned her back to gain access to her breasts. Then he sucked on one nipple as he used his fingers to knead and stroke the other.

Briana kissed his forehead and leaned towards his ear, trying to reach his skin, but not interrupt his wonderful assault on her breasts. She scooted down a little further, eager to have him inside her. This caused her dress to push up further along her thighs. She was frustrated by his shorts and her panties, which caused an unwanted barrier.

Her movement caused a tortured sound to emit from his throat. Colin left her breasts and brought his lips back to her mouth, suckling and biting her lips, as he pulled her closer to him and lifted her off of the counter.

He carried her back to his room, but before placing her on the bed, he pulled away from her and looked into her eyes.

"Is this okay?" he asked, clearly trying to keep his control in check, even as she rocked against him once more.

"Yes," Briana said with total confidence. "Please."

That was all the affirmation he needed. He laid her down and took off her clothes. Then he took off his. He laid next to her on the bed, stroking her skin with his hands, as he placed light kisses down her body. He started with the nape of her neck, then travelled along her collar bone to her breasts. After licking and nibbling her nipples again, he continued his descent along her stomach to her thighs.

He moved down the bed so he was in front of her, and nudged her legs, asking her to open them for him. She did as he requested, the blood pumping hot through her veins.

He kissed his way up her legs, starting at her knees, and ending in the one place that burned the most. When his mouth touched her, she felt momentarily embarrassed. No one had ever kissed her like this before, and she wasn't sure how she felt about it.

One second later, when his tongue began to lick her and he looked up to make sure she was okay, she lost all thoughts of embarrassment and let herself be taken away by the feelings he evoked.

It didn't take long for the tension to build in her core, causing her to buck and thrash against his mouth. He took that as a sign of encouragement and began to lick faster and deeper.

She came with a shout and a moan. She couldn't believe she was being so vocal, but she was no longer in control of herself.

Colin kissed her thighs once more, before kissing a trail back up her stomach to her chest. Her sensitive nipples tingled when he stroked them. She worked to catch her breath.

When he was fully on top of her, she moved appreciatively at the feel of his weight. His skin felt silky and slick and she knew that he had to be ready to explode himself. She felt him throbbing against her.

She couldn't help the large grin of satisfaction that spread across her face, as he said, "I need to be inside you."

She felt him reach for the condom and heard the packet crinkle as he tore it open.

She pulled her knees up anticipating the feel of him inside her.

He slid in slowly, making her breath catch. Her eyes closed as she let the pleasure of this intimate joining overcome her.

When he was fully inside of her, he momentarily stilled, and looked into her eyes. Emotion washed over her. She lifted up to kiss him long and hard. She pulled her knees up further and wrapped her legs around him, lifting her pelvis up off of the bed and bringing him further inside of her.

His control snapped. He started pumping in and out of her, and she held onto his shoulders for support. She rocked her hips up, causing him to rub roughly against her. She felt the orgasm begin to spread through her limbs once more. When she knew she was about to come, she suckled on his earlobe, then bit it.

"Oh, God. Yes, *Now*."

Her throaty words caused him to intensify his thrusts, and they both came with moans and shouts of satisfaction.

Briana lay there, stroking Colin's back and wondering about how he had just made her feel. He had brought things out of her that had never happened before.

She couldn't help but smile, as she closed her eyes and kissed the side of his neck.

"I think I just died and went to heaven," he muttered, his face in the pillow.

She giggled.

"If that's what death is like, I'm ready to die. Repeatedly."

Colin chuckled, then lifted his head up to look down at her. "You're amazing." He kissed one corner of her mouth, then the other, before kissing her fully on the lips.

"I think you're amazing too." she admitted, gazing up at him with happiness and hope in her eyes.

He smiled down at her, then cocked his head to the side and said, "What the hell is that beeping?"

"Oh, no." She tried to move him off of her so she could get up. "My chicken. Has it been going off long?"

"I'm not sure," he admitted, letting her up. "Let's go check on it."

They got up and ran to the kitchen to try and salvage their lunch.

Chapter Fifteen

After Briana left to get ready for work, Colin got on the computer and continued researching coaching at the college level. He was really excited about an opening at the University of Texas in Austin. He called his former coaches and asked if they would give him letters of reference, which they agreed to do. He looked at all of the requirements for the application and was excited at the prospect.

When he opened his email, he noticed another message from Shawn. All it said was "Call me, 911." He really didn't think there was anything left to say to her. He had no interest in getting involved with her again, or hearing about her latest conquest, so he deleted it.

While he was taking a shower before work, he couldn't help but think back to his afternoon with Briana.

Damn, she was hot.

He figured years of pent-up sexual tension probably hadn't hurt in making their first time together amazing. Lord knew he'd wanted her in high school. Bad. She hadn't been ready then and he'd respected her and her wishes, but it had been difficult.

She was better than he'd ever imagined in his fantasies, and there had been plenty of those throughout the years. He turned the temperature of the water down and tried to cool himself off.

Once he was dressed and ready, he headed to the store to meet his dad for inventory. When he pulled up, his dad's car was already there, so he went inside to meet him. He found him in the back storeroom.

"Hey, Pop," he greeted his father. "You been here long?"

His dad looked up from his inventory sheet and gave him a broad grin. "Hey, Colin. Not too long. Your mother made sure I sat down for dinner before she let me leave the house. She's worried that I'm not eating healthy enough. She made me eat steamed vegetables," he said with a grimace.

Colin chuckled. His dad hated eating healthy. He was a meat and potatoes kind of guy.

"Where do you want me to start?" he asked.

His dad turned to him, dropping the clipboard to his side and looking seriously at his son. "Your mother and I had a long talk about you over supper," he said.

Colin blinked over the unexpected turn in the conversation. The mirror image of his own, and felt his heart ache at the sadness in them.

"What about?"

His father put his hand on Colin's shoulder and squeezed. "Look, Colin, we know how much getting injured has affected the plans you had for your life. We're so sorry that things turned out this way. Initially I thought that when you came back here, things would fall in to place… that you'd learn about the store and eventually take over. But it's obvious that you're not happy. I know that you love me and your mother, and that you want to help us and make us happy. But son, you settling for less than your dreams won't make us happy. Would I have been happy if your dream had been to run the store and pass it along to your children? Heck yeah. But that's my dream, not yours."

Colin throat tightened. He looked down and tried to get a handle on his emotions.

"Thanks, Pop. That means a lot to me. I don't want to disappoint you, and I know you're ready to retire. I want that for you. You work so hard. It's time for you to enjoy your life with Mom."

His father's face burst with pride. "You're a wonderful son Colin, more so than your mother and I ever could have imagined. We don't want you to put our wants ahead of your own. There are other people in our family who can run the store. Your cousin Steve has always expressed an interest. Maybe I'll give him a call," his dad said. "We want you to do something that is going to give you a full and happy life."

Colin pulled his dad in for a hug, holding on a little longer than normal. He cleared his throat before he spoke, "Actually, they're hiring assistant coaches at UT. I was thinking about applying."

His father grinned again. "That sounds perfect. Now, we'd better get to work. These items aren't going to count themselves."

Colin was in dry storage when Rich came shuffling in through the door.

"What're you doing here, man?" Colin asked him.

"There's nothing going on tonight. This town is dead, so I thought you might be able to use an extra set of hands for inventory," Rich answered with a shrug.

"Sounds good." Colin pulled a page out and handed it to Rich. "There are pens and another clipboard on the desk. Thanks."

While they worked, Colin asked Rich how things had gone after he'd left the evening before.

"Nothin' much happened," Rich replied. "I made sure that Pete and Kara were okay. She sobered up pretty quickly. She was fawning over Pete, amazed that he'd stood up for her and taken a punch like that. Shit, I was pretty amazed myself. Who knew Pete had it in him. Anyway, Pete said he would make sure Kara got home safely, and they left. Kent was hanging out in the corner, drinking himself into a stupor, and growling at any chick who tried to talk to him. I think Bree messed him up pretty badly."

"Yeah, she said that she told him that she didn't want to see him anymore. But she said they only dated casually, I don't know why he was so upset."

"I guess he was more into her than she was into him," Rich speculated. "He'll be okay. There was no shortage of girls willing to help him get over Bree, that's for sure."

"As long as he stays away from Bree, I don't care what he does," Colin said mildly.

"Are you guys back on then?"

"I hope so. I think she is beginning to trust me again."

"That's great, man. I hope it works out. You two were always great together."

"Thanks," Colin said with a smile. "What about you? Any prospects on the horizon?"

"Well, I know it's probably playing with fire, but I can't stop thinking about Roni."

"Kent's sister?" Colin asked with a shake of his head. "I don't think that's a good idea, Bro."

"I know, I know. And to be honest, she doesn't seem the least bit interested," Rich stated with a wounded look on his face. "I talked to her for a bit yesterday, just to get to know her a little, and, man, she wasn't giving me the time of day. It was like pulling teeth trying to get her to open up about herself. Usually girls like to spill everything, but not this girl. Maybe that's what I like about her."

"Just be careful, man. Kent already tried to warn you off. I know you're always up for a challenge, but you may want to let this one go."

Rich shrugged, then gave Colin a cocky grin. "Look who's passing out dating advice. One night with Bree and you're an expert."

Colin chuckled and punched him good-naturedly on the arm. "Get to work."

Friends & Lovers Trilogy

Chapter Sixteen

Briana hadn't had an opportunity to speak with Kara since the party at Rich's house. She was dying to know what had happened between her and Pete. But Kara wasn't home, so Briana went into work early, hoping to catch her before their shift started.

When she walked into the back room, she stopped dead in her tracks.

Kara and Pete sat at the break room table. Kara was sitting in his lap and they were kissing each other heatedly.

Briana cleared her throat, which caused them to jump apart. Kara caught herself before she fell to the floor, giggling. Pete's fair skin colored instantly.

"What's going on?" Briana asked.

"Shh." Kara responded, holding a finger to her lips. "I don't want Pam coming back here."

"Why not? What's going on?"

Pete stood up and headed towards the door. "I'll leave you two alone so you can talk."

He winked at Kara and walked out. Briana started out after him, then turned to Kara, who was smiling wider than she'd ever seen.

"Did I just enter the Twilight Zone?" Briana quipped, which caused Kara to giggle again.

"OMG, Bree things are totally crazy."

Briana had never seen Kara look or act this way, like a lovesick girl.

"Are you guys, like, together now?"

Kara sobered a bit and tried to look more serious, but she was so happy that even without the smile, she glowed.

"I'm so sorry about what happened the other day, Bree. I never should have started drinking, I knew we had to work, but one drink led to another and the next thing I knew, that asshole started looking pretty good. I should have listened when you came over and tried to get me to leave with you. I feel so bad about the way he treated you, and the way he treated Pete." She got a dreamy look on her face. "God, Pete. Can you believe the way he stood up for me? I mean, I always knew that he was a great guy and that he was crushing on me, but I've never had anyone do that for me before."

"What happened after I left, Kara?" Briana asked, taking a seat as she spoke, baffled by the look on Kara's face.

"Well, Pete took me back home. I was sorry that he'd gotten hit, but I was pretty pissed that he'd butted in. At least, at the time I was. I yelled at him and told him to mind his own business, that I wasn't his problem. He just watched me with that calm way he has, and let me rant. When I was done, he told me that I was a wonderful person, and that I deserved better than some drunken asshole pawing all over me at a party. That set me off again and I started yelling at him. When I was done he told me that he loved me, that he's loved me for the past year, and that he wants to spend the rest of his life proving to me how amazing I am." Her eyes began to fill as she spoke, and Briana started to get choked up.

"Then what happened?"

"I stopped yelling and started talking. I told him about my father leaving when I was a baby, and my mom blaming me for it. I told him how she'd lock me in a closet so she could go out and hook up with guys. I told him how she told me every day that I was worthless. I laid it all out for him and then explained that I wasn't good enough for him. He's a great guy and he deserves better than me." Kara smiled through her tears. "He got mad and told me that if he ever heard me talk about myself like that again, he'd bend me over his knee. Ha. Then he said that I was exactly who he wanted and needed and that if he needed to, he would remind of that every day. Can you believe it?"

Briana smiled back at her, through tears of her own. "Yes, I believe it. You're wonderful and Pete is the most amazing guy alive. You both deserve each other and you deserve to be happy."

They hugged each other and cried softly in each other's arms. When they pulled back Briana looked at the clock and said, "We'd better get cleaned up and get to work."

She passed Pam's office as she walked towards the kitchen, and noticed Pam talking to Nicole.

"Bree," Pam called out to her.

Briana poked her head into the office. "Hi, Pam. What's up?"

"Nicole is going to start serving next week. I was wondering if you knew anyone who might be good for the hostess position, before I post it in the paper."

Briana looked at Nicole and smiled. "Congrats." Then she turned back to Pam. "I might. I think I saw her in the dining room when I walked in, let me go check and see if she's still here."

Walking into the dining room, Briana spotted Roni sitting at the bar eating a salad and headed over to her.

"Hey, Roni, how's it going?"

Roni looked up from her salad, but when she noticed it was Briana calling her, her face closed up.

"Hi."

Briana grabbed the stool next to her and said, "Look, I know things between me and Kent are weird right now, but honestly, all we have ever been is friends. I know he's upset now, but I also know that we'll work it out, and I don't want things to be strained between you and me in the meantime. I know we just met and all, but I'd like to think that we're becoming friends."

Roni considered this as she looked down at her salad, then looked Briana in the eyes.

"Yeah, he told me that you guys had an understanding and that you were never his girlfriend. But you hurt him. I've never seen him this upset over a girl before."

Briana looked at Roni with regret.

"I'm sad to hear that. I hate to think that Kent is hurt, and that I'm the cause, but I don't feel that way about him. I just don't, and I think it would've hurt him more in the long run if I hadn't let him go." Briana paused for a moment as her words registered. She had to admit, at least to herself, that she finally understood Colin's reasons for breaking it off with her before he left for college.

Roni nodded. "I get it, and sure, we're cool. I just have to stick up for my brother, ya know."

"Of course," Briana assured her. "Listen, I know you're here temporarily, but I was wondering if you were interested in getting a job while you're here."

"Actually, I'm going to be staying longer than I originally thought, and I've been looking for a job and maybe an apartment. I love Kent, but I can't live with him anymore."

"We have a hostess position opening up here and Pam, the boss, asked if I knew anyone who would be a good fit. It's not the best pay, but it's a job and it's a good place to start. Kara and Nicole both started as hostesses here. I can take you back to talk to her if you're interested."

Roni smiled, her dimple flashing, and Briana had to blink at the brilliance of it. Roni's beauty would have been intimidating if she wasn't such a cool girl.

"That sounds great. Are you sure she would want to see me now? Do I look okay?" Roni smoothed her fitted top and pretty grey skirt.

"You look amazing I'll go back and ask Pam if she's ready to talk to you now. Oh, and I think Nicole is looking for a roommate, so if you're looking for a place, you should talk to her."

"Thanks, I will." Roni smiled and looked excited about the new developments in her life. Briana couldn't help but feel happy that she had a part in that.

Friends & Lovers Trilogy

Chapter Seventeen

Briana received a text from Colin, asking her to come over after work, so she cleaned the kitchen as quickly as she could and texted Colin that she was on her way.

She decided to walk, since it was just down the street, and left her car parked behind the restaurant. When she got about halfway down the street, she noticed Colin waiting in front of the store. He spotted her and started down the street at a jog in her direction.

"Hey," he said when he got close enough. "I would have come to get you if I'd known you were walking."

She ran into his arms and laughed when he swung her around. The streets were dark and still, and she heard the strained sounds of her coworkers closing up and leaving for the night.

"It's such a nice night, I thought I'd enjoy the walk," she replied. "I appreciate you waiting for me."

She snuggled her nose into the crook of his neck, then gave him a little nibble.

"Careful," he joked, "Don't start something you can't finish."

She pulled back and looked at him. "Oh, I plan to finish it."

He grinned. "Big talk."

She ran her hands over him, pausing at the denim that strained against her hand. She felt brave in the cover of darkness and stroked him seductively.

His breath caught and he closed his eyes, seeming to enjoy the contrast of the cool wind against his enflamed skin. He groaned softly. Her breathing grew shallow and her body went pliant in his arms. She was getting turned on by giving him pleasure and sensed that he knew it.

"We should go inside," he whispered in her ear, as he tried to move his body away from her eager hands.

She stepped forward, not willing to let him go that easily. Placing her hands on his hips to hold him in place, she rubbed her body against his as she kissed him.

"I don't want to go inside," she murmured, moving her hands up to stoke his hard nipples.

He shook his head, as though trying to clear it. He grabbed her hands by the wrists and kept them still.

"We can't have sex on the street," he said.

"Let's go behind the store then, Colin." She said, bringing their hands to her lips and kissing his fingers. "I want you outside."

Colin looked as though he'd been knocked upside the head. He threw her over his shoulder, and carried her around the corner to where his truck was parked and lowered the tailgate.

He placed her down on the edge, unbuttoning her pants, pulling them swiftly down her legs and throwing them to the ground. Her panties went next.

She grabbed him by the waistband and unzipped his jeans, pushing them down roughly, signaling for him to take them off. Colin needed no such urging and pushed them down his legs.

Briana wanted him so badly that she was losing patience. She scooted up to meet him and put her hand through the flap of his boxer briefs. She pulled his penis out and pressed the tip against her, eager to have him fill her.

"Wait," he said roughly, coming to his senses long enough to bend down to his jeans and pull out a condom.

She grinned, "You're optimistic."

He chuckled as he put on the protection. Once he was ready, he pulled her to him in a passionate kiss. He stroked her lips with his tongue, then bit her gently, before claiming her mouth.

He placed his hands under her bottom as he entered her, and held her in place as he thrusted. She held onto his shoulders, kissing, licking, and sucking any part of him that she could reach.

When the pressure began to build, she leaned her upper body back, causing her lower body to press even deeper against him. He thrust faster and she came apart, moaning softly and driving him over the edge with her.

Briana lay back in the bed of the truck, panting, and started to laugh. Colin looked up from where his head rested on her stomach.

"What's so funny?" he asked with a smile.

"I can't believe we just did that."

"I know. Who knew you were such a deviant?"

She slapped him playfully on the back. "Shut up."

He scooted off of her and pulled his pants up, handing her her clothes. Then they raced up the stairs to his house, laughing at their brazen behavior all the way.

It didn't take long for them to fall asleep once they made their way to his bed. Briana snuggled into his side and didn't move all night.

She woke to Colin kissing the tip of her nose, and she smiled up at him, thinking how happy she was in that moment.

"You're off today, right?" he asked.

"Yes, off today, back on schedule tomorrow,"

"Do you wanna spend the day together?"

"Absolutely."

He kissed her nose again. "Let me go grab a quick shower, then I'm taking you to breakfast."

"Sounds good," she said, stretching languidly and looking up at him with a smile as he watched the sheet slip from her body. "I'll go make some coffee."

He growled and lifted the sheet to cover her back up. "It'll be the quickest shower ever."

She laughed as he raced out of the room. Throwing on her clothes from the night before and wandered out in search of coffee.

She'd just hit the brew button when someone started pounding on the door. She heard the water running in the shower, so she went and opened the door.

Standing on the other side was a very tan, very pretty, very annoyed looking girl.

"Is Colin here?" she asked, seeming irritated that Briana answered the door and not Colin.

Briana crossed her arms over her chest and frowned.

"Who are you?" she asked. Not liking the feeling of jealousy that boiled in her gut.

"I'm Shawn. Who're you?"

"Briana."

"Oh…figures. I've heard about you," she said with a smirk.

"Funny," Briana spat back, "I've never heard of you."

"Was that fast enough?" Colin asked as he came out of his room wearing only a pair of unbuttoned shorts.

He stopped in his tracks when he saw who stood at the door. "Shawn, what are you doing here?" he asked, coming up behind Briana and putting his arms around her.

Briana wrapped her arms around his, grateful for his thoughtfulness. He probably knew that she'd be upset, and was showing her and the tanning bed victim at the door, that he was one hundred percent with her.

"I tried emailing you and texting you, but you ignored me. I figured if I showed up in your little town, you'd be forced to deal with me." Shawn explained.

"We ended it back at school. I ignored you because we have nothing left to say to each other."

"Maybe you were just busy hooking up with an old flame." She replied, not hiding her derision as she looked Briana up and down.

"What do you want, Shawn?" Colin asked, his tone conveying his impatience.

Shawn brushed past them and walked into the living room, forcing them to move aside and follow her in. She walked into the kitchen and came back out a few seconds later with a cup of coffee in her hand.

"Make yourself at home," Briana said sarcastically.

"Thanks, I will."

"What is this, Shawn?" Colin asked again, running his hands through his still damp hair. "You need to just leave."

Shawn smiled over the rim of her cup, obviously enjoying the tension she was causing.

"I'm pregnant."

It was like a bomb had been dropped in the center of the living room. Colin exhaled and crumpled down onto the couch. He looked at Shawn in disbelief.

Briana couldn't think, couldn't process. She went with her first instinct, turning on her heel, and walking out the door.

When she reached the other side, she stopped and leaned back against it. It was silent. Then she heard the faint sounds of Colin and Shawn talking inside.

Shawn was pregnant.

Briana closed her eyes and thought about what this meant. She knew Colin, so she knew that he would do the right thing, which meant he would help Shawn with this baby.

She knew that he had feelings for her, and didn't have feelings for Shawn, so she didn't think that he would offer to marry Shawn, but she supposed there was always that chance.

Could she handle it if he chose to marry Shawn?

Yes, but she really hoped that didn't happen.

Could she handle being with Colin as he went through Shawn's pregnancy, then as he helped raise a child with her, if he didn't marry her?

She thought that she could.

She breathed deeply in and out, trying to clear her head, and calm her shaking body.

She knew that what she and Colin had was special, and she wasn't willing to walk away without letting him know that she was going to stick with him no matter what. She knew what she had to do.

Chapter Eighteen

Colin sat in silence, his head in his hands, trying to make sense out of what Shawn had just said.

"We always used protection," he said quietly, unable to accept her declaration as the truth. "Are you sure it's mine?"

"Fuck you," Shawn replied, finally losing the smirk that had donned her face since her arrival. "You know I never cheated on you, and I haven't started seeing anyone new... yet."

"I thought you said you were on the pill, and we used condoms. I just don't get it." He hung his head, shaking it as he tried to come to terms with yet another life changing event.

This didn't have to ruin his plans, he assured himself as it sank in. He could be a coach and help Shawn raise their child. People did it every day.

When he looked up, Shawn was staring at him as she drank her coffee, studying him as if his every thought played across his face.

"All right," he said loudly, as if speaking at a higher volume would convince him that everything would be okay.

Before he could finish his thought, Briana came storming back in the door. He was surprised at the relief he felt at seeing her. She walked over to him and sat down, putting her arm around his shoulder.

"Are you okay?" he asked, kissing her lightly on the cheek and brushing her hair back from her face.

She nodded, closing her eyes briefly at his touch.

"I just needed some air," she explained, giving him a small smile that didn't quite reach her eyes.

Colin held her gaze and tried to convey his feelings for her. He hoped that she trusted him enough to understand what he was about to say to Shawn.

Then he looked at Shawn again. She looked very annoyed at having to wait for him to respond to her little bombshell.

"All right," he began again. "I'll help you with whatever you need. I'll be there with you through the pregnancy. I'm sure we can get you a place here if you want to be close until you have the baby. Then I'll share joint custody with you and help you raise the baby. I'll help with expenses and be a part of his or her life in every way possible."

He turned back to Briana, to see if she was freaking out at what he'd just said, but she nodded and held her hand out for him to hold. She squeezed it and relief flooded through him.

She was going to stick with him.

He noticed that Shawn still hadn't said anything. She was staring at him with her mouth open, as if surprised by what he'd said.

"Have you lost your mind?" she sputtered, putting the coffee cup down with a thud. "You actually think I'm going to keep this baby? You think I'm going to ruin my body for some washed up loser? No. I plan to marry someone who can take me places, and that won't happen with a snot nosed brat at my hip."

"What are you talking about, Shawn? Why are you here then?"

"I'm going to have an abortion," she stated coldly. "I want you to pay for half."

Colin stood up and faced her, his face turning red with anger. "And that's it? You tell me that you're pregnant with my kid, but I don't get any say in whether it lives or dies?"

"It's my body, Colin. The decision is mine."

"Why'd you have to come here then?" he asked, his anger fading to sadness. "Why'd you even tell me about the baby if you never had any intention of keeping it?"

"I thought you should know," she said smugly. "You're just as responsible for this happening as I am, so you should pay half."

Briana couldn't stay quiet any longer. She stood up and got in Shawn's face. "So you agree that he is partly responsible for this baby, but you don't agree that he should have a say in what happens with the baby, is that right?"

"Yup," Shawn responded. She put her finger in Briana's face. "You, however, have no say in any of this, so why don't you sit your ass down?"

"Hey," Colin exclaimed, stepping in front of Briana to block her. "Don't talk to her like that. You're the one who is unwelcome here, so how about you tell me what you want and get out?"

"I made an appointment for next week. I just need you to send your half of the money to this address." Shawn handed him a business card. "All of the information is on the back."

"I'll take care of it. Now please, just go."

Shawn did as he requested and left as quickly as she'd arrived.

He walked back into his room and lay down on the bed, wondering how he'd ever recover from this latest development in his life.

Chapter Nineteen

Briana followed him and lay down next to him, cradling his body with hers.

"I'm sorry," she said.

He turned to face her, his eyes glistening as he spoke. "I'm not mad at her for her decision. She never wanted to have kids, I get that. But for one moment there, I was a father, and I found the possibility...exciting."

She pulled his head to her breast and caressed his hair, letting him come to terms with the loss of a precious thing that he'd never really had. She couldn't help but wonder what would have happened to their relationship if Shawn had been there to tell Colin that she was keeping the baby.

Briana was positive that he would be an amazing father. Although she knew that she wanted to focus on school and wasn't ready to have a child of her own, she didn't think that Colin having a child would have effected them negatively.

She had to admit that seeing the way he'd reacted to Shawn's news had really made her proud, and nothing could have endeared him to her more.

More than she ever had before, she loved the man he was today.

I love Colin, she thought to herself, the smile building until it took over her face.

She continued to play with his hair until he fell in to a light sleep, then hugged him to her and wondered what their future would hold.

When Briana went to work the next evening, she was happy to see Roni and Nicole manning the hostess stand.

"Hey, Roni. It looks like you got the job. Congratulations."

"Thanks, Bree," Roni responded with a smile. "I appreciate the hook up. Nicole was just explaining everything to me before she goes to train with Kara. I think this will be fun."

"Remember you said that in a few weeks, when you want to kill me for getting you into this," Briana said with a chuckle as she walked towards the back. She noticed Kent sitting at the bar and wondered how long he'd been there. He looked like he was pretty hammered.

She went back to put her things down, and noticed that she had a text from Colin.

Bree, I know I said this already, but you're so amazing. It really means a lot that you were there for me yesterday. That was the craziest moment of my life, and you being there made it much more bearable.

Briana smiled to herself and replied, *Anytime. Really. I'm happy that I was there. I'll talk to you after work.*

She put her phone away and figured that she'd better man up and go out there and talk to Kent. She really did want to remain friends with him. She knew she wouldn't be able to handle it if he hated her. He just meant too much.

She approached Kent and leaned against the bar next to him. "Hey, Kent," she said softly. "How's it going?"

He peered at her with bloodshot eyes. He looked like he hadn't shaved in over a week, and he may not have showered in just as long.

"Hey, Babe," he slurred. "You coming back?"

Briana felt sad in the pit of her stomach, unable to believe that he was this affected by her rejection. She knew that he liked her, but thought it was more of a passing fancy.

"No, Kent. I'm sorry. Why don't you put the drink down and go home and get some rest?"

His face went from hopeful to angry. "How 'bout you mind your own business?"

Nicole came up and stood in between Briana and Kent. "Is everything okay here, Bree?" she asked, looking pointedly at Kent.

Before Briana could answer, Kent reached up and snagged Nicole by her waist, pulling her into his side and squeezing her tightly.

"See, Bree? I don't need you, either. There are other girls who are more than happy to take your place." Kent leaned forward and tried to kiss Nicole, grabbing her bottom and trying to hold her to him.

She smacked him and pulled away. "Stop it, Kent. Don't act like this," Nicole pleaded.

"C'mon, Nic, don'tchyawanna hang out with me?" He gave her a bleary smile and tried to give her a pinch.

Her face flashed with hurt and embarrassment before turning to anger. "I'm not going to be one of your rebound girls, Kent."

Then she turned and stormed off into the back of the restaurant.

Briana looked at Kent, who stared after Nicole with a confused look on his face.

"I wasn't trying to make her mad," he said.

Briana turned as Rich walked up beside them.

"Why don't I give you a ride home, Bro?" he asked Kent, putting his hand on the other man's shoulder.

Kent looked up at Rich and let him help him up off of the stool. "Hey, Rich. You don't think Nic's mad at me, do ya? I was just messin' around."

Rich grunted under the weight of the larger man and responded, "Nah, man. I'm sure she's okay. Let's get you home."

"Thanks, Richie," Briana said as they walked towards the exit.

"No problem, Bree," Rich responded with a wink.

Roni came up and put her hand on Briana's arm before Briana could walk into the kitchen.

"Don't take it personally, Bree," Roni implored. "It's not just you that has him upset, so please don't feel bad. There's some stuff going on with our parents, and Kent hasn't gotten any of the job offers that he was hoping for…all of that on top of what he sees as your rejection has just become too much for him. He's going to be fine, he always is. He's always been the strong one in our family. He just needs a little time to pull himself together."

"Okay, Roni. Thanks" Briana said, instinctively pulling the other girl in for a quick hug. "Let me know if you need anything, okay?"

"Sure," Roni said with a smile, then went back to the hostess stand to wait for the dinner rush to start.

Briana went back to check on Nicole before getting the kitchen set up the way she liked it. Nicole said that she was fine, that Kent had just surprised her, but Briana could tell by the look on Nicole's face that there was more to it than that. It was obvious that Nicole didn't want to talk about it anymore, so Briana didn't press her.

Once the dinner rush started, she was happy to be in the weeds. With all of the drama going on recently, it was nice to just cook and not have to think about anything.

Kara came in and out with Nicole, explaining the process of putting in the order, checking back on it and sometimes getting the condiments ready. Nicole seemed a little frazzled, but Briana was sure it was just first night jitters.

When it was time for her break, Briana went out on the floor to see how things were going. Roni was working her way through the crowd with a table of four, Kara and Nicole were waiting on a group of rowdy guys, and Briana noticed Rich and Colin sitting at the bar.

She went up behind Rich, wrapped her arms around him and gave him a loud kiss on the cheek.

He turned around with a grin and pulled her onto his lap, kissing her soundly on the mouth.

"Hey," Colin objected. "Get your hands off my girl."

Briana giggled and smacked her lips in an exaggerated way as she kissed Rich back. "Thanks for taking Kent home," she said, turning serious for a moment. "I really appreciate it."

"Sure thing," he replied with a wink, letting her off of his lap and turning to Colin. "*Your* girl?"

Colin looked sheepish for a moment, then pulled Briana over to him and looked into her eyes. "If she'll have me."

She met his lips gently at first, then deepened the kiss before pulling back and smiling brightly. "She'll have you," she replied.

Colin's face broke into a wide grin. He reached over to bump fists with Pete, who watched the whole exchange from behind the bar.

"You hear that, Petey?" Colin sang. "Looks like we've both hit the jackpot in the girlfriend department."

"Better ya'll than me," Rich quipped taking a drink of his two dollar draft.

"You say that now," Colin laughed, "But just you wait. When the right girl comes along, you'll be right there with us."

"Fat chance," Rich said, but Briana saw him watch Roni's progress back to the hostess stand through the mirror over the bar.

"Briana, could you please not sit on the customers?" Pam requested as she came through the kitchen door.

Briana giggled and climbed off of Colin's lap.

"Sorry, Pam. I was just finishing up my break."

Pam rolled her eyes and told her to get back to work.

"You okay?" Briana whispered to Colin before going back to the kitchen.

He nodded at her and gave her a small smile.

As she went back to work she heard Rich ask, "So, what's up dude? What did you want to talk to me about?"

She was leaving Colin in good hands with Rich. As much as he loved to joke around and have fun, Rich was the most loyal friend she'd ever known, and she knew without a doubt that he would be there for Colin now.

Chapter Twenty

Briana hung up the phone. Then she started jumping up and down and squealing.

"What?" Kara asked, running out of her bedroom. "Is everything okay?"

"Yes," Briana shouted, jumping over to Kara and pulling her in a hug, jostling her around. "Everything is wonderful. I just got off the phone with the culinary school. They accepted my application and want me to start school in the fall."

She broke apart from Kara and did a booty dance, shaking her butt and circling Kara.

Kara couldn't help but laugh as she started dancing around the room with her.

"Yay! That's wonderful." Kara enthused. She stopped suddenly. "Wait a minute…that means you're moving to Austin."

She pouted prettily, which made Briana laugh.

"It's just to Austin," Briana assured her. "You'll come visit me and I'll come visit you."

"Promise?"

Briana pulled her into a big hug. "Of course. You know I love you, girl."

"I love you, too."

"We still have a couple weeks together. Oh, I'll have to give Pam notice. I feel bad about that, but she knows this is what I really want to do, so I think she'll be happy for me."

"She will be. Don't worry about that, Bree. Everyone is going to be happy for you. I'm so proud of you for going after what you want." Kara's eyes misted over.

"Thanks, Kara. Oh. My. *Gosh*. I have to tell Colin," Briana said. "I'm going to see if I can catch him at the store. I'll see you at work, okay?"

"Sure," Kara laughingly responded to Briana's retreating back.

Briana parked and ran into the store, looking for Colin through the aisles. She stopped at the counter where Rich was making a shake for a little boy. He looked up at her and she mouthed, *Colin?* He pointed his head toward the back office and she gave him a huge grin before she went through the door to the back.

She found Colin sitting at the desk when she walked in. He was starting at the computer, a notepad in front of him and a pencil in his mouth, His brow was furrowed in thought.

He looked adorable.

She walked up behind him and wrapped her arms around him. He jumped, then smiled and leaned back to nuzzle her neck.

"Well, this is a nice surprise," he said in between kisses along her jaw.

His hair smelled spicy and delicious. She closed her eyes and enjoyed the feel and smell of him.

"I have some good news," she whispered

He turned in his chair so he could face her. "I'm always ready for good news."

"I just got off of the phone with the culinary school. I've been accepted to start in the fall." She said it so quickly that by the time she got to the end of the sentence her voice was a few octaves higher than normal.

"That's awesome," he replied, pulling her in for a quick kiss on the lips, his pride in her evident on his face. "I knew they'd accept you. It's so great that your dream is coming true."

"I'm so glad you think so, 'cause I'm super excited." Briana squealed and gave him another quick kiss. "I'm gonna tell Pam tonight. I know it's too soon to give notice, but I don't want to keep it a secret. I want to tell *everyone*. And I want her to have a chance to hire someone else that I can train before I go."

"I'm sure she's going to be thrilled for you," he assured her. He held her hands in his, looking up into her beaming face. "I love you, Bree."

Briana's mouth formed an O and her expression changed from excitement to surprise, and finally to happiness.

Colin continued talking before she could say anything. "I know now may not be the best time. You've just started to trust in me again, and it may seem too soon, but I swear, I've never stopped loving you. These last few weeks having you back in my life have been the happiest of my life, and I don't want another moment to pass without you knowing that."

Tears began to form in Briana's eyes. She felt lighter, happier, than she ever had. It seemed like things were finally turning out the way she had always hoped they would.

"But I'm leaving for Austin."

"That's okay," he tried to reassure her. "Austin isn't that far. We can see each other on weekends and stuff. Don't worry about that, we'll work it out."

She smiled even wider and nodded her head once in affirmation.

"I love you, too." she exclaimed.

Colin beamed at her, bringing each of her hands to his lips. They heard a throat clear and jumped at the interruption.

"Sorry," Colin's father said gruffly. "I needed to get something off of the desk. I didn't mean to intrude."

"You could never intrude, Mr. Grayson," Briana said as she bounced over to him and gave him a hug. "I have to get to work, anyway." She looked over her shoulder and winked at Colin. "I'll see you later."

Colin's father chuckled and patted her back. "It's good to see you two so happy again."

She gave him a quick kiss on the cheek and bounded out of the office. She was a little early for her shift, but that gave her time to talk to Pam, so it worked out perfectly.

Just as everyone predicted, Pam was as excited about her attending the school as she was, and she was happy that Briana would be able to train a new short order cook before she left.

When she was in the break room clocking in and putting up her stuff, Kara and Pete came in laughing and holding hands.

"Close your eyes, Bree," Kara instructed. "We have a surprise for you,"

Briana glanced between them with suspicion, but did as she was told.

She heard the sound of shuffling feet and muffled voices and couldn't keep a smile from forming.

"Okay," Kara said loudly. "Open 'em."

Briana opened her eyes and saw every available shift worker piled into their small break room. In the center of the table was a delicious looking chocolate cake that read, "*Congratulations, Bree. We are so proud of you.*"

Briana didn't even attempt to hide the tears that streamed down her face.

"Thanks, guys. This means so much to me."

Everyone took turns giving her hugs and wishing her luck. The people who had to get on the floor got back to work with the promise that cake would be saved for each of them. Everyone else stayed to have a piece.

It was the best cake Briana had ever eaten.

Epilogue

The last couple of weeks before Briana left for Austin flew by. She spent every spare moment with Colin, which only strengthened their relationship.

The day that Shawn texted him to tell him that she had gone through with the abortion was difficult, but they got through it together. Colin was sad at the loss, but admitted that it probably wasn't the best time for him, or them, to start a family. He was adamant that he did want to have kids someday, which made Briana even more excited about their future.

She knew that long distance relationships didn't always work, but she had faith that after all that they had been through, they would find a way to make it work.

She trained the new hire at the restaurant and felt confident that he would work out just fine.

Nicole and Roni found an apartment together and were having fun picking out decorations. The biggest surprise came when Kara revealed that Pete would be taking Briana's place in their apartment.

"I know it sounds crazy. And fast. And crazy," Kara admitted to Briana when she told her. "But he needs a place and I've got a room opening up…it just makes sense. It's not like we're living together…I mean, yes, technically we're living together, but not living together."

Briana chuckled at Kara's rationale and said, "You guys will be great."

It was a sad day for both of them when it was finally time for Briana to leave.

"I'm going to miss you so much, Bree," Kara said between sniffles.

"Me, too," Briana whimpered back.

They hugged, squeezing each other tight. When Colin's truck pulled up, they were still locked in their embrace, not ready to let the other go.

"Hey, ladies, don't cry," Colin said when he got out and started loading Briana's things into the bed of his truck. "Please?"

Briana and Kara broke apart and wiped their faces, then Briana picked up one of her bags and went to put it in the truck. She paused before she lifted it in, looking at Colin in confusion.

"What are all of these other bags?"

Colin and Kara exchanged glances and turned to her with wide grins.

"I got hired on as an Assistant Coach at UT," he said. "I'm going to Austin with you."

Briana dropped her bag with a thud, her mouth wide with shock. The tears once again began to fall down her face.

"Oh. My. God."

She jumped into Colin's arms, wrapping herself around him and screaming in his ear. "I can't believe it."

He laughed as she pulled back and began to cover his face with kisses.

"I love you so much," she exclaimed.

"I love you, too, Bree," he replied. "And I promise that this time, we'll make it last."

Friends & Lovers Trilogy

Keep reading for Nicole and Kent's story, *I Choose You*, followed by Roni and Rich's, *Trust in Me*. At the end of Trust in Me, I have included a bonus ending for each couple, but please wait until after you have read all three stories, since they are in sequence, and the bonus endings will have spoilers if you read them first.
Thank you, Bethany Lopez

Friends & Lovers Trilogy

I Choose You

(Nicole & Kent)

Friends & Lovers Trilogy

Prologue

Nicole knew that she was going to have to face her parents and let them know that the plans they'd had for her were not the same as the plans she had for herself. She didn't want to marry Jake or start a congregation.

She knew it would be difficult, and that they were going to be disappointed in her, but first she had to face Jake.

She pulled into the parking lot of the city park where they were meeting.

Jake was already there. He was sitting on the bench facing the pond and watching the ducks that floated by.

His light brown hair blew in the soft breeze and his expression was peaceful.

Nicole's stomach clenched at the thought of what she had to do. What she should have done three years ago, but had been too afraid to.

"Hey Jake," he turned and stood up at the sound of her voice.

They were almost the same height, so she could see his eyes light up as she walked up to him.

"Hey Nicky," he said warmly as he put his arms out, expecting the hug that she always greeted him with.

She walked into his arms willingly, taking stock of the familiarity of his hold, while breathing in the scent of his familiar cologne.

She knew Jake, had known him since they were small children. He would never forgive her for what she was about to do.

She squeezed him tightly one last time, before pulling back to look him in the eyes.

Jake looked back at him, confusion spreading across his handsome face when he noticed the look on hers.

"What is it?" He could always tell when something was wrong.

"Can we sit?" Nicole asked, gesturing to the bench. She had to sit before her knees gave out.

"Okay," Jake said slowly, as if already beginning to dread what she was going to say next.

"Jake," she began, clasping her hands nervously in her lap as she forced herself to look at him. "I'm sure you've noticed that I've changed over the last few years. Things aren't the way they were when we began dating. First, you went away for school… then I left for school. Since then, most of our relationship has been spent over the phone or on the internet."

Jake nodded, waiting for her to get everything off of her chest.

Nicole bit her lip, then continued, "Look, I have to admit that I haven't been honest with you, or my parents, for some time now. I changed my major to English. I don't want to study Youth Ministries and come back here to start a congregation. That was always my parents' dream, and yours, not mine."

Jake looked over her shoulder, as if processing what she had just said, then looked back at her.

"That's okay, Nicky. I mean, I'm not happy that you lied, but I'm glad you told me now. You don't have to run anything if you don't want to. You can just be The Minister's Wife. There will be plenty to keep you busy, even without running Youth Ministries."

Nicole sighed. She knew what she had to say next was going to hurt him, and decided it was best to tell him quickly.

"No Jake, I'm sorry, but it's more than that. I don't want to live here at all. I don't want to be 'The Minister's Wife'. I don't want to be your wife." She stressed, not wanting to hurt him, but wanting him to understand.

Jake's face fell, hurt and confusion taking over.

"What?" Jake asked, as if unable to believe what she'd just said. "You don't want to marry me? We have been engaged for three years, and you've never acted like you had second thoughts about us. I don't understand."

Jake stood up and walked to the edge of the water. He raked his hands through his hair, then in his pockets, as if unsure what he should do with them.

The pain on his face tore Nicole apart, and she knew that she should have talked to him when she had first begun to question their betrothal.

"Jake," she whispered softly as she walked up next to him. "I'm so sorry. I love you and you are the last person I ever wanted to hurt."

He turned to her at that, anger flashing in his eyes.

"If you loved me, you wouldn't be hurting me."

Nicole felt a hot ball of tears begin to form at the back of her throat, and turned to leave before she made matters worse.

"I'm sorry, Jake," she said again, a little more loudly. "I promise that I'll stay away and let you live your life. I wish you every happiness."

When she got to her car, Nicole turned back for one last look at Jake.

He stood in the same spot by the water, looking out at nothing, as his shoulders softly shook with sadness.

Two Years Later...

Friends & Lovers Trilogy

Bethany Lopez

Chapter One

Nicole was nervous and excited about Roni moving in with her.

She and Roni only met a few months ago, so she didn't know that much about her. All Nicole knew was that she needed someone to help pay the rent and utilities, or else she was going to be in a lot of trouble.

When she'd brought up the fact that she was looking for a roommate, her friend Bree had mentioned that Roni was looking for a place to live.

Bree and her boyfriend, Colin, had left the weekend prior. They'd moved to Austin, where Bree was going to culinary school and Colin was working as an Assistant Football Coach at UT. Nicole was looking forward to heading to Austin in a few weeks to see their new place.

She and Roni worked together at the local Bar & Grill. Roni had taken her job as a hostess, when Nicole had been promoted to server. She'd shown the other girl the ropes, and had a chance to talk to her a bit.

So far they got along; Nicole guessed they would find out pretty quickly, if they would get along as roommates.

Over the past few weeks, she and Roni had gone shopping in anticipation of the move. They'd

157

decorated Roni's room and some of the common areas, so the apartment was looking really good.

This was the first day off they'd both had in some time, so Roni was officially moving in. Nicole had gotten up early to make sure everything looked clean and presentable. She wanted Roni to be welcomed into a home that she could be proud of. Plus, Nicole knew that Roni's twin brother, Kent, would be helping her move today, so she wanted the apartment to look nice the first time he saw it.

He was very protective of his sister, and Nicole knew that he'd tried to talk her into staying with him, but Roni wanted to get out on her own.

In an effort to relax, Nicole sat down with a cup of coffee and her laptop, when she heard the sound of excited voices coming up the stairs.

When she heard Roni's bawdy laugh, she opened the door with a smile, and was faced with a faded grey t-shirt stretched across the sexiest chest she'd ever seen. Without looking up, she knew the owner of that chest. She'd been crushing on him ever since her first day in this small town.

She felt the familiar tug in her belly, as she allowed herself a moment to draw her gaze slowly up his chest, over his broad shoulders, and into his striking face.

Kent was the most gorgeous man she'd ever met, and no matter how many times she saw him, she always got butterflies when he was near.

He grinned down at her.

"Hey, Nic." Kent was the only man who had ever called her that, and she felt her heart trip every time he did.

She tried to speak, but no sound came out. She tried to clear her throat inconspicuously. "Um, Hi."

"Kent, could you please move your butt? This box is heavy," Roni's voice said from behind him.

Nicole moved a few steps back and out of the way so he could come inside, allowing Roni access through the door.

She chided herself for acting so weird every time she was around Kent. She thought he was out of her league. She knew that he could get any girl he wanted, and she was nothing like the girls he usually went for.

"Let me take that," Kent said to his sister, easily lifting the box from her hands and taking it to the room that Nicole indicated was Roni's.

"Hi roomie!" Roni squealed, jumping and doing a little spin around the room.

Nicole couldn't help but smile at her excitement, then watched, confused, when Roni's demeanor changed at the voice in the hall.

"Hello... I'm looking for the apartment housing the hottest ladies in town," Rich yelled out as his face came into view.

Roni rolled her eyes and turned to walk into her room.

Nicole barely had a moment to register Roni's behavior, before she was enveloped by Rich's strong arms.

"Hey baby doll," Rich said with a smile. "Kent told me his sister was moving in today, so I thought you guys might need some help from a big, strong, sexy man."

Nicole giggled at his words and the wink that accompanied them.

"Thanks, I didn't realize you were coming by, I would have stocked the fridge." Nicole responded.

"I've got it covered," Rich said, pulling a six pack from behind his back.

Nicole smiled and took it from him. She went to put it in the fridge and said, "Leave it to you to think of everything,"

Kent came back out and walked up to Rich, his arm extended to shake his hand.

Nicole caught herself watching his movement across the room, and quickly averted her eyes before anyone else noticed.

"Hey man," Kent said in greeting, "Thanks for coming out to help."

"No prob," Rich responded, his eyes following Roni as she came out of her room. "I don't have much going on since Colin and Bree left, at least not until school starts back up next week."

"Oh, does that mean you'll be leaving town soon?" Roni asked a little too eagerly.

Rich just smiled at her.

"Yeah, Sugar, I'll be leavin'," he drawled with a wink. "But don't you worry; I'll be back before you have a chance to miss me."

Roni rolled her eyes again and snorted.

"No danger of that happening."

"Hey," Kent said with authority. "You - turn off the charm," he said pointing at Rich. Then turned his finger on his sister, "And I know you have better manners than that. Use 'em."

Rich just laughed and asked Kent what he needed help with as the guys headed downstairs to unload.

"What was that about?" Nicole asked Roni quietly, once they were alone.

"What?" Roni asked.

"That thing between you and Rich?"

Roni snorted again, "I know a million guys like him and believe me, there is no *thing* between me and Rich. I just don't buy his *aw shucks*, southern stud act."

Nicole chuckled good-naturedly and slung an arm around Roni as they headed out to help the guys.

"Oh, it's no act… Rich is a true southern stud."

They laughed together as they descended the stairs to help the guys.

Chapter Two

For their first night as roommates, Nicole picked up some wine and brownie mix. Once the guys left, Nicole got the brownies ready and put them in the oven, then went to help Roni unpack.

Nicole paused at the doorway of Roni's room, struck by how beautiful the other girl was.

"You know, if I didn't know you, I'd probably hate you," Nicole said, startling Roni, who had her head in a box.

Roni straightened and looked at Nicole with a confused expression.

"Why's that?"

"You're gorgeous," Nicole replied. "And not just, wow, look at that pretty face. The whole package. Perfect face, perfect body, perfect hair… shoot, even the perfect feet."

Roni looked down at her perfectly polished bare feet.

"Perfect feet?" She asked.

Nicole shook her head in mock disgust.

"Yeah, I mean, look at my ginormous feet compared to yours." She walked up and put her foot up against Roni's. "See, yours are positively dainty."

"If you say so," Roni answered with a laugh. "I'm just a girl you know. And you're one to talk; you aren't exactly hard to look at yourself. You want to talk about body… I'd kill for yours."

"Okay, now that we have complimented each other to death," Nicole said, picking up the box of linens and walking over to the bed. "What do you say we get your stuff put away, then get to know each other over some wine and brownies?"

"Sounds like a plan," Roni replied, and started unpacking boxes while Nicole made the bed.

Since they'd already decorated most of the common areas, it didn't take long to get Roni's room set up the way she wanted.

They were sitting on the couch with a brownie in one hand and a glass of red in the other in no time at all.

"So," Roni asked, "What made you move here from Dallas?"

"Well, long story short, I was engaged to my high school sweetheart, with whom I was supposed to start a congregation, and grow old with in Dallas. Unfortunately, that was my parents dream, not mine." Nicole put her glass down and looked at Roni with a sad expression. "I realized that I wasn't in love with Jake, and that I really wanted to be a writer, not a Youth Minister."

"That must have been tough," Roni encouraged her to go on.

"It was," Nicole admitted. "Jake is a great guy, and I hated hurting him, but I knew we wouldn't be happy in the long run. My parents were livid when I told them, and they said that they weren't going to support me or my decision… so I left. I just picked a random spot on the map, and here I am."

"Wow," Roni said her grey eyes wide. "So, you haven't spoken to your parents or Jake since?"

"No," Nicole admitted. "It's been two years. I haven't heard from anyone since I left."

"Well, I'm sorry about your parents, but wow. Good for you!" Roni exclaimed.

Nicole picked her wine glass back up and took a drink before asking, "What about you? What brought you here?"

"I married my high school sweetheart right after graduation, but he ended up not being the man I thought he was, so I left him." Roni looked down at the amber liquid in her glass as she spoke.

"I had no idea you'd been married," Nicole said softly. "I'm sorry it didn't work out. So, rather than staying with your parents, you decided to come here?"

"My parents are going through a rough time, and stuff with my ex got too intense, so I asked Kent if I could stay with him for a while." Roni smiled absently. "I can always count on Kent. Anyway, once I got here, I realized have nothing to go back home for, so I decided to get a job and move in with you."

It was obvious to Nicole that there was more to the story, but that Roni wasn't ready to open up about everything, so she refilled their glasses and changed the subject.

"Are you really not attracted to Rich?" Nicole asked Roni with a big grin on her face.

Roni rolled her eyes.

"Like I said, I've met tons of guys like Rich. Smooth, sexy, flirts, who go through girls like they're disposable... My ex is the same type of guy." Roni admitted. "I'm not blind, of course I see that Rich is a very good-looking guy, but I'm not falling for that act again."

"Well, I haven't known him long, but I think there's more to Rich than that," Nicole said in his defense. "Sure he's a flirt, and he enjoys women, but from what I've seen, they enjoy him back. I wouldn't say he uses them."

"Well, until I see different, we will just have to agree to disagree where Rich is concerned." Roni replied. "I'm not in the mood for guys right now."

Nicole laughed at that, the wine started to make her feel relaxed and happy.

"I haven't talked to anyone since Jake," Nicole admitted. "Well, Jake's the only guy I've ever dated. That's horrible, right?"

"Really, you've only ever been with one guy?" Roni asked incredulously, grabbing the wine bottle and turning it upside down. "Looks like we need another bottle."

Nicole jumped up, and chose another bottle out of her little wine rack on the counter.

"No fear," She giggled. "We have more."

She uncorked the wine and refilled their glasses before settling back in on the couch.

Roni nudged Nicole's knee with her toe to prompt her to keep talking. She put her feet up and stretched out to get more comfortable.

"So… you were saying, just Jake." She prompted.

Nicole looked at Roni, trying to figure out how honest she wanted to be. She had a feeling that she and Roni were going to be friends for a long time. She trusted her enough to tell her the truth.

"Yeah, I was saying Jake's the only guy I ever dated, and was engaged to, but I've never *been* with any guy." Nicole waited for Roni's reaction.

She didn't have to wait long.

Roni sat up quickly, causing the wine in her glass to slosh around. She looked at Nicole in disbelief.

"You're a *virgin*?"

"Yes," Nicole admitted. "My family is very religious and I was raised to believe that sex is something that takes place between a woman and her husband."

"Whoa… I can't believe it," Roni said shaking her head and chuckling slightly. "You have a body that guys drool over, and you've never used it… Wow. I mean, I think it's totally cool that you made that decision and stuck to it… I just can't believe it."

Nicole laughed at Roni's candor.

"It's never been a problem, or a hard decision," Nicole explained. "Jake had the same values, so we always planned to wait. The whole time I was in college, I was engaged and since I've been here there hasn't been anyone that I've been interested in."

"Do you still plan to stick to it?" Roni asked, curious. "I mean, if you did meet someone, or decided to date casually, do you still plan to wait until you are married?"

"Yes." Nicole said.

"Wow," Roni said again. "I don't know if I could marry someone without knowing whether or not the sex was good."

That made Nicole laugh, and Roni joined in.

"Wait… I'm not a slut or anything," Roni clarified. Then she looked back at Nicole and said, "Well, shoot, I guess compared to you, I am."

Nicole shook her head fervently, feeling the room spin slightly as she did.

"No way. Don't talk like that. You don't have to compare yourself to me or worry that I'll judge you. This is a decision I made for myself. Besides," Nicole said with a wicked grin. "Just because I haven't had sex, doesn't mean I haven't done other stuff."

Roni poured some more wine, then scooted dramatically closer with a big laugh.

"Oh goody, do tell. Make me feel better about myself."

Nicole laughed at Roni, then sighed and smiled at her new roommate.

"I think this is gonna be great. You and me, together in this town… I think we're going to be lifelong friends."

Roni smiled widely and picked up her glass to clink it with Nicole's.

"Me too." She responded. "Now quit procrastinating and get to the good stuff."

Friends & Lovers Trilogy

Chapter Three

Kent stretched languidly as he drifted out of sleep the next morning. He'd gone out with Rich for a few more beers after they'd dropped off Roni's stuff, but he didn't feel any worse for it.

He slowly opened one eye, happy for the blackout curtains he'd hung in his bedroom.

He was not a morning person.

Kent glanced over at the clock, his forearm brushing against the empty sheets next to him, and he wondered how long it had been since he'd had a woman in his bed.

Shit, at least since Roni had come to town and stayed in his house. Well, now that she had moved out and he had his space back, he would have to remedy that.

His mind wandered to Briana, and he wondered how she was doing in Austin. He couldn't help but smile.

Although he was sad that she'd taken Colin back and moved away, he couldn't help but be proud that she'd followed her dreams.

He could think of her now without feeling like he'd lost her. He knew that she'd never really been his to lose in the first place, but he'd still felt bereft when she'd told him she didn't want to see him anymore.

He wasn't naïve enough to think that he'd loved her, but he knew that he could have, if she'd given him the chance.

"Oh, well," he thought as he pushed himself up in the bed and threw his legs over the side. "No use wishing for something that was never going to happen. Time to move on."

He sat still for a moment, allowing himself time to wake up, before standing up and heading into the bathroom to take a shower.

Although he worked at the local newspaper, Kent had always been smart with his money. He'd started saving as a young child, and had received a scholarship to go to school, so he'd worked and saved all through college as well.

Growing up poor had taught him determination.

He was determined to never live the way his parents had, to never settle for someone who didn't love you, and to make sure he was always prepared to care for himself and his twin.

Kent loved his house. It was a small, two bedroom home on the outskirts of town. He'd paid to have it renovated, and enjoyed the small luxuries that he'd put in the house.

Even more, he liked knowing that it was bought and paid for, and was solely his.

Of course, Roni knew that it was available to her whenever she needed, as was anything he owned, but like him, she wanted to make her own way. He was proud of her for that.

As the hot water from the dual shower heads streamed over his back, he wondered what he would do now that he was a free man again.

Maybe he would go out that night and try to break his slump.

Even as the thought crossed his mind, he couldn't stop the flash of a certain beautiful, busty blonde from creeping in.

Damn, Nicole was hot.

Kent could tell she was attracted to him. It had been apparent by the way she'd stood there staring at his chest yesterday, he thought with a chuckle.

He didn't know much about her. Just that she was sweet and kinda quiet. He hadn't seen her with any guys since he'd met her, and wondered about that for a minute.

He knew he'd upset Nicole one night at the bar. It was after Bree had told him that she was seeing Colin and didn't want to see him anymore. Kent had been drinking and was trying to prove to Bree that he didn't care about her and Colin, and he'd hit on Nicole in front of her. He'd apologized and Nicole seemed to understand that he'd meant it.

He wondered if she was as sweet as she seemed. If so, she was probably the last thing he needed right now.

He needed someone who was the opposite of sweet.

The opposite of good.

The opposite of anything that was going to make him *feel* things.

He just needed to get laid.

He stepped out of the shower and toweled off with his plush full body towel, then hung it to dry, as he went naked to the mirror to shave for the day.

As he walked from the bathroom into his bedroom to get dressed for the day, he thought, "Yeah, it's good to have my house back."

While he drove into town listening to his favorite Country station, Kent decided to give Rich a call to see if he wanted to hit up the bar that evening.

He had only just gotten to know Rich, he'd met him and Colin at the beginning of the summer, and although he didn't think Colin was good enough for Bree, he couldn't help but like both of the guys.

He and Rich had been hanging out quite a bit, and it was nice to have someone to chill with. Too bad, Rich had to head back up to school soon.

He pulled up to the newspaper office and went inside. He'd been putting out applications recently to newspapers in big cities, but the newspaper business was on such a downward slide, no one was hiring.

Kent brushed off the disappointment and pulled out the charm when he rounded the corner and encountered the Editor in Chief's secretary.

"Morning, Marla," Kent started with his most charming smile. "You're looking lovely as always. Is the boss in?"

Marla turned a jaundiced eye on him and drawled in her best Clint Eastwood impression, or maybe that was just her voice after fifty years of smoking a pack a day.

"Don't think that smile is going to get you anywhere with me, young man. The boss will see you when he's ready, and not a second sooner."

"Yes, Ma'am," Kent replied, keeping the smile in place as he walked to his cubicle.

He hoped that all of the crap he'd put up with since being hired on here would eventually pay off.

Chuck, the Editor in Chief, had been reluctant to hire someone right out of college with no experience, but Kent had managed to get the job anyway.

Chuck and Marla had both been working at the paper since the dawn of time, and Kent had convinced Chuck that he could bring them up to speed with this century, and help them keep the doors of the paper open.

He'd been working his ass off to keep his promise, but it seemed like the two of them had fought him every step of the way.

He got the paper online, set them up with Twitter, Facebook, LinkedIn and every other account he could think of to keep the small paper relevant.

There were a couple interns from high school and the local community college, as well as a photographer, but that was it for staff.

Kent sat at his desk and checked the notes left for him from the night before, turning on the police blotter as he settled in.

A buzz on his phone notified him of a message, and he smiled when he saw that Rich was "game on" to meet at the bar for some beer and food.

He hoped a night out would take his mind off work, and Bree, and get him back in the game.

Chapter Four

The bar was pretty full that night and Nicole had a full station. She had never considered waitressing before she'd moved here, but she really was having a fantastic time.

She laughed at something an older couple said as she refilled their sweet tea, then turned to go to the kitchen to check on her orders, when she noticed Kent and Rich standing at the hostess station talking to Roni, who seemed to be ignoring Rich altogether.

Nicole's heart jumped in her chest at the sight of Kent. He had on jeans and a t-shirt, nothing fancy, but the way the t-shirt hugged his muscular body, had her belly tightening. And a glance at his biceps bulging from beneath his sleeve, almost made her walk straight into Kara.

"Distracted much?" Kara asked with a smirk and a raised eyebrow.

"Hmmm?" Nicole replied absently.

Kara laughed and made a production of looking over at Kent and then back at Nicole.

"Stop it," Nicole whispered, when she saw how obvious Kara was being.

"Oh, please," Kara said with a laugh as she grabbed Nicole's arm and pulled her into the kitchen. "It's as plain as the dreamy look in your eyes, that you have a thing for Kent."

"It is?" Nicole asked, suddenly worried that it was obvious to everyone, including Kent.

"Duh," Kara said, stopping in front of the prep table and looking to see if any of the plates were for her customers. "Don't worry, I doubt it's obvious to everyone, but I've been watching you since you started working here. I know that you haven't given any of the guys who have hit on you the time of day, but when Kent comes into the bar, Woo-Hoo... Sparks fly."

"You think so?" Nicole asked, picking up a few plates and arranging them on her tray.

"Honey," Kara drawled. "You look at him like he's a tootsie roll pop and you want to lick your way to the center."

Nicole blushed at that and was about to ask Kara what she thought of Kent, when Pete came walking in from the back.

Kara squealed, "Hi baby," as she ran over to give Pete a hug and a kiss.

Pete grinned broadly and seemed to enjoy his beautiful girlfriend wriggling in his arms.

"Not at work, Kara," He chided, his face showing the pleasure that his words did not.

"Oh, you're such a rule follower," Kara replied, kissing him loudly on the lips. "I love that about you. Now, get your cute butt behind the bar, so I can watch you break all the poor girls' hearts."

"Please," Pete said with a laugh. "There are no other girls, but you."

Nicole groaned good-naturedly, as she headed back out into the dining room. "Give me a break. You two are so corny."

Once she dropped off the meals, she checked on some of her other guests, before going to Rich and Kent, who had just been seated in her station.

"Hey, Darlin'," Rich said with a suggestive look. "How's everything going with your new roommate?"

Nicole couldn't help but smile at Rich's flirting.

"It's great." She said truthfully. "Thank you both so much for helping us. Can I get you started with something to drink?"

She worked up the courage to turn in Kent's direction, and was immediately caught in his direct gaze.

His lips turned up slightly as he looked her up and down.

"You look lovely this evening, Nic." His grey eyes twinkled and she began to feel light-headed.

"Thanks, so do you." She blushed slightly once the words were out of her mouth. She cleared her throat before turning back to Rich, who made her feel much more comfortable.

"I'd like a draft to start," Rich said with a wink. She smiled back at him before turning once more to Kent.

"Make that two," Kent added.

Nicole turned to go, but was stopped by Kent's hand on her arm.

"What time are you off?" He asked, making her stomach flutter wildly.

"Um, eleven," She replied breathlessly.

He just smiled and released her arm.

Nicole walked off towards the bar, wondering why he'd asked.

The night went by very quickly. Even after the dinner crowd thinned out, the number of people eager to hang out and have drinks and appetizers never seemed to die down.

Nicole counted down her drawer and went in the back to clean up and get her stuff, when Roni walked into the back room.

"Oh, my poor feet." Roni said dramatically.

"Busy night, huh." Nicole replied, realizing how badly her feet throbbed. "What do you say we have a drink before we go home?"

"God, Yes. That sounds great." Roni picked up her purse, then linked her arm through Nicole's and they walked out into the bar.

They were about to grab a stool when Kent called out Roni's name. He and Rich had moved up to one of the tables by the bar after they'd finished dinner, and had been hanging out watching a game and talking.

Roni looked at Nicole when Kent waved them over, Nicole shrugged.

She wanted to go and hang out with them, but she didn't want to be obvious about it.

Nicole walked behind Roni until they got to the table, and was about to sit next to Rich when Kent said, "Nic, why don't you sit over here by me?"

She looked over at Roni, who seemed a little surprised at his request, then rolled her eyes when Rich chimed in, "I've got a spot for you right here, Roni."

Nicole couldn't help but chuckle at the interaction between the two of them. She felt her palms begin to sweat when she sat down next to Kent, her arm brushing his as she settled in.

He lifted his arm and laid it across the bench behind her head, then leaned over and whispered in her ear, "Thanks. I've been waiting all night for the chance to talk to you."

"You have?" Nicole asked disbelief apparent in her voice.

He leaned back and asked, "Why is that so hard to believe?"

Nicole blushed again, cursing herself for her lack of finesse when it came to talking to guys.

"Because you could talk to any girl in here," she replied honestly.

Kent laughed, delighted at her candor.

"You're the only one who's been on my mind lately, and that's a fact."

Nicole couldn't hide the delighted smile that spread across her face. She was still smiling when Kara came up to get their order.

"Well, well, Ladies. You've got yourself some fine company this evenin'. What can I get you to drink?" Kara leaned against the edge of the booth, as if her legs were struggling to keep her upright.

"Can I get a Gin and Tonic," Nicole asked.

"I'll have a draft and four shots of Jack," Roni added.

"Oh, no shot for me, please," Nicole said to Roni.

"C'mon," Roni cajoled. "One won't hurt."

"I'll make sure you're okay," Kent promised, rubbing a hand over her shoulder to reassure her.

Nicole shivered at his touch and gave Kara a nod and a smile.

"So, Rich," Roni asked dryly, "when are you leaving again?"

Rich just chuckled and settled back in his seat. "I leave day after tomorrow."

"Hmmm, that's too bad," Roni said sarcastically.

Rich took a sip of his beer, then looked at Roni seriously. "Did I do something?"

"What do you mean?" Roni asked defensively.

"Well, is it guys in general that you dislike, or just me?"

Roni was saved from answering when Kara came back by the table with the drinks. She put a shot out in front of each of them, and said to holler if they needed anything else.

They each picked up their shot glass and lifted it.

"To friends and family," Roni offered, then they brought their glasses together in "cheers" and downed their respective shot.

Nicole felt the burn of the liquid as it splashed through her mouth and down her throat. It hit her belly and she had to concentrate to keep it there.

Yuck. She hated shots, and she really hated whiskey.

Everyone else seemed to have no problem with their drinks and quickly slammed their glasses back down on the table.

Nicole shifted slightly, and when her leg brushed up against Kent's, she moved quickly away as if she'd been burned.

She felt Kent's chuckle at the side of her face, and turned, only to realize that their faces were merely inches away from each other.

She sucked a breath in sharply, and felt the warmth spread through her body, as his eyes focused on her lips and dilated slowly.

She couldn't stop her tongue from darting out to moisten her lips, and grew heady as Kent groaned softly.

"You wanna get out of here?" Kent asked quietly, leaning closer to her, never lifting his gaze from her lips.

Nicole's head cleared at that, and she backed slightly away from him. Yes, she was totally attracted to Kent and knew that he was probably used to girls jumping at the chance to go home with him, but as much as she wanted the chance to get to spend more time with him, she knew they had different ideas on how that time would be spent.

"Oh, ahhh, I'm sorry. I can't."

Kent blinked, trying to hide his surprise.

"No problem." He pulled his arm back from behind her and straightened in his seat. He picked up his beer and turned to say something to Rich.

Nicole felt her stomach drop with disappointment. If Kent was so turned off by her not wanting to go home with him tonight, what would he think about her not wanting to have sex before marriage? She knew the answer; he wouldn't want anything to do with her. He was a sexy, single guy, who literally could have sex with any woman that he wanted. Why would he waste his time dating someone like her?

She took a swift drink of her Gin and Tonic, then excused herself to go to the restroom, before she embarrassed herself further.

When Nicole left the table, Roni reached over and punched her brother in the arm.

"Hey," Kent exclaimed. "What'd you do that for?"

"What'd you say to her, you jerk?" Roni asked angrily.

"Nothin'. Shit, Roni."

"It wasn't nothin'. She looked upset."

"God, Roni, this is the last thing I want to discuss with my sister. She's not into me, alright. All I did was ask if she wanted to get out of here." Kent managed to look indignant and slightly embarrassed.

"Jeez, Kent. She's not some floozy who you can just pick up for a one night stand." Roni said accusingly.

"I didn't mean it to come out like that, okay. I like her; I just wanted to get some time alone with her." Kent explained. "If she's not into it, whatever, I'll find someone who is."

"Don't be such a tool," Roni chastised her brother as she stood up. "Like I said, Nicole's not like these other girls. If you want to "hang out" with her, why don't you act like a grown-up and ask her out on a date? You guys are so immature."

She picked up her purse and Nicole's, then walked away without a further word for either of them.

"Hey," Rich piped in. "What did I do?"

"Don't worry about it man, my sister gets a little nuts sometimes. What do you say we pick up some beer and hang out at my house? I bet some of the guys would be game to come over for a poker game after closing."

"Sounds good to me," Rich responded.

They left some money on the table for Kara, then went to ask Pete if he wanted in on a game of poker.

Friends & Lovers Trilogy

Chapter Five

Kent woke to the sound of his phone buzzing. He whipped an arm out from under the strewn sheet and searched in vain for the annoying device.

Just when he started to drift off, the incessant buzzing started again.

He sat up angrily, his hand coming up to cradle his pounding head.

"Shit."

He may have played a little too much poker, and drank a few too many black and tans, the night before.

When his feet hit the floor, he swore under his breath when his heel made contact with his phone. When he felt the vibration under his foot, he grimaced and reached down to pick it up.

He gingerly opened one eye and flinched at the pain that seemed to radiate from his head.

How many shots had they done?

He was finally able to focus enough to look at his phone so he could see who the ass-pain that had been texting him all morning was…

He should have known, Roni.

Looked like she had been nagging him via text since early that morning.

"Nic is upset at your behavior last night... You'd better MAN UP..."

She had sent the same text twenty times in the last three hours.

Psycho.

He threw his phone down on the bed, then went to get some aspirin and a little 'hair of the dog'.

Two hours later Kent was standing in front of Roni and Nicole's apartment, headache free, holding a bunch of flowers and wondering if he really wanted to get this invested in a girl right now.

His six foot frame had him taking up most of the space in the narrow hallway. He paused before knocking, debating internally with himself.

He felt bad about offending her, and he really did want to get to know her better, but was he sending the wrong message by showing up on her doorstep, with daisies, to ask her on a date? Was he really interested in dating right now?

An image of Nicole flashed in his mind.

Yes, she was blonde, beautiful, and had a killer body, but she also had a wonderful innocence about her. A sweetness... And when she smiled, his heart seemed to shift in his chest.

That image alone should have sent warning bells off in his head; but instead, he raised his hand and knocked loudly.

"Where's the fire?" Roni asked when she opened the door. "Jeez, Kent, it sounded like you were bustin' down the door."

"Is Nic here?" Kent asked quickly, hoping to bypass his sister and get the groveling over with.

He should have known better.

Roni leaned against the doorjamb and grinned up at him, leaving him no choice but to continue to stand there awkwardly in the hall.

"Oh, you're here to see, Nic, huh?" Roni teased. "Did you get my texts?"

Kent rolled his eyes at her and said, "Yeah, all nine-hundred of them." Then he put his hand up and easily moved her out of his way.

He walked inside and looked around their living space.

"Is she here?" He asked Roni, turning back to her as she closed the door.

"Yeah," Roni replied as she went back to the couch and turned the volume on the TV up. "She's in her room. Don't disappoint me, Bro."

Kent decided to ignore her taunt, instead walking over to the closed door and raising his fist to knock again.

"Come in," Nicole called from inside her room.

Kent took a deep breath and opened the door. He stepped inside and shut the door quietly behind him, watching Nicole with every move he made.

She sat in the corner of her room at a small wooden desk. She was facing her laptop and typing furiously. Her hair was up in a messy bun, and she had on running shorts and a Nike t-shirt.

She looked amazing.

Kent cleared his throat loudly, hoping to get her attention, but Nicole seemed oblivious to anything except whatever she was working on.

He walked up to her and placed a hand on her shoulder, causing her to jump and whip her head towards him.

Her mouth formed a pretty O, and Kent noticed that she was wearing pink glasses.

It took her a moment to process what was happening, and he could tell the moment that it registered.

She flung her glasses onto the desk and rose quickly, hitting her hip on the desk as she did.

"Shoot." She yelled, rubbing her hip and looking at him warily. "Sorry, I didn't realize it was you at the door."

"That's alright," Kent chuckled. "You okay?"

Nicole nodded and took a step back, suddenly all too aware of the fact that she was alone, with Kent, in her bedroom.

"What's up?" She asked nervously.

Kent gestured to the reading chair she had next to the window. "Do you mind if I sit?"

Nicole shook her head no, then sat back down in her desk chair, seeking safety from the desk that stood between them.

Kent started to sit, then realized that he was still holding the flowers.

"Oh, I um… got these for you," He said awkwardly as he thrust the bouquet towards her. He cursed himself for acting like a freaking schoolboy, but couldn't help but feel happy at the look of pure pleasure that crossed her face as she accepted the daisies.

"Thank you," Nicole said softly, burying her face in the happy blossoms.

"Sure," Kent said absently, his body tightening swiftly as he looked at her. He backed up to grab a seat and told himself to just spit it out already.

"Look," he began, "the last couple times we've met up I've really made an ass of myself. First, that night at the bar when I man-handled you in front of Bree, then last night. I acted the way I always act with girls I'm interested in, but I know that I need to treat you differently."

"What?" Nicole tried to deny what he was saying, while in the back of her mind, the fact that he'd said he was 'interested' in her was making her insides go haywire. "I know you didn't mean anything by it. You don't have to treat me differently."

"I do, Nic. You aren't just one of the girls that I usually pick up in the bar. I know you, I like you, and you're my sister's roommate. I should have treated you with more respect, and I apologize."

"I like you too, Kent, just the way you are. I don't want you to think you have to act differently around me. I'm nothing special, honest." Nicole said worried that he was already putting her in the friend zone, and that she would never get a chance with him.

Kent stood abruptly and walked over to her, bending down and lifting her chin so that he was looking directly in her eyes.

He wanted her to see that he was telling her the truth, and to make sure that she heard him.

"You are special, Nic. You aren't just looking for a good time, and you don't deserve to be treated like you are. I swear that when I asked you to come to my place, I wasn't expecting you to hop into my bed; I just wanted to get to know you better. I approached it totally wrong, and I don't want to make that mistake again. I came by today to make amends, and to ask if you'd like to go out on a date with me."

Nicole blinked slowly, her brain working hard to catch up with her pounding heart.

"Yes," She said breathlessly, caught by the intensity of his grey eyes. "I'd like that."

Kent's grin was swift and broad.

"Great. When's your next evening off?" He asked softly, his gaze dropping momentarily from her eyes to her lips, as he released his hold on her chin.

"Um, Thursday," She replied, licking her lips to moisten them. Her mouth had gone dry under his perusal.

Kent stood upright, pausing to brush a disheveled lock of hair behind her ear before he turned to walk out of her room.

He paused at the door and turned to her before exiting.

"I'll pick you up at six." Kent promised with a smile, then he walked out, leaving Nicole sitting at her desk, smiling softly at the empty doorway.

Friends & Lovers Trilogy

Chapter Six

Nicole was so nervous, she felt like she might be sick. Her clothes were strewn across her bed, chair, and desk. She couldn't find anything to wear on her date with Kent.

Roni stood in the doorway, watching Nicole search frantically through her belongings, and couldn't stop the laugh that escaped her.

Nicole turned quickly at the sound; the look on her face betrayed her nerves.

"It's just Kent," Roni assured her. "He won't care what you're wearing."

Nicole threw her hands up in the air in frustration.

"I've seen the way he dresses, I know he cares... And besides, I care," Nicole argued. "I want to look nice for our first real date."

"Nic, you look great in sweats. Plus, you have *amazing* clothes. I would kill for your wardrobe." Roni walked in and started going through the clothes on the bed. "What are you thinking? A dress? Or maybe jeans and a cute top?"

"I don't know," Nicole wailed as she threw herself atop her clothes and covered her eyes with her hands.

Roni picked a pretty navy blue dress off of the pile and held it up. "This."

Nicole uncovered her eyes and peaked out at Roni.

"You think?" She asked.

"Yes. I love the tiny flowers and the neckline. I bet it looks great on you." Roni held it out to her and nodded, encouraging Nicole to put it on.

Once she put the dress on, it was easy to accessorize and finish getting ready. She just finished putting her makeup on when she heard Roni letting Kent in the apartment.

Her stomach started to jump and dance at the sound of his voice on the other side of the wall.

Nicole took one last look in the mirror and smiled. She couldn't believe she was actually going on a date with Kent.

She took a deep breath and opened her door. Kent and Roni were talking in the kitchen; he turned at the sound of her approach, and smiled broadly at her.

"Wow," he exclaimed, looking her up and down with appreciation. "You look beautiful."

He walked out of the kitchen to take her hand. She couldn't help but melt a bit when he brought it to his lips.

"Thank you," Nicole replied softly.

"Oh, Lordy." Roni stated.

They both ignored her as Kent guided Nicole to the door, by placing his hand at the small of her back.

"See you later," Kent said to his sister as they left.

"Don't stay out too late," Roni called after them with a chuckle.

As they slid into Kent's truck he said, "I hope you like barbecue."

Nicole turned to look at his handsome profile with a smile.

"I *am* from Texas."

Kent chuckled at that and pulled away from the apartment.

Nicole realized that neither Roni nor Kent had ever mentioned where they were from, so she figured it was the perfect time to ask.

"I grew up in Dallas, where are you from?" She prompted.

Kent didn't reply right away, but debated with himself about how much he was willing to reveal. He didn't usually talk to people about his family. Not even Bree knew about his upbringing that was knowledge shared by him and Roni alone.

"Detroit," he said finally.

"Really?" She asked, surprised. "I never would have guessed. I've never been, do you miss it?"

Kent bit back a bitter laugh, instead shaking his head.

"No." He realized how abrupt he must sound, so he tried to shift the conversation to Nicole. "How about you? Do you miss Dallas?"

Nicole looked out the window, realizing that Kent didn't know anything about her. She had discussed her past with Briana and with Roni, but this was her first real conversation with Kent. She knew she would have to tell him everything eventually, if she hoped to have any sort of a real relationship, but she wanted to keep it light tonight.

"No, I'm happy here," she replied.

"Me too," he admitted. "I never planned to settle down here, and have been putting my resume out, but I have to admit this town is growing on me."

"Are you applying at newspapers, or are you looking for a different line of work?"

"Newspapers. I've applied to all of the big city papers, but it's a rough time to get hired in journalism right now."

Nicole's stomach dropped at the thought of Kent getting hired on somewhere else and moving away, but she didn't say anything

Kent pulled into a parking spot and turned to her. "Have you ever been here?"

Nicole looked at the barbecue joint and shook her head. "I've heard its good, though."

"Let's go find out," Kent said, and they got out of the car.

Once they had ordered and picked up their food, Kent led her out the back door, and Nicole was surprised at the set up outside.

A stage took up the entire backside of the property, with a dance floor in front of it, and picnic tables filling in the rest of the space. There was another bar outside, and the place was decorated with old signs and bar paraphernalia.

There was a band warming up onstage.

Nicole couldn't help the pleasure that coursed through her, and smiled widely at Kent as she joined him at a table.

"This is amazing." She exclaimed.

"Yeah," he replied. "I've heard it was great and always wanted to come, but never had a chance to before tonight."

They sat down and began to tear into the meals before them: pulled pork, brisket, creamed corn, corn bread, and macaroni and cheese.

"So, you never said what you went to school for. Are you applying for jobs?" Kent asked her in between bites.

She didn't want to go into her whole backstory on their first date, so she just said, "I majored in English. I haven't been applying anywhere yet."

Kent nodded as he worked on his corn on the cob. "Do you know what you want to do next?"

Nicole looked at him shyly as she picked up her corn bread. "Actually, I'm a writer." She looked down at her hands. This was the first time she'd ever told anyone what *her* dream was and was afraid of what reaction she would see on his face.

"Really?" He asked simply, a small smile on his face. "Well, it looks like we have something in common."

Nicole looked up at him quickly, took in his smile, and returned a brilliant one of her own.

They sat in a comfortable silence as they ate, then Kent looked down and Nicole's plate and realized that she was keeping up with his gusto.

He used a wet nap to clean his fingers and gazed at her with appreciation in his eyes. "I love that you actually eat."

Nicole stopped savoring her corn bread long enough to look up at him with a puzzled smile. "What do you mean?"

"Well, I love to eat, and it makes me happy to see that you do too. I was worried that you would want to just order a salad or something."

Nicole laughed and admitted, "Sometimes I like to eat salad, but I love to eat too, and there is nothing I enjoy more than Texas barbecue."

They grinned at each other, then Kent reached over to get some sauce off of Nicole's face, and her grin disappeared, her eyes glazing over at his touch. When he put the same finger into his mouth and licked the sauce off of his finger, her mouth closed and she found it hard to breath.

Kent looked at her intently as he tasted the sauce, then smiled seductively at her, "Dance with me."

Nicole smiled absently and took the hand he offered.

When they got on the dance floor, they fell easily into the two-step, Kent leading Nicole around the dance floor as if they had been dancing together forever.

Nicole allowed herself to just enjoy dancing with Kent. They looked into each other's eyes as they moved, and she felt her body warm under Kent's gaze.

He was one sexy man.

When the band began to play a slower song, Kent gathered her into his arms and they swayed to the music.

Nicole's head rested against his strong chest, and she enjoyed the feel of being in Kent's arms.

They danced for hours, and didn't end up leaving until the band started to pack up at the end of their set.

They rode back to Nicole's apartment in a comfortable silence, and Nicole replayed the evening they'd just spent together, over in her mind.

Nicole came back to reality when they pulled into her place and Kent said softly, "We're here."

He walked her to her door, and they both paused before she went inside.

"I had a wonderful time. Thank you so much for everything," Nicole said as she looked up at him.

"It was my pleasure," Kent replied as he reached a hand up and gently touched her hair. "You're so beautiful."

Nicole felt her face grow warm with pleasure and started to deny his claim, but stopped when he reached his other hand out to touch the side of her face. He leaned in slowly to taste her lips with his.

Nicole felt like she'd been waiting for this moment for months. Without thinking, she reached her hands up to pull his head in closer, moaning softly as she opened her mouth and greedily invited him in.

Kent paused for a moment, shocked at her response, then his instincts took over and he pushed her up against the door. His hands moved lower to explore her body, and they both got swept away in the moment.

When his hand brushed the underside of her breast, she turned her head to catch her breath, causing him to stop and back up a step.

"Sorry," Kent said quietly. He ran his hands over his face in an effort to gain a semblance of control. "I didn't mean to move so fast."

Nicole smoothed out her dressed, then looked up at him with a smile. "You don't have to apologize; I enjoyed every bit of that kiss." With that said, she gave him an embarrassed smile, then leaned in to give him one more quick kiss on the lips, before opening her door and going inside. "Goodnight."

"Night," Kent replied as she shut the door.

He stood there for a minute, his body screaming out at the loss. Taking it slow with Nicole was going to be harder than he thought.

He was going to have to go home and take a cold shower.

Chapter Seven

Nicole and Roni decided to have a small housewarming party, and invited everyone over after work. They didn't want anything big, just a small gathering with drinks and appetizers.

They cleaned up and prepped everything before work, so they would just have to come home and get changed.

Nicole finished getting ready first, so she was setting the food out on the counter when the first knock sounded on their door.

She tucked a stray stand of golden hair behind her hair, and opened the door. She was caught off guard when Kent swept her up and kissed her until she was breathless.

When he put her down she was laughing.

"What was that for?" She asked.

"I missed you today," Kent said softly, as he bent to plant a kiss right below her ear.

Nicole shivered slightly and admitted, "I missed you too."

He pulled away and smiled into her eyes. "Good."

"Really?" Roni asked incredulously as she walked out of her room. "We're about to have our first party, Kent, it's not make out time."

Kent wiggled his eyebrows at his sister.

"Oh, it's always make out time."

He grabbed her by the waist and started to pepper her face with kisses. Roni broke out in laughter, and yelled, "Uncle."

Nicole smiled and felt a moment of envy at how close the twins were. Her family seemed so cold in comparison.

Kent released Roni when there was another knock on the door. Roni tried to smooth out her hair and clothes before she opened it.

"Hey," Kara said, giving Roni a quick hug as she and Pete came inside. She held out a bottle of wine and said, "This is for you guys."

"Thanks," Nicole said, as she walked over to hug both Kara and Pete. "Thanks for coming."

She was showing them to the kitchen when some more people from work showed up at the door. Roni greeted their guests, and Nicole began to make sure everyone had a drink.

Kent came up behind her in the kitchen and thanked her when she handed him a glass of crown and coke.

"How'd you know this is my drink?" He asked her when he took his first sip.

"I pay attention," She responded with a sly smile.

Kent leaned over and nuzzled her neck.

"You're a good hostess."

"Oh, my momma made sure of that," she replied wryly.

He watched her as she passed out drinks to her guests and wondered about her comment.

Kent moved to the couch and started a conversation with Pete about football. He enjoyed talking with the other man. Pete always had a kind word for everyone, had a good sense of humor, and was a killer poker player. He was one of the people in town that Kent could really call a friend.

As they talked, Kent watched Nicole work the room, and wondered again about her earlier statement. It was obvious from the way she carried herself, that she'd had a very different upbringing than he had. He couldn't imagine his mother ever being so at ease entertaining in her home. He found himself comparing his life with Nicole's. He was sure that they were from different worlds and wondered what she would think of him if she knew where he came from.

When he saw her slip into her room, he excused himself from his conversation with Pete and followed her.

Nicole grabbed the lip gloss off of her dresser and applied it, before turning to go back into the living room. She stopped when she saw Kent enter the room.

He stepped inside and closed the door, leaning against it as he smiled.

"You sure know how to work a room. I don't know why, but the way you move is really hot. I've been waiting for the chance to get you alone," he pushed up off of the door and walked over to her, offering her the glass of wine he'd poured for her.

"Thanks," Nicole said as she took a sip of the chilled wine. "Mmmm, that's good."

"I noticed you were so busy serving everyone else, that you never had a chance to enjoy a glass yourself."

"Well, a good hostess has to make sure her guests are happy."

Kent looked at her quizzically. "That's the second time you've made mention of that. Tell me." He said simply, and gestured for her to sit.

She looked at the closed door, then back at him. "I guess it's okay to disappear for a minute."

Kent chuckled at her response as he settled on the bed next to her.

Nicole knew that she would to have to tell him about herself eventually, and figured now was as good a time as ever. She hoped it wouldn't totally change the way he saw her, and that he would still want to date her once she told him everything.

She took another sip of wine, then took a deep breath, before looking at him and saying, "I grew up in Dallas, as you know. My parents are very wealthy and enrolled me in private schools. They are very active in the church and had high expectations for me and my future."

Nicole figured it was best to tell him everything at once, but felt the nerves bouncing in her belly in anticipation of his reaction. She really liked him.

"What kind of expectations," he prodded.

"They wanted me to go to SAGU, study Youth Ministries, get married, and start a congregation with my husband as the minister." She spit it out quickly, in one breath, then took a sip of wine and looked at him over her glass.

Kent brushed her hair back in assurance, then asked, "Did they have the husband picked out?"

"Yeah, Jake," She felt a small pang in her heart when she said his name. He'd meant so much to her for so long, she found that she missed the friendship they'd shared.

"We started dating in high school, and he fit the mold perfectly. We were engaged for three years and everything was going according to plan until I got to school."

"What happened at school?"

"It was my first time being out on my own, away from my parents, and I began to realize how controlling they were and that their dreams weren't necessarily my dreams. I changed my major to English without telling them, and I fell in love with my creative writing courses. As I got closer to graduation, I began to understand that Jake's dreams mirrored my parents, not my own, and that I didn't love him in the way a woman should love her future husband."

"Wow," Kent said, taking her hand in his. "How did they take the news?"

"Well, I haven't spoken to my parents or Jake since the day I told them that I no longer wanted to get married or work in the church, so I guess they didn't take it very well," Nicole said with a dry laugh.

"I think it's admirable that you were strong enough to give up everything you knew to start fresh and do what you want," Kent said, his finger caressing the top of her hand.

"There's something else you need to know," Nicole began, a little more confident after his easy acceptance of what she'd shared so far.

"What is it?" He asked, curious at what else she could tell him about her past.

"Well, I said my family is religious, and they raised me with strong Christian values, which I still live by." Nicole stopped, suddenly overcome by nerves at the thought of his rejection.

"Go on," Kent prodded.

"I was raised to believe that sex should be shared between a husband and a wife. I'm a virgin… and I'll remain a virgin until my wedding night." Nicole spit it out as quickly as she could, then watched Kent's face for his reaction.

His finger stilled on her hand, and his facial expression remained frozen as he processed what she had just told him.

A virgin.

Kent looked at her stunning face, surrounded by her beautiful long blonde hair, which currently covered the most stunning pair of breasts he'd ever seen.

He felt suddenly bereft at the realization that no matter what kind of relationship he strove to have with Nicole, he would probably never get to have sex with her.

He'd seen what an unhappy marriage looked like, he'd grown up in the middle of one, and he'd always told himself that marriage was probably not in his future. He didn't want to take the chance of ending up like his parents, and he knew that he had to keep Roni as his number one priority. No woman he knew would ever accept coming in number two to his twin.

Kent cleared his throat awkwardly, as he thought about what to say.

Did he want to get to know Nicole better?

Yes.

Did he think she was funny, beautiful and fascinating?

Yes.

Did he think they had the potential to have a good relationship?

Yes.

Could he spend the unforeseen future with Nicole, and not have sex with her?

Not have sex with anyone?

"I know it's a lot to take in in one night," Nicole started. Her stomach dropped at his silence. She needed to let him off the hook and get some space before he could tell she was upset. "You don't have to say anything. I get it. You're a very good-looking, single man, and you didn't realize that sex was off the table when you asked me out. Don't worry about it; let's get back to the party."

In that moment he realized that, yes, he could handle it. She was worth the nights of torment that he was sure to have.

He put his hand out to stop her from leaving when she rose.

"I hope you don't think so little of me, to believe that I'd run off because you're a virgin. I think it's great that you have such strong beliefs, not many people do nowadays."

A smile broke out across her face, leaving Kent momentarily breathless at her beauty.

"Really?" She asked slowly, to allow him the chance to change his mind if he wanted to.

Kent stood up and pulled her into a hug.

"Yes, really. You're an amazing woman, Nic, and I want to continue to spend time with you."

Nicole pulled back and smiled.

"I'm so happy to hear you say that," She admitted.

"We'd better get back to the party." Kent said, picking up their glasses.

"Okay," Nicole replied, and took the hand he offered to escort her back out into the living room.

Friends & Lovers Trilogy

Chapter Eight

A couple days after their housewarming party, Nicole got up early to meet Kent for a hike on the outskirts of town.

She had worked the last few nights, and he had deadlines to meet, so they hadn't been able to find any time together.

She was excited to see him again, but couldn't help but be a little worried. The last time she'd seen him was when she'd told him she was a virgin. They'd talked and texted a couple times over the past few days, but he'd seemed a little distant.

When the knock came, she was in the living room ready to go. She let him wait a few seconds, so she didn't seem too eager, but her heart leapt when she opened the door.

Kent's work-out clothes accentuated his well-defined muscles, and showed plenty of tanned skin.

When Nicole's eyes finally made it Kent's face, she smiled brightly at him.

"Hi."

"Hey, Nic," Kent returned her smile. "You ready?"

She turned to grab her water bottle, and he groaned at the site of her perfectly rounded ass in her spandex shorts. He felt his body tighten in response, and wondered how he was going to make it through the day.

Nicole walked out, leaving him to shut the door and follow her down the stairs.

Her hair was swept up in a high pony tail that swung back and forth. Kent tried to focus on her hair, rather than the sway of her other body parts as she bounded down the stairs.

The drive to the trail was a short one, but it gave them enough time to catch up on their days apart.

"Kara asked me if I want to go with her to Austin this weekend to see Bree and Colin. We have the same days off this week, so we thought it would be fun to go and see their new place," Nicole said.

Kent was silent for a moment, then replied, "That's cool. I'm sure you'll have fun. Austin's a great city."

"I've never been there, and I've always wanted to go, so I'm excited. Plus, I really want to see Bree again."

Kent just nodded. Nicole figured she'd better change the subject. "How's your week been?"

"My boss has actually been talking about retiring. I don't know what his plans are for the paper, but I'm going to approach him about taking over the paper myself. I know I don't have a lot of experience, but I think I can bring a lot to the table, and I have a vision of where I want the paper to go."

"That's wonderful, Kent," Nicole hoped that meant that there was a chance he would stop looking for jobs in other places, but she didn't feel confident enough to ask him. She didn't want it to look like she was pressuring him.

He parked his Mustang and they got out and began to stretch. Kent tried to focus on something other than Nicole as she bent and flexed her limber body, but he couldn't stop his eyes from taking in the sight of her. He closed his eyes as he finished warming up.

"Ready?" He asked once they'd stretched for a few minutes.

Nicole smiled and nodded.

Kent motioned to the left, to indicate what direction the trail began, and they took off at a brisk pace to begin their hike.

Kent cleared his throat and tried to will the fog in his brain to fade away.

"So, Nic," He began, "You said that you're a writer, what do you write?"

Nicole stumbled a bit and felt the heat begin to rise up her neck. She hadn't been kidding when she'd said she'd never told anyone that she wanted to write. She knew she could trust Kent, but she was worried that she was falling too hard, too fast.

"I write fiction, Horror actually."

Kent stopped walking, causing her to stop and turn to look at him.

"Horror?" He asked, looking slightly amazed. "You are full of surprises, aren't you?"

He started walking again and she fell into step behind him, her face flush with uncertainty.

"Is that a good thing?" She asked.

Kent grinned down at her, "With you... Yeah, it is."

Nicole couldn't help but return his grin.

They picked up the pace as they started up an incline.

"Have you finished anything?" He asked.

"Yes, actually, I have," Nicole admitted. "I have finished the first draft and I've been editing it."

"Is that what you were doing on your computer when I brought you the flowers?"

"Yeah," She said as she smiled at the memory. "I was so focused that I didn't know it was you that came in my room."

"That's amazing, Nic." Kent replied. "I think it's wonderful that you're going after your dreams. You're very focused. I think we have that in common."

"Oh? Why do you say that?" Nicole asked him.

Kent figured after everything she had told him about herself, he needed to open up a little bit as well, no matter how much he hated talking about his personal life.

"Well, I've always known that I didn't want to live the way my parents did, so I've worked my whole life to make sure that didn't happen."

He stopped and offered her his hand, then helped her over a small crevice in the path.

"How do you mean?" Nicole asked, intrigued to learn something new about him.

"My parents never saved a dime and we were always scraping by. My dad couldn't hold a job, so my mom would get odd jobs cleaning houses or babysitting, meanwhile, Roni and I would go days without eating. When I got old enough to start mowing lawns, I vowed that Roni would never go hungry again. I also promised myself that I would be smarter with my money, and I would never be worried about where my next paycheck was coming from."

Nicole slowed down and took his hand in hers. "I think the way you look out for Roni is wonderful, and I'm amazed at the strength you had at such a young age."

Kent pulled her hand up to his lips and kissed it softly.

"Thanks, I'm glad that you can appreciate how important Roni is to me," he looked up to get his bearings. "We're about halfway through this trail. We'd better speed it up if we're going to get you home in time to shower before work."

They hit the trail hard. Nicole used the time to clear her head and to reflect on what Kent had told her about his childhood.

They'd led very different lives, and Nicole couldn't imagine the obstacles he'd dealt with growing up, but she was very impressed with the man he was today.

Kent made sure they did some cool down stretches before getting back in the car.

He'd worried briefly that Nicole would look at him differently when he'd told her a little about his upbringing, but he was happy that he had. He wasn't ready to tell her everything yet, but he was comfortable with what he'd told her.

He drove her back to her apartment and walked her to the door.

"Do you want to come in?" Nicole asked him, her face was flush from exertion and glistened prettily.

Kent felt a strong urge to gather her in his arms and take her to her room, kissing and stroking her gloriously toned body along the way. He imagined carrying her into the shower and lathering her up.

He shook his head, trying in vain to calm his raging hormones. He felt like a teenager again: unbearably horny and unable to find release. Well… At least not the way he wanted to.

"Um, no," He replied gruffly. "I'd better not. You have to get ready for work and I have some stuff to do at my house. I'll give you a call later."

He leaned down and gave her a kiss on the forehead, then turned and jogged down the stairs, leaving her there staring off after him, the confusion she felt apparent on her face.

Friends & Lovers Trilogy

Bethany Lopez

Chapter Nine

Nicole was finishing up packing her bag when she heard a knock on the front door, indicating Kent had arrived with dinner.

Kara was going to be picking her up to go to Austin in a couple hours, and Kent had offered to bring dinner over for her and Roni before she left.

Roni had to work this weekend, so she couldn't go on the Austin trip, but Nicole was excited to get away and see Bree and Colin. She was sure that Roni would enjoy having the apartment to herself for a few days. They were getting along great so far, but it was always nice to get some alone time.

Nicole zipped up her bag and took it out into the living room to set it by the front door. She prided herself on being punctual, and didn't want to make Kara wait when she arrived.

Roni had let Kent in and they were setting the table for dinner.

"Hey Kent," Nicole said, walking over to give him a hug.

"Hey babe," He replied, giving her a quick squeeze before releasing her. "I was just asking Roni if she wanted to spend some quality time with her big brother this weekend."

"Really? Big brother? You are like two minutes older than me." Roni said wryly.

"Still counts," Kent countered with a wink.

"Mm mm, that looks delicious," Nicole said, her stomach grumbling as they opened containers of tacos, beans, rice, salsa, and guacamole.

"The best you'll ever eat," Kent promised.

"That's a big statement," Nicole replied. "We have some excellent Mexican food in Dallas."

"Yeah, but this place is run by a sweet old lady who moved here from Mexico in her teens, and makes her own tortillas." Kent boasted. "I'm telling you, no one makes a meal like Señora Garza."

"Let's stop talking about how good it's and dig in," Nicole counted with a laugh. "I'm dying over here."

Kent and Roni sat down and Nicole began to make their plates. Kent couldn't help but smile as he watched her, always the perfect hostess. He thought briefly at how perfectly he could see her in his life, long-term, then scowled; the last thing he needed to be thinking about was what a wonderful wife Nicole would make.

"You okay?" Roni asked him. "You look like you got a bad bite."

Kent shook off the annoying thoughts and smiled at his sister. "No, I haven't even tasted it yet. I was just thinking of something."

"Well stop thinking and start eating," Roni said with a laugh.

Nicole was already savoring the delicious combination of flavors, so she just smiled absently at the twins. She'd always wished she'd had siblings. Growing up as an only child, her parents had made sure she never wanted for any material things, but she'd always longed for a sister or brother.

Kent smiled at her obvious enjoyment of the meal.

"I'm right, aren't I?"

Nicole could only nod as she enjoyed every bite.

"Rich called me and said he would be coming home for Halloween," Kent said.

"Great," Roni groaned.

"What's your problem with Rich?" Kent asked her. "I didn't raise you to be rude, but you seem to be every time you're around Rich."

"I've seen too many guys like him, that's all," Roni answered.

"Rich is nothing like Hank, Roni, he's a good guy. You should give him a break."

"Hank?" Nicole asked curiously.

"My ex," Roni stated.

"Rich said it looks like he's on track to graduate in December, so it looks like you'll have to get used to him being around full time." Kent informed Roni.

Roni didn't reply she just went back to eating with a scowl on her face.

When their bellies were full, Roni went to her room to wash up, while Nicole and Kent settled in the living room to wait for Kara.

Kent sat down, picked up Nicole's feet and placed them on his lap. He picked up one perfectly manicured foot and began to massage it gently.

Nicole settled back and closed her eyes, groaning softly and smiling reflexively.

"That feels wonderful," She said in a soft tone.

Kent quickly realized his mistake when he couldn't pull his eyes from her beautifully curved mouth and his vision blurred at the sounds emitting from her throat.

God, she was hot.

He continued rubbing and pressing his fingers deeply into her skin, and tried not to dwell on the fact that her other foot was pressing perilously close to his hard cock.

"Shit, when is Kara gonna get here," he wondered miserably.

Nicole lifted her other foot, and pulled the one he was rubbing out of his hands, indicating that she was ready for the other one to be massaged.

She opened one eye and grinned saucily at him, so he picked up the other foot and began rubbing, laughing in spite of himself.

When she put her other foot down, it inadvertently landed right on top of his strained jeans, causing him to jolt and her eyes to fly open.

Nicole sat up and moved closer to Kent, as he watched her warily.

He'd never been so afraid to have a girl coming at him like she wanted to eat him alive. This was unchartered territory.

Nicole had felt his erection, so she knew that he was turned on, but the look he gave her indicated that he was anything but. She wasn't sure what to do. She really wanted to kiss him. She wanted to be in his arms and feel his hard body pressed against hers, but she was afraid of rejection.

She was debating with herself whether she should ask him what was wrong, or just throw herself at him, when there was a knock on the door.

Nicole got up to answer it, but not before she noticed the look of relief that crossed Kent's face. She felt her stomach jitter with disappointment.

Had he changed his mind about dating her?

She opened the door and Kara came bounding in.

"Road trip!" Kara yelled.

Nicole laughed as she watched Kara dance around the room with excitement.

Roni came out of her room and said, "Hey Kara, don't you look cute."

Kara had a teal blue tank top on with a long white skirt that was twirling as she spun around.

"Thanks, Roni," Kara said, stopping to give the other girl a hug. "I so wish you didn't have to work and were coming with."

"Me too," Roni said with regret. "But I do have a hot date with my brother to look forward to."

"Best date in town," Kent chimed in, as he came over to give Kara a hug hello.

"I'll say," Kara said with a wink. "Hey, Kent, I was going to ask if you wouldn't mind giving Pete a call to hang out one night while I'm gone. I want my man to have some fun and not just sit around missing me."

Kent chuckled at that.

"Sure, we could probably get a poker night together or something. No worries, I'll take care of him."

Kara beamed at him.

"Thanks."

She turned to Nicole, "You ready?"

Nicole nodded and walked over to pick up her bag.

They all walked down to Kara's car and Nicole put her bag in the backseat, opening the front zipper and pulling out a water to keep in the front with her.

She walked over to the curb where Roni and Kent were saying goodbye to Kara.

"Tell Bree and Colin we say hi," Roni was saying to Kara.

Kent didn't say anything about Briana or Colin. He hadn't since she'd brought up the trip, which made Nicole wonder if he still had feelings for Bree.

"I have to get going too," Kent said, looking briefly at his watch. "You girls have fun," he said to Nicole and Kara, then turned to Roni and said, "I'll give you a call to set something up."

He turned to each of the girls and gave them a kiss on the cheek before he walked away and got into his mustang. Nicole was left staring after him, as the other two girls looked on.

"What was that?" Roni asked Nicole.

"I'm not sure," Nicole replied. "Ready, Kara?"

"Sure thing, girl," Kara replied with one more smile for Roni before she got into the car.

"See ya," Nicole said as she got into the car, then waved as the pulled out of the parking lot.

Nicole looked out the window and thought briefly that getting away for a few days might be the best thing for all of them.

Chapter Ten

It only took about two hours for them to arrive at Briana and Colin's apartment in downtown Austin.

When they pulled up to the apartment complex, Briana noticed Kara's car and started jumping up and down. Kara pulled up alongside her and rolled down the window.

"Hey, pretty lady, can you put us up for the night?" Kara asked, followed by a booming laugh.

Briana jumped in the backseat and told Kara how to get into the parking garage.

"I'm so excited that you guys are here," Briana squealed with delight.

"Me too!" Nicole said, turning around in her seat to look at Bree while she spoke.

Briana looked as pretty as ever, her long chestnut hair was pulled back in a fat braid and her brown eyes sparkled with excitement.

When Kara parked they all jumped out of the car and gave each other a round of hugs. When Kara and Nicole hugged each other, they all laughed at their exuberance.

"Do you need help with any of your bags?" Bree asked.

"No, we each only brought one bag," Kara assured her as they got their bags out of the car and followed her to the elevator.

"This is a beautiful complex," Nicole observed.

"Oh, my gosh, we love it!" Briana gushed. "We looked around a lot, and decided to go with a loft, just so we could have the other amenities that this building offers. It has a gym and a pool, there is a Trader Joe's next door, a hiking trail nearby, and we are within walking distance to 6th street."

"What's 6th street?" Nicole asked.

"You'll see," Kara and Bree said with a laugh.

When they reached her floor, Briana walked them down the hall and let them into the apartment. It was a large open space with wood floors. Briana and Colin had decorated it in country style, and managed to reflect their personalities. There were sports memorabilia scattered amongst the pictures and wall hangings, and the kitchen looked like a chef's dream.

"I hope you don't mind, the sofa is a sleeper, so the two of you will share that." Briana mentioned as they set their bags in the corner.

"That'll be fine," Nicole responded.

"Where's Colin?" Kara asked Briana.

"He's at work. They had evening practice, but he'll catch up with us later. I have to admit, with him working and me going to school, we don't get much chance to socialize, so I'm really looking forward to going out tonight. He's going to meet up with us later."

"Let's get ready then," Kara exclaimed, unzipping her bag and pulling out her make-up case.

"Yay," Briana said happily.

They all put on fresh make-up and fixed their hair, then set out for a night on the town.

Nicole hadn't been in a city since she'd left Dallas, so she was looking forward to hanging out somewhere other than the bar and grill.

They walked down 6th street, and Nicole was surprised how many people were milling around.

"Wow, this is a lot different than being home," She observed with a laugh.

Bree nodded her consent, then ushered them into a bar that already had a crowd on the floor, dancing to a local band.

They made their way to the bar and Bree spoke loudly so they could hear her. "They don't have a cover here and have a special on pitchers, so this is where we usually hang out. Is beer okay with you guys?"

Kara and Nicole both nodded and Kara said, "Sure, but let me get the first round."

They each had to show I.D. in order to get a glass, but they were quickly given their pitcher and Briana led them to a booth in the back of the bar. Close enough to see the band, but far enough away that they could still talk.

At the first sip of the cool brisk ale, Nicole smiled and licked her lips.

"I'm so happy to be here. Thanks for inviting me, Bree."

"Of course, I'm excited that you could come. I have been begging Kara to come out ever since we left. It was perfect that you guys had the same days off." Briana said with a smile, as she reached over to give Kara's hand a squeeze. "So, fill me in on all of the gossip."

"Well, Pete and I are doing great, "Kara said with a big grin on her face. "He has given up all pretense of living in your room and has moved all of his belongings into mine. Bree, he's just the sweetest thing!"

"Aww, that's great, Kara," Briana gushed happily. "I knew you two would be perfect together."

"I know you did, but I never imagined that I could love that red-headed stud the way I do." Kara was practically glowing as she spoke.

Nicole and Bree both giggled at that.

"How's everything going with you and Roni?" Bree asked Nicole. "You guys are officially roomies now, right?"

"Yeah," Nicole answered. "It's been great. Thank you so much for telling me that she was looking for a place, she really is the perfect roommate. I like her a lot."

"But not as much as she likes her twin," Kara divulged to Bree, causing Nicole to blush with embarrassment.

Briana looked at Nicole with obvious curiosity. "Really? You like Kent?"

Nicole was worried that Briana would be mad, or things would be awkward, and she really wished that Kara hadn't said something about her and Kent already. She'd wanted to tell Briana when they had a little more privacy.

"Um, well, yeah... We've been out a couple times." Nicole admitted sheepishly.

Briana smiled broadly and reached across to hold Nicole's hand.

"Nicole, that's great!" Bree assured her. "Kent is a terrific guy. The best. I can really see you two together. In fact, I remember him checking you out back when I was there. He's had a thing for you for a while now."

"Really?" Nicole asked with surprise. "You did?"

"Yeah. I think it was at our place at one of the parties and at the bar. I totally saw that he was interested in you."

"Are you sure it doesn't bother you?"

"Totally sure," Briana exclaimed. "Kent was never really mine, not in that way. I promise that I'm truly happy for the both of you."

"Awesome," Kara said loudly as she downed her beer. "Now what do you girls say we go tear up that dance floor, huh?"

They nodded and finished their drinks, then went out on to the dance floor to move to the music.

They danced until they were exhausted. That's where Colin found them when he walked into the bar.

He caught the stares of many of the male patrons, as they watched the three beautiful girls dance together on the floor. They were laughing, absorbed in each other and oblivious to the people watching them.

Colin walked up behind Bree and put his arms around her, matching her moves with his own.
He nuzzled her neck and was pleased to hear her intake of breath.

"Mmmm," Bree purred. "You really shouldn't do that; my boyfriend could be here at any moment."

She giggled and he spun her to face him and kissed her soundly on the lips.

"Hey baby," He whispered in her ear. "I missed you today." He pulled back and looked into her eyes, his dimples flashing as he smiled at her.

"I missed you too," Briana said, returning his smile full force.

Colin tore his eyes from Briana's and turned that heart-stopping grin on Nicole and Kara.

"How's it goin', Ladies?" He gave them each a hug, then asked, "You want me to grab another pitcher?"

They all nodded and made their way back to their table to wait for Colin to join them.

"You guys look like you're doing great," Kara said to Bree once they were seated.

"We really are," Briana gushed. "I couldn't be happier."

"That's so wonderful, Bree. You both deserve it." Nicole chimed in, a little envious at Colin's obvious adoration of Bree. She wondered again about Kent's recent less than affectionate behavior.

Colin poured them each a glass of beer before he sat, then settled in to enjoy a pint of his own.

"So, how's everything back home?" Colin asked.

They filled him in on the same things they had already told Briana, but Nicole also mentioned Rich helping Roni move in and the fact that he was on track to graduate in December.

"Yeah, he mentioned something about that last time we spoke, but it's been a few weeks. I've been so busy at work that I haven't had a lot of time to keep in contact with everyone."

"Kent also said that Rich is planning to come down for Halloween. I'm sure he doesn't want to miss the Halloween bash at the bar," Nicole added.

"Oh, babe, we should totally try to go home for that," Briana said to Colin. "Halloween falls on a weekend this year, and it would give us a chance to see our folks. Plus, it'll be great to see Rich again."

"Yeah," Colin agreed. "We'll see what we can do."

"Yay!" Bree exclaimed.

They finished the pitcher and decided to head back to the loft to drink and talk in a quieter environment.

When they got back, Colin excused himself and said he had to get up early and would give the girls a chance to catch up. He promised he would see them for dinner tomorrow and wished them a goodnight.

"I'm gonna go tuck him in," Bree said with a wicked gleam in her eyes. "There are beers in the fridge. Help yourselves and I'll be right back out."

Kara went into the kitchen to grab them each a beer, while Nicole went to the bathroom to change into her comfy clothes. When she was done, Kara went in to do the same, and Nicole sat down on the couch and took a sip of her beer.

She looked around the loft and thought about how much she would love to be at the point in a relationship that Bree and Colin were in. They were so obviously in love, it made Nicole's heart ache.

Kara came out of the bathroom in her flannel pajama pants and a t-shirt, with her hair piled on top of her head. She grabbed her beer and settled across from Nicole in a comfy looking oversized chair.

They were sitting there talking about how much they loved the loft, when Bree came walking out in her pajamas. She grabbed a beer from the fridge and joined Nicole on the couch.

"So, tell us everything," Kara prompted.

Briana smiled and filled them in on her classes in culinary school.

"I am having so much fun and learning something new every day. Colin keeps joking about having to hit the gym twice a day, since I started trying my recipes out on him." Briana looked so happy as she talked. "How's everything at the bar?"

"Oh, you know, same old thing." Kara said as she snuggled further into the chair. "Pam hasn't changed at all. Remember the time we stayed late after closing to wait for her, and then we realized that she wasn't in the backroom?"

Briana started laughing. "Yeah, she went home early and didn't tell anyone. We would have sat there all night if Pete hadn't gone back there to check on her."

"The day I came in for my interview, I thought Pam was a busser or something," Nicole chimed in with a chuckle. "I talked to her for about ten minutes before I realized that she was the manager and my interview had already started."

Kara and Briana cracked up at that.

"That is totally, Pam!" Kara chortled. When she calmed down enough to talk again, she looked at Nicole and admitted, "When I saw you, I thought you were going to be a Stone Cold Bitch."

"You did?" Nicole asked, surprised.

"Yeah, but it didn't take long after talking to you, to realize that you aren't. You just looked so perfect and put together, I jumped to conclusions." Kara said with a shrug. "I couldn't have been more wrong."

"Thanks."

"Well when I first met Kara," Briana cut in, trying to lighten the mood back up. "I knew Kara was a Bitch."

They all started laughing at that. Kara was laughing so hard that she almost fell off the chair.

They stayed up until four in the morning reminiscing and talking about the upcoming Halloween party.

When Nicole lay down to go to sleep, she realized that she finally had the kind of friends she'd always hoped for growing up. She'd never spent the night gossiping with girlfriends before. She fell asleep with a smile on her face.

Chapter Eleven

They slept in the next morning, then decided to put on their bathing suits and lay out at the pool.

Once the trio was settled into their lounge chairs Nicole decided to broach the subject that had been on her mind, but had been afraid to bring up.

"Hey, guys, can I get your advice on something?" She asked quietly, happy for the sunglasses that concealed the nervousness in her eyes.

"Sure, what about?" Bree asked.

"Kent," She stated simply.

"Oh, yeah, you can definitely ask our advice if it's about Kent," Kara chimed in with a saucy grin. "Spill."

"Well, I mean, I know Bree knows a little bit about my past, so I should probably fill you in on that first, Kara." Nicole started. "I was raised in a religious home, and was expected to go to college, then return home to marry my fiancé, Jake, and begin a congregation in Dallas. Once I got to college, I realized that those were my parents' dreams, not mine, and I changed my major, broke it off with Jake, and moved out on my own. That's the gist of it. Well, um, what I haven't mentioned is that because I was raised in that way, I don't believe in having sex before marriage."

Kara sat up, threw her legs over the side of her chair, and pushed her sunglasses up on her head. She looked into Nicole's eyes, the shock apparent on her face.

"Are you saying you're a virgin, and you've never had sex with *anybody*? Not even once?"

Nicole couldn't help but giggle at Kara's obvious disbelief. It helped ease her nerves, and she replied, "Not even once."

"Oh. My. God." Kara closed her eyes and shook her head, causing Nicole to laugh again, and Bree to reach over and punch Kara lightly on the arm. "What? I can't even imagine…"

"Stop, Kara," Briana chided.

"It's okay, Bree, I know it's surprising to people. I was with Jake for so long, and he had the same views on premarital sex, so it was never an issue before."

"But it is now… with Kent," Bree surmised.

Kara started laughing at that. "Oh, I bet Kent shit a brick when you told him."

"Kara!"

"No, Kara's right. That's pretty much the reaction I'd expected when I told Kent, but he really took it in stride. He didn't freak out, and he said he still wanted to see me. I gave him an out, but he didn't take it."

"But," Briana prompted.

"But since then, he hasn't touched me. I mean, not even a kiss." Nicole played with the frayed edge of her towel as she spoke. "Before I told him, we kissed and made out a bit, and it was really hot, but ever since I told him, he has given me a kiss on the cheek, or the forehead, but has made no attempt to really kiss me. Do you think that means he's not interested anymore?"

"Nicole, Kent may be a great looking, single, man who has no problem getting women, but he isn't a ladies man. I mean, he doesn't lie, and he doesn't treat girls like crap." Briana said in his defense. "If he didn't want to see you anymore, he would respect you enough to tell you, I swear."

"That's true," Kara put in. "Kent is always a straight shooter, he wouldn't lead you on."

"Then what do you think it is?" Nicole asked, hopeful that they could help her figure it out. She really didn't want him to pull away from her; she was beginning to care about him too much.

"Maybe he just doesn't know how to act." Briana suggested. "He's used to having sex with the girls he sees. Not to sound crass, but it's true. Maybe he isn't sure how to treat you, when he knows the end result will not include sex. I'm sure it's new territory for him."

"That's true," Kara added. "If I put myself in his shoes, I have to admit, I wouldn't know what to do."

"Well, I'm not going to have sex with him. No matter what my feelings for him are, I won't have sex with anyone who isn't my husband."

"No, and no one expects you to, least of all Kent. He's going to respect your beliefs." Briana assured her.

"I think you need to let him know that there are other things you can do besides have sex. Sexy things," Kara said with a wink.

"Yeah," Briana added. "Maybe you need to take the lead and show him that you want to kiss him, that you want to make-out with him, and any other things you may want to do with him."

Nicole knew what they were saying was probably true; she just worried that he would reject her advances. She would be mortified if that happened. On the other hand, she missed kissing him. She wanted him to see that she was a passionate woman, and she wanted to deepen their relationship.

"You guys are right," Nicole said aloud. "When we get home, I'll tell Kent how I feel, and let him know what I want."

"You go girl!" Kara said as she put her sunglasses back over her eyes and lay back on her lounge chair.

"Don't worry, Nicole," Briana said while she patted her on the shoulder. "I know it'll work out, and Kent will appreciate your honesty."

They all laid back and enjoyed the sun until it was time to go in and get ready for dinner.

Colin came home while they were getting dressed. Nicole finished getting ready first, and went to sit with him at the table while they waited for Bree and Kara.

"Would you like some wine while we wait?" Colin asked Nicole.

"Sure, that sounds great," She responded.

Nicole couldn't help but appreciate Colin's effort. He looked so handsome as he poured her a glass of red, and she thought again how lucky Briana was to be living the life that she wanted with the man she loved. Nicole hoped she could find a love like theirs.

She had loved Jake, but she'd never felt the passion for him that she felt for Kent. She'd never felt nervous around him, or excited just to hear the sound of his voice.

When Colin placed the glass in front of her and sat down, she tried to clear her head and focus on what he was saying.

"How's everything going at work?" He asked her.

"Pretty good," Nicole responded. "It can get hectic some nights, but the money's not bad, and I love everyone I work with. I know it's not a long term job, but for now, it's nice to go in and enjoy what I'm doing."

"Yeah, you can't ask for much more than that."

"How about you, how's the job here? Is it everything you hoped for?" Nicole asked, then took a sip of her wine.

Colin got a wide grin on his face, causing the dimples in his cheeks to deepen, and his eyes to twinkle.

"It really is. I love what I'm doing. I miss my folks and I feel bad that I can't take over the store for my dad, but this is exactly where I want to be. I can't believe how lucky I'm." Colin looked up and his smile got even broader when Bree walked over to where he was sitting. "Not only do I have my dream job, but I have the love of my life by my side. It doesn't get much better than this."

"Awe babe," Briana cooed as she leaned down to kiss him. "Ditto."

Nicole couldn't help but smile at the pair of them and their obvious happiness.

"Ya'll ready?" Kara said as she sauntered in from the bathroom. "This girl is starvin'."

They all got up and headed out to enjoy the girls' last night in Austin.

Friends & Lovers Trilogy

Chapter Twelve

It wasn't that Kent missed Nicole, she'd only been gone since yesterday, but as he got ready for the guys to come over for poker night, he couldn't help but picture her pretty face and wish she was there.

He poured some chips into a bowl and placed it on the granite counter top in his kitchen. He opened up the door to his walk in pantry, and found a container of salsa to put out with the chips.

He liked homemade salsa better, but didn't have any clue how to even begin to make it. He wondered if Nicole ever made fresh salsa.

He shook his head, trying to clear away the thoughts of Nic. He needed to get his head ready for the game and stop moping around like a love-sick idiot.

He looked around the kitchen to make sure everything was clean and straightened, the way he liked it.

He took in the glass cabinets, which were streak free, and showcased his matching dishware. The countertops were clutter free and his stainless steel appliances sparkled, and everything was put in its place.

The guys gave him a hard time about the fact that his house was always so clean and organized, and unlike most guys his age, he didn't live off of ramen served in plastic ware.

He could handle their ribbing. He liked the way he lived.

He noticed that they had no problem allowing him to host poker night. They had gone to one of the regulars, Steve's, house once. That was the first and last time that had happened.

As he walked through the tidy living room, with the black leather sofas and matching accent pieces, he thought about how much he wanted to see Nicole in his house.

He didn't know why he hadn't brought her here yet, but he realized that he could picture her here. He could see her helping him get ready for the poker night, or cooking in the kitchen, and was surprised by how much he liked the vision.

Kent was saved from his uncharacteristic thoughts by the knock on his door.

He opened it to a grinning Pete.

"What's up, Man?" Pete asked putting his hand out to grasp Kent's in a handshake.

"Not much," Kent responded with a smile. "Come on in. How's it going?"

"Pretty good," Pete said as he entered and headed towards the kitchen to put his beer in the fridge. "I miss Kara and all, but I have to admit, it's been nice to hang around in my boxers all day and watch Sports Center!"

"I hear that," Kent responded, although he'd probably never sat around in his boxers before in his life. If he wasn't dressed for the day, well, then he didn't wear anything. That was another benefit of having your own place.

Pete used the bottle opener to open a beer and offered it to Kent, before opening another one for himself.

"Thanks," Kent said, as he took a drink.

Pete went to go grab his seat at the table as another knock sounded on the door.

Steve and a couple of the other poker regulars came barreling in when Kent opened the door.

A chorus of "What ups" went around as everyone put their beer in the fridge and joined Pete at the table.

Kent joined the men and began dealing the cards as they all caught up on what had been happening in their lives since they'd last had a game.

After a few hands and numerous beers, they guys became louder and the money began to flow a little faster.

"So, Kent," Steve asked as he folded. "What's up with you and that smokin' hot waitress from the bar?"

Kent knew that this was normal conversation for their poker nights, but couldn't stop his jaw from clenching as he answered.

"Nic and I have been on a couple dates. Why?"

"No reason," Steve slurred slightly. "I've been asking her out for months, and she always turned me down. I thought she was frigid, but I guess not if she's seeing you."

Kent stared over his cards at Steve, and noticed that the rest of the guys had stopped talking and were looking back and forth from Steve to Kent.

"Be careful, Steve. I just told you I was dating her."

"Awww, chill out man, it's cool. I just wanted to know if you'd hit that yet, and if those titties are as luscious as they look."

Kent was out of his seat in a flash and was pulling Steve out of his by the back of his shirt before he had a chance to register what was happening.

It was a flurry of motion after that, as all of the guys jumped up from the table and tried to pull Kent off of Steve.

"Dude, that's just Steve," Pete was saying to Kent, trying to get his attention, as the larger man glared at Steve. "You know he didn't mean anything by it."

The red slowly began to clear and Kent's vision returned to normal. He realized that he had two of his buddies holding his arms, Pete was standing in front of him trying to reason with him, and Steve was on the floor looking up at him with confusion.

"I'm fine," Kent said gruffly, as he shook the other men off of him. He walked over to Steve and crouched down so he could look him in the eyes.

"Don't talk about her like that again," He said simply, then walked out his back porch and sat down on one of his deck chairs.

He was fighting to calm his breathing, while his brain was scrambling.

What the hell had come over him? He wondered. It was poker night. They always talked about women while they played. Sometimes the conversation got pretty graphic, much worse than what Steve had said tonight.

Pete came out and grabbed the chair next to his.

"You alright, man?" Pete asked softly.

"Yeah Pete," Kent exclaimed. "Shit, I don't know what happened; I didn't mean to go after Steve like that."

"It *was* crazy," Pete said with a laugh. "But I get where you're comin' from. I wouldn't like it if one of the guys was talking about Kara like that."

"Yeah, but Kara's your girlfriend. I mean, shit, you guys live together. That's different than Nic and I going on a few dates." Kent didn't know if he was trying to convince Pete, or himself.

"Maybe you like her more than you thought," Pete reasoned. "Hey, you chill here for a minute. I'll see the guys out and grab you a beer."

"Naw, that's alright, Pete." Kent said as he got up out of the chair. "I'll go fix this with Steve and see the guys out. Thanks though."

"That's what friends are for," Pete replied as he slapped Kent on the back.

Kent walked inside as the guys were cleaning up and grabbing their remaining beer from the fridge.

He went up to Steve and put his hand on the other man's shoulder.

"Sorry I flew off the handle like that, Steve." He apologized.

Steve looked up at him, the regret apparent on his face. "No man, I shouldn't have said that about your girl."

Kent was about to correct him, but realized that he did want Nic to be his girl, and for the other guys to know it.

"No hard feelings?" He asked.

"None," Steve replied. They shook hands, then Kent said bye to the rest of the guys and apologized for the way the night ended.

When he turned he noticed Pete was cleaning up and said, "Don't worry about that, Bro, I'll get it."

"It's no big deal. I don't mind, it's not like I have to rush home," Pete said with a wry smile.

Kent just nodded and went to clean up the remnants of poker night.

Friends & Lovers Trilogy

Chapter Thirteen

Nicole fell asleep on the way home from Austin. She woke up when Kara pulled into her parking lot to drop her off.

"I'm sorry. I didn't mean to fall asleep." Nicole said as she sat up in the passenger seat.

"That's okay," Kara replied. "It was a long night. I'm ready to go home and take a nap myself. Hopefully I can talk Pete into getting under the covers with me." Kara laughed and wiggled her eyebrows, causing Nicole to chuckle as well.

"Thanks so much for inviting me along. I had a lot of fun!"

"No problem," Kara responded as Nicole climbed out of the car and grabbed her bag. "I had a blast. See you at work!"

Nicole waved as Kara drove away. As she walked up the stairs to her apartment, she couldn't help but wonder what Kent was up to.

The conversations she'd had over the weekend kept coming back to her.

Kent had been acting strange ever since she'd told him about her beliefs, but she was positive that he was still attracted to her.

Well, almost positive.

She worried that maybe the fact that they wouldn't have sex would be a deal breaker for him. No matter what he'd said about being fine with it, it was obvious that he wasn't.

Nicole decided that she was going to take Kara's advice and show him that she wanted more from him than a kiss on the cheek.

After she put her bag in her room and saw that Roni wasn't there, she sent her a text to ask her where she was.

Roni shot back right away and said that she was having dinner with her brother at the bar.

"Are you back? You should totally come join us."

"Okay, I'll be right there."

Nicole brushed her teeth; freshened up her makeup, and put on one of the tops that Roni had made her buy last time they'd gone shopping.

It was a floral print that looked sweet off, but the cut was low enough to show off her ample cleavage and became much sexier when it was on.

She was hoping Kent would not be satisfied with a peck on the forehead when he saw her tonight.

She hurried over to the bar, then paused suddenly nervous before opening the big wooden door.

Nicole breathed in deeply, then went inside and looked around as her eyes adjusted to the dark room.

She walked around the hostess stand, looking around the booths as she searched for Roni and Kent.

She saw him standing at the bar talking to Pete. He looked so good, perfectly groomed, well dressed, and sexy as sin.

She started to walk over to him, when she noticed a perky little red head saunter up to Kent and say something, causing him to turn to her.

It was obvious that the girl was flirting with him. She had her chest pushed out, head cocked, and she was twirling a lock of that striking hair around her finger, as she looked up at Kent with big eyes and a sexy smile on her face. When Nicole saw the girls tongue dart out and lick her lips, the feeling went out of her body and her head felt like it was going to explode with jealousy.

Kent just looked down at the little siren and gave her a polite smile as he shook his head, then turned back to give his full attention to Pete, leaving the girl standing there.

When the girl frowned, then turned and stomped off, Nicole couldn't stop the smile that broke out over her face.

A sigh of relief escaped her, and the feeling slowly began to return to her body.

She hurried happily over to Kent and tapped him on the shoulder.

"Look sweetheart, I'm sorry, but I'm just not..." Kent stopped talking when he realized it was Nicole standing next to him.

Nicole knew she wasn't being subtle, but couldn't stop herself from going into his arms. She was so happy to see him.

Kent's arms came tightly around her and he pulled her in for a hug. She breathed in the scent of him and closed her eyes as she let the pleasure course through her.

"Hey, Nic," Kent said into her ear. "Did you just get back?"

She pulled back and nodded up at him. His eyes were drawn immediately to her cleavage. Since she was still pulled up against him, she could feel the reaction his body had to the sight of her exposed breasts, and she couldn't help the thrill that started at her toes and raced upwards.

Kent cleared his throat and backed up a step. "It's good to see you. Did you have fun?"

Nicole couldn't stop but smile at his attempt to get space. "Yes, it was great. Bree and Colin are just wonderful." She answered as she closed the gap between them and put her arms around his neck.

"I missed you," She said softly as she stood on her tip toes and pressed her lips to his.

Kent slowly smiled at her and admitted, "I missed you too."

Nicole beamed at that and said, "Good."

Kent chuckled at her, then looked up at the sound of his sister calling his name.

Roni was waving at them from her booth, so they walked over to join her.

"Sheesh, I was beginning to wonder if you guys were going to stand over there and make out all night, or if you were going to join me for dinner." Roni gestured at the food that was waiting at the table, but she smiled to soften her words, as she jumped out of the booth and grabbed Nicole in a hug.

"Welcome back. Was it great? Are they happy? Do they have a great place?" Roni shot the questions out, causing Nicole to laugh as she sat down next to Kent in the booth.

Nicole put her hand on Kent's leg and squeezed before leaving it there to rest. She was acutely aware of the heat generating from them as she answered Roni.

"Yes, it was great. They are totally happy, and their apartment is awesome. They have a gym and a pool and it's just a walk away from all of the restaurants and bars downtown. You will definitely have to come next time."

"Definitely," Roni agreed. "Here have half of mine; you know I'll never be able to eat it all."

"Okay, thanks," Nicole said as Roni began splitting her BLT and fries.

"So, did anything fun happen while I was gone?" Nicole asked as she picked up her sandwich.

Roni grinned and winked at her brother. "Kent had poker night."

"Oh," Nicole began as she noticed the dirty look that Kent shot Roni. "Did something happen there?"

Kent looked at her and shook his head, before shooting another dirty look at Roni, who just giggled.

"No, it was no big deal, just poker night."

Nicole decided to let it go for now.

Kent took a bite of his burger, and when Nicole reached a finger up to brush a bit of mustard from the corner of his mouth, he turned his intense gaze on her.

She smiled saucily up at him and touched her finger to her lips, letting her tongue dart out to lick the mustard off of her finger.

He cleared his throat, his eyes never leaving her mouth, and she felt heat run through her, making her wonder who she was trying to drive crazy him, or herself?

"Hello???" Roni said loudly. "Sister slash roommate is still right here in the booth with you, trying to eat her dinner. I'd hate to see you two after a week apart."

Nicole flushed with embarrassment, but Kent just grinned at Roni.

"Don't be jealous, Roni." He teased. "Rich will be home before you know it."

Roni rolled her eyes and said, "Please. Rich is the last guy I'd be interested in."

Nicole smiled as the twins bantered back and forth. She finished her food and placed her hand on her stomach to try and calm the nerves there.

She took a deep breath and smiled up at Kent through her eyelashes. "You have any plans for the rest of the night?"

He looked over at her, a wary expression on his face. "No, why?"

She picked her hand up and ran it through her hair, watching him as he tracked her progress. "Well, I haven't seen your place yet," She began. "I was hoping to get an invitation."

"You mean just the two of us?" Kent asked, glancing at Roni, who just shook her head at him.

"Of course just the two of you, you Dolt," Roni said in exasperation. "I'm not tagging along to watch the two of you paw at each other."

Nicole couldn't help but laugh at Kent's reaction to Roni's words. It was almost as if he was afraid to be alone with her.

She couldn't help but tease him, "Chicken?"

Kent looked down at his plate, then back into Nicole's eyes. "I can handle it if you can."

Nicole smiled at him, but she couldn't help but hope that he was right. That they would both be able to handle what she had planned for them that night.

Chapter Fourteen

They dropped Roni off and took the short trip just outside of town to Kent's house.

It was a nice house, well-maintained, with a well-manicured lawn. Nicole took in the large tree in the front yard, the wrap-around porch, and the wooden Adirondack chairs poised around the porch.

She loved his house immediately.

It had a comfortable, cozy look, and looked like a wonderful place to just be.

Kent seemed nervous as they walked up to the front door, which was uncharacteristic of him. She wasn't sure if he was nervous to show her his house, or nervous to be alone with her, but Nicole couldn't help but feel a little pleased at his nerves. She hoped it meant that he didn't think of her as just any girl.

Kent unlocked the door, then stepped back to allow her to enter.

Nicole was surprised when she walked in, although she probably shouldn't have been. Kent took care of himself and was always put together well; she should have realized that he would want his living space to be the same way.

She loved the fact that it was neat and clean, even though he'd had no idea she was coming over. She loved the muted tones and the leather furniture. It was definitely a male space, but still had a feeling of comfort.

She couldn't stop the sound of pleasure that escaped her when she walked into the kitchen. She ran her hand along the granite countertop and appreciated the glass front cabinets.

"It's really beautiful, Kent." Nicole looked at him, then pleasure apparent on her face.

He smiled down at her. His hand came up and softly caressed her face. "Would you like a glass of wine?"

"Sure," She said, then turned to check out the rest of his house. "You have great taste."

He walked up to her and handed her a glass of red wine, then gestured to the couch.

"Would you like to sit down?"

Nicole nodded and sank into the comfortable leather couch. She took a sip of wine, then set it on the coaster on the end table.

Kent sat next to her, careful to keep a bit of distance between them.

Nicole scooted closer and reached over to place her hand on his thigh.

Kent flinched slightly at her touch.

"What's going on?" Nicole couldn't keep the question to herself any longer. The mixed signals were driving her crazy.

Kent looked at her, a small frown on his face. "What do you mean?"

"You haven't kissed me since I told you that I was a virgin. You've barely touched me at all. Have you changed your mind about wanting to see me?"

Kent placed one hand over hers and used the other to tilt her head up towards him, so he could look directly in her eyes.

"No, I haven't changed my mind, Nic. I really like you."

"Then what is it? Why won't you kiss me?"

"This is going to sound crazy," Kent began, running his hand through his hair as he tried to gather his words. "I'm afraid to touch you."

"What?" Nicole asked bewildered. "Why?"

"I haven't had to worry about controlling myself since I was fifteen, Nic. I want to touch you, and kiss you, God knows I do, but I'm afraid I'll push you further than you want me to."

Nicole turned her whole body towards him and placed a hand on his cheek, forcing him to look at her.

"I trust you, Kent."

"I don't know if I can trust myself." He responded truthfully. "I want you, Nic. More than I've ever wanted anyone."

Hot flames licked through her body at his words.

"I want you too, Kent," Nicole said honestly. "We can still satisfy each other, even though we can't have sex."

His eyes darkened as they traveled over her face, then lower, then back up again. He shook his head, contradicting the expression on his face. "I can't... I can't touch you. I'm afraid I'll lose control."

Nicole felt empowered like never before. She stood up and put her hand out, willing him to take it. To put some faith in both of them and go with her.

Kent looked at her hand, then back at her face, pondering his decision before finally reaching out and allowing her to guide him off of the couch and towards his bedroom.

She led him to the bed and motioned for him to sit.

"You don't have to touch me," Nicole said huskily, her adrenaline fueling her with the confidence that she needed. "I'll take care of everything."

She pushed at him slightly, so he would sit further back on the bed. When he was settled up against the headboard, not saying anything, but following her with his stormy eyes, she put her hands at the hem of her shirt and lifted it slowly over her head.

She heard his intake of breath at the site of her pale pink bra, barely containing her breasts underneath.

Her confidence began to build with each passing second, so she placed her hands on the button of her jeans, watching Kent's reaction as she slowly allowed them to slide down her legs.

She crawled up onto the bed next to him, careful not to touch him… Not yet. He warily watched her approach, and started to say something when she put a finger to his lips and said, "Shhh. Stop worrying."

Then she placed her lips to his and allowed herself to do everything she had been dreaming about since she first laid eyes on him.

She started softly, her lips barely brushing his, reveling in the pressure that was slowly building within her. She peppered kisses along his lips and the corners of his mouth, before outlining his lips with her tongue.

His mouth opened as his breath caught, and she took the opportunity to kiss him fully. Her eyes opened to see his watching her, and a wicked smile played on her lips as she nipped at him slightly and took his full bottom lip into her mouth and sucked.

Kent groaned slightly, but made no move to touch her or try to gain control of the situation.

Nicole moved her mouth from his lips to his jaw and rained kisses along his jawline, then down his throat.

The soft humming sound that Kent was making in the back of his throat triggered something in her, and the teasing turned to hunger.

She took his mouth again and kissed him with a fierceness that threatened to break her own control. Her hands began to roam under his shirt, each feel of his muscular body fueled her frenzy and she reached down, eager to get his shirt off.

He sat up a bit, so she could get the shirt over again, then fell back against the headboard roughly, his breath coming out in gasps, as his hands clenched the blanket beneath them.

Nicole felt the blush begin to rise as she thought about what she was going to do next.

Nicole reached back and unclasped her bra, then slowly pealed it from her body. She looked down briefly, self-consciously, but when she looked up, Kent nodded his encouragement.

His hungry gaze devoured the site of her full breasts before him. The look on his face took Nicole to the brink of something she had never experienced before, and as he watched her, she brought her hands up to caress her breasts.

She cupped each breast, running her hands along them.

Kent closed his eyes briefly, as if trying to gain composure, before they flew open again, to watch her delicate fingers as she pinched her nipples into tight little nubs.

He groaned then, and shifted uncomfortably on the bed, licking his lips, unable to tear his gaze away from the site before him.

Nicole's long blonde hair spilled out over her shoulders. She was on her knees, rubbing her breasts, and watching him watch her.

The site of her beautifully aroused face, and her body clad only in the sweetest pair of pink panties, as she turned them both on, was enough to make him lose his mind.

The blanket was bunched up in his hands and it took every ounce of control he had not to say, "Fuck it" and bury himself in her.

Nicole leaned in, rubbing her breasts against his bare chest, as she straddled him.

Kent froze at the contact, as she began to rock back and forth on top of him, her mouth working its way up his chest.

He thought he might whimper.

"Nic."

She turned her hot eyes on him.

"Touch yourself for me."

She licked her lips, brought her hands up to her breasts and fondled them softly.

Kent watched her and said softly, "Lower."

Her eyes looked momentarily confused, then unsure as his words penetrated the haze that covered her mind. She faltered briefly, but was fueled on by the heat of his gaze.

Kent bit his lip and nodded as her hand began to slowly make a trail towards those pink panties.

The sight of her delicate fingers at the top of her panties almost did him in.

Overcome by need unlike anything he'd ever know, Kent watched as Nicole bucked against her hand and came apart in front of him.

Her head was thrown back, eyes closed, and her face was full of pleasure.

Nicole was breathing heavily as she slowly still, brought her head down and opened her eyes. She smiled shyly at him and leaned in to kiss him with her swollen lips.

When their bodies touched, she realized that he was still rock hard. His hands were red and taunt as he struggled to keep his hands where he'd promised, but he'd never been so close to the insanity he felt at that moment.

"Touch me," he said softly, his voice strained.

Nicole paused momentarily, before she moved her shaky hands to the front of his pants and undid the button of his jeans. She unzipped them slowly, the hiss that exited his mouth matching the hiss of his zipper.

She looked up at him again, for affirmation, then eased her hands into the opening in his boxer briefs.

Kent's breath caught as her smooth hand touched his pulsing shaft. Her touch was gentle and unsure, the combination of which drove Kent crazy. Surprisingly, it didn't take long for his release. Kent was amazed at the pleasure he experienced at her touch, but was relieved to finally be satiated.

They both laid back, struggling to catch their breath, both of them smiling, before Kent reached out and pulled Nicole to him. He cupped her face with his hands and kissed her, before running his hands up and down her body.

"God, I really wanted to touch you." Kent admitted as he smiled against her lips.

"I trust you, Kent. You don't have to be afraid with me," Nicole said as she lay back down and rested her head against his chest, his arms cradling her.

Kent didn't say anything, he just ran his hands through her silky hair, as he realized that he'd never felt about anyone, the way he felt about Nicole. He couldn't help but worry that someone like him had no right to be with someone as pure as her.

Friends & Lovers Trilogy

Chapter Fifteen

When Kent woke up the next morning, he could still smell Nicole's shampoo on his pillow. He inhaled deeply and smiled, moving his hand along the sheet and opening his eyes when he realized he was alone.

He turned to lie on his back and stretched as his eyes began to focus and he became fully awake.

He heard sounds coming from the kitchen, and started to catch the faint smell of bacon drifting from beneath his bedroom door.

He swung his long legs over the side of his bed and ran his hands through his hair to try and tame it a bit before reaching for his jeans and pulling them up over his body.

He opened the door and paused, taking in the site of Nicole working in his kitchen. Her hair was pulled back into a ponytail, and she was wearing the t-shirt he had given her to sleep in last night.

It came to just above her knees.

She was fresh-faced and singing along to a song on the radio that was playing softly in the kitchen.

She looked amazing.

He walked up behind her and kissed her softly on the exposed side of her neck.

Nicole paused and turned into him, allowing him to take her in his arms, and turned her face upwards for a kiss.

Kent bent and kissed her softly, closing his eyes briefly to enjoy the sensation of her lips against his.

"Good morning," He said against her lips and he pulled slowly away. Reveling in the feel of her lush body pressed against his.

"Morning," she replied with a smile. "I hope you're hungry."

She turned back to the pans on the stove, flipping the bacon and scattering shredded cheese over the scrambled eggs.

"Starving," He responded, nuzzling her neck one more time before moving to the coffee maker. "This looks great."

He poured himself some coffee, then leaned against the counter, watching Nicole plate their breakfast as he drank it black.

"Can I help you with anything?" He offered.

"You can help me carry the stuff to the table," she replied, gesturing towards the condiments she had available on the counter.

They took everything over to the table, then sat down to enjoy their breakfast.

Nicole smiled at him over the rim of her coffee; the look in his eye caused his heart to thump loudly in his chest.

He took a few bites and grinned back at her.

"Delicious!"

"I'm glad you like it," she admitted.

They ate in a comfortable silence, until Nicole said tentatively, "Kent?"

""Something on your mind, Nic?"

"Well, I know it's kinda soon, but I got a text from my mother this morning," She began, then stopped mid-sentence to gauge his reaction. He nodded slightly, indicating she should go on. "Her forty-fifth birthday is next weekend, and she's throwing herself her usual self-indulgent party. She wants me to come, and since I haven't been back home since I walked out and moved here, I feel like I should at least show up. You know, to see if I can salvage our relationship."

"Yeah, I get it," Kent replied. "You should go and celebrate with your parents."

"The thing is… I was wondering if maybe you'd like to go with me." This she said with a shrug of her shoulders and a hopeful smile.

Kent felt his stomach begin to knot as her request sunk in. He didn't do well with parents, and from everything he'd heard about hers, he doubted that he was the type of guy they had in mind for their celestial daughter.

"I don't know, Nic," He replied, trying to figure out how he could get out of this without upsetting her. Lord knew he hated the thought of spending time with his own parents, let alone meeting hers.

"Please?" Nicole pleaded. "I wouldn't ask, but I'm terrified of going by myself. I haven't seen my parents since I ruined their dreams for me, and I'm sure that she will invite Jake in an effort to get us back together. I'd be able to handle it a lot better if you were there with me."

His stomach turned at the mention of her ex, and he was torn between the fact that he really, *really*, didn't want to go, and the possibility of her parents or ex upsetting her.

"I don't know that my being there will make things easier for you, Nic." Kent reasoned.

"It will, truly." Nicole promised.

Kent could only imagine the kind of people that would be at her mother's party… The kind of people that would have looked at him and his family with pity and contempt.

As uncomfortable as he knew he would be at the party, he looked at her sweet face, so full of hope, and couldn't bring himself to deny her request.

"Okay," Kent said reluctantly, smiling when she let out a squeal of delight. "But we're just going there for the party and coming back. I don't want to stay for the entire weekend."

"No problem," Nicole agreed, jumping up from her chair and settling on his lap. "Thank you so much! This means the world to me."

She peppered his face with kisses, causing him to chuckle, then grasped his face in her hands and deepened the kiss.

His arms came up around her, holding her tightly to him, as the need began to build within him.

Nicole pulled back slightly, smiling down at him, her hands caressing the hair at the nape of his neck.

"I'm going to owe you big time for this," She said with a devious grin.

"I'm sure I can think of a few ways you can repay me," Kent countered. He lifted her easily as he stood, and carried her back to his bed, as she nibbled softly on his ear.

Chapter Sixteen

Nicole turned to wave at Kent as he drove away. She opened the front door and was surprised to be met by a blast of music.

She looked around when she walked in, and was surprised to see the living room furniture pushed up against the wall and Roni dancing fluidly around the room.

Nicole stopped and watched, unaware that the door was still open, or that she'd dropped her purse to the ground.

Roni was an amazing dancer.

Nicole was swept away by the emotion of the music and the gracefulness of Roni's movement.

She was speechless.

When the music ended, Nicole eyes filled. She was so moved that she sniffed, as her nose began to run, causing Roni to turn to where she stood.

"Hey," Roni said, breathless. "I didn't hear you come in."

"My gosh, Roni, you're amazing," Nicole gushed. "How come you never mentioned that you were a dancer?"

Roni picked up a towel from the table and wiped her brow as she walked past Nicole to shut the front door.

"I haven't danced in a few years," Roni admitted. "Hank wanted me to stop, so I did. I realized how much I missed it, and decided to give it another try."

Roni sat on one of their chairs at the table, drawing her knees up against her chest, and looked at Nicole with a smile of pure pleasure.

"It was even better than I remembered!"

Nicole pulled out a chair and sat down facing Roni.

"You're very talented."

"Thanks," Roni replied as she took a drink from her water bottle. "I'd always dreamed of become a professional dancer, but then I met Hank in high school."

"What happened?" Nicole asked encouragingly.

"I fell in love," Roni said mockingly. "I was stupid... I don't know what Kent has told you about our childhood, but it wasn't ideal. When Hank started talking to me in high school, I was swept away. I couldn't believe that he actually liked me."

Roni paused and took another drink, as if she needed a moment before she could finish her story.

"Kent has always been there for me, but I knew he was leaving right after graduation. He wanted me to go with him, but once I met Hank, I couldn't imagine leaving him behind. Kent wasn't happy about it, but he respected my decision, so he went off to school, and I stayed back with Hank. Once I graduated, my parents said I had to get out of the house, so Hank and I got married and moved into a little trailer in Detroit. Just a JP deal. He made me quit dancing almost immediately. He said it was too much money and it took me away from him and the house, so I quit. I really wish I hadn't." Some of the joy left Roni's face, and she started to peel the label off of her water bottle.

"What happened?" Nicole asked, curious, but reluctant to pry.

"Let's just say he wasn't the man that I thought he was. We were together for about three years, then I finally worked up the courage to call Kent and tell him what was going on. He came to get me right away. I thought he was going to kill Hank when he got there, but I didn't want them to fight, I just wanted to leave."

"Oh my gosh, Roni. I'm so sorry that you had to deal with that. I'm happy that you were able to get out when you did."

Roni looked down, then shook her head as if trying to regain her composure. She looked back up and looked Nicole in the eyes.

"I'll never let a man control me like that again. When we were dating, Hank said all the right things and I was sure he was the love of my life… I won't make the same mistake again."

Nicole nodded and stood up to walk around the table and give Roni a hug.

"You're amazing," Nicole said as she held Roni tightly. "Please, never stop dancing again. You have a gift."

"Thanks," Roni replied, looking up over her shoulder with a sheepish smile.

"What are you thinking of doing?" Nicole asked as she sat back down across from Roni. "Are there any dance studios in town?"

"No, I looked," Roni replied. "That's why I rearranged our living room. I looked online and was hoping there would be a place nearby that I could join, but there isn't anything in town. The closest studio is in Austin."

"Oh, that's too bad," Nicole responded thoughtfully. "Well, feel free to rearrange the living room however you'd like. We'll have to be on the lookout and see if there is a better place in town for you to get back into it full time, if that's what you want."

Roni smiled at that and replied, "Well, I'm a little old now to have a professional career, but I definitely want to train again."

"Whatever you decide to do, I'll help in any way I can."

Roni smiled, then looked unsure before asking, "So, what's up with you and my brother? Please, no details or anything, because that would be gross, but… are you happy?"

Nicole couldn't stop the grin that spread across her face at the mention of Kent.

"Yes, I'm very happy. Your brother is wonderful and I can't believe he hasn't been scooped up by someone by now."

"Kent has been very wary of any girl that looked like she wanted something serious, other than you and Bree, of course."

When Nicole's smile fell a bit at the mention of Kent and Briana's relationship, Roni bit her lip and apologized. "Shit, I'm sorry, Nic. I shouldn't have said anything about him and Bree. You know their relationship was never serious."

Nicole tried to smile back at Roni, but didn't quite pull it off. "That's okay. I was there; I know he really liked her, even if she didn't feel the same way. I just have to believe that our relationship is different. He agreed to go home with me for my mother's birthday party next weekend."

Roni's feet hit the floor with a thump, and she leaned across the table, an incredulous look on her face.

"Seriously??? Kent is going to meet your parents? This is HUGE!"

"No, it's not a big deal. I don't want to face everyone alone, and he said he would come with me as back-up." Nicole explained, trying to play off the situation.

"It's a big deal," Roni argued. "Kent never meets the parents. Like, ever! Did he really say he would go with you?"

Nicole laughed at Roni's expression of disbelief. "Yes, he did."

"Wow," Roni leaned back with a baffled smile. "I'd love to be a fly on the wall for that party."

Chapter Seventeen

Kent took his time getting ready the morning of Nicole's mother's birthday party.

He laid out his favorite suit and spent extra time grooming. He paired a pale blue tie with the charcoal grey suit and white dress shirt.

He hated the nerves that were plaguing him and wished like hell that he'd never agreed to go with Nicole.

He grimaced at himself in the mirror as he finished styling his hair, then he recalled how excited Nicole had been when he'd agreed to go, and how grateful she'd been since, and he vowed to be on his best behavior.

When he couldn't delay any further, he headed out to pick Nicole up at her apartment.

He knew he'd waited too long when he pulled up and saw her waiting outside.

She was breathtaking.

Her blonde hair flowed freely in waves around her shoulders, and the form-fitting black dress was deceptively simple. His body tightened at the way her curves were showcased in the material.

He hopped out and kissed her on the cheek.

"You look amazing."

Nicole flushed with pleasure.

"Thank you. My mother gave me this dress for graduation, so I figured it would start us off on the right foot if I wore it."

"She has perfect taste."

"That she does," Nicole said with a nervous giggle, as she followed him around to the passenger door. She thanked him again when he opened the door for her, and waited for her to be settled inside before closing it.

Kent looked up and saw Roni peering out the window. They waved at each other, and Kent knew by the look on Roni's face, that she understood the turmoil that was building in him.

As they headed towards Dallas, Nicole placed her hand softly on Kent's knee.

"Are you okay?"

Kent looked briefly at her, then back at the road. "Yeah, I'm fine. How about you? Nervous? Excited?"

"I'm a little nervous." Nicole admitted. "It's been a while and they weren't pleased with me last time I saw them, so I'm not quite sure what to expect."

Kent just nodded as he wondered what her parents would think of the newest development in her life.

Him.

Nicole pulled him from his thoughts when she said, "Oh, I forgot to tell you, I saw Roni dance the other day. She's so amazing."

Kent couldn't help the smile that formed at her words. He'd been hoping that Roni would start dancing again.

"She is, isn't she? She has loved to dance for as long as I can remember. Becoming a professional dancer was always the only thing she wanted to do, then she met that asshole, Hank, and she totally lost her focus. I'm so happy to hear that she's getting back into it."

They rode in silence for a while, as memories of Roni as a little girl flashed through his mind.

When he was eight years old, he'd started mowing lawns in the neighborhood to pay for her dance classes. He remembered the look of pure joy on her face when he'd come home with a well-worn tutu that he'd found at the Goodwill. She wore that thing to every lesson.

His heart ached when he thought of the way she'd always scanned the crowd before a performance, hoping to see their parents, and smiling bravely at him when she realized that once again, they hadn't showed.

He felt the familiar stirrings of anger and despair, that occurred anytime he thought about his parents, and knew it stemmed from the impending introduction to Nicole's.

He tried to shake it off as the city came in to view, but he couldn't quite let go of the bitterness in his gut.

Nicole gave him directions, and his trepidation grew at the site of the mansion that she led him to.

He pulled up to the gate and entered the code Nicole gave him. The gates opened slowly, and the massive house seemed to grow larger as they inched along the circular drive.

He parked behind a silver Bentley and exhaled slowly as he pulled the key out of the ignition.

He turned slightly and noticed that Nicole was wringing her hands nervously as she looked out the window at her parents' house.

"That's quite a place," Kent said teasingly, trying to ease the tension in the car.

Nicole turned to him with a small smile, but her eyes were filled with worry.

"Are you ready?" He asked.

She nodded slowly, so he got out of the car and walked around to let her out.

As he rounded the car, the front door opened and a tall grey haired gentleman stepped outside and waited on the top of the stairs, watching Kent but not saying anything.

Nicole took his hand and he helped her up. She stood and smoothed her dressed, then stilled when she noticed the man at the door.

Nicole walked slowly to the stairs. When she got to the base she said, "Hello, Daddy."

Her father nodded slightly and simply said, "Nicole."

She walked up the steps and kissed the side of each of his cheeks lightly, then stood off to his right and gestured down to Kent.

"This is my boyfriend, Kent."

Kent climbed the stairs and put his hand out to shake Nicole's fathers'.

"Kent, this is my father, Gordon."

"It's nice to meet you, Sir," Kent said as they clasped hands.

"Nice to meet you too, Kent." Her father said his voice deep and low. He turned to Nicole and stated, "Your mother is waiting for you in the drawing room," then he turned and walked back into the house, leaving Nicole and Kent no choice but to follow him.

"We have about a half an hour before the guests arrive for drinks," Nicole said in a whisper. "I'll take you in to meet my mother, then I will be expected to greet the guests with her. You can mingle and enjoy a cocktail, and I will come to you as soon as I'm able. We will have an hour for drinks, then dinner will be served. Afterwards there will be drinks and desert and maybe some dancing. Then we can head back home."

Kent tried to comprehend everything she was saying, but it all seemed pretty complicated for a birthday party. The last birthday he celebrated with his mother was when Roni baked cupcakes, their father got drunk, and their mother ended up crying as she blew out her candle.

Now that he thought about it that sounded like all of his mother's birthday celebrations.

He tried not to stare at the opulence of her parent's home, but he couldn't help but be impressed.

He heard the high pitched tone of what he assumed was Nicole's mother's voice as she spoke with Nicole's father.

"She brought a date?" The shrill voice asked in a hushed tone.

Great, Kent thought when he heard her mother's question, then he turned to Nicole who was looking at him sadly.

"Did you say something about a drink?" He asked under his breath as they entered the room.

"Darling," Nicole's mother cooed as she glided towards her daughter, arms stretched open wide.

Kent could tell that she had probably been nearly as beautiful as Nicole when she was younger, but she'd had so much work done to her face, she could no longer hold a candle to her daughter's fresh beauty.

And she resented it.

He knew by the way she looked Nicole over with hard eyes, before going in for air kisses, that Nicole's mother resented her daughter's effortless beauty.

He hated her on sight.

When she was finished putting on a show for her own benefit, she turned to Kent with a fake smile.

"And just who is this handsome gentleman?"

Nicole smiled at Kent as she spoke to her mother, as if trying to soften the sharpness of her mother's tone.

"This is Kent, Momma. My boyfriend."

Kent took the hand her mother offered and brought it to his lips, obligingly.

"It's nice to meet you, Ma'am."

"Psht. Ma'am? Please, call me Kitty." She drawled softly, her hard eyes never stopping their appraisal of him.

"It's nice to meet you, Kitty," He amended, thinking it was a ridiculous name for a ridiculous woman.

"So, Kent, how did you meet our little Nicky? Are you from Dallas? Do I know your family?"

Kent realized the interrogation had begun, and gratefully accepted the drink that Gordon offered him.

"I met Nicole at her work. No and no." He replied pointedly, hoping Kitty would get the hint and leave him alone for a moment.

No such luck.

Kitty pulled back a bit, affronted by his abrupt tone. Kent could tell he wasn't gaining any points, but he couldn't bring himself to kiss her ass.

"Where are you from?" Kitty asked, taking a glass of wine from her husband without so much as a smile of acknowledgement.

"Detroit."

Kitty wrinkled her nose slightly, as if she had just smelled something rotten, and was just about to speak, when she was distracted by a movement by the door.

"Jake," Kitty practically purred as she turned to greet her new guest, leaving Kent without a word.

Kent turned to see the man that Nicole had been engaged to, and was less than thrilled to see a very good-looking, obviously well-off, young man.

He sipped his drink and watched Kitty fawn over Jake, who didn't seem to mind in the slightest. He felt Nicole's arm wrap around his waist and she leaned in to whisper to him.

"Don't mind her, she doesn't mean anything," She followed his gaze to the door, and he felt her arm stiffen.

"You okay?" He asked, wondering if she stiffened because it was awkward to see Jake again, or if she felt something for him.

This party was already making him crazy.

"Yeah," Nicole replied softly. "I mean, I figured he'd be here, but it's weird seeing him again."

She pulled away slightly when Jake walked toward them, and Kent felt the separation instantly. He wondered why he'd ever agreed to come; it was obvious that he didn't belong here.

"Nicole," the shorter man said softly as he approached. He pushed his hand nervously through his light brown hair, and Kent got a whiff of his expensive cologne. Kent knew the brand, it was one of his favorites, but he would bet that Jake had never scrimped and saved to buy that cologne.

He watched as they kissed each other in greeting. No air kisses this time, he noticed. No, they were actual kisses.

He walked over to pour himself another drink and heard Nicole asked Jake how he'd been.

He looked out the window and paused, his drink frozen inches from his lips.

Their backyard extended further than the eye could see. The lawn was manicured and perfectly green. The trees were lush and full, and there was a large sparkling pool with a large patio surrounding it, and what looked like a pool house.

The pool house was larger than the house he grew up in, the house his parents still lived in.

Kent shook his head slightly and took a long drink.

"Kent," Nicole put a hand on his back to get his attention. He turned to see her standing behind him with Jake. "This is Jake."

Kent couldn't stop himself from stretching to his full height, making him practically tower over Jake.

Jake offered his hand and said, "It's nice to meet you."

Kent looked at him for a moment, before accepting his hand and shaking it. "You too, man."

He hated to admit it, but Jake actually seemed pretty cool. He couldn't fault the guy for loving Nicole, she was pretty amazing.

Nicole smiled up at him, her gratefulness apparent, then she turned slightly at the sound of the doorbell.

"I'm going to go help my mother greet the arriving guests. I'll be back as soon as I can." She tiptoed up to kiss him on the cheek, before turning to go to her mother, who was standing at the threshold, watching them with evident displeasure.

"Is she always in such a party mood?" Kent asked wryly as he accepted another drink from a waitress who had started circling the room with a tray.

"Who, Kitty?" Jake asked with a grin. "You get used to her… eventually."

Kent just lifted his eyebrow questioningly and looked around the suddenly full room.

He'd never seen so many fake noses and boob jobs in one place, he thought with a chuckle.

Jake excused himself to go and talk to someone he knew, and Kent began to slowly wander around the room.

"Did you hear about the Truman's?" He heard Nicole's mom say in a loud whisper to a group of ladies dripping with jewels.

"From the Parish?" A tall bleached blonde asked.

"Yes." Kitty said her voice practically oozing excitement. "He was arrested for a domestic dispute. I guess he's an alcoholic and has been beating her for years. Can you believe it?"

"Oh my gosh, no." This came from a short portly brunette, who put her hand to her mouth in mock horror.

"I can't believe we've been going to the same church with them for all of these years," Kitty exclaimed, looking each lady in the eye to drive her point home. "Breeding always tells."

Kent felt his gut tighten and his face flush with a mixture of embarrassment and anger. He put his glass down on the nearest traveling tray and walked out of the parlor, down the hallway, and out the front door. Once outside, he breathed in deeply and tried to calm himself.

He could only imagine what Nicole's mother would think of his parents. Of his life. Of him.

He heard the door open behind him, but didn't turn. He knew it would be Nicole, coming out to see if he was okay, but he didn't want to turn and see her beautiful face. He didn't want to see the hurt that would inevitably end up there. But he knew he had to face her.

"Hey," She placed her hand on his back as she came up next to him. "I saw you rush out, is everything okay?"

He repressed the need to turn and hug her tightly against him. Instead, he steeled himself against his emotions and turned to her.

"No, Nic, everything's not okay."

Her hand dropped to her side when she saw the look on his face, and hers became a mask of confusion.

"What happened?"

"Let's just say I don't fit in with your world." He said tightly.

"Kent," Nicole reached towards him, but stopped before she touched him. The look on his face must have told her that he didn't want to be touched. "This isn't my world. What happened?"

"Nicole," He began, trying to think of the one thing he could say to make her realize that he was right, that they would never work. "My father is a drunk who uses his fists to get his point across. He beat on me from the time I was two until I was twelve." He stopped for a moment and breathed in deeply when he noticed the look of shock on her face.

When he felt composed enough, Kent continued to explain. "He raised his hand to Roni once and I took a bat to his knees. He never touched me again, and I made sure he never touched Roni, but my mother wasn't so lucky. He's been using her as his own personal punching bag since they got married, and she let him." He couldn't help the look of bitter disappointment that crossed his face. "I've tried countless times to get her to leave him, but she won't. They live together in misery."

He looked Nicole in the eye, trying to drive the point home, "That's what I come from."

Nicole's eyes filled with tears and she moved towards him, like she wanted to hold him.

Kent took a step back and put up a hand, causing her to stop.

"You deserve better than me." He stated simply.

"How can you say that?" Nicole asked softly, wiping the tears that were running down her face with the back of her hand. "You are amazing. How and where you grew up doesn't matter to me. You made yourself into the successful and wonderful man that you are today."

"Nic," He said harshly. "How could you ever believe that your parents would approve of me? That they would ever accept us as a couple? It won't happen. We're from two different worlds. C'mon, you can admit it… You're looking for marriage and children and a perfect home like this one. After seeing my parents' marriage, and Roni's, I just don't see it happening for me."

He watched as his words began to sink in, as she began to understand what he was saying. Her eyes began to fill again. He knew he had to finish it now, before he caved, crushed her to him, and begged her to stay with him forever.

"We both know that this will never work. We are too different, and want different things. I think it's better if we just walk away now, before it gets more difficult."

Nicole looked up at him, her beautiful eyes shined with tears and her full lips quivered. "You want to walk away?"

Kent felt the burn begin in the back of his throat and slowly start a descent down to his stomach.

"Yes. I think it's best if I leave now. You should stay, and be with your family. I can send Roni back to pick you up."

Nicole sniffled slightly, then raised her chin and looked him in the eye. "Don't do me any favors. I'll get my own ride back."

Kent nodded curtly, then turned to walk down the steps and towards his car.

When he heard the door open, he turned and saw Nicole rush into Jake's arms, her shoulders quivering.

He felt like he'd been punched in the gut and fought the urge to go back up the steps and rip her out of Jake's arms.

Instead he turned, got into his car, and drove back home.

Friends & Lovers Trilogy

Chapter Eighteen

A few days later Kent was sitting at his desk writing a piece on the upcoming local election, and trying unsuccessfully to not think about Nicole, when Marla's gravelly voice shouted to him from the other room.

"Kent, the boss wants to see you."

Kent saved his progress before pushing back from his desk and walking back to Chuck's office. The door was open, so he knocked on the door jam and waited for Chuck's invitation before entering.

"Come on in, Kent. Shut the door behind you and have a seat."

Kent did as requested, curious as to what Chuck would have to say to him behind a closed door.

"I know we have discussed this briefly in the past, and I know you have been applying to other papers in bigger cities than this one, but after a long discussion with the wife, I have come to a decision." Chuck paused for affect before continuing on. "Kent, I'm going to retire and I'd like you to take over the paper."

Kent didn't say anything. He knew Chuck's penchant for long pauses, and figured he wasn't finished saying everything he wanted to say.

He was right.

"Now, before you say anything, I want to make myself clear. I want to fully retire and enjoy the rest of my days, never having to think about this paper again. What I'm offering here is not just a chance for you to run the paper, but to buy it from me outright. I know you're a smart business man, and we could come up with a good payment plan with the bank, so I feel totally confident that you could own this paper and run it well."

Kent was silent as everything the other man said really sank in.

He'd own his own business.

He already owned a home in this town, and his sister was here. He could put down roots and settle here forever.

He thought briefly of his dreams of living in a big city and realized that it didn't have the pull for him that it once had.

He wasn't a spontaneous person by nature, but he knew a tremendous opportunity when he heard one, and when he thought of all of the possibilities that owning his own newspaper held, he knew what his decision had to be.

"Yes, Chuck, I'll take you up on your offer." Kent stood and held out his hand to Chuck, who took it and shook it enthusiastically.

"Outstanding son," Chuck said with a wide grin. Then he reached under his desk and pulled out a bottle of whiskey. "Let's have a drink to celebrate."

Kent couldn't help but chuckle to himself as he pulled into his driveway later that evening. He and Chuck would be going to the bank the next morning to start getting all of the necessary documents in order.

Kent parked and was about to head inside to get ready for Rich's visit. He'd texted him earlier to say that he'd arrived in town and asked about getting together that evening. Kent had told him to stop by, and he had a few minutes to get settled before Rich showed up.

He was surprised, but pleased, to see Roni waiting on his couch when he opened the door.

"Hey, Roni," He said with a grin when he saw her. "I tried calling you earlier; you aren't going to believe what happened to me today."

Roni put her hand out, indicating he should stop talking, then she stood up, put both of her hands on her hips, and shot him a dirty look.

"You're news can wait," Roni said harshly, her grey eyes flashing dangerously. "I have tried giving you some space, but I couldn't take it any longer. What did you do to Nicole?"

Kent looked down at the ground before glancing back up at her with a shrug. "What did she say? How's she doing?"

Roni threw her hands up, exasperated. "She hasn't said anything… At least not to me. Jake brought her home from her parents' house, and I could tell she was upset, but she said she couldn't talk to me about it. All she would say is that you ended things."

"She shouldn't be taking it out on you," Kent began.

"She's not taking it out on me, you bonehead. She's friendly and we talk about other stuff, but she won't tell me what happened. She won't confide in me and let me help her through this, because I happen to be related to you and she doesn't want to put me in the middle. I gave you a few days to realize that you'd made a mistake, but here you are, so I'm here to hear it from you. What happened?"

Kent walked over to her and motioned for her to sit back down on the couch, then sat next to her.

"I told her it wouldn't work. In the long run. Look, Roni, you didn't meet her parents or see the place she grew up in. It's the polar opposite of what we had as kids."

"So?"

"So... I just didn't fit in there. Nicole deserves a man that can give her everything she's ever dreamed of. She's good, sweet, and pure. She deserves someone that'll make her proud and be proud of everything that she's."

Roni looked at him like he had a screw loose.

"And why aren't you that man?"

"C'mon Roni," Kent stood up, frustrated, then started to pace around his living room. "You know the things I dealt with growing up, and the things that I've done. I'm not that man."

"Now you're pissing me off," Roni began, standing herself and walking over to him. "Nicole would be lucky to have you. You're the most loving, generous, and protective man that I've ever met. You would be there for her and give her everything you are capable of giving. Don't talk about yourself as if you're not good enough. Do you think that I wouldn't be good enough for a nice man or a man who was raised with money?"

"No Roni, of course not," Kent replied as he ran his hand through his already disheveled hair. "You deserve the best."

"So do you, and so does she." Roni put her arms around his waist and looked up at him. Into his eyes. "You guys deserve each other. Don't be a horse's ass, Kent."

She hugged him to try and soften her harsh words, then pulled back to look at him again.

"What was your good news?"

He kissed her on the top of her head, then smiled wryly down at her.

"Now you want to hear my news? You tear me a new one and now you want to hear it?" He laughed softly as he said it, but the smile didn't quite reach his eyes.

"Yup," Roni grinned back up at him.

"Chuck offered to let me buy the paper from him. He wants to retire."

"That's wonderful, Kent," Roni broke free and did a little happy dance around the room. "You said yes, right?"

"I did," Kent admitted. "I think I can be happy here, and you're here, so as long as you think this is somewhere that you would like to stay, then I think it would be good for us to have a solid home."

"I like it here," Roni said with a smile. "I'm so happy for you!"

She ran back to him and gave him a hug. He put his cheek on the top of her head and asked, "Is she okay, Roni?"

Roni was about to answer when the doorbell rang once, then the door opened and Rich walked in.

"Ugh," Roni groaned when she saw him.

"Nice to see you too, sunshine," Rich said with a grin and a wink as he walked in. "What's up, man?"

Kent walked over and gave Rich a slap on the back, then paused when Colin walked in behind him.

"I hope you don't mind, I asked Colin to come with me." Rich explained. "He called to say he was in town, and there's something I want to talk to the both of you about."

"No problem," Kent said, then walked over and held his hand out to Colin. "How's it going, Colin? How's Austin?"

Colin shook Kent's hand and said with a smile, "It's great, man. Nice house."

"Thanks."

"Hey Colin," Roni greeted her friend's tall good-looking boyfriend. "So, if you're here, does that mean Bree is too?"

"Hi, Roni," Colin responded with a flash of his dimples. "Good to see you again. Yeah, Bree was actually headed over to your apartment to see you and Nic. I think Kara's meeting her over there too."

"Awesome," Roni said as she turned to her brother. "You're off the hook for now, but you'd better come to your senses soon. I'll see you later. Bye, Colin. Rich," She said dryly when Rich winked at her.

"Your sister really likes me," Rich grinned at her retreating back, then laughed out loud as she flipped him off before closing the door behind her.

"How long are you both here for?" Kent asked as he walked into the kitchen. "You want a beer?"

They nodded, then followed Kent out onto his back deck and sat down to catch up.

"'Til Sunday after Halloween," Colin answered first.

"Yeah, me too," Rich replied. "But I'll graduate in December and be back for good. I'm so ready to be done with school."

"What are your plans when you get back?" Kent asked the slightly younger man.

Rich set his beer down and looked at the two of them, his hazel eyes flashing with excitement.

"That's what I wanted to talk to the two of you about, actually. This may sound like it's coming out of left field, but I have been doing my research for a little over a year now." Rich ran his hand through his shaggy brown hair, then took a deep swig of his beer before finishing. "There's an old warehouse over on Fifth Street, and… Well, I bought it."

"You did?" Colin asked. "I know the place you're talking about. What are you going to do with it?"

"I'm going to make it into a Rec center. For kids," Rich began to talk more quickly. "You know how we spent all of our time shooting hoops and playing catch growing up?" This he directed at Colin.

"Yeah."

"Well, I want to build a place where kids can come hang out, and be active, in a safe and controlled environment. I plan to have a baseball diamond out back, courts inside, and different areas for classes."

"What kind of classes?" Kent asked eagerly, getting caught up in Rich's excitement.

"Karate, music, dance... I don't know everything. I haven't worked it all out yet, but it's going to be great."

"That sounds amazing, man," Colin said. "I would have loved a place like that growing up."

Kent nodded in agreement, "Me too. And I've noticed that there isn't a Y or any sort of Boys and Girls club here, so that would be great."

Kent went in to get another round of beers. He could see the enthusiasm his friend had for this idea and agreed one hundred percent that the kids in this town needed and would utilize a Rec Center like that.

He believed in the idea so much, that when he got back outside with the guys he said, "I want in. Not as an owner or anything, that's your deal, Rich, but I want to help. Be a silent partner or something, and maybe offer a journalism course or something."

Colin looked up at him with a grin as he handed him a beer. "Dude, I was just saying the same thing. I would love to be involved, and although I'm not here full time right now, I'd love to help out when I am."

"You guys are awesome," Rich said as he cleared his throat. "I'm just glad you didn't laugh at me."

"Hell no. Why would we laugh, it's a great idea. And, I know an amazing dancer that could help you with classes, but she may be a hard sell." Kent said with a chuckle.

Friends & Lovers Trilogy

Chapter Nineteen

The girls surrounded Nicole on the living room floor. They had blankets, throw pillows, and a pitcher of margaritas.

"Okay," Briana began, as she lifted her margarita to her lips and brushed her freshly cut bangs from her forehead. Her long chestnut hair was pulled back in a ponytail and the bangs framed her pretty face. "Tell us exactly what happened at the party."

The other girls nodded their encouragement to Nicole, who sat cross-legged in her yoga pants and an oversized sweatshirt.

"Well, it was okay in the beginning. My dad wasn't bad, but as soon as Kent met my mother, things started to go downhill. It's funny; I forgot what a snob she can be. I guess I've been away from her for a while. Anyway, I could tell right away that they didn't like each other," She paused to take a deep drink.

"Why do you say that?" Kara asked as she turned over to lie on her stomach, "Kent's a pretty likeable guy. I'd think he'd be a parent's wet dream!"

Nicole giggled at that, the tequila slowly starting to take effect.

"Not my mom, her idea of a suitable guy is someone exactly like Jake. From an upstanding Dallas family, with deep roots in the church, and someone who thinks social status is important."

"Well...that's definitely not Kent," Roni said with a snort.

"No," Nicole agreed with a small smile. "Kent is so much better than that."

"What happened to make him leave?" Briana asked softly, laying her hand on Nicole's arm.

"My mom was rude to him from the get go, and once her friends arrived, she ignored him all together. He overheard her gossiping about someone from the parish who'd been arrested for domestic violence, and he just walked out. When I followed him outside, he told me some stuff about his childhood," Nicole looked over at Roni, her compassion apparent in her eyes, then looked down at her glass as her eyes began to fill. "He said that we were too different, that we'd never work out, and he thought it was better to walk away now than drag it out."

Roni's arms came around her as the tears began to spill down her cheeks.

"My brother can be such an idiot."

"It sounds like he's just scared," Kara said quietly.

"What do you mean?" Nicole asked with a sniffle.

"We all know that Kent's the best. He's built himself into the sexy metro-sexual that he is today. He's a total sweetheart, and you can't deny that he's a wonderful brother to Roni. But..."

"But what?" Nicole asked as she sat up straighter and wiped her cheeks with the back of her hand.

"He's never been in a serious relationship," Roni answered. "Bree was the closest he ever got, and you see how that turned out." She looked over at Briana and said sadly, "Sorry."

"It's okay," Briana replied.

"We didn't have a good example of marriage, or love, growing up. Kent doesn't want to end up in a terrible situation like that, which would never happen, because Kent is the complete opposite of our father. But, because of them, he's never allowed himself to really trust a woman with his heart. He's afraid of being hurt and of not being the man that he wants to be."

Kara got up to grab the pitcher and poured them each another round. "Kent doesn't realize what a catch he is."

"He said that I deserved better than him," Nicole admitted.

Briana shook her head sadly. "You're going to have to tell him that he's the one you want."

"I tried, and he just walked away and left me there. What if I put myself out there and he still says no?"

"Do you love him?" Kara asked softly.

"Yes," Nicole smiled through the tears and nodded emphatically. "So much. I never thought I'd feel this way about anyone. He's the most amazing person I have ever met, and I feel stronger when I'm with him."

"Then you're going to have to take that chance," Briana said. "You might get your heart broken, but if you don't try, you'll never know."

"I know he loves you," Roni encouraged. "He's buying the paper. He's putting down roots here, and I know you're a big reason for that."

"He's buying the paper?" Nicole asked with wide eyes. "He's going to stay?"

Roni grinned at her, "Yes. I know he's stubborn and can be a total block head, but you're just going to have to make him see that you love him and you're not letting him get away that easily. Fight for him, Nic. I promise he's worth it."

Roni's eyes began to fill and Nicole leaned over to give her a big hug.

"I know he is. I love you," Nicole told the other girl as she pulled back. She looked around her living room at Roni, Briana, and Kara and her heart felt fuller than ever. "I love you all so much. You are the family that I always wanted."

"Awww," Briana said her emotion evident on her face. "I love you too."

"I'll drink to that," Kara exclaimed loudly. She lifted her glass and realized it was empty. "Time to make another pitcher. Let's fill up and figure out how we're going to help Nicole land her man."

They all laughed and stood up. They made their way to the kitchen to blend margaritas.

"I think we'll have to get you in a sexy costume for the Halloween party," Briana said with a wicked grin.

"Yes!" Roni agreed. Her face lit up as an idea began to form. "How about a sexy angel? Kent wants to put you on a pedestal and thinks that you're too good for him. Let's play with that."

"An angel?" Nicole asked skeptically.

"Perfect," Kara said with a smile as she put the ingredients in the blender. "He's not going to know what hit him!"

Chapter Twenty

The bar and grill was decorated with wall to wall Halloween decorations. There was a DJ in the corner spinning spooky hits, and there was a mass of monsters, sexily clad women, and people wearing simply a mask with regular clothes. Then there was Nicole.

She stood out in the room like a vision in white. Her hair was fluffed out and spilled over her back and wings in waves. Her ample bosom was showcased in the low cut slip dress. It fell well above her knees and her legs were covered in white fishnet stockings. She was wearing heels that looked like ice pics, and her face was made up dramatically with smoky eyes and ruby red lips.

She killed him.

When he'd walked through the door he'd seen her instantly, and had felt a simultaneous surge in his heart and in his pants. He'd never had a woman affect him the way that Nicole did.

He must have stopped and stared when he'd seen her, because Rich ran right into his back, causing him to stumble forward.

"Dude," Rich chuckled as he put his hand on Kent's arm to steady him. "You alright?"

Rich looked up and followed the direction of Kent's gaze.

"Wow, she looks fuckin' hot!"

Rich just chuckled again when Kent shot him a dirty look. He adjusted his hood to drape the way he wanted it, and checked his shorts to make sure they were in place.

"Is it on right?"

Kent looked at Rich's boxing costume and shook his head. "You look like a piece of meat, like you're just looking to get laid."

Rich gave him a big grin and a wink, "Then, mission accomplished!" He said as he sauntered off towards the bar.

Kent adjusted his cowboy hat and followed Rich. He stopped when he saw Colin and Briana at a nearby table. They were cute in a Top Gun themed matching outfit. Colin wore a flight suit and Bree had on a sexy little bomber jacket and short skirt. They both looked really happy.

"Hey, how's it going?" Kent asked. He shook Colin's hand and accepted Bree's hug when she leaned in to him. It had been a while since he'd seen her, but he was happy to say that he no longer felt a tug of longing when he held her.

"Great," Briana yelled over the music. "How are you? You look good."

"You guys look good too," Kent shouted back. "I'm gonna grab a drink. You guys need anything?"

He got their orders and went to join Rich at the bar. He couldn't help but notice that Nicole was surrounded by a group of horny monsters, and he felt sick to his stomach when he saw a tall dark vampire leaning in to speak in her ear. He forced his eyes forward and kept moving towards the bar.

He couldn't help but wonder if he'd been hasty in his decision to cut things off when he did. He still thought that she could do better than a guy like him, but he really missed being with her. He missed the sound of her laugh and the way she smiled to herself when she was writing. He missed her soft lips and the sweet smell of her hair.

He almost walked in to Rich when the other man called his name and snapped him out of his thoughts.

"Dude, you're out of it tonight. Let me get you a drink."

Kent thanked him and ordered the drinks for Briana and Colin.

"Gonna be a busy one tonight, eh Pete?" He yelled to his ginger haired friend. Pete nodded in agreement and turned to grab a couple beers. "Who are you supposed to be?" Kent asked when he saw the bow strapped to Pete's back.

"Hawkeye," Pete yelled, then he nodded towards the swinging door where Kara was coming out of the back with a full tray. She had on a red wig and a tight black body suit.

"Black Widow?" Kent guessed, and grinned when the other man nodded and handed him his drinks. "See ya in a bit."

When he got to the table to pass out the drinks, he noticed Rich was flirting with a hot blonde in a Grecian outfit. When he heard the snort and the sarcastic remark, he whirled the girl around and found Roni standing before him.

"What in the hell are you wearing?" Kent asked loudly.

"It's a costume," Roni answered wryly.

"Barely," Kent retorted as he took in the sexy shoes and what appeared to be a twelve year olds dress.

Roni just rolled her eyes at him and said, "Calm down. I'm going to go see Nicole."

He watched her walk away and then turned to see Rich was doing the same thing. "Hey. Stop it."

Rich just shrugged his shoulders and smiled at him, then tipped his head back to take a swig of his beer.

Kent watched Roni walk up to where Nicole was still talking to the lame vampire guy, and saw Nicole say something him, then turn to follow Roni. When he saw the guy put his hand on her arm to stop her, he saw red.

Kent walked quickly through the crowd and heard Nicole asking the jerk to let her go.

"Can you please let go of my arm," She asked loudly. "I'm going to go with my friend to get a drink."

"I'm not ready for you to go yet," the vampire replied, not letting go.

Kent walked right up to the shorter man and towered menacingly over him.

"She said let go."

The vampire looked up at him, his eyes already bloodshot and sneered. "Back off, man. Find your own bimbo."

"Kent," Nicole put her hand on his arm, as if to hold him back. "He's not worth it."

Kent looked down into her eyes and felt himself grow calm. He nodded at her, then reached over and peeled the guys hand off of her arm.

"Walk away." He said to the other man, then turned and dismissed him.

Nicole took her hand off of his arm, then turned to follow Roni.

"Nic, wait," Kent said quickly. "Can we talk?"

Nicole looked up at him, the hurt he had caused her apparent in her eyes, and for a second, he thought she was going to say no, but instead she held out her hand to him.

"Why don't we go over and say hi to everyone first and enjoy the party a bit," Nicole said as he took her hand. "We do need to talk, but just give it a little time, okay?"

Kent nodded, he'd give her all the time she needed, as long as she'd give him a chance to explain and apologize for hurting her.

When they got to the table, Kent heard Rich filling Briana in on his plan to open the Rec Center.

"Oh my gosh," Briana exclaimed, giving Rich a hug. "That sounds amazing. I would love to give some cooking lessons when I come in to town."

They all talked over each other about what they wanted to contribute to Rich's plan, and by the end of the conversation he was grinning from ear to ear.

"You guys are the best," Rich said sincerely.

Kent pulled Roni to the side while everyone continued to talk.

"Sounds like a great idea, right?" He asked her.

Roni looked at Rich thoughtfully, then smiled at her brother. "Yeah, it really does."

"He mentioned wanting to include dance lessons the other day. You would be great at that," Kent said.

"I don't know…" Roni replied.

"Just think about it."

Roni nodded and accepted his brief hug.

"I still think you should have more clothes on," Kent teased her, causing her to smile again and punch him playfully in the arm.

"Shut up."

Once it looked like the party was winding down and people were starting to leave the party, Kent scooted next to Nicole and asked if he could give her a ride home.

Nicole looked up at him and gave him a hesitant smile. "Sure."

They walked around and said goodbye to their friends. Kent stomach began to twist as he thought about the conversation they had to have. He knew after they did, there was a possibility that Nicole would be out of his life, at least romantically.

Friends & Lovers Trilogy

Epilogue

When they got outside, he realized that it was pretty cold out and she wasn't wearing much. As he looked down at her beautiful face, he wished more than anything that he had the right to touch her, to kiss her, to pull her into his arms and keep her warm.

They hurried to his car and got in. He turned it on to allow the heat to warm her chilled arms. Then he looked over at her and said, "You look amazing."

Nicole looked down at her scantily clad body and tried in vain to pull the dress down over her legs, but smiled softly at his compliment.

"Thanks." She looked up and into his eyes.

He looked at her sweet face, so full of hope, and he worried that he'd never be able to give her everything she deserved.

He grew nervous and started to wonder if his initial decision to let her go was right. Was he just being selfish by trying to keep her in his life?

"Kent?" She questioned softly when he didn't start driving.

He turned to look at her and said, "I don't know exactly what to say, Nic. I mean, I know that I hurt you the other day, and I wanted to apologize for that. But I also want to say that I miss you, and I hate to think that I have caused you any pain."

"I won't lie to you," Nicole replied. "You did hurt me, but I understand where you were coming from."

Kent nodded, happy that she understood him, but sad that she may in some way agree with him. Agree that he wasn't good enough.

"I'm sorry for the things that you went through as a child, but where you come from and how you were raised is not a factor in the way I feel about who you are now." Nicole put her hand on his cheek; she wanted to make sure he was looking in her eyes as she continued. She wanted him to see that she was sincere in what she said.

"Kent, I think you're the most wonderful, talented, kind-hearted, amazing person that I've ever met. When I'm with you, I feel strong and invincible. You make me believe that I can be anything I want to be."

She smiled shyly at him and continued, "Kent, I'm in love with you."

Kent couldn't help the pride that he felt at her words. The way she described him is the way that he always hoped people would perceive him. Not as his father's son, or the boy who came from nothing, but as the man he was today. He was still afraid and unsure, but he felt he owed it to Nicole to tell her what was in his heart as well.

"Nic, I think you're a strong, beautiful, and capable woman. The way you stood up for yourself and your beliefs, even when you knew that your parents wouldn't understand, amazes me. You have a kind heart and are the sweetest woman I've ever met. I want to strive to make you proud of me and hope that you'll always look at me the way you do now."

He looked deep into her eyes and declared, "I'm in love with you, Nicole."

Nicole smiled broadly and a single tear fell down her face.

Kent wanted to kiss her, but he had to make sure that she understood everything he was feeling.

"I love you. That's why I think you deserve better. You deserve a man like Jake. One who is as innocent as you, who hasn't seen and done unmentionable things. Any man would be lucky to be able to marry you and raise children with you, and I want you to be sure that you can see a future with me."

He paused to give her a moment to process everything he'd said. "Your parents will probably never approve of me, and my parents will never be in the picture. It'll just be us... and Roni. I don't want you to feel that you're settling by staying with me."

Nicole took his hands in hers and held them tight.

"We have Roni, Rich, Bree, Colin, Kara, and Pete. They're our family. I don't need anyone else. If my parents won't approve of you or our relationship, then I don't need them in my life." She squeezed his hand in hers and said, "I don't see being with you as settling. I feel like the luckiest woman in the world when I'm with you. Jake's not the man that I want or need, you are."

Kent saw the truth in her eyes and relief flooded him.

He finally did what he'd wanted to do since he first saw her that evening. He pulled her to him kissed her thoroughly, putting everything he felt into the kiss.

When they pulled away, Nicole looked happily up at him and said simply, "I choose you."

Friends & Lovers Trilogy

Trust in Me
(Roni & Rich)

Friends & Lovers Trilogy

Prologue

Roni tried to brace herself for the blow before it landed, but she was still knocked backwards into the stove. Her hands flew out, instinctively covering her face, as her hip caught the corner of the stove and she collapsed onto the jaundiced linoleum.

She curled into the fetal position and brought her arms up to cover her head, but his boot still found its way to her ribs. Roni cried out in pain as her husband kicked her repeatedly.

Hank shouted obscenities at her as he grabbed two fistfuls of her long blonde hair and dragged her towards their dingy living room.

Roni tried not to struggle as she was pulled along the floor, worried that her hair would be yanked out if she did. She kept her eyes and mouth shut, she'd been in this predicament before, and knew she'd end up with more cuts and bruises if she struggled.

She saw her opportunity when Hank stopped in the threshold and loosened his grip.

Roni rolled backwards and sprang to her knees. In one fluid motion, she gained her footing and turned to sprint towards the backdoor. Since her back was turned, she didn't see Hank raise his leg to kick her, but felt his foot make contact with her back right before she went sprawling face first back onto the linoleum.

She didn't pay attention to the blood that started oozing from her nose; instead she boosted herself up on to all fours and began crawling towards the exit.

Hank's dry chuckle turned her belly cold, but Roni tried to push through the fear and stay focused on her goal.

This wasn't the first time her husband had used physical violence to make a point. When she'd first met him, she thought he was so handsome and strong. She'd thought he'd take her away from the nightmare that she'd grown up in and protect her, the way her twin brother always had until he went away to college. She couldn't have been more wrong.

The first time he'd hit her, she'd been beyond shocked. She'd never been struck a day in her life, her brother, Kent had made sure of that. When she'd told Hank she was going to leave him, he'd been full of remorse and promises, and she'd been foolish enough to believe him.

The last straw had come the night before, when he'd punched her in the stomach after they'd returned from the local bar. She'd been dancing to the band, by herself, but he hadn't been pleased. As soon as they'd walked into their small trailer, he'd blind-sided her and called her a whore.

When she woke up this morning, she'd called Kent and told him the truth about her marriage. He'd been angry and appalled, but agreed to come and help her leave Hank, just like she'd known he would.

Kent was the one man she could always count on.

The surprise came when Hank had come home early and found her packing her things. She'd said she was leaving when her brother arrived and tried to walk out of the trailer quickly, but Hank had caught up to her in the kitchen.

Her thoughts seemed muddled in her mind and she crawled as quickly as she could. She felt like she'd been crawling forever, but had only made it a few inches, before she felt Hanks boot on her ass. Roni sprawled on the floor, then quickly tried to curl back into the fetal position and protect as much of her body from him as she could.

She felt his hot breath on her cheek as he leaned down and whispered, "I will never allow you to leave me."

Roni braced herself for the next blow, then opened her eyes when she heard scuffling and the cold, hard tone of her brother's voice.

"I should kill you right now," Kent said in a low dangerous voice as he pulled Hank from her and flung him back towards the wall.

Roni scrambled up off of the floor and ran to the bedroom to grab her bags. When she got back, Kent was pummeling his fists into Hanks face.

She ran over to him and put her hand softly on Kent's shoulder. "Stop. He's not worth it. Let's just get out of here."

She heard Kent breath in deeply. He pulled back and Hank slid slowly down the wall. He landed on the floor with a thud.

"You will *never* see my sister again," Kent explained to his brother-in-law, then he turned, put his arm around Roni, and led her out of the trailer.

When they walked outside, Roni winced at the bright sunlight. Kent stopped and turned her towards him.

She was ashamed to look him in the eye, so she kept her head down. He put his finger under her chin and brought her face up so he could examine it, his grey eyes filled with worry.

"It's just my nose," Roni said softly. "Hank doesn't like to mark up my face."

Kent swore under his breath and pulled her gently into his arms. "Why didn't you call me sooner, Roni? I could've helped."

Roni felt her eyes fill and her throat get hot and scratchy. "I was ashamed. You always protected me from Dad, then I go and marry someone just like him. I was afraid you'd be disappointed."

"I could never be disappointed in you," Kent replied as he kissed her softly on the top of the head. "I'm taking you back to Texas with me; we'll figure everything out once we get there, okay?"

"Okay," Roni said with a small smile. She let her brother walk her to the rental car and settle her into the passenger seat. While he shut the door and walked around the car, she settled back in to the seat and closed her eyes.

Roni felt Kent get into the car and heard him start the engine. As they drove away from the tiny trailer she'd called home, she finally felt safe.

Six Months Later...

Friends & Lovers Trilogy

Chapter One

"Where are you going?" The tiny brunette next to him asked with a pout. Rich smiled down at her and gave her a kiss on the forehead as he moved one hand under the covers to search for his underwear.

"I gotta go finish packing up. I'm heading home tonight."

The brunette sat up quickly, not bothering to grab the sheet that fell from her naked body. Confusion crossed her features as she asked, "Are you going home early for break?"

Rich paused his search and took a moment to appreciate her perky breasts, then looked into her deep brown eyes. "No, doll, I'm going home for good. I finished my last class yesterday, that's why I was at the bar last night. We were having a going away party of sorts."

Her mouth formed a small O, then turned down into a pretty little frown.

"So, you mean I won't ever see you again?"

Rich finally found his boxer briefs and swung his legs over the side of her queen sized bed to put them on. He stood up to pull the underwear over his slender hips, and reached down to grab the jeans that were peeking out from under her bed. He pulled them up, but didn't bother with the zipper; instead he crawled back onto the bed and kissed her full lips.

"Probably not, doll. I don't have any plans to come up here again anytime soon."

She kissed him back, then watched him scoot back off of the bed and grab his shirt from the top of her dresser in the corner. He felt her eyes on him as he pulled the dark gray shirt over his head. Rich brushed his hands through his shaggy brown hair in an effort to tame it a bit. He slipped on his shoes, then went back to the bed to give her a final kiss goodbye.

She grabbed his face in her hands to intensify the kiss. She trailed her lips across his jaw, pausing to pay homage to the cleft in his chin.

"Bye, doll."

"Do you keep calling me 'doll' because you don't remember my name?" she asked.

"No, I call you doll because you are as sweet and delicate as a doll," Rich said with a wink. "I never forget the name of a woman I've spent time with, Sam. I promise you that."

When he left her room, she was still sitting in the middle of her bed. Bare from the waist up, her dark hair flowing around her shoulders, and a beautiful smile on her face.

God, he sure did love women!

Rich walked to his car with a grin on his lips and a hop in his step. He couldn't wait to load up his car and leave campus, Sam already a fond memory. He opened the door of his rusty old Charger and paused to rub his hand along the dashboard the way he always did when he entered his car.

He'd bought the car recently out of necessity. She wasn't new by any stretch of the imagination, but she was reliable. He couldn't afford to buy a new car right now, since all of his hard-saved money was going towards his dream of opening a Rec Center for the kids in his hometown. One day he'd be able to get the car of his dreams, but for now, he wanted to make sure his car knew that he appreciated her every time he started her up.

He kept the windows down as he cruised toward the house he'd shared with some buddies over the last couple years. He was sure he'd miss hanging out with the guys, but he was excited about going back home and seeing his family and friends full-time.

The last time he'd been home had been for Halloween, and he'd had a great time hanging out with everyone. Bree and Colin had come home for the party, and he'd been thrilled to see how happy they were. Shoot, it seemed like all of his friends were hooking up. Kara and Pete were still going strong, and since he talked to Kent quite often, he knew that his friends' relationship with Nicole was moving along pretty rapidly.

His parents wanted him to move back in with them until he got settled, but Rich was ready to be on his own. He'd had the contractors renovate the back part of the warehouse that would be the Rec Center so that he could live on site. He figured it would work for a few years while he got the center up and running, then, if things went according to plan, he would rent it out to employees once he was ready to invest in a house of his own.

For now, he was ready to be a "grown-up".

And, if he was being honest with himself, he was looking forward to seeing a certain tall blonde again. Sure, Roni acted like he was a pain in the ass every time she saw him, but he couldn't help but like that about her. Most of the women he encountered enjoyed his company, even went out of their way to get it. It was kind of nice to meet someone who didn't drop her panties when he turned on the charm.

He didn't believe that she found him as repulsive as she pretended to, but she sure didn't make anything easy, he thought with a chuckle. That was one of his favorite things about her, and there was a lot about her that he liked.

Getting Roni to give him a chance was a challenge that he was really looking forward to accepting.

Chapter Two

Roni felt the sweat trickle down her back and she moved with the music. Her head was clear as she let the beat guide her. She felt freer than she had in years.

She danced for over an hour before she felt like she needed to stop and get some water. She stood and looked out the window as she drank. She couldn't keep the smile from stretching across her face.

She felt happy here. Not only happy, but content and safe. She loved being close to her brother, and was thrilled that he had found someone like Nicole. The two of them were so cute together, it bordered on nauseating, but it was wonderful to see Kent so in-tune with another person.

Roni loved the apartment she shared with Nicole. It was basically her apartment now, since Nicole spent most of her waking hours at work or with Kent.

Roni enjoyed the time alone.

She'd gone straight from her parents' home, to the one she'd shared with Hank. When she'd first arrived here, she'd bunked with her brother, and now she was living with Nicole. This was the closest she'd come to having a place of her own, and she found that she really liked having the time to herself.

She looked at the clock and realized that she'd have to shower and get ready for work at the Bar & Grill soon. She'd been hostessing for a few months now, and she liked the job and the people she worked with, but it wasn't what she wanted to do long term. She really wanted to start dancing full time again.

Roni understood that she would never become a professional dancer at this point, she'd been away from it for too long, and wasn't getting any younger, but all she'd ever wanted to do with her life, was dance.

There weren't any dance studios in town, which she thought was not only sad on a personal level, but for the kids in town who didn't have the opportunity to take classes.

Dance had helped her get through her childhood.

She'd been thinking a lot recently about what Rich was doing with the warehouse downtown. As much as he annoyed her, she had to admit that he was producing something wonderful for the community, and the children in it.

A Rec Center that would offer classes and a place for the kids to go to was a wonderful idea, and she couldn't help but want to be a part of it. Her brother told her he thought it would be great for her to teach dance lessons there, but she had another idea. She just had to bite the bullet and talk to Rich about it.

Roni knew that this center was his baby, but she really wanted to own something of her own, now she just needed to find Rich and see if he would buy in on it.

She'd heard that he was back in town and staying on the construction site. She thought if she got ready now, she'd have time to talk to him before her shift started.

After she was ready, she drove to 5th street and stood nervously outside the warehouse. It was so much bigger than she'd imagined, and looked like the unused warehouse that it was, but she could see the potential in it. She felt a flutter of excitement in her belly.

She made her way through the warehouse, careful to avoid the areas that were currently being worked on, towards the back of the building. That's where Kent said Rich's rooms were.

When she came upon a white door slightly ajar, and heard the music streaming out of the room beyond it, she figured she'd found the right place.

She pushed the door open and peered inside. Her jaw dropped and her eyes seemed to freeze open at the site before her.

There was a makeshift bed in the corner, boxes strewn about the room, and a door that led into a small bathroom. In the center of the room Rich stood in nothing but basketball shorts. His very toned and naturally tanned body glistened with sweat as he worked the speed bag before him, his fist moving rapidly as they punched.

The quick curl of lust in her belly shocked Roni. She'd never had such an intense and immediate reaction to a man before. Even more shocking was the fact that it was Rich that caused her body to suddenly feel infused with liquid heat.

He hadn't heard her enter. The music was too loud, and he was totally focused on pounding the bag.

Roni couldn't look away. She felt a visceral need to touch. As the muscles rippled under his skin with each movement, her hands itched to feel.
Roni shook her head briefly. What was she thinking? This was Rich. A player. A Flirt. The exact opposite of the kind of guy she needed in her life.

Someone needed to explain that to her legs, she thought. They were about to give out.

Suddenly she realized that the movement before her had stopped. She shouted out, "Hey," to get Rich's attention, before he turned and caught her staring at him. The last thing she needed was for Rich to think she thought he was hot!

Rich wiped at his brow and turned, a grin spreading across his face when he saw her in the doorway. He held up a finger, to tell her to give him a second. He crossed the room towards the docking station and bent to turn down his iPod.

Roni stifled a grown at the sight of his ass as he bent over. Who knew a man's ass could be so freakin' tight? And his back… Good Lord!

Roni composed herself as he turned back towards her, but couldn't help the jitters of happiness in her stomach when he didn't reach for a shirt.

"What's up, Roni?" He seemed truly happy to see her.

"Hey," She responded, trying to focus on his face. His brown hair was curling at the ends, damp with sweat. She didn't understand why she found that so attractive. Maybe it had been too long since she'd had sex. It shouldn't feel like she had to make a concerted effort not to throw herself at him. "Um, not much. I hope I'm not intruding."

Rich picked up a towel and used it to wipe the sweat from his face, then he moved passed her to grab a water bottle from the fridge. "You're not. Would you like a water?"

"Sure," Roni said when she realized that her throat felt dry. "Thanks."

"Sorry, there's not much room around here for entertaining," Rich said with a chuckle as he looked around his small space. "I haven't had a chance to do much with it yet; I've only been back a few days."

"That's fine. I can't stay long. My shift starts soon."

When she didn't say anything, Rich smiled at her and the familiar twinkle lit his eyes.

"You just came by 'cause you missed me?"

That broke Roni out of her sex-crazed daze. She rolled her eyes at him and snorted. "That'll be the day. Actually, I came by with a proposition."

"Even better," Rich said, his grin widening at the look on her face.

"You wish," Roni retorted. "I'm talking about a business proposition."

"Okay," Rich said with one last wink, before the flirty smile left his face. "Shoot."

"I know you're planning to use the space to offer different classes to the kids and the community. I want to start off by saying that I think it's a wonderful idea, and all joking aside, I love that you're actually doing it."

"Thanks," Rich said with a sincere smile. "I appreciate that."

Thrown off temporarily by his change in demeanor, Roni cleared her throat, took a deep breath, and laid out her proposition.

"I'm a dancer. It's been a while since I've been able to train, but I've danced since I was a little girl. I'd love to open up my own studio, since there isn't one in town. Since you have all of this space, and are looking for ideas of classes to offer, I thought I would bring my proposition to you."

She paused to look at him momentarily, so she could gauge his reaction. He looked intently at her and nodded for her to go on.

"My long term goal is to own my own studio, but that just isn't plausible right now. I thought maybe you could rent space to me here. I don't want to just be hired on as a teacher; I want to own my own business. I want full creative control to use the space as I see fit. Of course, since it's your building, and I would be renting from you, I would consult with you. But I want to be fully in charge of the studio and what I do with it."

Roni breathed in deeply again, holding her breath in as she waited for his response.

"I didn't realize that you're a dancer," Rich began. "Kent told me he knew someone I could contact about instructing, but never mentioned it was you."

He paused to consider that for a moment before continuing, "First of all, I'll say that it sounds like a great idea. You're right, I do want to offer dance lessons here at the center. I hadn't thought about renting space, but that doesn't mean I object to doing it."

Roni chewed on her lip as she waited for him to continue.

"This is a lot to take in and I know you have to get to work… Can I get back to you?"

Roni exhaled and nodded.

Rich continued, "I have to talk to a few people and I'll think over your proposal. I'm having auditions/interviews in two weeks for the people who are interested in setting up classes here. I can set up a time for you now, or you can wait until I get back to you on the rental idea."

"Now would be good," Roni said with a small smile. "I appreciate you considering my idea."

They settled on a time for the interview and Rich walked her outside to her car.

"Thanks," Roni said again, as she opened her car door.

"Anytime," Rich said the saucy grin back on his face. "I look forward to seeing the way you move."

Roni rolled her eyes at him as she got in her car, but she waited to drive away until she'd enjoyed the view of him walking away.

Chapter Three

Rich stood under the shower and let the hot water massage his aching muscles. Eyes closed, he allowed himself to think about Roni and the proposition she'd brought to him. She'd looked so pretty standing amidst his cluttered room. He'd wished briefly that he could throw her over his shoulder and ravish her long, lean body on his sorry excuse for a bed, but he'd controlled himself when he heard what she had to say.

Now that he was alone, he could take a little time to remember how her shirt had been snug in all the right places, and her little skirt had swayed slightly, flirty toned legs that seemed to go on forever.

When his body started to stiffen, he changed the course of his thoughts and admitted that her idea was a good one. He stepped out of the shower and toweled off. He hung the towel on the rod, and walked out into his room to find something to wear.

"Jesus, man," Kent said as he watched his friend stride into the room.

Rich just looked at him, a cocky smile on his face. "Guess you shoulda knocked."

"There's a freakin' work crew out there," Kent exclaimed, gesturing towards the men on the other side of the door. "I didn't think you'd be prancing around with your door open, naked as the day you were born."

"I ain't got nothin' they haven't seen before," Rich said with a chuckle as he pulled on a pair of jeans.

"Shit," Kent laughed. "And he's going commando." This he said with his eyes rolled upward.

"What can I do for you?" Rich asked as he picked up a t-shirt, smelled it, then pulled it over his head. "Other than the free show."

"I was wondering if you were up for a beer later. I was driving by on my way to the paper, and thought I'd ask in person. Gives me a chance to see the progress on this place."

"Actually, I was gonna call you later. Colin and Bree are coming in for the weekend, and Colin asked about us getting together tonight. Just the guys. You mind if he comes with?" Rich asked as he looked around the room for his keys and wallet.

"Yeah, that's perfect actually. I'd love to get both of your opinions on something," Kent smoothed his hands over his dress shirt, as if to assure himself that he didn't look as disheveled as Rich. "You guys okay to come by my house and hang out, rather than go to the bar. I don't want a lot of ears around."

Rich slipped on some flip flops and looked at Kent curiously. "Sure, man. I'll let Colin know. Everything okay?"

Kent smiled at him and said, "Yeah, everything's great. You do realize you're wearing flip flops… In December."

Rich looked down at his feet, then back up at Kent, "Yeah, I'm just running to my folks for a bit, then by the bank. No dress code."

Kent shook his head at his friend as they walked out of the warehouse.

"Alright, man, I'll see you tonight. Let me know if you guys want me to order some pizza or something."

"Will do," Rich said as he got into his Charger. "Later."

He murmured to the car as he started her up, then headed a few blocks down to his parents' house. He'd been home a few days, and knew his mother was going to be salty that this was the first chance he'd had to stop by.

When he opened the front door to his childhood home, the smell of baking cookies greeted him, and he couldn't help but smile.

"Somethin' sure smells good," he yelled as he took off his shoes and made his way towards the kitchen in the back of the house.

"Hmmm, that sounds suspiciously like my long lost son," his mama said with a hint of sarcasm. "Can't be though, because *my* son would have come by the second he'd gotten back to town."

"Now, Mama," Rich said as he dropped a kiss on the top of his mother's head, snatching a cookie as he narrowly missed the back side of her wooden spoon. "I told you I wanted to get settled at the warehouse first."

She gave him a wry look that made him chuckle. He bit into the peanut butter cookie and moaned as the flavors hit his tongue.

"I swear you make the best cookies in the state of Texas," Rich said with a wink.

As he knew it would, the frown fell from his mother's face, replaced by a big grin. She was the most wonderful person he'd ever met. The site of her familiar grin warmed his heart and reminded him of how happy he was to be back home.

Trying to keep the grin off of her face she said, "Boy, don't you try to butter me up with that charm of yours. You know it shouldn't take three days for you to unload your boxes."

"Leave the boy alone, Martha," Rich's dad, Frank, said as he walked in from the back porch. "He doesn't need you laying guilt at his feet; he's a grown man now. With a place and a business of his own."

Martha shook her head and went back to plating cookies, as Frank smacked Rich on his back.

"We're real proud of you and what you're doing over at the old warehouse, Son." Frank smiled around the toothpick that was always in his mouth.

"Thanks, Pop," Rich replied. "They're making headway already; you'll have to stop by."

"How about some food?" His mom asked, "Have you eaten anything yet today?"

"That'd be great, Ma," Rich said as his stomach grumbled in anticipation. "I haven't had a chance to eat anything yet. I worked out this mornin', so I could eat a small cow."

"Well, you're kind of in between meals," Martha said as she eyed the clock. "You in the mood for breakfast or lunch?"

"I'd kill for some of your biscuits and gravy."

"Bacon?"

"You know it," Rich said with a grin.

"Come on back, I'll show you what I'm working on," his dad said as he headed towards the back door.

Rich paused to grab his mother in a big hug and kiss her on the cheek. "I've missed you, Mama."

Martha squeezed him back and patted him on the cheek. "I'm happy you're home. Now go on outside with your daddy, this food won't cook itself."

Rich followed his dad out into the backyard. He'd missed this. He'd missed them. He really was happy to be back home. Funny, he'd always thought he wanted nothing more than to get away from here when he was growing up. Now he knew there was nowhere else he'd rather be.

Chapter Four

Roni was leaning against the hostess stand talking to Kara when her brother walked into the Bar & Grill.

"Hey, handsome," Kara said with a grin as she walked around to pull Kent into a quick hug. "How've you been? We haven't seen you around much lately."

"I'm good, getting everything squared away with the paper," Kent gave her a quick grin and lifted a hand in greeting to Pete, who was tending bar. "How're you?"

"Things are great here too. Pete's been itchin' for a guy's night though, you gonna have a poker night anytime soon?"

"Actually, Rich and Colin are stopping by tonight, I was gonna ask Pete if he was busy," Kent said, then looked at his sister. "I need to talk to Roni first though, then I'll see what he's up to."

Roni looked up at him, curious, "What's up?"

"Can you take a quick break?" He asked.

"Yeah, I haven't had my break yet, and it will be at least a half an hour before we start getting busy for dinner. Let me go tell Pam."

Roni walked back and told the manager she was going to take a break. Kara said she'd keep an eye on the door, so Roni followed Kent outside.

Kent walked over towards the outdoor seating, pulling a chair out for her before sitting himself.

He was smiling, but Roni noticed that his leg was bouncing up and down and he was picking nervously at his shirt. She began to worry that something was wrong.

"What's going on, Kent? You're kinda freakin' me out."

Kent reached out and grabbed her hand. He let their hands rest on the table and smiled broadly at her. "I wanted to talk to you about something."

"Okay," she prodded, wishing he would just spit it out already.

"I've been thinking about this for a while, and I'm actually gonna talk to the guys about it tonight, but I wanted to talk to you first. Get your opinion."

Roni nodded her encouragement for him to go on.

"I know I haven't been with Nicole for that long, but I know I've never met anyone like her, or felt this way about anyone before her. Mom and Dad weren't the best role models, and I know neither of us hold much stock in the sanctity of marriage, but Nic does. I'm going to ask her to marry me." His grin got so big; it looked like he was beaming from the outside in. He chuckled lightly and continued, "I know it's crazy, but I think we can make it work. I don't care about getting her parents' blessing, and Lord knows, I couldn't care less what our parents think, but I wanted to make sure that we have your blessing. Do you think I'm crazy?"

Roni felt her throat tighten and the tears begin to form, as her heart beat wildly in her chest. She'd never seen her brother so happy, and although she was surprised at how quickly their relationship was progressing, she trusted Kent's instincts more than anyone she'd ever known.

"You're not crazy, Kent. Of course you have my blessing. I love Nicole, and I think the two of you are perfect for each other. I know you'll have a marriage that lasts. It'll be nothing like Mom and Dad's, or mine for that matter. It's wonderful. Nicole is going to be thrilled. When are you going to propose?"

"I'm taking her away this weekend. I have the guys coming over tonight, and I'm going to have them help me get everything set up. I can't wait to see the look on her face." Kent reached into his pocket and pulled out a small velvet box. "This is the ring I picked out for her; do you think she'll like it?"

Roni gasped and put her hand over her mouth, "It's beautiful."

She reached for the box, so she could look more closely. The platinum ring had a petal design with diamonds all along the band. It was delicate and beautiful, and would fit Nicole perfectly.

"She's going to love it."

"You think so?" Kent asked eagerly.

"Absolutely," Roni couldn't help the pang in her stomach. Seeing that ring reminded her of her engagement to Hank, or lack thereof.

It had been the day before her high school graduation. She and Hank were sitting in his car after having pizza, and she was telling him that she wasn't sure what she was going to do next. Her parents were going to kick her out, and she didn't want to leave Hank, but she had nowhere else to go other than Kent's. Hank said he didn't want her to leave, and suggested they move in together. She'd told him that she wasn't sure her parents would allow her to live with him. Although they didn't want to support her, she was pretty sure they would go crazy if she attempted to move in with Hank.

She'd never forget that moment as long as she lived. Hank had shrugged his shoulders, took a drag of his cigarette, and said, "I guess I'll marry you then. Make it legal."

She'd been young and in love enough to be excited by his statement. Now she realized how foolish she'd been. Looking at Kent, seeing his excitement and obvious love for Nicole, she saw everything that had been missing from her relationship with Hank.

Roni shook the memory off and looked into her brother's bright eyes. "Congratulations. You deserve to be happy, Kent. I'm so excited for you."

Kent got up and walked around the table to pull her up into a big hug.

"Thanks, Roni. I love you."

"I love you too."

He pulled away and looked into her eyes. "You'll find someone who deserves you, don't worry." He ran a hand over her hair and put his finger under her chin, lifting it so he could look her in the eyes. "You *will* find your happily ever after. In the meantime, don't spill the beans to Nicole."

Roni smiled up at him, nodded and said, "I promise."

Kent pulled her into another hug.

"Alright, I'll let you get back to work. I've gotta go get ready for the guys tonight and make sure everything is set for this weekend. Wish me luck!"

"You don't need it," Roni assured him.

She laughed as she watched him walk away with a spring in his step. It felt great to see him so totally happy.

As he drove off she sat back down in the chair and slowly tore apart a napkin. She couldn't help but feel envious of Nicole and Kent's relationship. It was so different than her relationship with Hank.

She'd been young and stupid. Totally disillusioned. And she'd paid a price for it. Not just the broken bones and surface injuries, but she was worried that she'd never be able to trust herself again.

She'd been so wrong about Hank. She'd always wanted a happily ever after.

Friends & Lovers Trilogy

Chapter Five

When Rich walked into the Bar & Grill, his eyes automatically sought out Roni. She was walking back from seating a party in the center of the room, a small smile played across her lips. He felt the lust pool in his belly. Just watching her walk across the room turned him on. He'd been thinking about her way too much, for way too long. The kicker came when she noticed him standing by the hostess stand. She seemed to miss a step, started to fidget with the ring on her right hand, and her smile was replaced by a scowl. God, she was sexy.

"Hey, Sunshine," Rich said with a cocky grin. "Happy to see me?"

He got the eye roll he'd been hoping for and leaned over onto the stand, purposefully invading her space. As she grabbed two menus from the slot underneath, he grabbed her free hand and brought it to his lips. Roni froze and stared at him.

"What the hell are you doing?"

Rich let his lips linger for a moment, enjoying the feel of her soft skin. He inhaled deeply, letting the scent of strawberries fill him momentarily.

Roni broke out of the temporary shock and pulled her hand away.

"Just wanted to say hi, sugar," Rich drawled as he stood up and gave her space.

"You can say hi without touching me," Roni said between clenched teeth.

Rich couldn't help but grin at her. Roni liked to act like he made her skin crawl, but he was sure she couldn't be completely immune to him. The tension was palpable, at least on his end. She had to feel the chemistry between them, didn't she?

The door opened behind him and he turned to see Colin walk in.

"Hey, brother," Rich said, slapping Colin on the back. Then he turned to Roni and said, "It's just the two of us."

Colin wore a U of T Jersey and a smile. His dark hair was ruffled a bit and he looked relaxed and happy.

"Someone got lucky this morning," Rich said under his breath to Colin as Roni led them to a table.

Colin chuckled deeply, put his hand on Rich's shoulder and squeezed. "A great way to start the day."

"Don't I know it."

They sat down in the booth and took their menus. Rich held Roni's hand before she could turn to leave. "Thanks, sunshine," he said with a wink.

Roni just looked at him and turned to walk away, but Rich could've sworn she was hiding a smile as she walked away.

"Well, I know you had a great morning, anything else new since we left each other last night?"

Colin leaned back in the booth and put his arm up over the bench. He really did look happy. "Nah, not really. That was some pretty great news Kent had last night though, huh?"

Rich thought back to the look on his friend's face when Kent had told them that he was going to propose to Nicole this weekend. He'd never seen the man so excited. Kent always seemed pretty reserved and put together; it was great to see him acting like a little kid on Christmas morning.

"Yeah, it's awesome," Rich agreed. "I think those two are great together."

"It's hard to believe how much has changed in the last year," Colin added.

"You ain't kiddin'," Rich began. The waitress came over and they ordered some coffee and their breakfast. When she turned to put in their order he looked back at Colin and continued, "I never would have guessed I would be back home opening a Rec Center, or that you and Bree would be living in sin in Austin, that's for sure."

Colin's grin got wider at the mention of Briana's name. "Things are better than I ever could have hoped. I love my job. I love my girl. Life is good!"

Rich chuckled and brought the coffee that had just been dropped at the table to his lips. He inhaled deeply, then opened his eyes and caught Roni watching him from her stand in the front. He nodded slightly to acknowledge he saw her, took a sip and smiled when she frowned and turned away from him.

Colin followed the direction of his gaze and said, "Anything new on that front?"

Rich turned his eyes back to Colin and shook his head, "Not in the way you mean."

Colin raised an eyebrow and Rich's response. "In what way, then?"

"She stopped by the warehouse and asked about renting space for a dance studio."

"I didn't know she was a dancer."

"Me neither. Kent had mentioned knowing someone who could run a dance class at the Center, but I'd never imagined he was talking about Roni. She doesn't just want to run a class, though, she wants to rent the space and open a studio. Have full creative control."

"What are you thinkin'? Were you planning to rent space?"

"It hadn't occurred to me, but I'm not opposed to it. Lord knows, I know nothing about dance. I figured I'd offer classes and leave the logistics of those classes to the people I hire to run them, but I can see the benefit of having a permanent studio on site. We don't have one in town."

"That's true," Colin agreed. "And it'd be no different than having the gym and the boxing ring. Those services are permanent, and you have plenty of space to hold other classes."

"I agree," Rich said with a nod. "I'm holding interviews and auditions in the next few weeks, and I've schedule an audition for Roni. If she has the talent and a strong business plan, I think it would be great for the center."

"An audition, huh?" Colin asked with a grin.

As their food was brought out, Rich looked at Colin, "I'm taking this business very seriously. I want to make sure the people who are offering classes are talented, as well as able to teach, and have patience with the kids. Hence, auditions as well as interviews."

Colin nodded as he picked up a piece of bacon and took a bite.

Then Rich grinned, "But I will admit that I'm looking forward to seeing Roni move."

Rich poured some hot sauce on his eggs and scanned the room to find Roni. She was standing by the bar talking to Pam, an easy smile on her face as she laughed at something the other woman said. The lone dimple on the left side of her face peaked out when she laughed, and he let his gaze trail over her long lean body. Her long blonde hair reminded him of the sun, all soft and golden, which was why he couldn't help but call her sunshine whenever he saw her. She drew him in.

Colin cleared his throat, causing Rich to turn back to his friend, who winked at him and said, "You've got it bad this time, brother."

He couldn't deny what his friend was saying. He could admit to himself that he liked Roni. A lot. Not just the way she looked, which was spectacular, but he loved her saucy attitude. The way she loved her brother and her friends. She was loyal, and that was a trait he admired in a woman. From his experience, it was hard to come by.

He looked back over at Roni, then brought his eyes back to Colin and nodded at his friends' words, "Yeah, I think I'm in trouble."

Friends & Lovers Trilogy

Chapter Six

Roni was a little unsettled by her recent reaction to Rich.

First, there had been the physical reaction to seeing him working out in his room, then, when she'd seen him standing at her podium yesterday, her heart had jumped and she'd nearly stumbled. She kept finding her eyes drawn to him while he and Colin had eaten breakfast, and when their eyes met, she felt a warmth flow through her.

She'd never had a reaction like this to a man before, and she hated that her body was betraying her this way. Rich was a total playboy. Why couldn't some sweet, boring, accountant set her blood on fire? Why did it have to be the ladies' man with the killer body?

She tried to clear her head of all thoughts *Rich* as she stretched, but she couldn't help but feel excited at the thought of her upcoming audition. Excited and nervous. The more she thought about having her own studio, the more she loved the idea.

Her body moved naturally to the music as she envisioned what having a studio would mean for her. She wondered if there would be enough space to have a small boutique as well. She could sell shoes, leotards, and tutus. Her face bloomed at the thought and smiled as visions of pink tights and sparkly hair ties bounced through her head.

She was beginning her cool down when she heard what sounded like a herd of elephants bounding up the stairs to her front door.

She turned as the door busted open and Nicole came bounding inside. Roni braced herself as Nicole ran full throttle and launched herself into Roni's arms.

Roni started to laugh until she realized her friend was sobbing in her arms. "Hey, are you okay?"

Nicole pulled back and smiled threw her tears. "I've never been better. I'm getting married!"

Nicole laughed loudly and pulled her hand free to show Roni the sparkling ring that sat happily on her finger. "Isn't it perfect?"

"Yes, it is," Roni agreed. "I'm so happy for you."

Nicole hugged Roni tightly, then pulled back and kissed her squarely on the lips. "We're gonna be sisters."

Roni felt her eyes fill at that and nodded at Nicole, "Yes, we are."

"I'm so happy, Roni," Nicole put her hands on either side of Roni's face and looked into her eyes. "Will you be my Maid of Honor?"

Roni felt a tear slide down her cheek. She nodded as she pulled Nicole back into a hug. "I'd love to."

Roni looked up as her brother came walking into the apartment.

Well, it was actually more like a strut. The look on his face was pure bliss, which turned to tenderness when Nicole turned to him. "How are my favorite women in the world?"

Nicole turned from Roni and walked over to hug her fiancé. "I love you," she said as she reached up to kiss him.

"I love you too."

Roni felt like her heart was going to burst, she was so happy for her brother and Nicole.

"I know Kent already told you he was going to ask, but I had to come tell you first, and ask you to be my Maid of Honor." Nicole said with a smile. "We're going to go and tell Briana and Kara next."

"He did tell me he was going to propose, but not how he was going to do it," Roni said. "Tell me everything."

Nicole seemed to bounce up and down and smile more broadly, if that was possible, then started to speak, "He told me to pack an overnight bag, that he'd talked to Pam and gotten me a couple days off so we could go on a trip. I was really excited about going away together; I had no idea that he was going to propose." Nicole stopped long enough to turn and give Kent a big kiss on the lips, causing Roni to laugh at her friends' exuberance.

"Anyway, we drove for a couple hours, then pulled up to the sweetest B & B I've ever seen. It was a pretty blue with white shutters, a wraparound porch, and a white picket fence. The total dream. When we checked in the owners told us about the amenities: hot tub in each room, gardens in the back, and wine tasting in the evening. I loved it immediately, but the best part came when we got to the room," Nicole paused again and grabbed Kent's hand tightly in hers, smiling up at him.

"Kent opened the door and let me walk in first. The room was decorated beautifully, all white and lace and antique furniture. Pink rose petals covered the bed in the shape of a heart. More rose petals led a trail to the balcony, where the hot tub was bubbling and the champagne was on ice. There were even chocolate covered strawberries. He thought of everything," Roni got a little misty at the look of pure delight on Nicole's face. Who knew her brother was such a catch?

"While I was admiring the view from the balcony, Kent came up behind me. When I turned to tell him how beautiful it was, he was on bended knee. I couldn't breathe," Nicole laughed out loud at the memory. "He looked so handsome, smiling up at me with the small box in his hand. When he opened the box and showed me the perfect ring inside, I couldn't help but squeal. I was saying yes before he even had a chance to ask."

Nicole hugged Kent again, then Roni, before looking at her watch and saying, "Sorry we can't stay, but I really want to tell the others before work. I'll see you tonight."

"See you tonight, and congratulations," Roni said as they all walked to the door. She hugged her brother, then Nicole and watched them walk hand in hand down the stair.

She closed the door and leaned against it allowing the tears to fall freely.

She really was happy for them. Thrilled, in fact, that her brother would finally have everything he deserved.

Deep down she knew she also cried for her failed attempt at marriage. In a few weeks the marriage she'd naively thought would be a fairytale for her, would officially be over. She didn't miss Hank, their house, or the life that they'd shared, but she did miss the dream.

She sank down to the floor and allowed the tears to purge the regret from her soul.

Chapter Seven

Rich couldn't believe how far things had progressed in the last week. His boxing ring had been delivered and was set up in the back corner of the warehouse. It was in a large enclosed room, which housed the ring, speed bags, heavy bags, and had an entrance into the men's locker room. It was his favorite part of the Center so far.

That was about to change, since he'd just gotten a call from the guy driving the truck which carried his workout equipment, and he'd said he'd be arriving in about thirty minutes.

Rich walked through his door, past the kitchen, taking care to avoid the parts of the warehouse that the crew was currently working on. He made his way towards the workout area. One section would hold the weights and there would be an adjoining room for the cardio equipment.

He wasn't starting with a lot, just a complete set of weights, machines for a full circuit, and four of each cardio machine. He had room to grow if he needed to, but figured it was smart to wait and see how much use the fitness portion of his Rec Center got, before he invested too much in it.

His focus was going to be on the kids, but he also wanted to offer classes and activities that the entire community could enjoy, and he thought a fitness center would bring in a profit. When he allowed himself to dream really big, he admitted that he'd love to eventually put a lap pool in behind the building, but knew that would be much further down the road. For now, he was really pleased with how smoothly everything was coming together.

He'd used the boxing equipment last night, and couldn't wait to try out his weights when they arrived.

When he was satisfied that the rooms were prepped and ready for the delivery, he turned to go back towards the front of the warehouse. His first interview was scheduled to start in five minutes.

Before he made it, a small brunette popped her head around the corner.

"Hi," the pretty woman said with a smile and an outstretched hand. "Are you Rich?"

"I am," Rich responded, trying to conceal his surprise. "Are you Alex?"

When his dad had asked him to set up an interview with a Karate instructor from his parents church named Alex, the last person he'd envisioned was the petite woman before him.

"Yes. I was thrilled when your parents told me what you were doing here. I loved taking Karate lessons when I was growing up, and I'd always hoped to get a chance to lead my own class someday."

"Great," Rich said with a smile. "If you want to follow me, we'll go ahead and get started. I'll ask you some questions, then see your demonstration. Afterwards, I'd be happy to answer any questions you may have."

"Okay. Your dad mentioned an audition and an interview, so I thought it was best to wear this first and then change into my karategi. Is that alright?"

"Of course," Rich replied. "Once we're done, you can get changed in the women's locker rocm. It isn't completed yet, but the restrooms are fully functional."

Rich led her to one of the rooms that would be used for Karate lessons. He had a couple chairs set up for the interview portion. The room was complete with hard wood floors and a floor to ceiling mirror covering the back wall.

Rich asked her the questions he'd prepared and was impressed with her answers and her demeanor. Alex worked for the Mayor and was very intelligent.

The position he was hiring for was part time. Week nights and weekends, so the fact that she had a full time day job wasn't a problem. He found out that she was single without any children, and she wanted to dedicate her spare time to teaching and keeping her skills current.

While she was getting changed, Rich moved the chairs to the corner of the room and waited for her to return. Alex seemed like a perfect fit for the job. As long as she didn't fumble through the audition, Rich was prepared to offer it to her.

She nailed it.

She was strong, confident, precise, and loud. Boy, was she loud.

Alex took off the outer jacket portion of her uniform and draped it over her arm as they walked out of the room. She wore a white tank top underneath, which showcased her firmly toned arms.

"The job is yours if you want it," Rich was saying to Alex when Roni rounded the corner. He looked up at her and smiled, holding a finger up to let her know he'd be with her in a minute, then went back to his conversation with Alex.

Rich's heart thumped in his chest at the sight of Roni in a black button up with a red pencil skirt. Damn, she looked good.

He said goodbye to Alex, then turned to where Roni was waiting. "I just have to go sign for a deliver, then I'll be right with you. You can wait in here if you'd like," he said, gesturing to the room he'd just exited.

"Okay," Roni said with a nervous smile.

Rich hurried to the loading dock. He found the driver and his crew had already started unloaded the equipment. He picked up the paperwork and asked the driver, "You need me to sign here?"

"Yup."

"Okay. Hey, Jason, can you check the items off as you unload them to make sure that everything is here. Let me know if you have any issues. I have another interview to conduct, then I'm done for the day. I'll come back to help get everything set up."

He waited for Jason's answer, then went back to where he'd left Roni. She was sitting on a chair, ankles crossed, fidgeting with the hem of her skirt. She looked up and met his hazel eyes.

"Sorry about that, you ready?" Rich asked as he took the seat across from hers.

"Yes."

"We'll start with the interview portion, then I'll show you where you can change for the audition. Afterwards, I'd be happy to walk you around and answer any questions you may have," he explained.

Roni nodded and clasped her hands together, placing them in her lap.

"Relax. It's just me, and it's just you," Rich said with a warm smile.

"I know," Roni said, "but this is really important to me, and it's been a while since I've danced in front of anyone."

"You'll be great," Rich assured her. "So, I want to start by saying that, as long as everything goes well today, I'm open to renting the space to you for the studio."

Rich was rewarded with a dazzling smile. It took his breath away. He cleared his throat and went on, "I'd like to hear your ideas for the space."

"I want to run the studio full time, and for all ages. I'll start off with ballet and tap for the youngest dancers, and offer contemporary to the more serious dancers. Ballet and tap teach the fundamentals, so it's a great place to start. If I get enough interest, I'd offer more classes in different styles, but I think these will be a good place to start. I have some money saved, and would like to focus on the studio full time. I'll still work part time at the Bar & Grill, at least for now, but eventually, I'd like this to be my only priority. I'll train each class for an end of year performance that we could hold at the town theater. I'll look into all that, but, basically, I want to offer a full-fledged dance studio to the community." Roni's eyes had lit up with each sentence, her excitement over this opportunity apparent.

Rich couldn't help but become enthused along with her.

"That sounds great, Roni."

"Can you show me the space you were thinking of? I'd be interested in including a resale section, where I can sell dance attire and accessories, if possible."

Rich led her towards the largest studio space, which he'd had finished with the dance studio in mind.

"Well, there is a small room off the back of the studio, which I figured could be used as an office, it's not really big enough for resale. However, we will have a resale section here at the Center. We will offer attire, equipment, and accessories for the different classes we have here. I planned to get with each instructor and see what items they wanted to have available for resale to start. As time goes on, we can add or takeaway items as needed. You would have a say in what is sold, if that works."

Roni grinned up at him, "You've thought of everything."

Rich smiled back at her, pleased that she seemed to share his enthusiasm. "I really hope so."

They stood there, smiling at each other for a moment, until Rich realized that he was still conducting an interview.

"Let me show you to the locker room. You can change and meet me back in the studio."

Roni nodded and followed him to the women's locker room, which was on the other side of the room he was staying in.

"Did you pick a room next to the locker room on purpose?"

That made Rich chuckle, but he just shook his head and walked away, giving her time to get ready.

Rich moved the chairs back out of the way, placing his in the back corner, in order to give her access to the entire space.

When she walked in, his breath caught and his entire body seemed to stiffen.

Her hair was piled on top of her head, black boy shorts showcased her long, lean legs, and a small black tank molded to her slender form. Her feet were bare. For some reason that last bit of bare skin made Rich feel like he was going to lose his mind.

She padded softly across the wood floor to the radio and hooked her iPod in. She stretched languidly in front of the mirror, seeming to have forgotten Rich's presence.

With each stretch, Roni became more limber, and Rich became harder. He was starting to think this audition was a terrible idea.

Terribly awesome.

When she was finished stretching, she pressed play on her iPod and positioned herself in the center of the room. As Christina Perri's voice filled the room, Roni began to move.

Rich couldn't have uttered a sound if he wanted to. He was completely, and utterly mesmerized.

Her body seemed to be made for this. The movement was so natural, so sensual, Rich had to focus on keeping himself in the chair… his entire body seemed to scream at him to get up and go to her.

As the music stopped, Roni turned to him, her chest heaving as she fought to catch her breath.

"That's the contemporary. It'll be for the advanced classes. I can show you the basic ballet and tap steps for the younger classes if you'd like."

Rich tried to speak, but squeaked instead.

He felt his face grow warm as he cleared his throat and tried again, "Um, no. That won't be necessary."

Roni stretched a bit as she walked towards him, a puzzled smile on her face.

"You okay?"

Rich stood, willing his legs to hold him as he tried to look cool and unaffected. "Yeah, I'm great."

Roni stopped in front of him, looked shyly at her foot, then back into his eyes. "Did you like it? Can I rent the space and work here?"

A stray piece of hair fell from her bun, down the side of her face. Without thinking, Rich reached over and tucked it behind her ear, his hand stopping as it touched the side of her face. He watched as Roni's pupils dilated and her tongue darted out to moisten her lips.

Shit, he thought, this was going to be harder than he'd anticipated if the state of the throbbing in his pants was any indication.

"I loved it. You're an amazing dancer," Rich said, his hand gently caressing her cheek. "You can rent the space."

She surprised him by launching into his arms and throwing hers around his neck. She hugged him hard, then pulled back with a laugh. "Sorry, I'm all sweaty."

He may have whimpered at that, but he'd sure as hell never admit it. Instead he smiled back at her and nodded, then pulled away from her until he could no longer feel the glorious slippery heat of her skin.

Roni gathered up her stuff and bounded out of the studio with a shout of joy. She said she'd see him later as she walked out the door, leaving him hot and hard, as he turned and headed towards the men's locker room.

He was going to need a cold shower. Glacier cold.

Chapter Eight

Roni still felt the adrenaline pumping when she walked into the Bar & Grill to meet her friends. She'd felt great during the audition, although the thought of Rich watching her did make her self-conscience, it had also been invigorating.

She walked up to the table where Nicole, Briana, and Kara were already sitting, and was greeted by a chorus of "Hello's".

Nicole was showing off her engagement ring when Roni scooted in next to Briana. She gave the other woman a hug and said, "It's good to see you again Bree."

"You too," Briana said as she brushed her dark hair out of her face. "I'm so happy we could come home for the holidays."

Briana looked up and smiled when the door opened again, she waved at Rich as he walked in. Roni watched as he walked over to where Pete was tending bar. As he said something to Pete, the new bartender, Claire sauntered over to him.

She was a beautiful, bawdy redhead that had been on the job for about two weeks. She seemed intent on showing Rich all of her assets. Roni could hear the deep tenor of Rich's voice as he said, "Howdy, darlin'."

Roni rolled her eyes and turned her focus back to the girls.

Rich was nothing but a flirt.

Briana, Nicole, and Kara were all watching her, then looked pointedly at Rich.

"Whatchya lookin' at?" Kara said with a saucy grin.

"Just Rich, doin' what Rich does best," Roni replied dryly.

"Oh… He's pretty good at that, but I wouldn't say that's what he does best," Kara said with a big laugh as she nudged Briana.

Roni narrowed her eyes at the two of them.   "What do you mean?" She asked.

"Let's just say, there is a very good reason that the ladies love Rich," Kara replied. "He knows how to treat women."

"You've slept with him?" Roni asked in a whisper as she leaned over the table towards Kara.

"Sure," Kara shrugged. "Before Pete, of course. You can always count on Rich for a good time."

"Kara," Briana warned in a low voice, "You know that's not all Rich is… A ladies man." She looked over at Roni and smiled. "I mean, it's the truth, he does know his way around the female form, but he's so much more than that."

Roni choked on the water she'd just sipped, "Wait a minute… You too?" She looked around at her friends. "Is there anyone he hasn't slept with?"

Nicole raised her hand, causing them all to laugh.

"Roni, Rich has been single for as long as I've known him. He makes sure that the girls he's with know that he isn't looking for anything serious. He's not a heartbreaker or a *dog*, he's just a man that loves being with women," Briana explained.

"Hey, whatever he wants to do is his business, not mine," Roni said, all of her suspicions about Rich had just been confirmed by her friends.

"He's a great guy, Roni," Kara said.

"The best," Nicole agreed.

"Don't hold his past against him," Briana added.

"Guys, there's nothing going on between Rich and I," Roni said.

Just then, Rich turned to see them all staring at him. He grinned broadly and Briana waved her fingers at him. He gave them a wink, said something to Pete and Claire, then walked over to their table.

"This must be my lucky day," Rich drawled as he got closer. "Such a beautiful group of women."

"Hi, Rich," Nicole, Kara, and Briana said in unison, causing them to giggle and Rich to raise an eyebrow.

He looked over at Roni, "Hello again."

Roni just said, "Hi."

"You coming to the party at Kent's on Christmas?" Nicole asked him.

"Absolutely, what time are ya'll lookin'at?"

"Around four. That will give everyone time with their families, then we can have some drinks and apps before dinner."

"Sounds perfect," Rich said. "Do you need me to bring anything?"

"Well, we figured we'd pull names for gifts, so I'll text you with the details. Other than that, just bring yourself," Nicole replied.

"Great," Rich said. "Well, I gotta get back, so I'll leave you ladies to your meal. Oh, and Roni, thanks again for the dance earlier. You were magnificent."

That said he gave them each a smile, then walked back out the door. Once he was gone, they all turned to look at Roni.

"The dance?" Nicole asked with a big grin.

"I had my interview and audition today," Roni replied. "I'm going to rent space at the Rec Center and open a Dance Studio."

"That's wonderful," Briana said. "This Rec Center is really turning into something great. I'm so happy for Rich, and for you. I can't wait to see what they've done so far. Especially in the kitchen."

"What I saw today looked amazing," Roni admitted. "What's this about Christmas?"

"That's what we were talking about when you walked in, before we were all distracted by Rich's hotness," Kara said with a laugh.

"I just talked Kent into it last night," Nicole said. "I thought it would be fun for us to all get together and spend Christmas with each other. Have a nice meal and exchange gifts. You in?"

"Of course," Roni said. She loved Christmas.

They all started talking about the holidays and the Rec Center. Roni couldn't help but think about what everyone had said about Rich. Lord knew he was hot. There was no denying that. Nor could she deny the attraction she'd been having to him lately. With everything she knew about him though, she didn't think she could ever act on it.

She just wasn't interested in a guy that was so obviously opposed to commitment, and who'd been with so many women.

He was he exact opposite of what she needed, wasn't he?

Chapter Nine

Rich broke down the last box, grabbed the bag of trash and the rest of the boxes, and headed out back to the dumpster. He'd finally finished unpacking his room. There wasn't a lot to it, but it felt great knowing that it was all his.

The small space held his bed, his speed bag, and had a flat screen mounted on the wall. With the small bathroom attached, the amazing kitchen a few feet away, and his office in the front of the warehouse, he figured he had everything he needed. Add to that the access to his own fitness center and boxing ring, and one might say he was living the dream.

After unloading his trash, he entered the warehouse through the back by the boxing ring; he stopped in when he noticed Jason using the equipment.

"Hey, man," Rich said to his new friend and manager of the boxing/fitness portion of the Rec Center. "How's the equipment?"

Jason kicked the heavy bag one more time, then turned to Rich, "It's great, Rich. I used the weights, tried out the cardio equipment yesterday and today, and have been in here for the past hour. Everyone's gonna love it. I know I do."

Rich went over to the mini fridge and pulled out a water for himself and Jason. He held onto the water as Jason ran a small towel over his face, and his short jet black hair, then handed him the bottle.

"I'm getting really pumped for the grand opening," Rich said. "Everything is coming together and we are on track for the opening on January 2nd. I can't believe it's only a couple weeks away. I have some friends coming in for a tour in a bit, then a couple more interviews this afternoon. If you wouldn't mind taking a look at the web page I've been working on, I'd appreciate it."

"Sure thing," Jason replied. He paused then asked, "Hey, I was just wondering, did you hire that tiny brunette?"

"Who, Alex?" Rich asked. "Yeah, I did."

"What's she gonna teach? Art or something?"

Rich chuckled, "No, Karate."

Jason looked surprised, then smiled, "No, shit?"

"Why you askin'? Interested?"

Jason looked at Rich, then down at his own arms, which were covered in tattoos. "Yeah, right. I've seen her around town; she works for the Mayor's office. I don't think she'd be interested in a guy like me."

"What, you mean a smart, good-looking boxer, with the pre-requisite "bad boy" tattoos and motorcycle? Yeah, doubt she'd find that attractive," Rich said dryly with a smirk. Then he looked at his friend seriously, "Don't sell yourself short."

Jason nodded at him and slapped him on the back, then turned back towards the bag and started kicking.

Rich headed out towards the office and was almost there when the door open and his friends came piling in. He smiled at their ooohs and aaahs.

"It looks beautiful," Briana said as she gave him a hug.

"I can't believe how great it looks," Nicole said as she waited her turn for a hug. He obliged, then turned to give the hand-clasp, half-hug to his friends.

"I'm glad ya'll could come by," Rich said. "There are still a few spots that are under construction, but you'll get the idea."

Briana jumped up and down, "Can we see the kitchen first?"

"Hold your horses, shorty," Rich said with a chuckle. "We'll start here, then make our way around the Center."

"O-kay," Briana said with a mock pout.

They started with the office. It held two large dark oak desks with leather chairs. There was a sofa along one wall and a large white board along the other. It was simple and uncluttered now, but would surely be the hub of the Rec Center.

"Hey, my dad said he talked to you the other day. Said you called to set it up," Colin said as he looked around the room. "How'd that go?"

"Great. I figured who better to get advice about opening a business in this town, than your father. He's been running the store for years. He gave a lot of insight," Rich answered his friend.

"That's good. He's very smart and one helluva business man," Colin said. "It was smart of you to contact him."

"I have my moments," Rich said with a chuckle as he led them out of the office and towards the kitchen.

Briana started to squeal when she caught her first glimpse of steel, and took off running for the kitchen.

Colin laughed at his girlfriends' excited shouts. He turned to Rich, "She's going to want to cook in there every day until we go back to Austin."

"You won't get any complaints from me," Rich said with a smile. "I've been living on frozen meals and bar food."

They walked in to find Briana running her hands along the stainless steel countertops and gazing lovingly at the appliances.

"I can't wait to break it in," Briana said.

"Just let me know when you're ready," Rich replied.

After a few minutes of adulation, Briana allowed Rich to continue with the tour. They went into the women's locker room, where the girls voiced their appreciation of the separate showers with shampoo and conditioner dispensers and the sauna.

They poked their heads into Rich's personal space briefly, then made their way to the studios.

"Is this the one that Roni will be using," Kent asked.

"Yup," Rich answered. "There is a small room in the back that she can use as an office."

"I'm sure she's thrilled," Kent said with a smile. "I can see her in here. If you guys haven't seen Roni dance, you're in for a treat."

"She's amazing," Nicole added. Rich just nodded his head in agreement, then ushered them out of the space.

He gestured down the hall back towards the entrance, where the construction crew was working. "That will be a large resale area. I'll talk to the instructors for input on things that clients will need for their classes, as well as items they think would sell well."

"Oooh, goody," Briana said, her eyes brightening at the idea. "I have some catalogs I can show you."

Rich chuckled at her enthusiasm and said, "Sounds good, Bree."

He showed them the section that the construction crew would work on last. It was where the rooms for the other classes, such as Art and Music, would be built. They walked back towards the fitness center and Boxing area. Rich was excited about showing them his favorite part of the Center.

This time it was the guys turn to make sounds of pleasure and stroke the equipment lovingly, while the girls stood back and laughed.

"Would you like us to leave you alone," Briana asked in jest.

"Hey, we let you have your moment with the kitchen, give us ours, "Colin responded.

They walked around and tried out some of the equipment before heading back towards the basketball court.

"The guys bathroom is a mirror image of the women's, so we don't need to go in there," Rich said as the passed it. They stopped at the doors of the court and peaked in the windows. "They just laid the flooring and will put up the baskets before adding some bleachers."

"I am totally amazed at everything you have accomplished here," Kent said as they made their way back towards the entrance. "I think it's going to be wildly successful. I know I'll be first in line to join that gym and check out the boxing area. You should be really proud of yourself, Rich."

"Thanks, man," Rich said. "I wanted to ask if we could do an interview about the Rec Center for the paper. And take out an advertisement for the Grand Opening."

"Absolutely, "Kent said. "I'll check the calendar when I get back and I'll call you to set up a time."

"Great. Bree, I'll be finished with interviews this week, then I will contact everyone to set up a meeting about the Grand Opening. Start thinking about what you'd like to serve. Also, I'll come up with some mock advertisements for each of the classes, and I'd love your input on the cooking and baking flyers."

"Sounds wonderful," Briana said. "I'd love to help in any way I can before we leave. I almost wish we still lived here, so I could offer classes full time."

"Nah, we need you at Culinary School, so you can come back and teach the other instructors the things that you learn," Rich said as he gave her a hug. "Thanks for coming by guys."

"Thanks for letting us have a peak," Nicole said. "I will pull the names for the gift exchange tonight and will text you your person."

"Perfect, I'm looking forward to it," Rich said.

He saw them out, then walked back to his office to start on the paperwork.

Chapter Ten

Roni hung up the phone, walked to the window, and stared outside at the vast expanse of Texas land. She brought her hands together and squeezed, trying to minimize the shaking, as a single tear escaped and slid down her face.

She was officially divorced.

She was only twenty-two, and already had a marriage and a divorce under her belt.

She thought of all the dreams she'd had for herself just four years ago.

She'd graduate high school, go to New York, and become a full time dancer.

She was wrong.

Then she'd met Hank, and those dreams had changed. She thought they'd be married, have kids, and have a beautiful life together.

She was wrong.

Instead, the three years they were together had been a nightmare. A series of fights, fists, and tears.

Now she was here, and was truly happy.

Her new dream was to open her own dance studio, enjoy her friends, and be there for Kent and his family.

Was she fooling herself?

Was it even possible for her to ever be happy? How could she trust her instincts, when everyone she'd until now date had been wrong?

She should be happy that Hank was finally completely out of her life for good, but all she felt was emptiness.

Roni turned and grabbed her purse. It was getting dark, and the construction crews had probably shut down for the day, but she had to go see her studio.

She hopped in her car and drove over to the warehouse, worried that Rich would be out, and no one would be able to let her in. She wasn't getting her key until the next day, when everyone met for their first meeting to discuss marketing, resale, and the Grand Opening.

When she pulled into the lot, she saw his Charger and another vehicle. She got out and tried the door, and was relieved to find it still unlocked. She walked inside and saw Rich and the guys she'd seen hanging around before, Jason, maybe, walking down the hall.

Rather than announce herself, she walked straight to the studio.

She walked inside and spun slowly, inhaling deeply as she moved. The fresh paint and varnish smelled like hope. She perused the room, touching ever surface, trying to convince herself that this was real. This time her dream was going to come true.

As thoughts of Hank crept back into her mind, she lifted her leg onto the bar and began to stretch, not even conscious of what she was doing.

She felt foolish for believing he loved her, even after he'd started to hit her. He was the only man she ever kissed. The only man to ever touch her. She felt cheated thinking about it.

Roni felt unsettled and out of sorts. She needed something to bring her out of this funk. Something to prove that she was still desirable, that this divorce wasn't an ending, but rather, a beginning.

Roni stretched a bit more as her thoughts ran rampant in her head. She heard the front door shut, then the lock being turned. She walked quietly to the door of her studio and saw Rich turning from the front door.

She walked a little more loudly out into the hallway, causing him to start and turn.

"Shit, Roni," Rich said with a quick laugh. "I didn't know you were in here. I thought I was alone. When did you get...?" Before he could finish his sentence, Roni catapulted into his arms, her lips fusing onto his.

Rich stumbled back a step, taken off guard, before he caught himself and began to return her kiss.

She could tell he was surprised, but she had to hand it to him, he went with it.

Her back slammed against the wall and her legs came up around his waist, as their kiss became more frantic. Roni put her hands behind his head and in his hair, running her fingers through and pulling lightly. She suddenly became aware that their bodies were touching in every possible way, and she reveled in the feel of the liquid fire running through her veins. She rocked against him and felt the moan that rumbled through his chest.

She broke from his mouth and trailed kisses along his jaw, loving the feel of the roughness of his skin against her smooth lips. She licked his neck and began to suck on his earlobe, when she heard his sharp intake of breath. His response to her was driving her mad and she tried to press her body even closer to his.

Rich's hand came around to cradle her under her bottom as he backed away from the wall and began to lead her down to his room.

Roni latched on tighter; terrified that he would stop and ask her questions.

He didn't.

Rich kicked open his door and maneuvered around his space until he reached the bed. He lowered them both slowly, Roni still attached to his body, then rocked into her once they reached the mattress.

Roni moaned loudly, the sensations she was having were amazing. She didn't know if it was because it had been so long since she'd been touched this way, or because it was Rich that was touching her, but she knew she wanted to go on feeling this way forever. Utterly alive.

Rich kissed down her neck and over the swell of her breast. He brought his hands up to cup her breasts, kissing and suckling her nipple through the fabric of her shirt, before he sat up, looked down at her button down top and ripped it open. Roni gasped and lifted off of the bed so he could undo the clasp of her bra, eager to have his mouth on her flesh.

He didn't disappoint her.

He removed the rest of her clothing and kissed, nipped, licked, and sucked every inch of her skin. Each touch made Roni more frenzied. The feel of his lips, the rough contrast of his jeans against her, and his fingers. Oh… his fingers. They seemed to be everywhere all at once. Intent on giving her pleasure unlike any she had ever known.

Roni reached for the hem of his t-shirt and tugged, urging him to lift it over his head. Then she worked the button of his jeans, her breath catching when he slid them down, revealing his nakedness underneath.

That first touch of skin on skin felt wonderful. Roni writhed a bit underneath him, wanting to feel his satin skin sliding against hers.

"Holy shit, Roni," Rich moaned against her lips. "You're going to kill me."

The fact that he was so obviously turned on made her feel powerful. She pushed him lightly, so he turned and lay on his back, giving her the ability to gain more control.

She looked down into his handsome face, then leaned down to kiss the cleft in his chin, before claiming his mouth once more. She felt totally confident and comfortable with him. She wanted to do and say things she'd never felt able to do before, and she was certain she was safe with Rich. Certain he wouldn't judge her, or be turned off by anything she did or said.

Roni felt her courage rise with each intake of Rich's breath. With each moan, and with each whimper. She couldn't believe that she'd just made him whimper, it pushed her over the edge.

She told him to keep his hands above his head, then started her descent down his body with her lips. She loved how smooth his skin was over his hard muscles. She kissed across his chest and down over his abs. Then she went back and sucked on his nipples, her body tightening at the sounds he was emitting.

She ran her hands along the length of him, pausing to caress his shaft, her vision greying when he told her to slow down. She slithered back up his body, licking her way up his neck to the soft spot behind his ear before whispering throatily in his ear, "I want to fuck you now."

Roni brought her lips up to his and kissed him as he stared into her eyes. Pupils dilated. Rich reached a hand out and opened the drawer next to his bed. He pulled something out, closed it, then handed her a condom.

"Be my guest," Rich said with a saucy grin.

Roni smiled back at him, then moved down to open the condom and slide it over him.

The smile left her face as she rose back above him and looked down into his hazel eyes. She kept her eyes locked on his and she lowered herself onto him, her body expanding to accept the length of him inside.

"God, you're so tight," Rich murmured, closing his eyes momentarily, letting the sensation fill him.

Once he was fully inside, he jerked his hips involuntarily, telling her to move.

She began to move up and down, the pressure starting to build within her. She moved faster and faster, moving her body to find the right spot. When she found it she began to move quickly, bending down to kiss him briefly, before pulling back and moving even faster. Rich put his hands on her hips to help her stay in place.

Roni didn't worry about trying to keep her building passion to herself. She moaned and shouted to Rich, making sure he didn't stop what he was doing.

Her orgasm shot through her, lighting her body on fire and causing bright dots to color her vision. She wanted to slide down into a puddle on Rich's bed, but his hands at her hips kept her going until he reached his own release.

Roni lay down on top of him, vaguely aware of their sticky bodies and pounding hearts, melding together as they tried to catch their breath.

Her head was next to his on the pillow, her hair fanned out, and she softly kissed the side of his neck, since it was right there.

As their heart rate returned to normal and reality started to set in, Roni began to come out of her sex crazed haze.

Shit, she thought, what did I just do?

She closed her eyes and tried to steady her breathing. God that had been the best sex she'd ever had in her life. Was that normal? Was it always supposed to be like that?

Rich turned his head and she opened her eyes to look into his.

"Hi," he said with a smile, reaching out to move a strand of her hair off of her face.

"Hey," she responded.

"I'm not complaining or anything, but what the hell was that?"

His question brought her fully out of the haze and she sat up abruptly, moving off of him, gathering up her clothes, and walking quickly into the small restroom.

Roni cleaned herself up, got dressed and splashed some water on her face. When she felt composed, she walked back out with a smile on her face.

Rich was still on the bed, only now he was sitting with his back against the wall and a sheet thrown haphazardly over the bottom half of his body. His chest and abs were still visible. Taunting her with their magnificence. Now that she'd tasted him, she was eager for seconds.

"You want to talk about what just happened?" Rich asked.

Roni looked at him and shook her head, "Not really."

Rich chuckled at that.

"I've got to get going," Roni started as she started to inch towards the door.

Rich got up off of the bed, the sheet sliding to the floor as he walked over to reach her.

Roni stood frozen in place at the site before her.

Holy shit, she knew he'd looked good, but seeing him in his full glory almost knocked her on her ass.

She cleared her throat and tried to look in his eyes.

"You're leaving?" He asked when he reached her. He put a hand behind her head and pulled her in, kissing her thoroughly before letting her go.

"Yeah," Roni said. Her voice barely above a whisper. "I've got some stuff to do at home."

Rich rubbed his thumb over her lips, causing her to shiver, and said, "Okay. But we *will* talk about this, Roni."

She nodded at him, then turned and fled.

Friends & Lovers Trilogy

Chapter Eleven

Rich was excited.

Today was going to be his first official meeting with his new employees. He felt like everything was finally real. They were going to discuss schedules, supplies, marketing, and the Grand Opening, plus anything else that came up.

He never thought he'd be so excited for a meeting, but he really was. It was his meeting, in his warehouse, with his employees. Talk about a dream come true.

He may have gone a little overboard, he thought with a chuckle. He had pastries and coffee on the table, with a tablet and pencil at each seat. He had an easel with a white board and markers, ready to show them his ideas and annotate theirs.

Rich looked at his watch, saw he still had fifteen minutes until the meeting started, and headed towards the back to find Jason.

"Hey, man," Rich said when he saw him walking out of the fitness center. "You about ready?"

"Yeah," Jason replied. "I was just making sure everything looked good for the tour."

"Great," Rich said. "I can't thank you enough for all of your help."

"No Problem. I love it here, Rich. I'm happy you took a chance on me."

Rich slapped the other man on the back and they started back towards the front just as the door open and the other employees started to trickle in.

Rich went into his office to give himself a moment to collect his thoughts. He took a few deep breaths and looked at his notes to remind himself what he wanted to talk about.

He walked back into the kitchen and saw that most of the people were seated and had pastries in front of them. No one was talking yet, but at least they were taking the food.

"Go ahead and make yourselves comfortable," Rich said. "Get some coffee and pastries. I'll wait a few more minutes before I begin."

He went to the head of the table and placed his items in front of him as he sat. Jason sat down next to him and grabbed a muffin from the tray. Rich watched as Jason looked over at Alex, who was sitting across from him and in the middle of the table. She looked very petite amongst the boxing trainers that flanked her.

Alex looked up and smiled at Jason when she caught his stare. Jason quickly looked away, causing Rich to chuckle softly. Alex shrugged slightly, then went back to putting creamer in her coffee.

Briana and Roni came into the room laughing. Rich smiled and said, "Morning." He indicated that they should take their seats, his stomach dropping at the site of Roni.

Her hair was back in a ponytail and she wasn't wearing any makeup. She looked like she was on her way to work out, in yoga pants and a form fitting dry-fit top. He couldn't stop the image of her above him, her face full of passion as she'd found her release.

Shit, he thought, he needed to focus on the meeting or he wouldn't make it five more seconds without taking her right on the table in front of everyone.

Rich counted to twenty in his head and thought of the highlights he'd watched on ESPN this morning, to clear the images from his mind.

"Thank you all for coming," Rich began, "We'll go ahead and get started. I want to begin by going around the room. I'll ask each of you to introduce yourself and let everyone know what you will be teaching here."

As his new employees introduced themselves, he thought about what he wanted to talk about next. When Alex was talking, he noticed Jason staring at her with his mouth slightly open, so he kicked his friend under the table.

Jason jerked slightly, and closed his mouth, turning to Rich with a question on his face. Rich gestured with his hand, telling Jason to ease up on the staring. If his friend had any sort of chance with the pretty Karate instructor, he needed to keep the creepy factor down to a minimum.

When it was Briana's turned, he smiled at her enthusiasm as she told the group about the cooking classes she wanted to offer.

He tried to holster his own creepy factor as Roni spoke. He made sure he looked around the table, rather than get caught up in her beauty. But, damn, she was beautiful.

When the introductions were complete, he talked to them about the resale store. He passed out catalogs and told them they had a sheet in front of them that listed websites that they could utilize as well. He said he needed their initial orders to him by the end of the week, so he could have the merchandise on the shelves for the Grand Opening.

"We'll give them free lessons all day during the opening, utilizing the merchandise that you tell me to order for the store. That way, if there are any specific items you need them to purchase in order to take your class; we will have the items readily available. This will make it easier for you and the client, and you will earn money off of the profits." Rich explained as they looked through the catalogs.

"Now, can you tell me what classes you plan to offer during the Grand Opening?" Rich asked. Once again having them go around the table.

When everyone had a chance to speak, Rich asked if anyone had any questions for him, or each other, before moving on to the tour. No one did, so he took them out and showed them around the Center.

Once they had the complete tour, he released them to go to their own respective work areas and said he would be in his office if anyone needed anything before they left.

As she was about to walk away with Briana, Rich called Roni over and asked if he could talk to her for a minute.

"Hey," Rich said softly. "How are you doing?"

"Good," Roni said simply, not quite meeting his eyes.

"Are you busy later?" He asked.

"I have to work."

"When's your next night off?" Rich prompted.

"Why?" Roni asked, looking down at her feet.

"Roni," Rich said, putting his finger under her chin and lifting her face so she was forced to look at him. "What's going on? We need to talk about last night. I'd like to take you out to dinner... So we can talk."

"Dinner? You don't have to do that, Rich. Last night was no big deal."

Rich looked at her with a frown.

"I'm asking you to go out to dinner with me, Roni. What do ya say?"

Roni looked up at him, not saying anything at first, then replied, "I'm off tomorrow night, then I won't be off again until Christmas. We can have dinner tomorrow, if that's what you want."

Rich smiled at her, "Perfect. I'll pick you up at six."

Roni nodded before she turned and walked back towards the kitchen.

Rich went into his office, unsure what his next step with Roni should be. Obviously he'd dated before, but with Roni everything felt different. It wasn't just that he wanted her; last night hadn't changed that at all. If anything, he wanted her more now than he had before. But he felt more than just lust. There was something about Roni that made him want to take care of her. To make her happy. He couldn't dwell on it too much, or it would probably freak him out.

A knock on the door had him looking up. Briana was smiling at him from the doorway.

"Can I come in, boss?" She asked with a chuckle.

"Sure."

"I just wanted to tell you again how proud I am of you, Rich. This place is amazing, and I'm so happy to get to be a part of it. The Grand Opening is going to be amazing."

"Thanks, Bree," Rich said, coming around his desk to give her a hug. "That means a lot."

"I also wanted to remind you about Christmas," Briana said.

"I'll be there," he replied.

"Great, I'll see you then."

He walked her out and said goodbye to her and Roni as they exited the warehouse.

His cell phone buzzed in his pocket, telling him he'd received a text.

Hey, Rich. Just wanted to let you know, you've got Roni for the gift exchange. See ya then, Nic.

Of course he did.

Friends & Lovers Trilogy

Chapter Twelve

Why had she agreed to go on a date with him? Roni wondered as she looked for earrings to match her top. She knew that he was going to want answers for the way she'd behaved the other day. She should be avoiding him, not going out with him.

He'd just looked so cute.

And when she'd looked into his eyes, she would have agreed to anything he asked of her.

She was so confused.

Maybe once he found out about her and her past, he'd lose interest and things could go back to the way there were before she'd jumped him.

God, she still couldn't believe she'd done that. She'd never done anything so, well, *wild*, in her life.

She covered her mouth to suppress a giggle as she thought about it.

She'd never felt so free. Free to do what she wanted without fear of rejection or reprisal. It had been invigorating. And although she knew she was probably playing with fire, she loved the fire that coursed through her at the thought of that freedom.

Rich was a guy who liked to have fun. Maybe he wouldn't mind having some fun with her, totally free of strings or attachments.

Roni looked at herself in the mirror as she put in her earrings. Did she have it in her to have a casual relationship? It was something she'd have to think about.

At six on the dot, Roni hear footsteps on the stairs and took a deep breath. Her stomach jittering as she waited for the knock on the door. Even though she was expecting it, she jumped when Rich's fist connected with the wood.

She smoothed her hair down before she opened the door.

"Hey," Rich said with a smile that lit up his face. His hazel eyes glittered as they looked Roni over. "You look beautiful."

"Thanks," Roni said, returning his smile. She'd figured he'd be dressed casually, so she'd worn a new pair of dark denim jeans with a peasant top and a navy blue cardigan.

Rich nodded and asked, "Are you ready?"

Roni said she was and turned to lock the door as they walked out. She followed him down the stairs to the car.

She took a moment to appreciate the way he filled out his jeans as they walked. When he turned to say something as he opened the car door for her, she jerked her head up to meet his eyes. Her face reddened at the cocky grin that took over his face.

"You checkin' me out sunshine?"

Roni rolled her eyes and said, "You wish." She tried to play it off as she slid into the seat.

"So," Roni began as Rich started to drive. "What made you decide to open a Rec Center?"

"Colin and I were always goofing off, trying to find a field to play ball in, or shooting hoops at one of the neighbors' houses. It seemed like the days we couldn't find a place to get rid of some of that energy, we would end up doing something stupid and getting in trouble." Rich explained with a smile. "I thought if we'd had a place to go after school, and on weekends, where we could take classes in things that interested us, or play sports, we would have gotten into less trouble. Then I came up with the idea of opening a place for kids and adults in our community."

"It's a wonderful idea," Roni said, playing with her hair absently. "I'm so excited to be a part of it."

The drive to the restaurant was a short one, and they were pulling in before she knew it. He'd picked Italian, which was her favorite.

"How'd you know that I love Italian?" Roni asked him as they parked.

"I'm that good," Rich said with a cocky grin. When she looked at him wryly he chuckled and admitted, "I may have asked your brother."

A warm feeling spread though her at his words. He'd taken the time to find out what she liked. That was nice.

She smiled as he walked around the car to open her door.

"Thank you," she said.

"Anytime," Rich responded.

They went in and were seated in a quiet booth in the back corner of the restaurant. Rich asked if she wanted wine, and she said that she did.

They looked over the menu as they waited for the server to bring their wine.

"So," Rich began, "Are you ready to tell me what that was about the other day?"

Roni felt her face flush and her stomach drop at his question. "Really, that's what you want to start out with?"

"Better to get it out of the way," he said softly.

"Okay," Roni took a deep breath. "I don't want to go into the whole sordid story. I'll just say that I used to be married, and I'd found out that day that my divorce was final."

Rich looked surprised. It was obvious that no one had told him that she'd been married. She'd wondered if they would. It almost would have made this easier.

"Why did you get divorced?" he asked.

Roni smiled at the waiter as he poured her wine. She waited for him to finish and to walk away, before she answered Rich's question.

"He wasn't the person I thought he was," Roni explained, not sure how much information she wanted to divulge. "He was possessive, mean, and cheated any chance he got. He wouldn't allow me to do anything he didn't approve of. I just couldn't live that way anymore."

Rich was quiet for a moment, then asked, "Is that why you said you hadn't danced in a while?"

"Yeah," Roni answered a sad look on her face. "Hank hated how much time my dancing took away from our relationship. He not only made me quit, but he went so far as to cut up all of my leotards and he broke all of the figurines I'd collected throughout my life."

The memory of the day when she'd come home to see her treasures destroyed and strewn all over her bed brought back the despair she'd felt. That was the day she'd started to truly hate her husband.

"Hey," Rich said, taking her hand and bringing her focus back to the present. "You don't have to talk about it. I appreciate you telling me."

"It doesn't bother you?" She asked him bluntly.

"What?"

"That I was married," she said. "And that I basically used you for sex."

Rich almost choked on the wine he was drinking, causing her to laugh. He really was very sexy.

Rich quickly composed himself and shot her a grin and a wink, "You can use me for sex anytime."

Roni laughed; relieved that he wasn't making a big deal out of anything she'd told him.

"Seriously," Rich said. "It doesn't bother me that you were married, or that you are divorced. As for using me... I'm happy to help whenever you need it."

He winked at her again, then his face grew serious.

"I do hope, though, that eventually, you may see me as more than that." He looked down, as if he was nervous of what her reaction would be, or that he couldn't believe he'd just said that.

Roni sure couldn't believe it. Her belly fluttered and she squeezed his hand. She hoped he was serious about not caring that she was married before, but she didn't think she was looking for anything other than a casual relationship. At least not yet. She wanted to be totally honest with him, even if it meant him backing away.

"I don't think that I'm looking for anything more," she responded.

He looked back up at her, the disappointment apparent on his face before he quickly removed it with a smile.

"So you mean there's hope?"

Friends & Lovers Trilogy

Chapter Thirteen

Rich was disappointed at Roni's words, but he understood why she'd look to him for a casual relationship. Those are the only kind he'd had since he'd had his heartbroken as a teenager. He knew he would have to prove himself before she would trust him to be anything more.

He had to admit, he was totally surprised that she'd been married. He wasn't sure who knew about it, but he couldn't believe that he hadn't caught wind of it before now. He was being truthful when he said it didn't matter to him, it didn't. She was single now, and she was here with him. That is what mattered.

He could only hope that she would begin to feel for him the way he felt about her. Since the first moment Kent had introduced them at the Bar & Grill, he'd known that she was special, and that she stirred something in him that had been dormant for many years.

He watched her smile absently as she rolled her pasta around her fork and talked about her plans for the dance studio. She was absolutely stunning. He didn't know what kind of man her ex-husband was, but just from the little bit that she'd told him, and the look of sadness that had come over her face when she'd spoken about Hank, he figured the guy was an ass.

Rich hated that anyone could put that look on her face, and he hoped that she'd tell him more about her life. For now, he was happy just to be with her. The candlelight lit up her face, and he would gladly watch her all evening.

"Well, since you shared, I guess it's only fair that I do as well," Rich began, pushing his empty plate to the side and picking up his wine glass to take a drink.

Roni just looked at him and waited patiently for him to say what he needed to.

"I fell in love when I was sixteen," Rich began, his stomach churning at the memory. "Tara and I grew up together. Typical girl next door stuff. I think I began to love her when we were ten and she punched a kid on the playground who made fun of her skinny legs," Rich chuckled at the memory. "Anyway, when we were kids, the three of us were inseparable: Colin, Tara, and me." He paused and looked at her.

Roni smiled her encouragement, urging him to go on.

"Things started to change for us when we started high school. We still hung out together, but not all of the time. She started running with a rough crowd and Colin and I joined the football team. We were practicing all of the time, and although she lived next door, we lost touch. We reconnected the summer we were sixteen. I was on break from football, and school was out. Tara and I started spending every waking moment together. I fell completely and totally in love, like only a teenager can, I guess. I was oblivious to anything but Tara. I barely saw Colin at all that summer, but I didn't care. I only cared about Tara. When practice started back up, I began to hear things. Things about Tara and other guys. I got in a lot of fights, but I was afraid to ask her... I didn't want it to be true. Finally, Colin pulled me aside and told me that Tara had sex with over half of the football team," Rich shook his head and smiled sadly. "I didn't care. I loved her, and what she'd done in the past didn't matter, but then he told me that she'd been seeing other guys all summer, the entire time we were together."

Rich paused and took Roni's hand in his, "I know it doesn't seem like that big of a deal. Not now and not compared to your marriage, but at sixteen, I was absolutely devastated. When I confronted Tara, she admitted it flat out. She didn't think it was a big deal. We both said some nasty things and I vowed I'd never let another girl get me so wrapped up again."

Roni squeezed his hand, and he looked up at her, his grief apparent in his eyes.

"She died our senior year."

"Oh, my gosh," Roni exclaimed. "I'm so sorry."

"It's okay," he said. "I hadn't seen her since we'd had it out that summer."

"What happened?" She asked.

"Car accident. She was out with her friends and they'd been drinking. None of them survived," Rich took another sip of his wine and said, "Let's talk about something else."

When the waiter cleared their plates and asked if they'd like dessert, Rich looked at Roni and crooked his eyebrow.

"Oh, no, thanks," she said patting her stomach. "I'm totally stuffed."

Rich shook his head at the waiter and put his hand out to hold hers lightly.

"Would you like to go to a movie, or rent one?" He asked, hoping she wasn't ready for their date to be over.

"Nicole and I have a bunch at the apartment, I'm sure we can find something to watch," Roni answered.

His stomach dropped and cock jumped. "Is Nicole home?"

"No," Roni said with a smile. "She spends most nights at Kent's. She won't officially move over there until after the wedding, but she essentially lives there already."

Rich felt a flash of heat as he thought about being alone with Roni at her place.

Jeez, his body was reacting like he was fifteen again. He needed to get a grip.

"Okay, sounds great."

Roni chatted about the items she wanted to get for the resale store while they made the trip to her house. Rich tried to listen, but his hormones were going haywire.

When they'd had sex before it had been totally impulsive and unexpected, he hadn't had time to think, only to react. Now, it was all he could think about. He realized that they might not even have sex, at least his mind did. The rest of him was fully tuned in and ready to go.

Roni's perfume teased him every time she shifted in her seat, the timber of her voice rolled over him as she spoke, and he gripped the steering wheel tighter to keep from stroking her long blonde hair. His every sense seemed to be on high alert. It was all he could do not to pull over and ravage her in the front seat.

Oblivious to Rich's thoughts, Roni reached out and touched his bicep as she spoke. Rich bit back a groan and thanked God when they pulled into the apartment parking lot.

Rich watched the sway of her hips as she climbed the stairs. She paused to put her key in the lock; he leaned in and breathed in slightly. Shit, not only did she look like sunshine, she smelled like it.

Roni opened the door and flipped on the light. Rich looked around briefly, making sure they were indeed alone, before walking up behind Roni and pressing his lips on her shoulder. He felt the shiver run through her body and he lost the ability to think clearly.

"Are you okay with this?" Rich asked breathlessly. He wanted her badly, but he wanted to make sure she was as into it as he was.

"Oh, yeah," Roni said with a smile, letting her head fall to the side to give him better access to her neck.

His tongue replaced his lips, causing Roni to groan. Rich turned her slowly, until her eyes met his.

"I know that you want to keep this casual," Rich said softly. When she nodded he continued, "But while I'm sleeping with you, I am sleeping with *only* you. I would appreciate the same from you."

He didn't want to scare her or put more pressure on her than she wanted, but he couldn't bear the thought of anyone else touching her.

Roni looked up at him and put her arms around his neck. "I don't think that'll be a problem, since my ex-husband is the only other man I've slept with."

Rich's eyes widened slightly and his stomach coiled with need. He brought his mouth down to hers, kissing her thoroughly as he lifted her and urged her legs around him. He carried her back to her bedroom and set her gently on the bed.

He walked over and turned the light on, then walked back towards the bed, stripping his shirt as he moved.

Roni leaned back on the bed and watched him, her eyes growing heavy with desire. Rich decided to have a little fun with it and began to dance slowly as he took his clothes off. Roni began to giggle at his exaggerated movements.

When he was wearing nothing but a smile, he went to her and leaned his body into hers.

When he put his mouth to hers she said, "Leave the dancing to me," then she laughed out loud.

His muscles strained as he held himself over her, only their lips touching. He kissed her until she was no longer laughing.

Her lips felt plump and soft beneath his. He could kiss her all night and never get tired of the way they felt against his. He laid his naked body against her, freeing up his hands to roam over her.

He worked on getting her sweater off, not wanting to separate his lips from hers, but needing to feel her skin against his.

Roni pushed up off of the bed to help him remove her clothes, causing her body to rub him in all the right places. Rich got up to give her the room she needed and helped her remove her clothes. By the time they got to her socks, they were fighting over who got to take it off.

After wrestling with the sock, they were both laughing so hard they had to stop to catch their breath.

The comic relief had helped to bring him out of the craze. When he looked down at Roni's naked form, he was ready to enjoy every inch of her with a clear mind.

Roni scooted back on the bed, a sexy little smile still lingering on her face, and laid her head on a pillow. Her golden hair fanned out around her, and the look in her eyes had him crawling up to her.

Where last time was fast and feverish, this time he planned to take his time and savor their time together. What she said about him being only the second guy she'd ever been with, made him want to show her how much pleasure he could bring her.

He took his time on her throat, loving the sounds she made as he licked and sucked the sensitive area below her ear. His mouth traveled down to savor each breast. Her back arched and he knew she was as turned on and ready to burst as he was. He continued his descent, taking a moment to kiss her flat stomach lightly, the quivering of her muscles causing his body to grow harder.

Roni's legs opened and fell to the side as his tongue traveled lower. He felt her heat and her pulse as he kissed his way to the place he most wanted to be. Her hips thrust up and she moaned loudly as his tongue found her. He nuzzled her slowly, taking his time, using his mouth to make her come. She started to whimper and her body jerked slightly, letting him know she was almost there. He concentrated on the pressure of his tongue and brought his lips together to suck softly. His hands moved under her firm behind and lifted her even closer to him.

Her release almost caused his own. His senses were alive with the taste, smell, and feel of her. He was surrounded.

He grabbed the condom off of the floor and rose above her. He put the protection on deftly and looked into her eyes as he slid inside of her, inch by inch.

He wasn't in a hurry. He moved slowly in and out, kissing her face gently, before pulling back and locking his hands with hers. He watched her, feeling more connected to Roni than he'd ever felt to anyone. Watching her eyes as he moved within her was the most erotic thing he'd ever felt. He held off his own release until he saw the pleasure building on her face. When he did, he let go of her hands and brought her legs up over his shoulders. He saw her eyes dilate at the deeper sensation and began to thrust harder, running the tip of his cock against her g-spot.

"Yes," Roni said softly, biting her lips and closing her eyes as she tried to focus on what she was feeling. "Right there."

He loved that she wasn't afraid to be vocal. It turned him on that much more, and the look on her face nearly did him in. He kept thrusting until she started to gasp and he felt her tighten around him. Her legs dropped off of his shoulders as he came. He kept his hands on her hips until he was spent.

Her legs relaxed on the bed and he laid himself gently on top of her, careful to keep most of his weight on his arms.

It took a few minutes to catch his breath. When he did, he rolled to the side and curled her in to him. He kissed her forehead and rubbed her back slowly.

When they were both breathing normally he asked, "So, you ready to watch that movie now?"

Roni laughed and looked up at him. "Sure." She kissed him softly, then pulled back. "Rich?"

"Yeah?"

"Can we just keep this simple?" She asked. "I mean, keep it between us for now?"

At this point, Rich thought, she could have asked him to dance around the room in a cat suit and he would have agreed. He chuckled slightly and responded, "Sure."

Chapter Fourteen

Roni felt a little awkward spending Christmas Eve and Christmas at her brother's house. She didn't want to impose on Kent and Nicole's first holiday together, but she didn't want to be alone either.

Briana and Colin were spending the holiday with their families, Rich was with his, and Pete had taken Kara home to meet his parents in Vegas. She certainly wasn't going to go back to Detroit to spend Christmas with her parents, so when Kent had told her to come stay with him, she'd agreed.

"Are you sure I won't be an imposition?" Roni had asked him.

"Roni," Kent had replied, holding her face in his hands. "You're my family. You could never be an imposition. It should never be a question; we will be spending all of our holidays together."

He'd pulled her into a hug and Roni closed her eyes and let the peace that Kent always offered her, overcome her.

When she'd walked into Kent's kitchen, where Nicole was making Christmas Eve dinner, she'd wanted to make sure her friend was okay with her being there too. She didn't want to cause any trouble between the couple.

Hey, Nic," Roni said, giving the other girl a hug. "Merry Christmas."

"Merry Christmas, Roni," Nicole responded with a big grin.

"I hope it's okay that I'm here."

Nicole had stopped what she was doing and put her hands on her hips. "Of course it's okay. Kent is your brother. I know how close you are, I envy you both for that. You will always be welcome here, not matter what the occasion. You're my family too, Roni. We are the only family we have, and I hope we spend all of our important moments together."

Roni felt her eyes tear up at Nicole's words. She pulled her into another big hug, then pulled back and wiped her eyes with the back of her hand. "Do you need any help?"

They made dinner and enjoyed a quiet night together. They'd exchanged gifts between the three of them and Roni had gone to bed to give them some time together.

Now they were in the kitchen again, this time prepping for their Christmas get together with their friends.

Roni was wearing the new emerald green blouse that Nicole had given her for Christmas.

They were putting out appetizers when the first knock sounded on the door. Kent opened it and said, "Merry Christmas," to Briana and Colin as they walked in. Briana handed him a bottle of wine and Colin asked where to put the presents.

They were all hugging and saying hello when Rich snuck in behind them.

"Merry Christmas," Rich bellowed, announcing his arrival. "Let's get this party started!"

He gave Kent a half hug, then asked where he should put the two bottles of champagne he'd brought. When he passed Roni on the way to the fridge, he leaned in close and whispered in her ear, "Merry Christmas. I've been waiting to see you all day."

Roni didn't respond, but she felt the shiver spread from her ear down to her toes. She just smiled and took his coat, along with the others, and put them on Kent's bed. When she turned to go back out, Rich was standing in the doorway, a dangerous look on his face.

She started to speak, but only managed a squeak before his lips were upon her.

When he pulled back she was breathless, "What was that for?"

"You smelled so good, I wanted a taste," Rich said with a wicked grin, before turning and walking back out the bedroom door.

Roni gave herself a moment to regain her composure. She pulled out her chapstick and ran it over her lips, before returning to the party.

She went into the kitchen to help Nicole pour the champagne and pass it out. When she had her glass, she took a big sip and breathed in deeply, closing her eyes as she thought, "Rich is harder to resist than I thought he would be." She bit back a giggle before joining the group in the living room.

They were settled in listening to Briana and Colin talk about their Christmas Eve with his family and Christmas day with hers, when a cheerful knock sounded on the door. Roni wasn't sure what tune they were trying to play, but it brought a smile to her lips. The smile bloomed fully as Kara came bounding in, dragging Pete behind her.

"We got married!" Kara yelled.

Everyone got to their feet, scrambling to get to Kara and Pete and shouting their congratulations. Pete's face turned as red as his hair, but the look on his face was pure bliss.

"Oh. My. God." Briana yelled. She held Kara's hands in hers and they jumped up and down. Shouting and laughing.

Rich slapped Pete on the back and congratulated him, while Kent handed him a glass of champagne.

"Tell us everything," Nicole said over the shouts, her eyes glazed over with unshed tears. Roni smiled as her future sister searched out her brother and held him tight as they listened to Kara's excited explanation.

"So, we went and spent time with Pete's family and everyone was super sweet and nice to me," Kara held Pete's hand in hers as she spoke. "Pete's parents are unreal, like something off of TV. Anyway, we were having a great time and we decided to hit up some casinos. When we were driving down Las Vegas Boulevard and I saw all of the chapels it just hit me, so I proposed to Pete."

Pete's face was on fire, but he continued to smile and nodded, "She did. I've been wanting to ask her, but she was so against even starting a relationship, that I was afraid I'd scare her if I asked."

Kara reached up to give Pete a kiss. "I love you."

"I love you, too."

"So," Kara continued. "He was shocked for a minute, but then he said yes. We did all of the paperwork and stuff yesterday and got married this morning."

"What did you wear? Were Pete's parents there? Why didn't you call me right away?" Briana shot out the questions one after the other, causing everyone to laugh.

"I'm sorry, Bree," Kara said, hugging her friend. "I wanted to call you right away, but then we decided it would be more fun to tell everyone in person. Yes, Pete's entire family came, which I thought was pretty sweet, since we gave them one day's notice and got married on Christmas morning. And I wore my yellow dress with white lilies in my hair and in my hand. We have pictures, wanna see?"

Everyone went back to the living room and passed around the pictures of Kara and Pete's impromptu wedding.

Roni looked around at her friends, they were all so happy and in love with each other. She felt a tug in her stomach as she caught Rich's eye and he winked at her. She gave him a small smile, then focused on the pictures that were being passed her way. Kara and Pete were glowing in them. Roni laughed at Pete's expression in one, he was looking at Kara like he'd just won a million bucks. It was so sweet.

Nicole announced that dinner was ready. Everyone got up to make their plates and sat around the table. They feasted on ham, sweet potatoes, green beans, salad, cranberries, and sweet rolls.

Roni ate so much that she considered opening the top button of her pants. Rich was finishing up his second plate and Roni just had to say, "How can you keep eating, Rich?"

"I gotta maintain this sexy physique," Rich answered back with a grin as he pushed his stomach out to make it look like he had a big belly instead of the hard as steel abs he possessed.

Roni rolled her eyes and shot back, "It'll take more than a good meal to make you sexy."

"Jeez, would you two just do it already?" Colin asked with a grin.

Roni blushed as Kent yelled, "Hey, watch it Colin."

Roni avoided looking at Rich, but she felt his eyes on her. She got up and started to clear the table. The girls all helped while the guys went into the living room to catch up on the football game.

"Why do the guys always get out of cleaning up?" Roni asked. She was not a fan of doing the dishes.

"Kent usually helps, but I figured since it's a holiday and football is a Christmas tradition, I won't give him a hard time about sitting this one out." Nicole said.

Once they had everything cleaned and put away, they went out to join the guys and Briana said, "Present time!"

Nicole went to the tree and started bringing presents over, passing them out, she said, "Let's wait until everyone has their present before we start. Do we want to open them one at a time or all at once?"

"One at a time," Briana said eagerly. "I want to see everyone open theirs."

Roni hated everyone watching her as she opened presents. She always worried that she'd get something she didn't like, then she'd have to try and pretend she did. That was how just about every Christmas had gone while she was growing up. Her parents always got her the most random gifts: a toaster oven, a pack of knee high socks, a candy bar… One year she'd opened a six pack of beer. She was eight. It turned out it was for her dad, but still.

Colin began to open his first. She'd had his name and had asked Briana for some suggestions on what to get him. There limit was twenty dollars, but she'd been able to find a place to engrave his name and team logo on a name plate for his desk.

"This is great, Roni," Colin said with a smile. "I'll put it on my desk as soon as I get back."

He stood up and she met him for a hug. "Merry Christmas."

They went around the room opening their gifts. Briana got an apron that said *Kiss the Cook*, Kent got a couple new ties, Kara got the new Florence and The Machine C.D. with temporary tattoos, Pete got a deluxe wine opener set, Rich got a new Dallas Cowboy's hat, and Nicole got a new bracelet. Kent picked Nicole's name and admitted he went over the twenty dollar limit.

Roni was the last person to open her gift; she looked down and turned the box in her hand. It was from Rich. She looked up at him, but he didn't smile or wink at her, he just watched her with a serious expression on his face.

She swallowed, trying to remove the nervous lump from her throat, then carefully opening the present. It was a plain brown box. She struggled to get the tape off, so Kent grabbed some scissors and handed them to her. She felt all eyes on her and wondered if the agony would every end.

She finally got the box opened. She pulled out tissue paper only to find that whatever was inside was wrapped in bubble wrap and taped up.

She took the scissors again and began to cut at the tape. When she got all of the tape cut and unraveled the bubble wrap, her breath caught in her throat and she carefully lifted each piece up. There were three figurines, each in a different stage of dance. She looked at each one reverently, holding it up and turning it, so she could memorize the beauty of each piece.

Roni looked up at Rich, and cradling the figurines to her chest, walked up to him, put her hand behind his head, and drew his lips to hers. She kissed him deeply, allowing her tongue a moment to sweep through his mouth. She pulled back and rested her forehead against his.

"Thank you."

It took her a moment before the comments from their friends began to register.

"Whoa," Pete exclaimed.

"I guess they already did," this came from Colin.

"What the heck?" Kent's voice said softly.

"Shhh," Nicole replied.

Roni pulled away and smiled sheepishly at her friends, avoiding her brother's eyes, then she turned back to Rich.

"So much for simple," Rich whispered with a smile.

Friends & Lovers Trilogy

Chapter Fifteen

Since there were only a few days until the opening of the Rec Center and Briana and Colin were returning to Austin the day after that, everyone decided that they wanted to go out dancing.

Well, the girls decided… The guys just went along with it.

Rich slapped some cologne on, made sure there weren't any holes in his jeans or t-shirt, and figured he was ready. He turned off the lights as he walked through the Rec Center, locking up before turning to get in the car with Kent and Nicole.

As they pulled out and headed towards Roni's, Kent asked the question Rich had been dreading since Christmas.

"What's up with you and my sister?"

Rich met his friends' eyes in the rear view mirror. "We're just hanging out, nothing too serious, just like Roni wants."

"What do you want?" Kent asked softly.

"I like her, man. I have since you introduced her to us," Rich admitted.

"You like a lot of girls," Kent said, not giving Rich an inch.

"I know," Rich said. "I'm not going to lie to you and say that I haven't touched another girl since I met your sister, but there's been no one else since I moved home. And there won't be, not while I'm with Roni. I really like her."

"Be careful with her," Kent replied. "She hasn't had a lot of good guys in her life. I hope you'll change that."

Rich smiled and said, "Thanks, man, I will."

When Roni got into the car, everyone was silent. She scooted in next to Rich and looked around.

"Were you guys just talking about me?"

"Why would we want to do that?" Rich asked playfully.

Roni leaned forward, hit her brother on the shoulder, and glared at him in the rearview mirror.

"Kent, my sex life is none of your business."

Kent turned to glower at Rich, who turned to look out the window.

Roni was going to get him killed.

When Kent stopped glaring at the side of his head and pulled out of the parking lot, Rich turned to Roni.

She looked stunning in a black skirt with a charcoal grey sweater. Rich leaned over to whisper in her ear.

"Aren't you going to get hot, dancing in that sweater?"

She grinned at him and responded, "I have a tank top underneath, so if it gets hot, I'll take the sweater off. And, I can put my hair up."

His body got hot as he thought of her taking off her sweater. Suddenly, his jacket was stifling, and he had to take it off. Roni chuckled and snuggled in to his side.

"This is going to take some getting used to," Kent mumbled from the front. Nicole punched him lightly in the arm and said, "Get a grip, Kent."

"So, is everyone else meeting us there?" Rich asked, trying to change the subject.

"Yeah, Bree, Colin, Kara and Pete are riding together. Bree texted me a while ago, saying they are on their way. They'll probably beat us by a few minutes," Nicole said.

Rich sat back and enjoyed the feel of Roni's hand in his as he and Kent discussed the latest Cowboy's game. Roni intertwined her fingers in his, her thumb stroking him softly. He shifted uncomfortable in his seat, causing her to giggle, and Kent to look at them suspiciously in the mirror.

Rich felt relief when they pulled into the lot of the club. He needed a beer.

When they walked inside, they saw everyone else in a large booth in the corner of the club by the dance floor.

It was a Country & Western Bar, so during the day they served food and played music, at night it became a twenty-one and over club. It had a mechanical bull, country lessons in the corner, and a big floor for dancing. Since it was the only bar of its kind in town, it didn't only play country music. On Saturday nights, it would play some Top 40 and dance music, as well as the country music that kept the regulars happy.

When they got to the table, there were a few pitchers already waiting, so Rich poured himself a glass.

"What do you want to drink?" He asked Roni, leaning in to be heard over the music.

"Can you get me a vodka and cranberry?" She asked with a smile.

He nodded at her, then asked if anyone else needed anything, before heading to the bar with Pete.

"How's married life treating you?" Rich asked Pete.

"It's awesome, man. I swear, I was so relieved when she asked me. I'd been trying to figure out how to ask her for months," Pete replied with a laugh. "I still can't believe it."

Rich smiled at his friends' obvious joy and love for Kara. That is what he wanted. To be in love and married and ready to start a family. He thought of his parents' marriage, and knew that they'd showed him how to make love last.

He knew Roni would freak if she knew his line of thought, but deep down, he always knew that he wanted what his parents had. He'd been devastated by Tara, and had gone a little wild while in college, but at his core, he'd always been a family man.

They paid for the drinks and took them back to the girls.

Roni said thanks, took the glass from Rich and began to drink as she talked with Briana. Rich refilled the beer he'd downed while at the bar, then sat down next to Colin. He was happy he'd been able to spend so much time with his friend over the holiday, and knew he'd be sad to see him go.

The song changed and the girls started to yell something about needing to dance, that this was their song. Rich tried to get out of the way as Nicole and Kara climbed over him to get out of the booth and join Roni and Bree on the dance floor.

The guys stayed in the booth. Enjoying their beer and the sight of their girls moving on the floor.

After a few more trips to the bar for vodka cranberries and pitchers, Rich was feeling pretty good. He had enough liquid courage to join Roni on the floor. The way she moved her body to the music was like a beacon, pulling him towards her.

He was very turned on by watching her dance for the past couple hours, so when he finally got his hands on her, his body throbbed in response.

The song changed to a slow love song and Roni wrapped her arms around his neck, pressing every inch of her body to his.

Rich felt the hot sweat glistening on Roni's skin, which only turned him on more; that combined with her body rubbing against him, made him feel like he was about to go insane.

Roni writhed against him to the music and he tried not to think of their friends possibly watching him slowly lose control.

Rich captured her mouth with his, his tongue sweeping in to deepen the kiss. When she moaned against him, his hand came to the back of her head and his fingers tangled in her hair, pulling it softly. "You're driving me crazy," he said against her mouth.

Roni grinned at him wickedly, then moved away, putting her hand in his and pulling him towards the back. She pulled him down the hallway, past the women's and men's rooms, pausing in front of the Unisex bathroom to try the handle. When it opened swiftly, she pushed him inside, closing and locking the door behind them.

"What are you doing?" Rich asked.

Roni stalked closer to him, grinning when he came in contact with the sink. She jumped certain that he'd catch her as she brought her lips to his. He kissed her back, full force, turning so her bottom lay against the top of the counter around the sink.

"What if someone saw us?" Rich asked, trying to think through the fog in his head.

"No one did," Roni said breathlessly. "And if they did, who cares. They won't know anything."

As if to keep him from thinking, Roni reached down under her skirt and pulled off her panties.

"Shit," Rich said, before plunging back into her mouth. He thanked God he had a condom in his back pocket, ever the Boy Scout, then unbuttoned his fly.

Roni took the condom from him and opened it. "I love that you don't wear underwear," she said, as she slid the condom over him.

They stopped talking as he entered her. She wrapped her legs around him, then braced herself against the counter with her hands. When she was secure, Rich started driving into her. All thought of gentleness gone, they both strived for release, as the sounds of their moans and bodies joining together filled the small bathroom.

When they were done, Rich leaned down to help Roni with her panties before cleaning himself up. They both started laughing when they looked around and it really registered where they were. Roni splashed water on her face and pulled her hair up into a pony tail.

"I'll go out first and head to the table. You wait a few minutes, then join me," Roni said, kissing him as she opened the door.

Rich followed her out, then turned and went into the men's room to try and play it off like he'd been in there the whole time.

Chapter Sixteen

Roni chuckled to herself as she waited for Rich to come and pick her up. She couldn't believe the way she'd acted the other night. She'd been totally swept away. The way Rich wanted her made her feel so powerful.

Their quickie in the bathroom was going to the top of her list of favorite moments.

Their friends had been none the wiser when she returned to the table. She said there'd been a long line at the bathroom.

Rich had called her this morning and asked if she wanted to hang out today. She hadn't asked what they were going to do. She wondered if that should worry her. That she didn't really care, she just wanted to spend more time with him.

When she heard him on the stairs, her stomach jumped with excitement. Another clue that maybe he was starting to mean more to her than just a fling.

She wasn't going to worry about it though; she'd just be casual and see what happened.

Roni swung the door open before he could knock and threw herself in his arms, hugging him tightly.

"Hello, sunshine," Rich said, hugging her back. "You ready?"

"Yup," Roni said, reaching in to grab her purse. She locked up and followed him out to his car.

It looked like a storm was rolling in.

When they were both strapped in and the car was moving, Rich said, "I had fun the other night."

Roni returned his cocky smile with one of her own. "Me, too."

"Is everything set for the Grand Opening tomorrow?" Roni asked.

She couldn't help but laugh at the look of excitement that came over his face.

"Yup. I followed up with everyone today and everyone is good to go. Jason is putting up some last minute decorations right now, since I have a couple things to do, but other than that, we're all set." He smiled at her. "You ready for your first day of classes?"

"Yes. So ready," she replied. "I'm really excited to see everyone in action tomorrow."

When the car started to slow she looked up to see Rich's parents' house. She had been there once before for a party, but it had been a while.

"We're going to your parents' house?" Roni asked, suddenly nervous, all of her easiness gone. "Are they home?"

"Yeah," Rich replied. He parked then turned to her and took her hand in his. "It's no big deal. Colin called and said he and his dad wanted to meet me here to talk about something."

"You want me to meet your parents?" Roni asked, trying to understand why he'd brought her there. She suddenly felt very hot, even though it was cold enough to warrant a jacket. Her palms were sweating.

"Sure, why not?" Rich asked. "Roni, they're going to love you. Really, it's not a big deal. We'll be in and out. No pressure."

Roni looked back at the house and thought of the house she'd grown up in. She could just imagine taking Rich home to meet *her* parents. There'd be dirty dishes all over the kitchen, beer bottles scattered throughout the house, and the stale stench of urine and cigarettes.

"Roni," Rich prodded, bringing her back to reality. "If you really don't want to go in, I can run in and see what they want, or take you back home, but I promise, it'll be fine."

She tried to give him a smile of assurance, but her stomach was still tied in knots. She looked into his face and nodded. She could do this… They were just parents.

Rich kept a hand at the small of her back as he opened the front door, as if afraid she would take off running at the first opportunity.

The house was spotless. That was the first thing she noticed when they entered the foyer. That, the smell of baked goods, and the sound of laughter.

"There's my boy," Rich's mother said as she rounded the corner and gave him a hug.

"Hi, Mama."

The older lady turned to Roni, a big grin on her face, and asked, "And who is this beautiful young lady?"

"This is Roni, Mama."

Before Roni could say a word, she was engulfed in Rich's mom's arm. She stood there awkwardly, unsure of what she should do, but was released before she had to make a decision.

"Roni, I've heard a lot about you," she said, shaking her wooden spoon at Roni as she spoke. "You go ahead and call me Martha, darlin'. I have a feeling we are gonna be fast friends. Come on in and have a cupcake."

Martha was gone as quickly as she'd appeared, in a flurry of movement, her apron flapping as she rounded the corner into what Roni assumed, was the kitchen.

Roni looked up at Rich, slightly dazed, but he just returned a grin identical to his mothers and ushered her towards the back.

Colin sat at the table with two older men. They all stopped talking and looked up as Roni and Rich entered the room.

"Hey guys," Colin said. "I didn't know you were coming, Roni. I would've brought Bree."

"We're just stopping by to see what you wanted to talk to me about," Rich replied, squeezing Roni's hand as they neared the table. "Roni, this is my Pop, Frank," He said, pointing to the handsome man with a toothpick in his mouth.

"Hi'ya," Frank said.

"It's nice to meet you," Roni managed.

"And this is, Mr. Grayson, Colin's dad."

"Hello, pretty lady," Mr. Grayson said in a booming voice, startling her a bit.

She regained her composure and said, "Nice to meet you."

"Roni, why don't you come out back with me. We'll have some coffee and a cupcake, and leave the men to their business," Martha said, coming up behind her with two plates in her hand. "Here, you take these, I'll grab the cups."

Rich winked at her and walked to the back to open the door for her. She walked out, looking back at the guys longingly. She had a feeling she'd be much safer in there.

She walked over to the bistro set and placed the plates on the table. She sat down and waited for Rich's mother to join her.

How the hell had she gotten in to this mess?

Martha put the cups and saucers on the table. "Rich said you like a little cream and sugar, I hope it's okay," Martha said as she sat, wiping her hands on her apron.

Roni took a sip and nodded at Martha, smiling.

"So," Martha began as she unwrapped her cupcake. "Tell me about yourself. Rich has told me that you're a dancer and that you'll be renting space from him at the Center, but he hasn't said much else. Where are you from? Where's your family?"

Roni cleared her throat nervously and said, "Um, well, my twin brother, Kent, lives here."

"Oh, I know Kent. Such a gentleman," Martha cooed. "And you're a twin… That's really something. Must have been nice growing up."

"Yes," Roni could admit. "Kent is a wonderful brother. I wouldn't have made it without him."

Martha looked at her strangely, so she sputtered on, "We're from Michigan. Detroit. We were born and raised there."

"What made you come to Texas?"

"Kent."

"Oh, what about your folks. Do you ever get back to see them?" Martha prodded.

"No."

Martha looked at her pointedly and asked, "Any plans to go back, or do you think you'll settle here? Put down roots."

"We're staying," Roni smiled to try and make her answers less blunt, but she wasn't quite sure how to take Rich's mom. Was she just nosy, or was she looking out for her sons' welfare?

Martha grinned at her answer. "That's lovely dear. You know, you're the first girl Rich has brought around to meet us since Tara."

Roni looked up, startled at her statement. Rich had said this was no big deal, but it's obvious his mother didn't see it that way.

"Rich and I are just dating, Martha," Roni said.

Martha patted Roni's hand and said, "Don't be afraid of what's right in front of you, dear. My son is the kind of man a girl can count on. He'll make a wonderful husband and father."

Roni's blood ran cold at Martha's words.

Husband and *father*.

Rain started to fall in fat drops and a big gust of wind chilled Roni to her bones.

"Oh, we'd better go inside dear," Martha said as she stood.

They grabbed their dishes and went inside. The guys looked to be wrapping up their discussion. Rich had a huge smile on his face and was shaking hands with Mr. Grayson. He looked up at Roni as they entered and must have seen something on her face, because his smile disappeared and he went to her side.

"Everything okay?" He asked.

"Fine," Roni responded numbly.

Their exit was a blur to Roni. She knew she'd said goodbye to everyone, but before she knew it, they were pulling into the parking lot of her apartment building. The rain was falling in sheets and the thunder clapped loudly.

Rich was trying to ask her what happened, but she just kept saying she was fine, hoping he'd get the hint and leave her alone.

When she stepped out into the storm, she was swept back to another night, another storm. Hank had been gone for a week. Probably off on a binge, staying God knows where with God knows who. Those were her favorite nights. The nights he didn't come home. Unfortunately, when he finally did make it home, he was usually very drunk and very angry.

She was already in bed. Reading a book and hopeful that she'd get another night alone. There was a raging storm outside. Full of thunder and lightning. The best kind of night to be curled up with a book. She hadn't heard him come in, so she didn't even know what was coming.

He'd stormed in the room, slamming the door as he entered. He went straight for her feet and dragged her from the bed. Her body bounced against the floor as she fell, and she felt her wrist break when she tried to catch herself. He'd obviously been storing up a lot of anger, because he never said a word, he just beat her within an inch of her life.

He'd used his fists and feet, and when he got tired, he'd grabbed a bat.

The neighbors had heard her screams and called the cops. When she'd come to, she was in the back of an ambulance. She quickly retreated into unconsciousness and stayed there for a few days.

When she'd awoken in the hospital, she'd seen her mother sitting in the chair next to her bed. When her mother noticed her stir, she'd looked at her with the contempt she'd always shown her daughter. But this time there was a smirk on her face as well. Roni knew then that her mother was happy that she'd never gotten out and become a dancer, but that instead, she was living the same miserable life that her mother did.

She turned her head from her mother's stare, and closed her eyes, not opening them again until she was gone.

She never saw her again.

When the doctors came in, they'd explained how lucky she was to be alive. They'd talked about broken bones and internal bleeding. Then they told her she may never be able to have children.

Roni's heart had broken that day.

Roni walked up the stairs to her apartment, the rain soaking her with every step.

"Roni," Rich said from behind her, his voice desperate. "What they hell happened? Did my mother say something to upset you?"

Roni opened the door and walked in, her heart racing at the memories and the sound of the thunder echoing through the room.

Rich's phone rang and she heard him answer it. She turned to ask him to leave, and everything seemed to happen all at once.

The memories suffocated her as the thunder clapped. Rich's face turned angry and he began to yell in the phone. She didn't hear what he was saying, she only say his face and felt his anger. He hung up the phone and turned to her, his hands raised as he spoke and gestured. The combination scared her witless and she dropped to the ground. She low crawled to the living room, trying to find safety in between the back of the sofa and the wall. She held her hands over her head and whimpered, willing the feelings of terror to disappear.

"Roni," she heard Rich say gently. "Roni, I'm sorry. I don't know what's going on, but I'll do whatever I can to make it right. Please, talk to me, baby."

She saw him reach out a hand and recoiled. In the back of her mind, she knew that it was Rich, not Hank, that sat in front of her, but she couldn't seem to stop shaking.

"Go," she said softly.

"Shit, Roni. Let me help you," he pleaded. "I can't leave you like this."

She saw him sit on the floor a few feet away from her, his hands in his hair, and she wanted to go to him, but she couldn't.

"Kent," she said.

"Okay," Rich responded. He got out his phone and dialed.

She heard him telling Kent that he needed to come over, but she didn't tune in to everything he was saying.

She stayed huddled in the corner, and Rich stayed on the floor an arm's length away, as they waited for Kent to arrive.

When the knock came at the door, Roni heard Rich talking quietly to Kent. He explained what he could, then said something about having to get to the Rec Center to deal with a burst pipe. He asked Kent to have her call him when she was ready. He paused and looked back at her before he walked out the door.

Kent came up and put a hand on her shoulder, and she crawled onto his lap. Eager to accept the comfort that he offered.

Friends & Lovers Trilogy

Chapter Seventeen

Rich was exhausted. He'd spent the night with the plumber trying to deal with a pipe that exploded in the Men's locker room.

That, along with Roni's melt down the night before, had kept him awake long after he'd finally had the chance to lie down. Now, he was an hour away from the Grand Opening of the Rec Center, and he felt like he was half dead.

He'd texted Kent this morning to see how Roni was doing. Since she hadn't wanted him to stay last night, he hadn't been sure that she would welcome him checking on her this morning, but he had to make sure she was okay. It had really scared him to see her like that. So terrified, quivering in the corner. He honestly hadn't known how to react. Kent responded that she was doing better, wished him luck on the opening, and said he'd see him later.

Rich knew he'd see Roni soon, but for now, he needed to focus on one of the most important events of his life.

The Center was a flurry of movement, everyone was trying to get there last minute preparations done before the doors opened. Rich had done an interview with Kent for the paper, and had taken out an ad to promote the opening. He'd had a ton of people call, or stop him on the street, and say they were planning to attend and bring the whole family.

He walked into the kitchen to find Briana putting the finishing touches on dozens of cupcakes.

"Smells good, Bree," he said as he reached for a cupcake.

She slapped at his hand, as he knew she would, and clucked her tongue at him.

"Hands off, Mister. These are for the guests."

He grinned at her and picked up one icing covered hand, bringing it to his lips.

"Now, Darlin', are you sure we can't work something out?"

Briana laughed and pulled her hand away.

"Get out of here and make sure everything is ready for your big day. I'll save you a cupcake."

Rich smiled and winked, satisfied that he'd gotten what he wanted, then walked out to check on his other instructors, whistling as he walked.

This was going to be a great day. He felt it in his bones.

He paused when he got to the door of Roni's dance studio. Roni was inside lining up colorful tutus along the mirrored wall. Classical music played softly in the background, and she hummed while she worked. He walked hesitantly inside, clearing his throat as he entered, so he wouldn't startle her.

She looked up at him with a small smile, her eyes still a little troubled.

"Hey," she said. "You ready for today?"

Rich closed the gap between them, bringing his hand up to brush the hair from her face and leaving it there to cradle her cheek. "You okay?"

Roni closed her eyes and turned her face to kiss him gently on the palm. She opened her eyes and stepped back, putting some space between them.

"I'm okay. Let's focus on the Grand Opening today. You've been working so hard and I know it's going to be a great success."

Rich looked at her, then nodded, "If that's what you want, but let me know if you need anything, okay?"

Roni nodded back and he turned to leave, pausing when he reached the door.

"We *will* talk about what happened though."

"I know," Roni responded, then turned to finish getting ready.

As he walked through the building, he saw the Art room was set up, the music room had recorders and xylophones placed along the table, and Alex was warming up in the Karate studio.

"You ready?" Rich asked Alex, popping his head in briefly.

When she nodded to him, he gave her a thumbs up and kept going down the hall. Jason and the other boxing coaches were warming up and using the equipment. Jason nodded to him and he nodded back, then went to complete his walk through and head back out front to open the doors.

Within an hour the center was alive with the sounds of laughter and the excited chatter of children. It was better than Rich could have ever imagined.

By the time Colin, Kent and Nicole arrived, he had perma-grin.

"Wow, it looks like a great turn-out," Nicole gushed. She gave Rich a quick hug, then said she was going to see if Bree needed any help.

Rich smiled after her, then turned to his friends. "I can't believe it."

"I can," Colin responded. "This place is just what this town needed."

"Yeah, man," Kent agreed. "I can't wait to get my gym membership. In fact, I'll go back and see if Jason and the guys need a hand with anything."

Colin said he would catch up with Kent after he checked on his fiancé. Once they were gone, Rich went to his office to grab a water, before doing his rounds again.

He'd just opened the water and taken a sip when nervous giggles had him turning towards the door. Twin girls wearing pink leotards and pigtails stood watching him.

"Hello, ladies," Rich said with a wink, causing them turn to each other and giggle. "What can I do for ya?"

"Hi, Mr. Rich," the girl on the left said.

Her sister followed it up with, "Can you show us where the dance class is?"

"It would be my pleasure," he responded, placing the water on the desk so he could take each of them by the hand. "Let me be your escort," he said dramatically, as he led them towards the dance studio.

When they reached the studio, the girls were so excited they practically vibrated.

Roni was teaching a group of kids how to do a plié. He watched as she leaned down to whisper to a little girl who was having difficulties. The little girl smiled happily when she executed the simple move, and Roni's obvious joy caused his heart to flip in his chest.

He was falling in love with her. She was not only physically beautiful, but had a beautiful heart. The way she was with her brother and their friends, showed how selfless she was. He loved that she didn't take shit from anyone, including him, and that she always had a comeback. Seeing her dance and the way she interacted with the kids, just introduced him to more aspects of her, and so far, he was lovin' all of them. She was the total package.

Roni looked up and started towards him and the girls. Rich felt frozen in place as he tried to register what his heart was feeling.

"You guys here for a lesson?" She asked, smiling at the twins.

They both nodded quickly and let go of his hands yelling, "Thank you, Mr. Rich," as they ran into the room towards Roni. She gave him a small smile, then took the girls and got them situated with the rest of the class.

The rest of his day went by quickly. The bulk of it was spent making sure that everyone on staff had what they needed, and his guests were having a good time. He did get a chance to get in the ring with some of the teens who were interested in boxing, which made the day even brighter. It really proved to him that he'd made the right decision.

By the time the Grand Opening was finished, he and the staff were ready to drop. They'd taught countless classes and had been on their feet for over eight hours, but it had been totally worth it.

Although he was tired, Rich walked around and helped everyone clean up. He set up a time for them to meet and discuss what worked and what hadn't.

He was standing at the front, saying goodbye to everyone as they left for the night, when Alex walked up.

"Thanks again for doing a great job today," he told her.

"It was fun," she said. "And I think a good number of the kids that tried the class will be contacting you to sign up."

"Great," Rich replied. Then he remembered Jason and decided to do some recon for his friend. "So, you got a hot date tonight?"

Alex looked a bit puzzled and replied, "Nope. I'm perpetually single."

"Perpetually?" Rich asked with a chuckle.

Before Alex could respond, Roni cleared her throat behind them. Rich looked up and wondered at the look on her face.

"Everything okay?" He asked.

"Yup," Roni responded. "I just need to get going."

Alex smiled unsurely at her, before turning back to Rich and saying, "Well, thanks again, Boss. I'll see you tomorrow."

Rich said goodbye, then turned to Roni as Alex walked outside.

"You're leaving?" He asked, disappointed that she wasn't planning to stay so they could talk.

"Yeah," Roni responded, not quite meeting his eyes. "It was a long day."

"I was hoping you'd want to grab some dinner, and talk," Rich said, a little displeased by how needy he sounded.

"Not tonight," Roni replied. "We'll talk later."

"Alright, but you can always give me a call later, if you change your mind."

"Okay. Goodnight," she said as she walked out.

Rich watched her leave, as Jason came up behind him.

"Awesome turn-out tonight, Bro," Jason said, putting his fist out to pound Rich's.

"It was better than I'd ever imagined," Rich admitted.

"I'll be back early to get some training in before we open."

"Sounds good, I'll warm up with you," Rich said. "Oh, hey… Alex is single."

Jason stopped and turned to his friend, his eyebrow raised. "Oh, yeah?"

"Yup," Rich answered with a grin. "Told me so herself."

Jason returned his grin and said, "'Night," before walking out the door.

He locked up and did one last walk through, stopping in the kitchen to grab the cupcake that Briana had saved for him. He took it with him to his room, where he settled back on the bed and let the day's events replay in his mind.

He already had quite a few families' sign up for classes and they'd sold a good number of items in the resale store. Eventually his thoughts turned back to Roni and the way she'd reacted the night before. He couldn't help but wonder what was going on with her. He hoped she'd call so they could talk about it.

She never did.

Friends & Lovers Trilogy

Chapter Eighteen

Roni had a raging headache. She really hoped the aspirin would kick in quickly. She was on her way to the center. She knew she couldn't keep putting Rich off; she needed to talk to him. She'd done a lot of thinking last night, and she realized that she couldn't continue to have a relationship with Rich. Not even a casual one. Because it didn't seem to be as casual as it had started out to be.

Last night, when she'd heard Rich talking to Alex, she'd been slapped in the face by jealousy. Roni knew what it was like to be cheated on; she couldn't help but think of how Hank had slept with anyone that had given him the slightest invitation.

She didn't think that Rich was actually hitting on Alex, she believed him when he told her that he wouldn't cheat on her, but she didn't relish the feelings of jealousy. It brought back memories of the person she used to be.

Rich flirted with girls without even thinking about it, it was just his nature. She'd realized that even more after she'd met his parents. It's like he'd been brought up that way. She'd thought she was used to it.

But when she'd seen the cute little Karate instructor responding to Rich that she was single, she'd been overcome by the green-eyed monster.

She didn't like it. She and Rich were just having a fling, emotions shouldn't be involved. And the fact that they seemed to be, meant she needed to take a step back.

She needed them to maintain a good relationship, since they were going to be working together.

Roni felt a pain in her heart at the thought of telling Rich they needed to stall their relationship. She was surprised to realize that she was going to miss being able to touch him and be with him.

She checked his room first, but it was empty. She smiled at the site of his unmade bed and his clothes piled into a ball in the corner. He was such a guy.

That just reaffirmed that she was getting too involved, she thought, she should not think his messiness was endearing.

Roni shut Rich's door and made her way towards the back. She figured he was either in the fitness center or the boxing gym.

She heard them before she saw them, the grunts of guys and the sound of flesh hitting something. When she rounded the corner, the site before her stopped her in her tracks.

They were both shirtless, with boxing shoes and trunks on.

Jason had the boxing mitts on. His toned body glistened with sweat. His dark hair and strategically placed tattoos made a striking picture, but Roni only had eyes for Rich.

His muscles rippled underneath his naturally tanned skin with each punch he threw. He anticipated Jason's movements and met the mitts with his gloves, his hits fluid. The noises that he made seemed to resonate in the pit of her belly causing heat to pool there.

"They're something, aren't they?" Alex said as she came up behind her, causing Roni to jump.

"Oh, my gosh," Roni said bringing her hand to her mouth. "You scared me."

"Sorry," Alex said, stopping next to Roni to watch the guys who were oblivious to their audience. "I thought you heard me walk up."

Roni just shook her head, then turned to the other woman with her hand extended.

"I don't think we've officially met, I'm Roni."

"I know… You're the boss's girl," Alex said with a smile as they shook hands. "I've seen you around, but I guess we've just never had the opportunity to talk before."

"Oh, I'm not Rich's girl," Roni denied with a shake of her head.

Alex just smiled at her and shrugged her shoulders. "I think he would say differently."

They stood quietly for a moment, enjoying the sight before them. When the guys took a break and Jason put his head back to squirt water in his mouth and over his head before running a towel down his chest, Roni heard Alex's intake of breath and looked over at her face.

Roni smiled at her look of longing. Alex turned and blushed when she realized she'd been caught. She shrugged again and said, "I can't help it, he's pretty amazing."

Roni nodded her agreement, "And he's a really nice guy. You should go for it."

"Oh… no," Alex said with a small smile. "He'd never go for a girl like me. I work for the mayor and do Karate in my spare time. Not exactly his type, I'm sure."

Roni was surprised at the other woman's evaluation of herself, but Rich noticed them before she could take their conversation any further. He nodded and gave her the one-minute sign.

Alex turned to leave and said, "Well, I'm going to go check the messages and see if I've gotten any more sign-ups. I'm hoping to get my first class going by the end of the week."

"Okay," Roni responded with a smile. Then she turned and called out, "Hey, Alex. We should hang out sometime."

Alex smiled broadly and said, "Yeah, I'd like that."

Roni waved at Jason and turned to Rich who was walking up to her with a towel slung around his neck. She couldn't help but notice how perfectly toned his abs were, and she loved the cut of his muscles as they disappeared below his trunks.

Shit, she needed to focus.

"Hey, sunshine," Rich said with a beautiful smile before he leaned in and kissed her softly. Careful not to get any sweat on her.

"Hey," she responded, regretting the fact that she was about to lose the ability to kiss him softly.

As they walked towards his room he asked, "Did you have a good night last night?"

"Pretty much," Roni said. "I went to sleep soon after I got home. I was pretty tired."

"Yeah, it was a great day."

Roni hated to wipe the smile off of his face. She started to feel hot and sweaty all over, her hands dampening with the thought of hurting him.

Rich threw the towel in the corner with the other clothes, then walked over to the bed and threw the comforter up over the bed, trying to make it look more presentable, before turning to her.

"Sorry, the place is a mess."

"That's okay," Roni responded. "Do you have a minute to talk?"

"Yeah," Rich said, gesturing for her to sit next to him on the bed. "I have to grab a shower before I open the doors, but I have some time."

Roni sat next to him on the bed, her hair falling and covering her face, giving her a moment to compose herself and think about how she wanted to begin.

"Hey," Rich said, pushing her hair back over her shoulder so he could look at her. "It's okay. You can tell me anything."

"I don't think we should see each other anymore."

Friends & Lovers Trilogy

Chapter Nineteen

Rich felt like he'd been punched in the gut. He'd been so happy when he'd seen Roni standing in the gym talking to Alex. His first instinct had been to go to her and take her in his arms. He'd hoped her coming in early meant that she was ready to talk to him.

He'd never imagined she'd come to end it.

"Why?"

"This was always supposed to be a fling," Roni said in a tone that made him wonder if she was trying to convince him or herself.

"Well… it turned into more than that," Rich responded, hoping there was still a chance he could convince her not to do this. That she hadn't already made up her mind.

"Look, Rich," Roni began, "There are things you don't know about me."

"Tell me," he said simply.

"I'm pretty messed up," Roni said, pulling her hair back nervously and pulling it back into a bun. She looked so vulnerable, it broke his heart.

"Tell me," he said again.

"I told you that I was married, and that my divorce just came through, but… there's more to it than that."

Rich didn't say anything. He gave her a moment to gather her thoughts. It was obvious that what she had to say was tough on her, so he put his hand on her leg and squeezed it, offering encouragement.

"The first time Hank hit me was the day after we got married," Roni began. As her words registered, Rich's body tightened in response. He'd never imagined she'd been abused. He guessed he should've, after her reaction the other night, but he'd never been impacted by that type of behavior, so it never even occurred to him. He tried to calm himself down so he could hear her words clearly.

"I'd been putting my things away and he'd said something about making sure I put everything away neatly. I made some smart ass comment, just like I always do, without even realizing it. Hank came up behind me and pulled my hair, then smashed my face against the dresser, causing a cut right above my eye. I'd been so shocked I didn't know what to do. He'd apologized profusely and said he'd never damage my face again. It didn't register at the time, he didn't want to hurt my face, but he didn't say he'd never hurt me again."

Roni turned to him and took the hand he offered in hers, bringing it briefly to her cheek before letting it go.

"I guess I should tell you first about my parents, so you understand where I come from. I doubt Kent ever has," Roni looked off, unshed tears glistening in her eyes. "Our dad is an alcoholic, who routinely abuses out mother. I say abuses, because she refuses to leave him and he refuses to change. When I was little, Kent sheltered me from them as much as he could. I didn't really even realize what was going on until I was much older. I knew we struggled, and that my mom cried a lot, but I thought it was normal."

Roni paused to take a deep breath and Rich thought about how different her childhood had been from his. His parents had always been amazing. His mother was the heart of their house and his father the rock. He'd never realized how lucky he'd been.

"I found out later that Kent was taking beatings for both of us, and that when he was old enough to stand up for himself, all of Dad's anger was focused on our mom," Roni turned to look him in the eyes. "We tried to get her to leave him, but she won't. I think she was happy when Hank started hitting me, because it meant that I was no better than she was."

Rich couldn't even comprehend parents like the ones she was describing.

"Anyway, Kent went off to school and I couldn't go with him. My plans were to go to New York and dance professionally, but when I fell in love with Hank, I thought I could have both. It didn't take long for him to take dancing away, along with anything I tried to do outside of our home that didn't include him. Anytime I hung out with my friends, or spent a day at the studio, I ended up getting punished that night. I stopped doing anything, hoping I could make him happy and he would stop hitting me."

Roni looked at him, his hands were clenched and he felt like his blood as boiling.

"Don't feel sorry for me," she said sadly.

"Okay," he replied, exhaling a long breath and relaxing his hands. He wanted to hear what she had to say, even though it felt like his heart was ripping with each word she spoke.

"Hank cheated whenever he could, but by the end, I was happy when he did. It meant that he was leaving me alone. He'd go on these benders where he stayed gone for days at a time," Roni smiled sadly as she spoke. "Those were the best days of my marriage. I would read and escape into a book, pretending I was someone else, until he returned and brought me back to reality. It was after one of his benders that he beat me with a baseball bat."

Rich sprung from the bed at that, pacing as he tried to hold on to his anger. What kind of a coward used a bat against a woman, he wondered as he paced, and how was such a man allowed to live?

Roni watched him pace as the tears were finally freed and ran down her cheeks.

"I ended up in the hospital and the doctors told me that I may never be able to have children," Roni explained as she cried softly. "My mom came to see me, but she didn't try to help me, she just smiled. I never spoke to her again."

Rich stopped in front of her, his anger spilling over and asked incredulously, "She *smiled?* What the fuck kind of parent does that? Why didn't she get you away from that bastard?"

Roni just shrugged helplessly. She'd asked herself the same question a million times.

"When I was released from the hospital and we went home, Hank swore he would never touch me again. He was sorry that it had gone so far and I'd been hospitalized. I didn't really believe him, but at that point I felt numb. I didn't see a way out; I thought my life was doomed to be like that forever."

Rich crouched in front of her and took her hands in his, "What about Kent? I *know* he would've killed the bastard if he'd known. Did you ever reach out to him for help?"

Roni held his hands tightly as she spoke, "I hadn't at that point. I'd been too ashamed. I thought I was marrying a man as good as my brother, and I was embarrassed at how very wrong I'd been. The final straw came a couple weeks later. Hank had held true to his word and hadn't touched me since I'd been in the hospital. We went out to the bar to have a couple drinks, and I ended up dancing. I was in a good mood, feeling the effects of the liquor and the music spoke to me. I should have known better."

Rich's whole body twitched at that. He hated to hear her talk like anything she'd said or done warranted anything that animal had done.

"It was bad that night, and I told him I was going to leave him. I called Kent and asked him to come get me; he hopped on the next plane and flew out. Unfortunately, Hank didn't want me to leave, and he beat me again before Kent got there. Kent arrived while he was kicking me in the kitchen, and he pulled Hank off me. He nearly beat Hank to death."

"Good," Rich spat viciously. He only wished he'd been there to help his friend.

Roni smiled at him through her tears. She was amazing. He couldn't believe she had it in her to smile as she told him of the horror she'd had to endure at the hand of the man who was supposed to love and honor her.

Her earlier words forgotten, he leaned in and kissed her on the lips. Her tears salty on his lips.

"I'm so sorry you had to go through that," Rich said softly against her lips. "You're an amazing woman, and I'd kill that asshole if I could."

Roni pulled away and nodded, "Kent brought me here and I've slowly been building myself back into the woman I should have been all along. I'm grateful to be dancing again, and I can't thank you enough for your part in making that a reality for me."

Rich let his hands dropped and stood, before taking his seat back next to her on the bed again.

"But…" he prompted.

"But, I never meant for us to get serious," she began. "I was using you to help me gain my confidence back, and lord knows I've always found you attractive, even if I tried to pretend otherwise."

Rich nodded slowly, the empty feeling entering his stomach again.

"You're amazing," she said. "More so than I ever imagined. You're strong, sexy, and smart. You've started this amazing business, and your family is phenomenal."

She looked down at her hands as she picked at her cuticle.

"You know, I got so mad at Kent when he thought Nicole was too good for him, but I can see now where he was coming from." She put her finger to his lips before he could protest. "You deserve someone who isn't broken. A girl who won't fall to the ground if you raise your voice. Someone who can give you babies…"

Her voice broke at that statement, causing his heart to bleed for her, but he let her continue. To get out everything that she needed to say.

"I need this job. I need to be able to rent the studio from you and dance," Roni said. "I can't take the chance that something will go wrong, or that some other hot girl will come along, and that dance studio will be in jeopardy."

That pissed him off. He was with her until that point, ready to be understanding and supportive, but he took offense to her final statement.

"Don't do that," Rich said dangerously. "Contrary to popular belief, I'm not some man-whore who would cheat on you at the first opportunity. I've already explained that to you, and I thought you understood. I'd also never do anything to jeopardize your place here at the center. I'm enough of a man to separate business from my personal life. I think you're just looking for a reason to end this, and you're grasping at straws."

Roni nodded and rose from the bed.

"Maybe you're right, but that doesn't change the fact that I think we need to stop seeing each other. You deserve better."

Rich stood abruptly, grabbing her arms and pulling her to him. He kissed her swiftly and desperately, putting his heart into the kiss. He knew she wouldn't be swayed in this moment, but he wanted to give her something to think about.

"Don't tell me what I deserve," he said against her lips, before going in for another kiss. "Maybe you're the best thing that ever happened to me."

Roni looked up into his eyes, hers flashing with confusion. "I've got to go."

"Okay," Rich said, dropping his hands and letting her go. "But know this before you do, I'm falling in love with you, and I'm not giving up that easily."

Rich went into his bathroom and shut the door, leaving Roni in the middle of the room with her jaw dropped.

Fuck, he thought, he hoped he could get her to see that they were perfect for each other.

Friends & Lovers Trilogy

Chapter Twenty

"I don't know what I should do," Roni cried to her brother and Nicole. They were sitting in Kent's living room. Roni was still laying down on the couch with a cover over her and a nights worth of used tissues lying next to her on the floor. She'd come there after leaving her dance studio yesterday.

She hadn't wanted to go back to her apartment alone. Not with Rich's words replaying in her mind.

Roni had told them everything last night. Nicole was shocked, she hadn't been aware of the details of Roni's marriage or how horrible it had been. Some of the stories Roni retold, Kent had never heard before.

It had been a rough night, hence the tissues.

Roni had hoped a good night's sleep would bring clarity, but she felt just as confused as she had when she'd finally fallen asleep.

"What do you want to do?" Kent asked.

"I thought that the right thing was to end it now, before it got more complicated," Roni explained. "I'm renting the space from him, so we'll see each other every day. I don't want to mess up our working relationship, or our friendship."

"Why do you think you will mess it up?" Nicole prompted.

"Because he deserves better than me," Roni said throwing her hands up. "I'm a freakin' mess. Look at the way I freaked out the other day. His mom mentioned that Rich was "marriage material" and I wigged out. That information, coupled with the storm had me totally on edge. When Rich got that phone call about the pipes and raised his voice, I lost it. I was pulled back to all of those times when Hank got angry, and what the result was. Even though I *knew* that Rich is not Hank, I couldn't control my reaction."

"Honey, that just means you need help, not that you aren't good enough to handle a relationship with Rich," Nicole said. "He's a good man. I don't think he's afraid of a little work."

"Roni," Kent said, taking her hand in his. "Rich is the exact opposite of Hank. He's a man who believes in family, hard work, and loyalty. He's the kind of guy I have always hoped you'd end up with some day."

Roni looked at her brother with tears in her eyes. "What if I can't get over it? And what if I can't ever have children?"

"You will get over it, it just takes time," Kent responded. "And the doctor told you that you might not be able to have children, not that you can't. As long as you're honest with Rich, you guys can handle anything that comes your way… If that's what you want."

Roni nodded and took a deep breath.

"I'm going to go grab a shower and get ready for work," Kent said, kissing his sister on the forehead, before turning to Nicole and kissing her lips.

Nicole got up and motioned for Roni to scoot over and give her room next to her on the couch. Nicole put her arm around Roni and looked her friend in the eye.

"Do you want to have a relationship with Rich? One that's not just based on sex? Do you like him?"

Roni was silent for a few seconds as she processed Nicole's questions.

"I do like him."

"Well… What do you like about him?" Nicole prodded.

"He's sweeter than I thought he'd be," she began. "He's got a good heart and he's smart. He obviously loves his family and his friends, and would do anything for him. He's just a really good *person*, ya know?"

Nicole nodded as she smiled, her eyes misting over.

"He's one of the good ones," she agreed.

"And, of course, he's pretty easy on the eyes," Roni said with a laugh. "My goodness, that body."

Nicole laughed along with her, the tension receding a bit, until Roni stopped laughing and looked at her friend seriously.

"He said that he's falling in love with me and that he's not going to give up on me… I don't want to hurt him."

Nicole gave her a hug and pulled back to look at Roni's tear stained face.

"You aren't responsible for his feelings; you're only responsible for how you handle them. All you can do is be honest and try to take his feelings into consideration, not matter what you decide to do."

"Can you do me a favor, Nicole?" Roni asked as she chewed on her bottom lip.

"Anything."

"Would you tell Rich that I need a little time?" She asked. "I know I'll see him at work, but I need some time to think about what I want, and I don't want to have a serious conversation with him until I do."

"Sure, sweetie, I can do that." Nicole replied.

"Thanks." She smiled at her friend as Nicole got up and went back into her bedroom to get ready for the day.

Roni had gotten enough kids signed up to begin her first class, but she had a few days to prepare before they would begin training. She needed to take the next two days to think about what she wanted and how she was going to get it.

She got up and went to Kent's computer, logging on under her name. She searched for therapists in the local area. She figured that was the first place she needed to start.

Epilogue

The first few weeks after the Grand Opening were better than Rich could ever had imagined or hoped for. He wasn't in the black yet, but with the way things were going, he was confident that he would be within a year.

He was getting more and more local business owners, like Colin's dad, contact him about investing.

He'd been floored when he'd walked into his parents that day and Mr. Grayson had laid a check on the table and said he'd love to be a part of the center.

Rich didn't need to accept the money, but he loved that everyone seemed to want to be involved. It made the Rec Center more than just his dream, but something that really belonged to the whole town.

He'd been very busy, which was good since Nicole had stopped by to talk to him about Roni.

"She needs some time to figure out what she wants," Nicole has explained to him. "She's got a lot to work out, and just asks for some space while she does."

Of course, he'd agreed. He wanted to be with Roni, but he needed her to want to be with him too. He'd already been in a one sided relationship, and was in no hurry to go through that again.

So, he'd focused solely on his new business, and had been enjoying every minute of it. He and Jason trained in the mornings, then he showered and sat down at his desk for a few hours. Planning event, getting clients signed up for classes, and working on marketing.

Jason had really become his right-hand man, and was putting a lot of time and effort into managing the gym. He already had fifty gym memberships and was running a couple different weight classes already.

Rich was teaching the youngest class of kids. It was only once a week, so he had plenty of time to work on the business, but this was really why he'd had the idea of the Rec Center in the first place. He loved teaching the kids and seeing the love of the sport begin to show on their faces.

He was just finishing up his first class when Alex stopped by to speak with him after her last class of the evening.

"Hey, Rich," Alex said as she approached, still in her karategi. "I hope I'm not interrupting."

"No, we just finished class," Rich responded. "What's up?"

"I wanted to ask if you have time to meet tomorrow. I have some ideas that I wanted to run by you, and I have time in between my day job and tomorrows class," she said.

"Yeah, that sounds good. So, around five?" He asked, pausing to wave and say goodbye to a couple kids that were being picked up by their parents.

"Perfect," she said, turning to leave.

"Hey, Jason," Rich yelled, calling his friend over.

He saw Alex pause as the other man approached.

"What's up, Rich," Jason asked as he neared. "Hey, Alex," he said with a shy smile.

"Hi," she responded, smiling back prettily.

Hey, man," Rich started with a twinkle in his eye. "I know we were supposed to go out for a drink, but I'm not going to be able to make it. I've got some paperwork that can't wait."

"Okay," Jason said, a little puzzled by the statement. "No big deal, we'll catch up later."

"But, hey," Rich said, turning to Alex, "If you don't have any plans, Alex, you should take my place."

Alex looked at him, her mouth slightly open for a minute, before she turned to Jason, "I don't have any plans."

As the realization of what Rich had just maneuvered set in, Jason's face got flushed. He shot a look at Rich, but turned to Alex and asked, "Would you like to have a drink with me?"

Alex's face bloomed, causing Jason to smile broadly back at her.

"I would love to."

Rich shook his head and smiled as he watched them walk out. Funny how it was so obvious to him that they liked each other, but they were both utterly clueless.

Rich finished putting away the equipment, making sure everything was perfect before turning off the lights and closing up the gym. He was almost to his room when Roni appeared before him in the hallway.

He stopped and looked at her for a moment, eager to soak in her beauty and commit every bit of her to memory. He worried for a moment that she'd come to tell him that she'd thought things through and still wanted to end it. Rich wasn't sure he could take that. The last couple weeks of not being able to hold her and talk to her intimately, had only strengthened his feelings, and proven to him that she was the right woman for him.

He could only hope their time apart had the same effect on Roni.

"Hey," she said quietly, a small smile on her lips.

"Hi," Rich responded. They'd seen each other in passing, and he'd looked in on a couple of her classes, but this was the first time they'd spoken. It felt good to hear her voice.

"Are you busy?" Roni asked and her voice quivered with nerves.

"No. I just finished up with the kids, and was going to grab a salad out of the fridge and have a beer," Rich responded. "You want one?"

"No, I'm okay," Roni responded. "But I don't want to keep you from your dinner."

"It's fine, Roni," Rich said a bit desperately, afraid she'd take any opportunity to turn around and leave. "We can go talk. I'll eat later."

They walked back to his room and sat down.

"I really need to get some furniture in here or something," Rich said with a laugh. He turned to look at Roni. He love the way she looked with her hair swept back in a ponytail and no makeup on.

"It's okay," Roni said, fidgeting a bit with her hands, as if unsure of how to start. "First I want to thank you for giving me some time to think these last few weeks. I needed the time alone to figure out what my next step needed to be, and I really appreciate you understanding that."

"I'll give you anything you need, Roni. All you have to do is ask."

She smiled at his words, then took a deep breath and kept talking, "I also want to make sure you know that *I* know that you're nothing like Hank."

Rich took her hand in his and squeezed it slightly.

"When I broke down, it was from a culmination of memories, and the fear I had of commitment. I never thought you were going to hurt me, I'd just been holding everything in for so long, that I freaked out. I know you're a good man... A great man, really, and I want to make sure you know that."

"Thank you," Rich said sincerely, bringing her hand briefly to his lips, before placing it back in her lap.

"I've been to see a counselor," Roni told him. "I've had a couple sessions now, and I think she's really going to help me a lot. She already has. I told her about Hank, and I told her about you. She helped me realize that what happened with my parents and with Hank is not my fault, and that I do deserve to be happy. I have to be strong and confident in myself, before I can allow myself to truly be happy with someone else."

Rich felt his stomach drop. Did that mean she was telling him she needed to be alone?

He gave her a moment to compose her thoughts, hopeful that there was still a chance.

Roni stood before him and placed her hands on his cheeks, looking into his eyes as she continued, "I know that I want to be with you. You are everything that I have always dreamed a man could be, and I have to believe that I deserve the happiness that I know we will bring each other."

Rich couldn't help himself, he had to kiss her. He stood up swiftly and crushed her to him. He brought his lips to hers and entered her mouth eagerly, when she opened it for him. Their tongues danced and Roni moaned lightly, before he pulled back to look down at her face. He caressed her face with his hands, smiling at her as he said, "Sorry, I know you weren't done talking, but I couldn't stand not holding you for another second."

Roni leaned her forehead against him briefly, happy to be back in his arms again.

"It may take some time for me to get to the place I need to be, but I would be humbled and grateful if you would be there with me for the duration."

Rich held her close, kissed the side of her neck and promised, "I'll be here, for as long as you need, and however you need me. I want you to feel comfortable talking to me and know that you can lean on me whenever you need to. I plan to be with you for the rest of my life, Roni, and I want to make sure you know that I love you and you can *always* trust in me."

Bonus Endings

Friends & Lovers Trilogy

Briana & Colin

Briana couldn't believe Nicole and Kent's wedding was already here. It seemed like just yesterday that they were all friends working at the local bar & grill.

They'd spent the morning being pampered and primped, a perfect start to a magical day. She, Nicole, and Roni had been given massages, mani's, and pedi's, courtesy of Nicole's mother, Kitty.

The woman was a walking nightmare, but Briana had to admit that she and Nicole's father were making an effort to make Nicole's wedding a dream come true.

They were in the Bridal suite, getting the finishing touches on their hair and make-up, before putting on their gowns.

Nicole's blonde hair was pulled back into a loose french braid, in order to showcase her perfectly made up face, and the gorgeous veil that would be pinned to the back of her hair.

She, Kara, and Roni were wearing their hair down in fat curls. Their makeup was subtle and pretty. Perfect for the outdoor wedding that Nicole and Kent had decided on.

The three bridesmaids took turns zipping up their matching green strapless dresses. They were short with bows sewn into the skirt with a pink ribbon acting as a belt. They tied into Nicole's pink and green themed reception. The dresses were comfortable and would make dancing easy. Briana absolutely loved them.

As Nicole started to dress, Briana poured them each a glass of champagne. She felt her eyes fill as she watched her friend preparing for the most wonderful day of her life. She couldn't help the yearning that was building in her at the thought of planning her own wedding one day.

As Roni zipped up the back of Nicole's strapless wedding dress with a lace overlay, Briana couldn't help but say, "Oh… Nicole, you look so beautiful!"

Nicole smiled at Briana in the mirror, her eyes skimming over the A-line skirt and green ribbon belt that matched the color of the girls' dresses perfectly.

"You really do, Nic," Roni agreed. "You look radiant."

Briana handed Nicole her champagne flute as the other woman turned. They put their glasses in for a toast and Roni said, "To my new sister, may your wedding be everything you've ever dreamed of."

"And may your wedding night be perfect and magical," Kara added with a twinkle in her eyes.

"Ewww," Roni said, causing the other girls to laugh and the moment to lighten up. "I don't want to think about the wedding night."

"Nicole, are you ready, dear?" Kitty said opening the door a crack and peaking inside. She nodded when she saw the girls were dressed, then opened the door a bit further and allowed the photographer to enter the room. "Good, we'd like to get some pictures of Nicole in her dress and some of all of you together."

They took pictures in the room, posing and laughing as the photographer captured it all. Then they went outside, careful to avoid the guys, and got some pictures on the grounds of the venue.

Brianna knew the pictures of Nicole in front of the pond, with the sun shining and the brightly blooming trees behind her would turn out to be beautiful shots.

When the time for the wedding was finally upon them, they began their procession, with Kara in the lead.

Briana blew a kiss at Nicole before she started down the aisle, then began to walk towards the guys.

The outdoor venue was beautiful. The sun was shining, the grass was green, and the flowers were everywhere. It was perfect.

Briana smiled broadly when she caught Colin's eye, and kept her eyes locked with his as she walked, her pink and green bouquet held firmly in her hands. Her stomach jumped as she took in how handsome he was in his tuxedo. As she neared the alter, she smiled at Pete and Rich, before turning her gaze to Kent. He looked so handsome and happy; his face was glowing with the joy he felt. She grinned happily at him before joining Kara to wait for Roni and Nicole.

Once Roni was in place, the Wedding March began and Nicole came down the aisle on her father's arm. Her excitement was palpable and Briana felt adrenaline rush through her in response. She turned to see the look on Kent's face when he saw Nicole and didn't even try to contain the tears that flowed at the look of pure love she saw there.

The ceremony was short and sweet, ending with Kent sweeping Nicole into a deep dip and kissing her thoroughly. The small group of attendees jumped to their feet and cheered loudly, offering catcalls and whistle's for the duration of the kiss. Kent swept Nicole off of her feet and carried her laughing down the aisle.

Briana was chuckling at the site as she joined Colin to follow suit.

She put her arm through his and leaned in to whisper, "I love you."

"I love you too, Bree," Colin replied squeezing her hand before letting it go to follow Roni and Rich down the aisle.

They joined Roni, Rich, Kara, and Pete in the limo, popping a bottle of champagne as the driver pulled out of the driveway to go to the reception hall.

"I'm so happy right now," Roni gushed. "Did you see how totally ecstatic they both were?"

Rich leaned in to kiss her softly on the cheek before pulling a way and putting his glass out to the middle to toast. "To a wonderful marriage between two of the best people in the world."

"Cheers," they all chimed, smiling as they clinked their glasses together.

The trip to the reception was a short one. When the limo pulled up to the entrance, they took turns exiting, smoothing out their outfits and heading eagerly inside.

Briana's breath caught as she entered the ballroom that was holding Nicole and Kent's reception. Twinkling lights hung from the ceiling, and there were so many flowers, it felt as if the outside had been brought in. The tables were elegantly decorated with candles and white place settings. The overall effect was stunning, and she knew that Nicole would be thrilled.

The evening went buy in a blur. Eating, drinking, and dancing intertwining with each other and allowing everyone to enjoy all of the fun touches Kent and Nicole had to celebrate their big day.

From the open bar, to the elegant table service, and the Fondue station, to the choreographed dances... the night was a smashing success.

Briana was pleasantly full from the perfectly cooked filet, and more than a little buzzed from the free flowing champagne. As she danced in Colin's arms to the D.J.'s mix of wedding anthems, she smiled contently, and knew there was nowhere else she would rather be in that moment.

Nicole and Kent had already had their grand send off and were on their way to the airport. They were flying out to Acapulco, where they would be arriving in a few hours to begin their honeymoon.

Roni had caught the bouquet, to her chagrin, and Colin had caught the garter. They'd both decided to go against tradition though, and Briana was aware of the feel of the garter rubbing against her thigh as she moved.

The reception had been a mixture of laughter and tears. Most of the guests had left when the bride and groom had driven away, but their small group was still going strong; allowing the momentum of the evening to help them celebrate into the night.

Briana lifted her head off of Colin's shoulder when he stopped swaying to the music. She looked around and noticed that their friends were sitting at a nearby table, having champagne and talking. She and Colin were alone on the dance floor.

"Bree," Colin said seriously when her eyes met his. "You know that I love you. That I've loved you since we were a couple of crazy teenagers. When you agreed to give me a second chance, I couldn't believe how lucky I was. You're the only woman I've ever loved and the only person that I want to share my life with."

When he dropped to his knee and took her hand as he looked up at her, her world stopped. Her heart started to beat rapidly and her cheeks grew damp with the tears that began to flow. Briana gasped and brought her hand to her mouth when he opened the small black box to reveal the engagement ring inside.

The gorgeous princess cut diamond glinted up at her under the twinkling lights. It was everything she'd ever dreamed of as a little girl and if she was honest, in the last few months.

"Briana, I'd be honored and promise to love and cherish you for the rest of our lives, if you'd agree to become my wife."

Briana dropped to her knees and catapulted herself into Colin's arms, kissing him wildly as she said, "Yes, yes, yes!!!"

Colin slipped the ring on her finger and put his arms around her. As he kissed her, their friends stood and cheered and Briana knew that her life was exactly as she'd always dreamed it would be.

Nicole & Kent

The wedding had been everything Nicole had ever dreamed of and more.

She had been surprised when her parents said that they wanted to pay for everything, but then again, they had always been more generous with their money, than with their affection.

Nicole turned her head to look at Kent, her *husband*, as he slept. He was so handsome, she thought with a smile, and such a good man.

The plane hit some turbulence, causing her stomach to jump and her hand to clench Kent's.

"You okay, baby?" Kent asked sleepily, turning his head towards her.

"Yeah," she said. "Just a little bumpy."

"How long have I been out?" Kent asked, stretching his arms as much as possible in the confined space.

"A few hours," Nicole replied. "We are about to start our descent."

She opened up the shade so they could look out the window. They held hands as they watched Acapulco come into focus.

"It's so beautiful," Nicole said her voice full of the happiness that had fulfilled her since she'd walked down the aisle towards Kent and became his wife.

The plane landed smoothly, but they were both happy to get off the airplane and be on solid ground again.

When they stepped off of the plane, Nicole surveyed the area, trying to take it all in.

"I love it," Nicole cooed, peeling the already damp shirt from her sticky skin.

"This is just the airport," Kent said with a chuckle, putting his arms around her and pulling her close.

"We could still be on the airplane and I'd still love it," Nicole said, leaning in for a kiss.

She'd meant to give him a quick peck, but as soon as their lips met, she opened and he entered her mouth eagerly. She brought her arms up around his neck and felt his fingers dig into her hips and bring her even closer.

Nicole moaned softly as their kiss deepened and she felt Kent's arousal against her.

She was suddenly flushed and hot, and it had nothing to do with the Acapulco weather.

Kent broke the kiss, breathing heavily as he rested his forehead against hers. "Let's go get our bags."

Nicole nodded slightly, her breath not quite steady enough to speak yet.

They grabbed their bags, then headed out towards the front of the airport. Nicole squealed with excitement when she saw the jauntily dressed man holding up a sign with their names on it. They were escorted outside to the awaiting limo and slid inside as the driver took care of their luggage.

Nicole giggled as Kent popped the cork on the bottle of chilled champagne. She scooted closer to him when he offered her a glass, and snuggled in for the duration of their ride.

"Is there anything special that you want to do while we're here?" Kent asked. Nicole had been studying travel books for the weeks leading up to their honeymoon.

"I think I'd like to try ziplining and cliff jumping," she said. Nicole laughed at the surprised look on his face.

"Really?"

"Yeah," she said, leaning in to kiss him softly before settling back and taking a sip of the bubbly drink. "Why are you so shocked?"

"I don't know," Kent said with a shrug. "I shouldn't be surprised by anything anymore, but you always seem to manage to surprise me. I love it."

He bent over her and nuzzled his nose against hers, before leaning back and resting against the plush seat.

"Is there anything you want to do?" She countered.

"I'm open to whatever you want. I just want to enjoy every possible moment with my wife," Kent smiled at her.

Nicole moved in closer and pressed her lips to the base of his neck. She flicked her tongue out swiftly, then sucked softly, her body responding to Kent's quick intake of breath. Encouraged, she moved her lips up his throat and along his jawline, occasionally nipping and licking as she traveled. By the time she reached his mouth, he'd taken their glasses and set them off to the side, allowing their hands free reign.

Kent lifted Nicole and she parted her legs to straddle him as their kiss deepened. Kent groaned as she moved against him, his hands fisting in her hair.

When the car began to slow, Nicole gradually came to her senses and pulled away, but not before going in for one last kiss. She smiled seductively down at him and said, "Welcome to paradise."

Kent swatted her butt playfully as she moved off of him. He handed her glass back to her and they were the picture of innocence when the driver opened the door and welcomed them to their hotel.

They exited the limo and checked into the hotel. When they were walking to their bungalow, Nicole noticed Kent's unease with the opulence around them and took his hand in hers.

"It's just you and me, babe," she said with a smile as they passed through the garden.

Kent returned her smile, his eyes still uneasy. "I feel a little out of place," he admitted.

"Mission accepted," Nicole said saucily.

"What?"

"By the time we leave here, you'll know that you have as much right to be here as anyone else," she promised.

"Oh yeah?"

"Yup," Nicole said, reaching down to cup his ass as they walked.

"Hey," Kent said, jumping away in shock. "What're you doing?"

"Don't be such a prude," Nicole laughed. "This is our honeymoon, and I want everyone to know that you're mine."

Kent looked down at her, eyes smoldering and said, "Two can play that game."

Before she realized what he meant, she was swept up in his arms. She threw her arms around his neck and her head back, laughing with delight.

He carried her over the threshold, trying to pay attention to where he walked as he kissed her senseless.

"Wow," he said simply, when they got to the back of the bungalow.

Nicole turned her head and her breath caught as she took in the beautiful four poster bed, surrounded by glass walls that opened up to a deck with a hot tub bubbling seductively.

The view showcased teal blue water crashing against the sand. Kent opened the doors leading from their bedroom to the deck and the sound of the waves crashing brought a beautiful smile to his face. Nicole felt her stomach flip and a hot flash seemed to zip through her. He had never looked as gorgeous as he did in that moment.

"Wanna go in the hot tub?" She suggested.

He turned and grinned at her, "Absolutely."

Nicole grabbed her bathing suit out of her bag and took it into the bathroom to get changed. She wasn't quite ready to change in front of Kent yet, husband or not.

She looked at the skimpy white bikini, and didn't know if she should curse or thank Briana for talking her into buying it. Nicole inhaled deeply, before opening the door to join Kent. When she walked out, she saw him stepping gingerly into the hot water, his eyes focused on the gorgeous scene before him. She padded softly out onto the deck, willing herself not to cover her exposed skin with her arms.

Kent turned towards her even though Nicole was certain she hadn't made a sound. His eyes widened, along with his smile, and his pupils dilated slightly.

"You look amazing."

"Thanks," she said shyly.

He scooted over and sank into the water, giving her room to enter the Jacuzzi.

Nicole lowered herself into the hot water and sighed softly as it slid silkily over her skin.

"That feels wonderful," she murmured.

Kent cleared his throat and she opened her eyes to see him looking at her hungrily. She followed his gaze and was mortified to see that her white bikini was practically transparent in the water.

She moved to cover herself, but Kent growled, "Don't," and she stilled her movements. The look he was giving her turned the blood in her veins into molten lava. Her hands fluttered out over the water nervously and she gasped as Kent pulled her swiftly into his arms. His mouth was on her before she had time to register what was happening.

Their mouths fused as their bodies came together. The sounds of their passion mingled with the bubbling tub and the waves behind them, but they didn't hear any of it.

Nicole whimpered against Kent's lips as the friction of their bodies threatened to drive her wild.

Kent stood, lifting her and exiting the jacuzzi in one swift movement. They entered the room and he brought her softly down to rest on the bed.

"I'm so happy I waited until I found you," Nicole said breathlessly, her eyes shining with unshed tears.

"God, so am I," Kent exclaimed gruffly, then proceeded to claim Nicole as his wife. Forever.

Roni & Rich

Roni stood staring at the pink plus sign, willing it to be correct. Her heart felt like it was about to burst with joy and disbelief.

The doctor had said she'd probably never be able to have children. Roni had made sure Rich understood that, and one of the reasons she loved him was that he wanted to be with her even knowing they may never have kids.

Roni had tried to come to terms with that fact, but deep down the possibility was a source of great sorrow for her.

Now here she stood, hopeful that the doctor had been wrong and terrified that it was a false positive.

A persistent knock sounded at the door.

"Well," Nicole asked from the other side. "Is it ready yet?"

Over the past few weeks Roni had been experiencing fatigue and her breasts were sore. She hadn't thought anything of it, until she realized she was a few weeks late getting her period. At first she'd been in denial that pregnancy was even a possibility. Even when she'd confided her symptoms to Nicole and her sister in-law had suggested that may be the case.

"You know what the doctor said," Roni had said to her friend at the time. "I'm sure I'm just late."

"Have you ever been late before?" Nicole asked, pushing her blonde hair behind her ear as she spoke. Being married suited her beautifully.

"Um, no… I guess I haven't," Roni admitted.

"Well, can you think back about six weeks and pinpoint a time when you and Rich could have gotten pregnant?"

Roni had blushed when she remembered the night she'd finally told Rich that she was in love with him. It had been about six months after Kent and Nicole's wedding. She'd been diligently attending counseling sessions, teaching dance, and spending every extra minute with Rich. Through it all he had been so supportive and caring, and their relationship had progressed beyond a blossoming romance and had become a stable happy relationship.

She'd stopped by the Rec Center after closing at the Bar & Grill, and had found Rich in the boxing ring sparring with Jason.

She'd watched him, getting turned on the more she watched his body move around the ring. By the time he finished up, Roni had worked herself up into a frenzy.

Rich had climbed out of the ring and she'd surprised him by jumping into his arms and kissing him thoroughly. His arms had come around her and he laughed.

"Happy to see me, sunshine?" He'd said between breaths.

He'd called goodbye to Jason as he carried her off towards his room in the back. Roni had taken the opportunity to devour his handsome face with her eyes and run her hands through his damp hair, which was in desperate need of a haircut.

Roni had thought about the day they'd met in the Bar & Grill, and how far they'd come since then, personally, professionally, and romantically. She looked into his hazel eyes and saw everything that she'd ever wanted staring back at her.

"I love you," She'd said, holding his face with her hands as she spoke, so she could see the grin that broke across his face and his eyes light up with pleasure.

"I love you too."

"Yes," Roni replied to Nicole, breaking out of the memory. "I know when it could have happened."

Now here she stood, the evidence in her hand, as Nicole eagerly waited on the other side of the door.

Roni opened the door swiftly, causing Nicole to fall into the bathroom.

"Well," Nicole asked again, catching herself on the bathroom sink before she did any harm.

Roni's eyes welled up as she showed the stick to Nicole. Nicole let out a squeal and pulled Roni into her arms, jumping up and down.

"Oh my gosh," Nicole said excitedly, tears starting to form in her eyes as well. "This is so great."

Roni nodded and smiled, then voiced her worries aloud.

"What if it's a false positive?"

"You know, most clinics offer free pregnancy tests. We can go and get your blood taken, and you will know for sure."

Roni nodded again.

"I just don't want to get Rich's hopes up, only to find out that the doctors were right after all," Roni admitted.

Nicole turned her embrace into a hug and patted Roni on the back.

"That makes sense. Let's go call some clinics."

An hour later Roni and Nicole walked out of the clinic and the two girls embraced once again.

"I have to get to my dance class," Roni said. "I'll talk to you later."

"Okay. Once they call you with the results, will you let me know?"

"Absolutely," Roni said with a smile as they walked to the parking lot and got into their respective vehicles.

The trip to the Rec Center was a short one, but it felt like it took forever to Roni. She wished she could get immediate results, but the lab had to run the test. At least they had told her she would find out before the end of the day. The uncertainty was torture.

Now that she felt a glimmer of hope that she would in fact be able to have kids, Roni really wanted it to be true. She knew with absolute certainty that Rich would be the best father ever, and that she was ready to show a child all of the love and affection that her parents had never been able to give her.

Kent would be a terrific uncle, she thought with a smile.

She wanted this so badly that her heart ached with the need.

Roni stuck her head into the office when she entered the Center, and saw Rich sitting at his desk, hands in his hair as he went over some paperwork.

He looked so hot.

She cleared her throat and he looked up. It took him a few seconds for his eyes to focus on her, but when they did; his face blossomed just like it always did when she entered a room.

Roni knew how lucky she was to have a man like him; after all, she'd once been married to his polar opposite.

"Hey, babe," Rich said as he got up from his seat and strode purposefully to her. He gathered her in his arms and she inhaled the scent of him deeply. Spicy, sweet, and totally male. "Headed to class?"

"Yeah," she responded, pulling back so she could look at his face. "I've got the little ones. We still on for dinner?"

"Nowhere else I'd rather be," he said with a smile. He gave her a kiss on the lips and a quick pat on the ass as she turned to leave.

Roni giggled at that, then went to her class to get ready for her pupils.

The beginning dance class was one of the most rewarding and fun, and by the end of the class, Roni's spirit was flying high.

"Thank you, Ms. Roni," one of the girls said as she walked out of the studio with her mother.

"You're welcome, Sophie. Great job today," Roni responded with a smile.

She cleaned up her studio and went to the kitchen in search of dinner. The last time Briana was in town, she'd cooked a bunch of meals and froze them. That was Briana's way of thanking Rich for allowing her to use his deluxe kitchen whenever she was in town, so Roni and Rich ate like kings for weeks after Briana went back to Austin.

Roni looked through the freezer and chose a pasta sauce. She put some water on to boil the noodles and got a pan out to thaw the sauce. She was cutting up the makings of a salad, when Rich walked up behind her and kissed her neck.

"Mmmm, smells good," Rich said softly in her ear, before taking a nip.

Roni felt the heat spark up and shoot straight down to her toes.

She was about to turn into him when her phone sounded off in her pocket.

Rich took over cutting as she pressed the button to receive the call.

"Hello?" Roni said softly, terrified of what news would be relayed to her. She kept her back to Rich and walked a few steps away.

She listened for a few moments, then hung up the phone. Roni stood stock still for a moment, before turning to Rich.

Roni looked at him, chopping vegetables in his sparkling kitchen. He wore a rumpled blue t-shirt, jeans, and flip flops. And knowing him, that's all he wore.

Rich looked up when he noticed that she hadn't spoken or moved for a few moments.

"Everything okay?" he asked.

"Come here," Roni said, turning to head out of the kitchen and into his room.

"Don't you have food on the stove?" Rich asked as he came in behind her.

"Sit down," she said, pointing to his bed.

"Okay…" He sat and looked up at her, a little wary.

Roni looked around his room.

It was a mess.

The bed was unmade, his dirty clothes were on the floor next to his hamper, and his furniture was old and tattered.

"This isn't going to work," she began. "You're a total slob. You need to make your bed and start cleaning up after yourself. I know you can do it, just look at the rest of the Center, it's pristine, but this room… not so much."

Rich shifted uncomfortably as he looked around his space.

"You've never said anything about the way this place looks before, why are you worried about it now?"

"Because you can't raise a baby in conditions like this," Roni said softly, unable to stop the smile that took over her face.

She watched the shock settle in as her words began to register, and Rich popped off the bed in a shot. He gathered her to him and tried to hug her tightly, without squishing her.

"Are you sure?" he asked, his face in her hair.

"That was the doctor on the phone," she said as tears began to slide down her cheeks. "She said we're six weeks along."

She heard Rich breath in deeply and his breath catch and she knew he was trying to compose himself.

Roni pulled back and looked into the face of her beautiful, sweet man, who was trying unsuccessfully, to contain his tears of joy.

Rich cupped her face in his hands and kissed her sweetly, their tears mingling together as they held each other close.

Rich stepped back and turned to his dresser, pulling something out before turning back to Roni.

When he dropped to his knee, Roni's heart threatened to gallop out of her chest, and she didn't think it was possible to feel any happier than she did at that moment.

Rich opened the box which contained a simple band with a round diamond in the center.

"Roni, this ring is only a fraction of the ring I want for you, but I offer it to you as a symbol of my heart and the life I want to spend with you. I've been carrying this ring around for the past eight months. I wanted the timing to be right, and I knew you weren't ready, but I wanted to have it handy once you were." She smiled at him, eyes shimmering with more tears, and she wanted nothing more than to scream yes, and be in his arms, but she let him finish.

"I want to share this Rec Center with you, buy a home and raise children with you. I want to be the shoulder you cry on and the person you share life's greatest joys with. I know I was only a shell of a man when I met you, and I hope to one day be the man that you deserve to have by your side as you grow old. Marry me, Roni, and make me the happiest man on earth."

Roni nodded spastically and said, "Yes," before putting her hand out for him to place the ring on her finger.

Once it was on he stood, and she put her hand out to admire it.

"It's the most perfect ring I've ever seen," Roni gushed before catapulting herself into the place that she wanted to be for the rest of her life. Rich's arms.

Friends & Lovers Trilogy

Keep reading for an excerpt from my Contemporary Fantasy

Nissa: a contemporary fairy tale

Available April 23, 2013

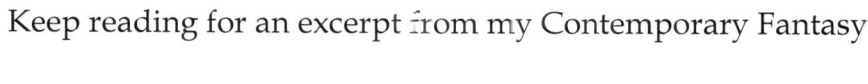

Friends & Lovers Trilogy

1

I'm only 900 years old, which is relatively young for a fairy godmother, equivalent to an eighteen year old human.

My clan is considered small amongst the fairies of our woods, as I only have six brothers and four sisters. Normally, woodland fairies cannot be godmothers or godfathers, but our mother was a fairy godmother before she partnered with my father, so it's in our bloodline.

My mother is a descendant of the Huldafolk. They're known for their kindness and generous spirit, which makes them ideal Godparents for humans.

My father is a Feeorin, a capricious lot, with a love of singing and dancing. We get our red hair from our father and pale skin from our mother, although I often wished for the green complexion of my father's family.

***

Despite the differences in their clans, my parents knew immediately that they were meant to be. My mother had returned from a mission and my father was singing at the Midsummer's Eve feast. It was love at first sight.

When fairies find the person they're fated for, we love each other for all eternity. Our bodies give us signs to help us realize that we have found the one.

My parents were lucky to have found each other when they had reached their mature forms and were old enough to be bound.

Once they met, fell in love, and The Fates determined they could be partnered; my mother was able to forgo her fairy godmother status and stay permanently in the woods with my father. She could, however, pass her status on to one of her children.

Our parents love to tell us the story of how they met and fell in love and how The Fates help all of us find love.

When you come in to contact with a fae that you have a strong connection with, your heart pounds like a drum, your right hand begins to tingle to the point of itching, and your eyes will momentarily turn pink to match your yearning heart.

When all of those things occur, you may appeal to The Fates for a blessing of your union. If The Fates do not agree that the union is everlasting, you will not be allowed to see each other again in this lifetime. If they agree that you are meant, the joining of your lives would begin in that moment and will not end until the passing of both beings.

"What happens if you never feel the signs, Mama?" my younger sister, Ella often asked our mother.

"Don't worry, sweet girl," Mother always assured her. "It's in our nature to enjoy lives full of love."

We all love to hear the stories and can't wait to feel the stirrings of fate. I always dreamed of finding my fate, but I also wished to follow my mother's path and be a Godparent. The thought of helping humans reach their potential or overcome a hardship, really called to me. I wanted to make a difference and be a part of something grander than the woods of my youth.

My brothers and sisters have no interest whatsoever in being a Godparent. They're content to rule the woods and live a happy and carefree life.

We all look alike, with our fair skin and bright red hair; our wings are the feature that separates us. Each pair is unique, a reflection of our personalities.

When it comes to personality, I'm the odd one of the bunch. Similar to my brothers and sisters, I love to frolic and dance, and I'm always ready to join them on a merry chase, but they often joke that if I can't be found, listen for signs of the injured or brokenhearted, I'll be there trying to fix the situation.

***

The day I finally gathered the courage to talk to my parents about my desire to follow my mother's path, I came upon them sitting outside our dwelling, enjoying the glow of a lightening bug.

My mother looked up at me, her pleasure at my approach evident, but I noticed the concern on her face, as if she had been awaiting my arrival and knew the outcome of our conversation.

"What's it sweet girl? We know something has been bothering you," my mother began as I walked nearer, my wings fluttering gently in the breeze of the cool morning. She held my father's hand in hers, as if it were an extension of her own.

"I've been thinking about this for a long time, but I haven't known how to tell you until now," I said softly, staring down at the ground. "I want to help people, as you did, Mama. I want to train to become a godmother."

They looked at each other, smiled, then looked back at me.

"Of course you do, honey," my father said with a quiet voice.

"You already knew?" I looked out over the pond outside our home relieved that they weren't upset.

"Nissa, of all of our children, you are the most like your mother: kind hearted, giving, and sensitive. Your siblings are content with life here and will be happy as they are, but we knew that you would be the one to choose this path."

They weren't sad about my decision, sad that it meant I would have to leave the woods. Knowing that this would make me happy and fulfill my destiny made it easier for them to accept.

***

In between helping humans, I was free to come home and visit my family for a while before I accepted on a new mission.

After finally finishing the three years training, which consisted of classroom education, use of magic, and finally, hands on experience, I was about to embark on my first project without my trainer, Fairy Godfather Titus, who had been with me since my first day at Headquarters.

***

When I volunteered, and was accepted to be a Fairy Godmother, I received the initial welcome packet. Once I had completed all of the entrance documents, I reported to Headquarters to meet my trainer and begin my years of training. I was given a room, and was instructed to wait there for my trainer.

"You must be Nissa," I was so nervous and unsure of my surroundings, that I hadn't notice the tall, grey haired fairy enter my room, until the boom of his voice startled me.

"I'm Titus," He said by way of introduction. "Follow me, so we can begin your training."

The frown never left his face, and before I had a chance to reply, I was rushing after him down the hall.

That was how my training began, and pretty much set the tone for the next three years.

***

The magic portion of the training was my favorite part. I loved feeling of calmness that passed through me when I knew the magic was working. I enjoyed manipulating objects and feelings, and the pride that came with success.

Classroom was a necessary evil, but I dreaded the days I had to stay inside. It was interesting to learn about the history of Fairy Godparents, and to read about past projects, but I longed to be outside practicing magic.

Once the magic and classroom training were complete, and Titus deemed me ready, we began the practical training.

For the first project, Titus took the lead. The second one we completed together. For the third project, I was the lead, but Titus was there as back up.

Now that I had completed all facets of my training, I was finally a Fairy Godmother.

I knew Titus was happy that my training was complete, not that I was a bad pupil or anything, he got very frustrated with my approach. He wanted me to be stern and detached with the projects, but I preferred to treat humans as I would my own friends and family. Being a Godparent would be very lonely, in my opinion, if I didn't make friends along the way.

Titus started in this business five thousand years ago and started as a trainer two thousand years ago. He only had one more fairy to train and then he could retire. Since fairies generally live anywhere from twelve to fourteen thousand years, he would have more than a few years left to enjoy his retirement.

He was more than ready to find a sweet little fae to settle down with and enjoy a quiet life, after dealing with young fairy pupils and the projects we took on.

As a thank you for the last few years, I decided to surprise Titus with a little gift.

Tomorrow he started training his new pupil and I began my new project. Once that happened, I would not see him again unless I was having problems, and he needed to come in and save me.

I really hoped that it wouldn't come to that, so I needed to say goodbye today.

***

I was in the cafeteria of the training building, putting the finishing touches on the dew drop sweetcake I made for Titus. I made it with boysenberry, his favorite, and decorated it with his initials. It looked delicious and I hoped he liked it.

Titus walked in to get his morning cup of hot nectar; if he didn't get his nectar you could forget about him acknowledging you. He was usually quite grumpy in the morning. I watched as he added a dash of bitter, to take some of the sweetness away, and took the first sip. He sat at his favorite table in the corner and opened the paper to read. Once he was settled in and sipping on his drink, I picked up the sweetcake and went over to join him.

The bells in my hair jingled as I walked, alerting him of my approach.

"You are no longer my pupil, Nissa, so our morning meetings are no longer necessary," Titus's voice came out in a big boom, but I knew he was really a sweetheart underneath all of his bluster. His hair was naturally grey and stuck out in wild tufts framing his face. I always wanted to reach out and tame it, but I feared he would be embarrassed, so I left it alone.

I smiled broadly at him and replied, "Good morning, Titus. I made you this sweetcake, your favorite, to say thank you and goodbye. I hope your next pupil is a quick study and you get to retire as soon as possible."

I set the sweetcake in front of him and saw him struggle to hide the delight that spread across his face. Without invitation, I sat across from him and grabbed one of his hands in mine.

"I mean it Titus. I'll miss you."

He looked into my eyes and said, "Nissa, you have the makings of a great godmother. You need to focus on the task you are given, not on the emotions of the project, and you will be fine."

I felt myself grow warm and the blush run through my body. Once it reached my wings they slowly lit up and shimmered with delight.

Sometimes being a fairy is so embarrassing.

"Thank you Titus, that means a lot to me. I'll let you enjoy your morning ritual before the work day begins. Good luck with your new pupil. I hope you enjoy the sweetcake." With that I stood to leave.

As I walked past him I stopped briefly to kiss his cheek. "Goodbye, "I whispered.

I walked out of the cafeteria and headed for my room to wait until my meeting with the mission specialist. The meeting would be held at the headquarters branch.

Now when I say branch, it's meant literally. Our "building" was in an old oak on the outskirts of the Redwood Forest, in Northern California. The branches contained different divisions: Headquarters, Administration, Housing, and Training.

As a Fairy Godmother, once I was assigned a project and left the headquarters, I would take on a human form, maintaining my basic features. Obviously I would lose my wings and ability to fly, and I would grow into a form more fitting for a human, but my hair, face and complexion would remain the same.

Friends & Lovers Trilogy

ABOUT THE AUTHOR

Bethany Lopez was born in Detroit, Michigan, and grew up in Michigan and San Antonio, Texas. She went to High School at Dearborn High, in Dearborn, Michigan, which is where she has set her Young Adult series. She is married and has a blended family with five children. She is currently serving in the United States Air Force as a Recruiter in Los Angeles, California. She has always loved to read and write and has seen her dream realized by independently publishing her first novels through Amazon.

Visit Bethany Lopez at:

www.bethanylopez.blogspot.com
http://www.facebook.com/#./pages/Bethany-Lopez/214630865247702
@BethanyLopez2
http://www.independentauthornetwork.com/bethany-lopez.html

28423682R00260

Made in the USA
Charleston, SC
12 April 2014